NEBULA AWARDS SHOWCASE 58

NEBULA AWARDS SHOWCASE 58

The Year's Best Science Fiction and Fantasy

EDITED BY

STEPHEN KOTOWYCH

Nebula Awards Showcase 58: The Year's Best Science Fiction and Fantasy

Cover illustration "Star Deity 2023" by Lauren Raye Snow
Cover design by M.L. Clark
Interior layout designed by Laurie McGregor / Page Turn
Typesetting by M.L. Clark

The stories, all names, characters, and incidents portrayed herein are fictitious. No identification with actual persons (living or deceased), places, buildings, products, or events is intended or should be inferred.

San Lorenzo, California, United States

ISBN 978-1-958243-04-6 (print)
ISBN 978-1-958243-05-3 (ebook)

2022 NEBULA AWARDS®

Presented at the Sheraton Park Hotel at the Anaheim Resort
and online on Sunday, May 14, 2023

Toastmaster: Cheryl Platz

Best Novel

Legends & Lattes by **Travis Baldree,** published by *Cryptid* and *Tor*

Spear by **Nicola Griffith,** published by *Tordotcom*

Nettle and Bone by **T. Kingfisher,** published by *Tor* and *Titan UK*

★ **Winner:** *Babel* by **R. F. Kuang,** published by *Harper Voyager US* and *Harper Voyager UK*

Nona the Ninth by **Tamsyn Muir,** published by *Tordotcom*

The Mountain in the Sea by **Ray Nayler,** published by *MCD* and *Weidenfeld & Nicolson*

Best Novella

A Prayer for the Crown-Shy by **Becky Chambers,** published by *Tordotcom*

"Bishop's Opening" by **R. S. A. Garcia,** published by *Clarkesworld Magazine*

I Never Liked You Anyway by **Jordan Kurella,** published by *Vernacular*

★ **Winner:** *Even Though I Knew the End* by **C. L. Polk,** published by *Tordotcom*

High Times in the Low Parliament by **Kelly Robson,** published by *Tordotcom*

Best Novelette

★ **Winner:** "If You Find Yourself Speaking to God, Address God with the Informal You" by **John Chu,** published by *Uncanny Magazine*

"Two Hands, Wrapped in Gold" by **S.B. Divya,** published by *Uncanny Magazine*

"Murder by Pixel: Crime and Responsibility in the Digital Darkness" by **S. L. Huang,** published by *Clarkesworld Magazine*

"A Dream of Electric Mothers" by Wole Talabi, published by *Africa Risen: A New Era of Speculative Fiction*

"The Prince of Salt and the Ocean's Bargain" by Natalia Theodoridou, published by *Uncanny Magazine*

"We Built This City" by Marie Vibbert, published by *Clarkesworld Magazine*

Best Short Story

"Destiny Delayed" by Ekpeki Oghenechovwe Donald, published by *Asimov's Science Fiction Magazine*

"Give Me English" by Ai Jiang, published by *The Magazine of Fantasy & Science Fiction*

★ **Winner:** "Rabbit Test" by Samantha Mills, published by *Uncanny Magazine*

"Dick Pig" by Ian Muneshwar, published by *Nightmare Magazine*

"Douen" by Suzan Palumbo, published by *The Dark*

"D. I. Y." by John Wiswell, published by *Tor.com*

Andre Norton Nebula Award for Middle Grade and Young Adult Fiction

Victories Greater Than Death by Charlie Jane Anders,
published by *Tor Teen* and *Titan*

★ **Winner:** *Ruby Finley vs. The Interstellar Invasion* by K. Tempest Bradford,
published by *Farrar, Straus and Giroux*

The Scratch Daughters by H. A. Clarke, published by *Erewhon*

The Mirrorwood by Deva Fagan, published by *Atheneum*

Every Bird a Prince by Jenn Reese, published by *Henry Holt*

The Many Half-Lived Lives of Sam Sylvester by Maya MacGregor, published by *Astra Young Readers*

Ray Bradbury Nebula Award for Outstanding Dramatic Presentation

Severance written by Dan Erickson, Chris Black, Andrew Colville, Amanda Overton, Amanda Ouyang Moench, Helen Leigh, Kari Drake, and Mark Friedman (Endeavor Content, Red Hour Films, Apple TV+)

The Sandman: Season 1 written by Neil Gaiman, Lauren Bello, Vanessa Benton, Mike Dringenberg, Sam Kieth, Catherine Smyth-McMullen, Heather Bellson, Jim Campolongo, Jay Franklin, Austin Guzman, Alexander Newman-Wise, Ameni Rozsa, David Goyer, and Allan Heinberg (DC Entertainment and Netflix)

Our Flag Means Death written by David Jenkins, Eliza Jiménez Cossio, Zadry Ferrer-Geddes, William Meny, Maddie Dai, Alyssa Lane, John Mahone, Simone Nathan, Natalie Torres, Zackery Alexzander Stephens, Jes Tom, and Adam Stein (Dive and HBO Max)

★ **Winner:** *Everything Everywhere All at Once* written by Dan Kwan and Daniel Scheinert (A24, AGBO, and IAC Films)

Nope written by Jordan Peele (Universal Pictures)

Andor. "One Way Out" written by Beau Willimon and Tony Gilroy (Bidangil Pictures)

The Green Knight written by David Lowery (Sailor Bear, BRON Studios, and A24)

Best Game Writing

Pentiment by Kate Dollarhyde, Zoe Franznick, Märten Rattasepp, and Josh Sawyer, published by *Obsidian Entertainment* and *Xbox Game Studios*

Journeys through the Radiant Citadel by Ajit A. George, F. Wesley Schneider, Justice Ramin Arman, Dominique Dickey, Basheer Ghouse, Alastor Guzman, D. Fox Harrell, T. K. Johnson, Felice Tzehuei Kuan, Surena Marie, Mimi Mondal, Mario Ortegón, Miyuki Jane Pinckard, Pam Punzalan, and Erin Roberts, published by *Wizards of the Coast: Dungeons & Dragons 5th Ed.*

Stray by Steven Lerner, Vivien Mermet-Guyenet, and Colas Koola, published by *BlueTwelve Studio* and *Annapurna Interactive*

★ **Winner:** *Elden Ring* by George R.R. Martin and Hidetaka Miyazaki, published by *FromSoftware* and *Bandai Namco*

Horizon Forbidden West by Ben McCaw, John Gonzalez, Annie Kitain, Ariadna Martinez, Nick van Someren Brand, Andrew Walsh, Adam Dolin, Anne Toole, Arjan Terpstra, Ben Schroder, Dee Warrick, and Giles Armstrong, published by *Guerrilla Games* and *Sony Interactive Entertainment*

Vampire: The Masquerade—Sins of the Sires by Natalia Theodoridou, published by *Choice of Games* and *Paradox Interactive*

Other Awards

Damon Knight Grand Master Award
Robin McKinley

Kate Wilhelm Solstice Award
Cerece Rennie Murphy
Greg Bear

Kevin O'Donnell, Jr. Service to SFWA Award
Mishell Baker

Infinity Award
Octavia E. Butler

TABLE OF CONTENTS

SHORT STORIES

"RABBIT TEST"   10
Samantha Mills published by *Uncanny Magazine*

"D. I. Y."   26
John Wiswell published by *Tor.com*

"GIVE ME ENGLISH"   38
Ai Jiang published by *The Magazine of Fantasy & Science Fiction*

"DICK PIG"   48
Ian Muneshwar published by *Nightmare Magazine*

"DOUEN"   62
Suzan Palumbo published by *The Dark*

"DESTINY DELAYED"   74
Ekpeki Oghenechovwe Donald published by *Asimov's Science Fiction Magazine*

NOVELETTES

"IF YOU FIND YOURSELF SPEAKING TO GOD, ADDRESS GOD WITH THE INFORMAL YOU"   88
John Chu published by *Uncanny Magazine*

"THE PRINCE OF SALT AND THE OCEAN'S BARGAIN"   109
Natalia Theodoridou published by *Uncanny Magazine*

"A DREAM OF ELECTRIC MOTHERS" 129
Wole Talabi published by *Africa Risen: A New Era of Speculative Fiction*

"TWO HANDS, WRAPPED IN GOLD" 145
S.B. Divya published by *Uncanny Magazine*

"WE BUILT THIS CITY" 175
Marie Vibbert published by *Clarkesworld Magazine*

"MURDER BY PIXEL: CRIME AND RESPONSIBILITY IN THE DIGITAL DARKNESS" 193
S. L. Huang published by *Clarkesworld Magazine*

NOVELLA (EXCERPT)

"EVEN THOUGH I KNEW THE END" 212
C. L. Polk published by *Tordotcom*

NOVELLA & NOVEL FINALISTS 218

MULTIMEDIA AWARD FINALISTS 227

SHORT STORIES

RABBIT TEST

Samantha Mills

It is 2091, and Grace is staring at the rabbit in the corner of her visual overlay. It is an Angora rabbit, fluffy and white, and when Grace picked the icon out, she did not realize how much she would come to dread the sight of it. She moves, and the overlay moves with her. A reminder. A threat.

There are three other authorized users with access to her rabbit test: her mother, her father, and the family doctor who installed it at their request shortly after her first menses.

In two months, Grace will turn 18 and at that point she can maintain or disable the app as she sees fit. But she doesn't have two months. Her period is six days late, and tomorrow her tracker will automatically administer a pregnancy test.

Grace pulls up the profile of her best friend, Sal, and sends their usual emergency alert: *Coffee??*

It is 1931, and Maurice Friedman and Maxwell Edward Lapham have just published "A Simple, Rapid Procedure for the Laboratory Diagnosis of Early Pregnancies" in the *American Journal of Obstetrics and Gynecology*, volume 21. This simple (very), rapid (by some standards) procedure involves one urine sample and one very unlucky rabbit.

(It is 1927, and Selmar Aschheim and Bernhard Zondek have just introduced the test *first*, actually, and theirs involves five-packs of mice. But the doctors, both Jewish, will soon flee Nazi Germany, and except for the occasional lab that prefers breeding mice over rabbits, it is the Friedman test that will catch on instead.)

Step One: Inject the urine sample into the veins of a live, juvenile female rabbit. Wait several days.

Step Two: Dissect the unlucky bunny. Inspect its ovaries. If they have enlarged and turned yellow, then congratulations or our condolences, this follicular maturation indicates a noticeable presence of hCG. You're pregnant.

Contrary to the parlance of the time, it is not the death of the rabbit that indicates a positive test. The rabbit always dies.

It is 2091, and the fine folks at Rabbit Test LMC do not have a laboratory farm. There are no animal casualties in the work they do. A very small minority of their users even understand the reference that inspired the company's name—it is a bit of trivia. Ancient history. An office joke.

Grace doesn't know, and doesn't care, and certainly isn't laughing. She waits for Sal at the coffee shop, and every sip of spark makes her stomach roil with nerves.

When Sal gets there—lovely Sal with her long brown hair and her nails painted like dragon scales—Grace can barely wait till they're in the parking lot to blurt it out.

"How?" Sal cries. "Didn't you map it, like I said?"

She had, she *had*, that was the thing. Grace had watched her cycle tracker like a surveillance drone over a labor march, and even though her parents disabled the setting that indicated her most fertile days ("Don't get any ideas," they'd said), she'd done the math on paper to map out her most *unfertile* days. At least, that's what she thought.

Now Sal is chewing anxiously on one of her nails (she'll ruin them that way, always does). "Did you tell Mac? Do you think he'll stick around? Will your parents—"

"I need a blackout," Grace interrupts. "Please, Sal. I know you've got some."

It's a glitch they've used before. An errant bit of update code that will block their apps for a day or two. Sal uses them to disable her blood alcohol test whenever her parents are out of town. They download patches every time, but she's a whiz at writing new ones, and that's all that Grace needs, just a day or two to corrupt the rabbit test. Under cover of the blackout, she can pull up the profile of one of those old ladies who sells pill packs out of their closets, hoarded up from before the ban.

She tries not to think about Mac, or that night spent fumbling in a sleeping bag in his dad's backyard. He's leaving for a deep-sea fishing gig in two weeks. He isn't even waiting for graduation, it's the old birthday-and-bounce, and everyone knows how few of those boys come back.

Sal is looking panicked—this is leagues beyond getting shitfaced on a Saturday night—but they're best friends, weekend witches, twins from different sins.

She whispers, "I'll do it."

It is 1940, and bioassays are already shifting away from mice and rabbits and on to frogs: *Xenopus laevis*, to be exact. It's a brilliant substitution, inspired by the research of Lancelot Hogben in the 1930s.

(The zoologist: British. His place of study: South Africa. Until he became disillusioned by the racism of the region, at which point he left the country behind and took a colony of frogs with him.)

Here is the genius of the development: within twelve hours of injecting the young frog with hormone-laden urine: *poof*, she lays eggs. Miles quicker than rabbit death row, and check this out: you can use the frog again!

There are obstacles in place (a doctor must decide that early diagnosis is warranted), but even so, tens of thousands of frogs will be exported from southern Africa each year to fill demand.

It is 1839, and there are no mice or rabbits or frogs in sight, but Catherine knows she is pregnant (she is all-too familiar with the signs), and she knows she cannot manage a fifth child on seamstress work.

She finds an ad in the *New York Sun*:

TO MARRIED WOMEN.—Is it not but too well known that the families of the married often increase beyond what the happiness of those who give them birth would dictate?...Is it moral for parents to increase their families, regardless of consequences to themselves, or the well-being of their offspring, when a simple, easy, healthy, and certain remedy is within our control? The advertiser, feeling the importance of this subject, and estimating the vast benefit resulting to thousands by the adoption of means prescribed by her, has opened an office, where married females can obtain the desired information.

The advertiser in question calls herself Madame Restell, and she takes clients at her Greenwich Street office between 9 a.m. and 10 p.m.

Catherine's grandmother swore by pennyroyal or tansy tea, but she also had more than one friend felled by a toxic dose. These are modern times, and Catherine would prefer something measured with more exactitude. In addition to the simple, easy, healthy, and certain remedy Madame Restell offers for people in situations such as Catherine's, she also sells Preventative Powder (five dollars per package) and Female Monthly Pills (one dollar apiece). Catherine isn't sure she can fit that into the family budget, but it would surely be a blessing if she could.

(It is 1839, and for enslaved women laboring against their will below the Mason-Dixon line there are no advertisements in the paper, there are no accessible offices on public streets, there is no quiet recovery in the privacy of their own homes, for they own nothing but their wits. For these women, forced to birth more children into the system that enslaves them, there is cotton root bark if they have the supply and the knowledge to use it, a remedy shared in whispers, a remedy that will bring down the foulest of punishments upon their heads if they are caught—but still they try.)

Catherine has no cause to know any of that, and if she did it would make her uneasy at best. She is not the sort of woman who attends abolitionist meetings or subscribes to their publications. She is a woman who scarcely has a moment free to tend her own problems, hence her need to tend *this* problem. Immediately.

She is lucky that someone has the means, the interest, and the entrepreneurial spirit to help her out.

It is 2091, and Grace is praying that someone might have the means, the interest, and the entrepreneurial spirit to help her out.

Within hours of installing Sal's blackout code, Grace feels her rabbit test commence. It's the barest prickle in her arm, the telltale tick of her med chip taking a blood sample. The scan goes straight to her tracker, and the animation of a laughing baby about stops her heart. But Sal's code holds true—her data is stored locally, and Grace deletes it with a desperate swipe before it can transmit to anyone else.

Grace sobs into her pillow for a good long while, convinced her plan has failed before it's even begun, because she can't do this, she can't do this, how did she think she could do this? She'll die and go straight to hell.

But her tears subside and she spends the rest of the afternoon scouring protest sites, seeking the ever-changing link to a link to a link that will land her on a temporary profile with the latest bot-evading slang for terminating pregnancy. She uses her bedroom ceiling for the projection, rapidly filling it with open pages, skimming one after another, trying to parse the euphemisms.

(It is 1840, and assorted Victorians are scanning the newspaper for *female regulators, cathartic pills*, anything that might solve *private difficulties* by *removing obstructions*. In 2091 there are no paper ads, but private difficulties remain.)

There. On a university black market page, buried among requests for machine-generated history papers and cafeteria access chips, Grace finds what she is looking for: *cheat sheets for rabbit tests.*

At least, she thinks this is what she's looking for. It could mean another blackout—or maybe it's just for birth control? Grace is vague on how the latter works.

The post is signed with the initials A.M.E. Grace rewrites her message a thousand times before settling on a hesitant, *What if I've already taken the test?*

Thirty excruciating minutes later, a reply pops up. *Give me your audio line.*

It makes sense not to have this conversation by text, blackout or no, but Grace's entire body begins to shake as soon as she sends her number. There is no way that she can talk to a stranger about this, there is no way she can make her confession to a possible-troll at best and a possible-cop at worst. When the call comes through her voice cracks on *hello.*

"You sound a mess," A.M.E. says, not without sympathy. "Tell me what you're looking for, babe."

It all spills out.

Over the next twenty minutes, Grace has one preconception challenged after another. For one thing, she had assumed all of the hoarders were old ladies, but A.M.E.—"Call me Ambrose"—laughs and assures her that he isn't *that* old, and he isn't a lady. Women aren't the only people worried about their uteruses, and Ambrose saw the writing on the wall long before the 2084 ban passed.

"I had the ol' womb exhume in the '70s," he says, "but I ordered as many pill packs as I could from overseas before the mail cracked down." He warns her that the pills have been expired for a year, but the worst-case scenario is they don't work, and she's already facing that.

He's charging four hundred dollars—he wants to help but hey, times are tough—and that's doable, barely, Grace can scrape that together between leftover birthday money and selling old toys on her market page. If anyone asks what the money was for, she'll say she took Sal out for dinner and a show.

And then he starts asking her questions that nobody has ever asked her before. What does she know about birth control? ("No, babe, taking it won't make you sterile for life. If only.") What are her plans after this? Not today, not next week, her *real* plans. Her life.

As Grace talks, she feels the decision taking hold. That's the gift Ambrose is giving her with this conversation, when he could have simply stated a price and a pickup location and left it at that. He isn't pressing her. He's giving her a moment to think it through, to own what she is about to do. It's her body.

"So," Ambrose says. "What's it gonna be?"

She's choked silent for a moment by a mudslide rush of fear and guilt. Grace can barely think the word in her own head (*abortion*) because it is so fraught, made dirty by her parents' strident warnings.

Her mother was there in 2084, you know, marching for stricter regulation of uterine care. People were killing their babies left and right before that, she said. It was easy. Untraceable. Rabbit tests were private, no requirement to inform a medical office; pills were on auto-order, so you'd scarcely notice the late date before a drone dropped a discreet package down the bathroom chute. And that was only the people who *weren't* hacking their natural biology, popping in gestational blocks like getting their ears pierced, as though the country wasn't in a population freefall, as though they weren't in dire need of sturdy white babies to survive the coming storms—(her mother's diatribes took many turns).

Grace still remembers hiding behind her mother's legs at that march, age nine and terrified of the crowd. She remembers the moment that her mother pulled her into the spotlight, and cried, "My miracle child! This is my miracle child!" And she told the entire story over amplification: how her prenatal pills had been swapped for baby killers (how could such a switch happen on accident? Grace would not question this until she was much older) and the doctor told her the chances of her child surviving were slim, even with immediate intervention, but she had prayed and prayed and prayed, and she'd saved Grace's life.

So yes, there is guilt. Mountains of it. Vast oceans, roiling with the rising temperature. Guilt the size of a rich man's space station.

But Grace is also exhilarated. She'll finish school. She'll be more careful. What are her plans after this? She doesn't know yet, but she desperately wants the time to figure them out.

"Tell me where to go," she says, and she means it.

It is 1978, and Alice is looking at an advertisement for the first FDA-approved home pregnancy test, now on shelves at pharmacies all over the country. It takes nine steps, two hours, an angled mirror, and a vial of sheep's blood, but for ten dollars you can investigate your own body in the privacy of your own home, and if the test comes up negative you can be eighty percent sure that it's correct.

It isn't merely the test that has taken Alice's breath away, but the coverage in *Mademoiselle*. For decades it has billed itself as the *quality magazine for smart young women*—those fashionable, sophisticated, career-minded girls of the '30s and '40s and '50s—and alongside the fashion editorials and the beauty tips it has boasted writers and editors such as Flannery O'Connor and Truman Capote, Shirley Jackson and James Baldwin, Joan Didion and Sylvia Plath.

But this is different.

The e.p.t In-Home Early Pregnancy Test is a private little revolution any woman can easily buy at her drugstore...Now its high accuracy rate has been verified here in America by doctors...That means you can confidently do this easy pregnancy test yourself—privately—right at home without waiting for appointments or delays...At last early knowledge of pregnancy belongs easily and accurately to us all.

The ad is remarkable enough, but it is the commentary on page 86 that has Alice close to tears. It is beautiful in its candor, its practicality—its *honesty*, baldly stating that the benefits of private and rapid results are that they give you a chance, if pregnant, "to start taking care of yourself...or to consider the possibility of early abortion."

To see those words printed openly in a national magazine?

She scarcely thought she'd see the day, because—

Because it is 1971, and Alice can't imagine how close she is to a future in which abortion is suggested with matter-of-fact sophistication in *Mademoiselle* and the rest of Condé Nast's women's magazine lineup.

Alice is a married woman with two children in school, and every afternoon she calls a list of complete strangers who have left messages for Jane. They are in dire need of help.

Jane does not exist.

Or rather, Jane is several women, and they provide a very specific service to the greater Chicago area. They call themselves the Abortion Counseling Service of Women's Liberation, but for the purposes of discretion, women in need can call the phone number on their flyer and leave a message for Jane, and Jane will get back to them soon.

(They are not the first group to think of this. There are Clergy Consultation Services in several states already—networks of pastors and ministers and rabbis lobbying for legalized abortion and referring women to legal clinics if they can afford to travel, and to discreet local contacts if they cannot.)

Once a week the whole crew meets up to assign phone numbers to the counselors for a callback. Alice is one of only a few Black members in the group. The rest are white. White housewives, white working women, white activists looking to do something tangible, something *now*. And they're helping thousands of people, there's no doubt about that, but the fact remains that as their service spreads through the South and West Side neighborhoods of Chicago, their clientele increasingly doesn't match their membership. Alice's goal is to provide these folks a reassuring and familiar face.

She joined as a counselor, driver, and sometimes-assistant after accompanying a friend to an appointment. *Call this number,* her friend's doctor had said. *They only charge what you can afford.* And sure as shit, Alice helped scrape fifty dollars together and fifty dollars is what it cost. She looked around that living-room-turned-waiting-room, full of frightened teenagers and weary moms-of-three, and she knew she wanted to help.

Abortion hadn't always been the purview of psych wards and hospital review boards; it hadn't always been a begrudging concession on one's deathbed or a desperate gamble in a germ-ridden hotel room.

It used to be the work of midwives and healers, friends and neighbors, those with wombs learning the workings of their own bodies.

Which is why the members of Jane are learning to perform the procedure themselves.

It is 2091, and Grace has no idea how a womb works, but *somebody* does, and she's heading his way.

Even with the blackout, she is too paranoid to hire a driver—everything leaves a trail, everything—and so she takes her little brother's electric scooter from the garage. Ambrose asked that she convert her money into gift cards rather than transfer it directly to him, and she's shaken by how many potential pitfalls she hadn't even considered.

Grace's destination—a parking lot with many exits, behind a hydroponic garden that used to be a mall—is fifteen miles from her home.

She leaves before dawn. Every streetlight is a searchlight, every passing face a spy. She's on that stage with her mother again, the bullhorn blaring *MIRACLE CHILD! MY MIRACLE CHILD!* And she's in her high school health class being told to abstain, make good decisions, have the integrity to wait, do not lift the veil of her body to an unworthy partner, and certainly do not lift it before being wed. She's failed her parents and her God and her teachers and her boyfriend and herself, but none of them need to know. She's going to hell, but not today.

Grace doesn't make it five miles before there's a horn blaring and her father shouting out the window and her mother sobbing in the passenger seat. Her father's wristband is flashing at the proximity—the scooter has an old geolocator tag that Grace had completely forgotten about.

Later she'll learn the details (Sal panicked and told her mother), but at the moment all she knows is that her parents are here, they've caught her, the door has slammed shut.

It is 2083, and Grace's mother is a single spear in a vanguard. Half the world is burning or flooding and the other half is arguing bitterly over who should take in refugees, if at all. (They'd postponed this future, a hard push in the '30s and '40s, a desperate revival of green initiatives, wholly reactive and far too late—but it was only a stall, in the end.)

Amelia is marching because she fears being outnumbered. She's marching because she believes it's her duty to save babies and place them in homes with good Christian values, because the scientific establishment is out of control, a cabal of demons on Earth locking an entire generation out of salvation.

She doesn't know or understand all of the terminology, but she's equally scathing toward every problem facing America today. Invasions at the border and children making up genders and godlessness in schools and lesbians in every sitcom and the greatest problem of all looming over the rest: the intrusion of technology into natural-born bodies. An entire economy of soulless elites enabling—encouraging!—people to tailor their hormones and alter their organs, to implant med chips and tracking devices, monsters who are giving their tech cute names like *rabbit test* when it isn't cute at all, it's a means to leap at the first sign of conception and take control of a natural process that ought to be left to God's will alone. (The hypocrisy of installing that same test in Grace will never occur to her; the right people have taken over monitoring it.)

The long and short of it is: her daughter will be raised better.

It is 2092, and Grace is a disappointment to her mother.

"*Breathe*," says the nurse.

Grace *is* breathing. She's also crying. She read what she could find about childbirth but nothing prepared her for the reality. At one point she is struck by the desperate, irrational desire to call Ambrose—at least he would tell her honestly what's about to happen. But that temporary profile is long gone; his number long disconnected.

"*Breathe*," says the nurse.

Grace is gasping. Her mother is at her side, but they are hardly speaking at this point. There are drugs, but she is in terrible pain. When the anesthesiologist ups the dose and half of Grace's body immobilizes, she has a panic attack.

The anesthesiologist's voice penetrates the haze. "...something for the anxiety?"

Grace's mother says yes. The drugs trickle in, and Grace can't remember most of what happens next.

It is 2092 and there is only so much comfort modern medicine can provide. Even if Grace's mother had hired a doula ("You don't need one," she had declared. "You have me.")—even if she had, what could a doula have said to make Grace feel any better? The deed is done.

A nurse holds up the infant, which is squalling in even more terror than its mother.

Barring any gender revelations to come: it's a girl.

It is 1817, and Asenath Smith is in love with an Episcopal preacher.

His name is Ammi Rogers, and he's been banned from the ministry in Connecticut for promoting separation of church and state. He works instead on the lucrative traveling preacher circuit, where he's grown exceedingly popular—particularly amongst the ladies.

Asenath, twenty-one years of age and grown up in a family of independent-minded women, met the controversial figure when he was giving comfort at the bedside of her dying grandmother, God rest her soul. She was smitten. She was smote.

When Asenath realizes she is pregnant, she goes straight to Rogers, secure in the fact of their upcoming marriage. They'll only have to hasten the date.

But Rogers won't marry her unless she ends the pregnancy. Most people ignore it when babies are born less than nine months from the wedding, but that courtesy will not be extended to him. His reputation is already under attack.

He gives her medication, but it doesn't take.

He attempts to use a tool, but that doesn't seem to work either, so he flees town. Several terrible, pain-ridden days later, Asenath gives birth: a stillborn.

The ensuing scandal is intense—the attempts at prosecution even more so. There is no seduction law in Connecticut, no statute banning abortion. He is arrested nonetheless.

The first trial fails when Rogers abducts Asenath and her sister, locking them up until they agree to withdraw their testimony. They keep their promise and refuse to cooperate at the second trial, but their former statements are presented anyway. In lieu of any charge more accurate, Rogers is convicted of sexual assault and sentenced to two years in prison.

The firestorm rages on. The coercion of Asenath Smith is central to the debate, but the debate does not include ways to ensure that women like Asenath can escape coercion. The General Assembly instead takes aim at medicinal abortion, eager to push midwives and grandmothers (many of them immigrants or formerly enslaved) out of the business—the first antiabortion legislation in the nation. Abortions approved and performed by doctors will remain protected for some time longer, putting these delicate bodily decisions into more authoritative hands.

This conclusion misses the point.

It is 2107, and Grace's daughter is fifteen years old. They've been living on their own for five of those years, finally out of Grace's childhood home and into a one-bedroom apartment in a downtrodden part of town. Most of Grace's neighbors are from India, and it's a relief to escape the constant scrutiny of her former neighbors, a relief to no longer be ducking her head in shame.

It isn't Olivia that Grace is ashamed of, even though that is what everyone expected of her. (She loves her daughter, despite it all.) Rather, she's ashamed of how long it took her to get out of that house. A decade of minimum wage shift work and listening to her mother's remonstrations about her character and the burdens of babysitting and social embarrassment, as if she hadn't kept Grace under strict supervision for eight months to ensure it would happen—

But it's over. These past five years have been peaceful. They've been revelatory. Her own life is under her own control (to the extent that working fifty-plus hours per week to afford pasta and imitation butter feels like control). Grace has cut ties to her church and only answers her mother's calls one third of the time. Life isn't what she hoped for, but she's learned to live with her life.

And then May comes.

In May, Olivia goes to a party after school and comes home sick. She can't remember a thing, but she's aching, she's distressed, she has nightmares that move like shadows in candlelight. They run a blood workup but whatever was in her system is gone without a trace.

Three weeks later she falls onto Grace's shoulder, panic-stricken, in disbelief, and in that second before the words tumble out of her mouth, Grace already knows. It's her rabbit test.

(It wasn't installed at Grace's request, or with either of their consent. Med chips are mandatory from age 6, the rabbit test from age 10. It's been a statewide law since 2102, and Grace can't afford to leave the state. The protesters who were so quick to condemn its use in private decision-making had no qualms about using it for surveillance.)

"What do I do?" Olivia cries. Over and over. "What do I do?"

Grace's mouth is dry. The words come out faintly. "I can fix this," she says. "If that's what you want."

"How?" Olivia whispers.

They stay up late that night, discussing the options. Grace tries not to reveal how badly she is shaking. She talks Olivia through the risks of trying to fake a miscarriage versus the risks of pregnancy and childbirth. She tries to give her the information she wishes she'd had, building the conversation without a blueprint.

"Have you run a search?" Grace asks abruptly.

"No, I came straight to you." Olivia reaches out hesitantly, as if to pull up a screen. "Should I...?"

"No!" Grace claps a hand over hers. "Don't search. Don't breathe a word to anyone, not even your best friend, do you understand?"

At the moment, the law only condemns the procurer. Olivia is a minor. Her body belongs to Grace in the eyes of the law, and therefore Grace is responsible for what comes next.

She does everything she can to cover her tracks. An anonymous account from a throwaway device, an exchange location in a terrifying part of town where the network is always down, an even more terrifying night spent rubbing her daughter's back, coaching her through the cramps and nausea, making note of the size of her blood clots and rehearsing the story they'll tell the doctor the next morning—

It isn't enough.

All it takes is one suspicious nurse to flag Olivia's paperwork. Why didn't they make an appointment when her rabbit test came up positive? Why didn't they go to the E.R. at the first sight of blood?

Grace's background is scrutinized, her location data inspected for mysterious gaps, witnesses contacted in regards to her character. And then, evidence where she didn't even know to destroy it: a drug test performed on their household wastewater line.

She is arrested for murder, but the public defender tells her they can get it knocked down to voluntary manslaughter if she attests that she was out of her mind, in a heat of passion triggered by the memory of her own thwarted abortion and the lack of a man's support. Grace doesn't want to be cast as a madwoman who shoved pills down her daughter's throat in a fit of old-fashioned hysteria, but it takes the sentence down from twenty years without parole to twelve.

She'll go away, and Olivia will be remanded into the custody of Grace's own mother.

And all Grace can think of as she's led out of the courtroom is: I had five years of my own. I had five years.

It is 1993, and she wants this baby *so much*, they have been trying and trying; there's a heartbeat, she can *hear* it, but there isn't a brain. Her body won't let it go, and the doctor says I am very sorry, but I will have to remove it myself.

It is 2015, and she has to sneak in on a Tuesday because her youth group is protesting the clinic on Saturday, and she needs a couple of days to recover or they'll wonder why she isn't there. She'll weep in the recovery room and call the nurse a murderer.

It is 1965, and she has to convince a hospital review board that she's suicidal, clutching letters from two separate psychiatrists, all for the privilege of spending two nights in a psych ward and having all her bits shaved for no clear reason, but it works, it's humiliating but it *works*, and she knows she's one of the lucky ones for finding a way.

It is 1150, and Hildegard von Bingen, the Sybil of the Rhine, is settling into life as the abbess of a monastery built in her honor. She is preparing to write the medical tomes *Physica* and *Causae et Curae*, in which, among many other remedies, she will list her most tried-and-true abortifacients. Officially, the Church considers the practice a sin, but it is not murder until the quickening, that moment four or five months along when the soul enters the body, and so a nun providing this care to her community is not remarkable, but merely practical.

The Romans have their silphium and the Chinese have achyranthes root. The Shoshone have stoneseed, the Lakota have sagewort, the Hawaiians have elixirs of hau, noni, 'awa, and young kī leaves. The Victorians have their tansy tea and savin, their ergot of rye, their black draught and mallow and motherwort. Millennials have got mifepristone and misoprostol, and the climate generation has gestational blocks and yellow pills droned straight to the bathroom chute.

It is 1750—seventeen fucking fifty—and Mary is consulting a dog-eared copy of *The American Instructor*, the greatly popular household textbook. It is not an arithmetic lesson that occupies her today—though math will come in useful—but an entry in the medical section at the back.

Mary is reading instructions on how to cure that most common of complaints among unmarry'd Women: the SUPPRESSION of the COURSES. Mary's courses are suppressed, all right, have been for weeks, and as a widow of certain means and a disinclination to marry again, it isn't the first time she's had to consult this home remedy. To cure her Misfortune, she's got to purge with Belly-ach Root and then drink Pennyroyal Water with Spirits of Harts-horn twice a day for nine days, then take three days rest, then go on again for nine more days. It's a pain, but better than the alternative.

(It is 1750, and across the vast tracts of North America there are dozens of Indigenous tribes with more than a hundred alternatives, but Mary has just got this book.)

She emits a light, "*Fah*," at the warnings and preventative measures listed at the end of the passage, as she always does. They conclude with a prim exhortation not to long for *pretty Fellows*, or any other *Trash* whatsoever. Her current fellow is not trash—he is really rather respectable—but Mary has no desire to shackle her person or her estate to another master, no matter how pretty. She watched her mother die on the birthing bed at age 42. She watched her sisters fade to shadows under the demands of overfull houses.

The death of her first husband has given Mary the freedom to move about as she wishes; to run her own household and control her own fate.

She isn't going to give that up lightly.

It is 2119, and Grace hasn't given up, but the years have been painful and slow. Today, she is getting out of prison.

She's not the same woman she was. She's angrier. She's hurting. She has a permanent cough from the last virus to run rampant through the prison population. But after twelve years, she's just as scared of reentering the world outside as she is of never seeing it again.

Olivia is waiting in the parking lot. They stare at each other for a moment that burns like a California wildfire and then they fall into one another's arms.

There's a child in the backseat of Olivia's car, four years old and squashed nose-first against the glass. He's named Raley, after the activist who made the marriage of his mothers possible after so many decades in which it was not. The tide is turning on bodily autonomy again. One generation's fight to choose their partners is fueling the fight to choose the size of their families—a reversal of the historic civil rights progression that will inspire dissertation topics for years to come.

"I missed you," Olivia says.

"I missed *everything*." Grace has held herself together for so long, she *refuses* to break down in the parking lot ten feet from the damn gate—but she comes close.

And then Olivia says, "I'm speaking at the decision next week. Will you come?"

Grace flinches. It's too much, too soon. Her world has been reduced to a handful of walls and familiar faces for years, and now Olivia is asking her to stand up in front of one hundred thousand people?

"*Please*," Olivia says.

Grace shuts her eyes.

The world continued to burn while she was gone. The last decade has seen ever more flooding and fire, hurricanes and heat waves, collapsing coastlines and viruses named for every letter of the alphabet. Some of these disasters hit the prison, in the form of power outages and spoiled food and illness and neglect, but others were only items in the news, dire glimpses of the life waiting for them outside. Grace has missed riots and assassinations. She's missed a national strike and no small number of election day bombings. But there are strides being made, small victories being won, and Olivia truly believes that a big one is coming next week.

It's happening. The final vote. Congress is on the verge of overturning the ban and returning some measure of bodily autonomy to more than half the population. There isn't a supply chain in place for abortion medication anymore; there aren't many doctors trained in the scant emergency procedures they are occasionally allowed to perform, and they certainly won't be welcoming any black-market midwives into their fold to make up the deficit. But they have a president waiting to sign. They have businesses eager to flood the market. They have a multi-million-dollar video campaign ready to roll out, complete with celebrity cameos.

If it passes. If.

If it doesn't, then things are going to get ugliest exactly where Olivia is asking her to be. There will be violence. Tear gas deployed by drone and skirmishes with National Guard robotics. There will be arrests in the thousands.

Grace imagines that chaos and suddenly she's nine years old again, being dragged into the spotlight as a poster child for uterine regulation. She's hearing her fate screamed through a bullhorn, she is stepping up to the mic and agreeing *my mother saved my life and your mother saved yours*, she is two months shy of turning eighteen and nursing the sting of a slap on her face, she is locked in her room except for mealtimes and exercise, she is locked in her cell except for mealtimes and exercise, she is watching her entire life pass by and wondering who she would have been if she'd been allowed to make up her own mind.

Her mother helped break this world. Her daughter is trying to fix it.

She looks at little Raley, his face still pressed to the car window, watching her, wondering what kind of person this prison grandmother of his is, and she's wondering the same thing. She says, "I'll go."

It is 2119, and Olivia is standing on stage with a dozen people behind her and a hundred thousand in front. Her wife is at her side, their marriage barely two years legal. Her son is wedged between them, dazzled by the lights.

The Senate steps are filled with shoulder-to-shoulder policing units, blue lights blinking on their boxy chests. The air is full of cameras—military surveillance and media coverage and endless proxies from supporters who could not make it in person.

It is Olivia's turn to speak. She is here to represent the grassroots group she joined the day she ran away from her grandmother's house, living couch to couch and paycheck to paycheck. She is here to represent everyone else who has struggled to build a life on an obstacle course.

She shouts, "There is no justification for obeying an immoral law!" and the roar from the crowd is deafening. She pulls Raley tight to her side, a child she chose, and she speaks of the past and the present and the future.

"At every turn, we've sought to know more about our bodies," she says. "And at every turn, that knowledge has been used to rope us in tighter, to set the deadline shorter, to put private decisions in the hands of public officials, as if we can't be trusted to choose for ourselves."

Olivia flings her other arm wide. She says, "We only want to control our own destinies! We want to decide the course of our lives, and not see every scientific advance weaponized against us. It is 2119, and I would not have this child if I'd been forced to term before I was ready, before I had a home worth sharing. And—"

It is 1350 BCE, and she is urinating on bags of wheat and barley seeds, waiting to see how quickly they will sprout. It works more often than you'd think.

She just wants to *know*, so she can plan, either way. And—

It is 1021, and she is watching the shah's physician pour sulfur over her urine, looking for the worms he believes will spring from the mix. It doesn't work any better than you'd think.

She just wants to *know*, so she can plan, either way. And—

It is 1658, and she is waiting at the home of the local piss prophet. He holds the matula up to the light, peering through the glass to assess the color of the liquid within.

She just wants to *know*, so she can plan either way. And—

It is 1998, and Lee Berger just identified the fungus causing a decades' long decline in Australian frog species. It was carried on the skin of our old friend *Xenopus laevis*, exported by the tens of thousands for urine-injection-pregnancy tests, and now it is threatening extinction to thirty percent of the world's amphibians.

It's unfortunate as hell for the frogs, but all of those people just wanted to *know*, so they could plan either way. Because—

—because she is still ten thousand dollars in debt from her *last* time giving birth.

—because if she stops taking her medication, she will die.

—because the thought makes him vomit, makes him faint, he wouldn't survive it.

—because if they don't finish school, they'll be raising this baby in their parent's basement.

—because she simply doesn't want to, she doesn't *want* to, she doesn't need to be on her deathbed or underage or running from a monster, her doctor said she couldn't get her tubes tied unless she had three children already, but where's the logic in giving birth to three children for the permission to have *none*?

It is 2084 and she is crying, "Our grandmothers fought so hard for this."

It is 2206 and she is crying, "Our grandmothers fought so hard for this."

It is 1878 and Madame Restell is bleeding to death in her bathtub rather than submit to another trial. It is 1821 and Asenath Smith is fleeing town in disgrace. It is 1972 and seven of the women of Jane have just been arrested in a raid. It is 2086 and Grace's medical record has been officially upgraded to that most precarious of categories: *potential to become pregnant*.

It is 2022 and it isn't over.

It is 2022 and it is never over.

Samantha Mills is a Nebula, Locus, and Theodore Sturgeon Memorial Award winning author living in Southern California. You can find her short fiction in *Uncanny Magazine*, *Beneath Ceaseless Skies*, *Strange Horizons*, and others, as well as the best-of anthologies *The New Voices of Science Fiction* and *The Year's Best Science Fiction & Fantasy 2023*. Her debut science fantasy novel, *The Wings Upon Her Back*, is out now! You can find more at www.samtasticbooks.com.

D. I. Y.

John Wiswell

People ask how Noah could possibly turn down the Ozymandias Academy. All they know about him is the headlines, and they think he's ungrateful. What you don't get is that attending Ozymandias was Noah's dream. Noah wanted it worse than anyone.

Do you know where he was on his fifth birthday? Sitting in the stained passenger seat of his mom's clunker, bouncing with excitement because she was driving him to mail his application. He clutched the envelope in both hands so there was no chance of dropping it.

He asked his mom, "Did you know Vamon doesn't need a wand?"

His mom teased him, "Vamon who?"

He sounded out the syllables. "Va-mon Kinc-tu-ar-in. He saved the whole world. He teaches at Oz-y-man-di-as."

"That's a big name. Did he listen to his mom?"

Noah sat up as though she had blasphemed. "Mom. He was an orphan."

"And he became a magician but didn't need a wand?"

Noah started wheezing, like he had crickets in his lungs. He said, "He could make daggers from nowhere, and one time he used bone magic so that all the skeletons in a graveyard fought for him. When he was too tired, he magicked his own bones to keep fighting against the Seraphs. All of it without a wand. Do you know what he used instead?"

"Honey, take a puff of your inhaler."

For a moment Noah removed a few fingertips from the envelope, wiggling them like they were shooting lightning through the windshield. "He did magic with his hands."

The next light turned yellow and his mom rolled the car to a stop. Under that yellow traffic light, Noah's wheeze became a brittle cough. It wasn't phlegm. His shoulders rocked against the seat and he hugged his application letter to his chest. Fighting through the coughing, he said, "Vamon's going to solve the drought. I'm going to help."

"Honey? Breathe. Where's your inhaler?"

"I'm going to do magic with my—" His proclamation gave way to a peal of strangled coughs.

His mom held the inhaler up for him, but he couldn't take the breath. The light turned red as she unbuckled herself to get at him. When she took him by the shoulders, he slumped into her side. That was the first time Noah blacked out.

When the paramedics got him, he was still holding his application.

If the Ozymandias Academy accepts you, the image of Vamon Kinctuarin visits you. He projects himself as a transparent green specter. It's tradition or something. The two of you are supposed to have an intimate conversation about the future of your education.

When he was ten, Noah had the transparent green action figure of Vamon on his person at all times. He asked it things.

"Are you proud of me?"

"Am I as brave as you were?"

"Are you fucking kidding?" his mom asked the receptionist at the clinic.

The receptionist barely moved, like this old white lady was so tired she didn't have energy left for nodding. She said, "They don't cover these tests no more. You should try St. Mary's."

"St. Mary's sent me here," his mother yelled, too angry to convince anybody, and too angry to stop being angry. "They're not accepting anyone on account of the drought. My son turned ten today and he has Cherub lung. Do you get that? Do you know what that means?"

Noah had heard it before, so he took his action figure and a pen from the nurse's station to fill out another Ozymandias Academy application. He'd already sent two that year, but there was a rumor online that they had some dropouts during spring break.

The receptionist said, "I didn't defund the plan. There's no money for anything no more. It's all going to the water crisis."

"I don't give a shit about water if my son isn't going to be here to drink it."

Their argument reminded Noah of something: The Ozymandias Academy had won a bunch of grants from the water crisis fund. He added a PS to his letter asking how their aquamancy program was going since he had some ideas for expanding it. His mind fuzzed out in the middle of writing.

The next thing he knew, he was on the prickly brown carpet, looking up at his mom. Cherub lung had made him black out again. That was getting more common.

He panicked until he found his application letter. It was underneath him. He asked, "Can we mail this wherever we're going next?"

Carrying him out of the clinic, she said, "If you want to be a wizard so bad, why don't you study that shit on your own?"

It was Noah's fifteenth birthday when Vamon finally visited.

It was midafternoon. Noah was in his bedroom with the blinds drawn like an appropriately pissy teenager, hunched over his concentrator rig. A concentrator is one of those "baby's first levitation" kits, a series of glass rods with minor magical charge that can float briefly in the air. Noah repurposed the kit to draw water from the air itself. After a week of tedious experiments, he had a cup one-quarter full of water. Or was that three-quarters empty?

The rest of the cup filled with green spectral presence, and there came the image of a wizened man wearing spectacles and a pointed hat. Vamon threw his arms out and bellowed, "Noah Byrne, I welcome you to this autumn's class of the Ozymandias Academy of Magic and Mystery. It is time to create what endures."

Noah held on to his desk as though to prevent himself from floating away, "Is this real?"

"It is."

Noah tried to swallow. "I got the scholarship? Really?"

Vamon's famous voice boomed, "There is very limited financial assistance for students who join the academy as late as you. The acceptance itself is a miracle."

"My mom just came off three back-to-back shifts. Please keep your voice down." Noah sure wasn't floating now. His elbow bumped a stack of bills and denial letters from health-care providers. He asked, "What did I qualify for? We're worse than broke."

Vamon folded his arms down at the fifteen-year-old boy. "Greatness requires sacrifices."

Noah felt a burn in his veins, like he was poisoned with a Seraph's venom. He gestured to the glass concentrator on his desk, and the quarter-full cup. "I made water. I used the magical processes I talked about in my application. It needs work, but it's real water. If you help me get in, I'll do whatever I can to make this fill Ozymandias's reservoirs."

The specter of his hero looked cursorily over the concentrator. "Quaint. Second-year students do better in their first week."

"Have you got water at Ozymandias?"

Vamon's voice shook the walls. "We have infinity. Are you going to turn down the invitation of a lifetime?"

"If you have infinity, can't you help me out? People helped you out when you were a kid."

"Me?" Vamon scoffed. "I got where I am by working harder than anyone else."

"Yeah, you worked hard," Noah said, an asthmatic rasp climbing in his voice. He reached for his inhaler. "But you had your inheritance, and those legendary guardians, and all your friends. With help, you stopped the Seraph. All I'm asking for is a little of the help you got."

"This is a disappointment, Noah," said his hero. "This acceptance should've gone to someone who actually wanted it."

Noah says he didn't cry, but whenever he tries to tell this story he winds up coughing until he passes out before he can finish. I know he tossed his inhaler at the specter and screamed every expletive he knew. What made him stop was hearing his mother stir in the other room, and the wave of guilt that brought on. He couldn't speak without yelling, and he couldn't yell without robbing his mom of sleep. Of course he collapsed.

He lay on the floor for hours after the phantom of his hero walked out on him.

You could tell Noah was a smart guy because he watched my channel. MX_ POTLUCK was (and still is, thank you) your one-stop shop for practical magic tips and horror movie opinions. At that time, my channel had already been banned twice for discussing forbidden arts. I always knew I was onto something when my channel got flagged.

Noah's was one of the whopping twenty-seven views I got on my first video about Seraph bones and the composition of wands. I was really into speculation on what Ozymandias did with Seraph bones to build their magical devices, and how much angelic magic lingered after the death of an angel. Meanwhile, Noah was scraping the internet for info on how to build his own wand.

He kept getting into fights in my comment sections. You can't tell everybody's age, but the zeal he had for arguing with randos screamed "teenager with too much free time."

And he was usually right. He wouldn't let anyone shit-talk my pronouns. My favorite was, *How're you going to memorize spells in dead languages if you can't even remember ze/zir?*

And if they made fun of my wheelchair? He'd spew flames before I even had the chance to ban them. I still banned them, after he murdered them with words. Eventually we started DMing, sometimes about magic, sometimes anime GIFs. We spent a lot of Friday nights sending each other "bone magic" jokes. We were so bad at flirting.

We were going to see one of those angel-themed horror movies that boomers say are tasteless because of the war, but I just can't get enough of them. Have you ever watched one? These whirling CGI nightmares of limbs coming after people who can't act? It's hilarious.

I picked the park where we'd meet. Noah was going to wear a pirate shirt and I was still so nervous that I wouldn't recognize him. I actually recognized him by his coughing.

He was the only guy on that sidewalk on his knees. This chonky white boy, this absolute unit with Starburst-strawberry-pink cheeks as he coughed like he was trying to expel his own lungs. Noah tried to prop himself against a mailbox and pose, as though he was merely casually dying.

Do you know how cute he looked? I wanted to put him in my pocket and keep him forever.

As his breathing calmed, he asked, "You're Mx. Potluck?"

I wheeled myself up the dip on the curb and over to him. "We're in public, dude. Call me Manny."

We hung out in Danielson Memorial Park, where the first Seraph was brought down. All the wreckage has been paved over, lives replaced with sculpture gardens. On hot days like that one, the place smells inexplicably of fresh rubber. I looked at the ground, feeling nostalgic. When I was little, before my kidneys turned against me, I used to come here all the time.

I scratched the toe of my shoe against the dirt and said, "I always wanted to find Seraph bones buried somewhere around here."

Noah turned a sour expression at the grass. "Yeah, I dug here too."

I asked, "Really?"

"Then I learned that Ozymandias had stripped every bone fragment out of the city long before we were born. They don't want anyone else doing magic."

I stuck out my tongue. "Yeah, we're so irresponsible."

Noah and I sat at the picnic table under the shadow of the wing of a statue of a dead angel, in a spot where the perspective meant all we could see was the wing, and not the conquering wizard standing over it. We bullshitted there for an hour, showing off the petty magic tricks we knew. He showed me how he manipulated water movements through air using his glass rods. I levitated his used tissues into a trash can. It was that embarrassing. When he made a playing card "disappear" up his sleeve, I choked on my own spit laughing.

The showtime for the movie was drawing near. I was working up the nerve to ask if he'd ever been on a date before, which was my super sly way of figuring out if we were on a date. Galaxy-brain teenager shit, right?

Then a fire truck screeched past us. Two more followed it, and Noah asked if we could skip the movie. I was going to mock him for being paranoid when I noticed how rough he looked. His lungs were almost as bad as my kidneys, and the smoke got him before I could smell it. We couldn't see the fire and it was killing him.

My place was the best option, since it was closer. We livestreamed the fire for hours. I'd felt how achingly dry it was without considering that old buildings might go up. It took the authorities another two hours to pipe in water to that district to begin fighting it. Somebody aimed a webcam at a nearby storm drain to film all the gallons of brown water that came streaming out of those ruined buildings. When we saw people try to drink that water, I turned it off. We watched a horror movie to try to take our minds off it.

The next day was what set Noah off.

Our city was in the top three worst hit by the drought in the entire country. The governor arranged a deal with magical institutions from around the globe to help. We begged for somebody to come stop apartment buildings from burning down.

The lowest bidder was the Ozymandias Academy. There were so many videos of their cavalcade of black cars rolling up to the capitol. Vamon Kinctuarin held a press conference from in front of an empty dam and said, "We are here to ensure no one suffers further indignity."

The Ozymandias Academy took control of all water supplies and municipal resources. That meant everybody on my block could expect our faucets to work for one hour a day. The same on Noah's block.

I didn't hear from Noah all afternoon. His mom took his phone and shut off the Wi-Fi so he couldn't say anything public and get in trouble. She's smart as hell.

She called me over. Noah had had two attacks in one afternoon triggered by his manic anger. And how swollen was his hand? He didn't have hand problems. He'd been punching his floor, leaving his fingers in several shades of baked ham.

I'd been that mad before. That's why I knew how to be constructively mean.

I asked, "How the fuck are you going to do magic in the hospital?"

Noah muttered, "Shut up."

"Like I ever shut up," I said. "Do you think Vamon felt that? Is he hidden under the floor?"

"Shut the fuck up."

"Because you beat your hand so bad you won't jack off for a month. Vamon doesn't give one tiny, miniscule damn. The city's carrying his bags while you're here picking your fingernails off the floor."

He looked at me. "So?"

"So do you want to keep hurting yourself, or do you want to hurt them?"

I asked, "How do we kill a drought?"

Noah sat back, smug, on his bed. "The way I start all my research."

Noah went to one of the big forums—I won't name it, but one the neckbeards in your life probably frequent. He used my VPN and created a new account. He typed up a post with the subject line: "WHY CAN'T THEY JUST DRINK OCEAN WATER?"

His post was trash. He thought every existing pipe system could take the same volume of water. He wanted to disperse water using aquamancy that "literally everybody knows how to do." His post called the government and the wizard industry lazy for not thinking of using oceans as water supplies.

I read it between my fingers. "It's salt water, Noah. You'd die of dehydration drinking it."

He posted it anyway. Thirty-two minutes later, a mod locked his thread.

In those thirty-two minutes, he got more than six hundred comments correcting every angle of his bad assumptions. More commenters than you'd think linked to external articles. We were barraged with starting points to our research.

Noah said, "There is no educational resource in the cosmos greater than a nerd who thinks you're wrong."

Every time we hit a wall in our plan, we made another account and trolled forums pretending to be someone who believed what we actually wanted to do was impossible. We never thought we were smarter than everyone else; we just had to trick people into making us smarter.

We didn't invent the wand or Wi-Fi or the keyboard. We wanted to add something to the big pool of ideas so everybody could use it.

I don't know which was harder: crunching the equations, or tutoring people and selling stuff to fund our experiments. We couldn't test most of our theories since we didn't have access to a wand. It was so exhausting, I didn't realize some of my problems weren't from exhaustion. I passed out a few times. Those were warning signs.

We were so excited. By researching cutting-edge water-treatment plants and new papers on the aquamancy of water disbursement and necromancies related to killing off bacteria and neutralizing pollutants, we got close to an idea.

I fiddled with the last horror toy I hadn't sold, and I asked, "Are we close to an idea that the Ozymandias Academy already has?"

Noah said, "If they can't do better than us with the entire world bankrolling them? Then screw them."

In the months we worked, Ozymandias had scarcely provided water to anybody. A few upscale neighborhoods got some relief—the ones where Ozymandias's big donors lived. You probably saw the video of the shirtless pharma bro watering his lawn and threatening to call the cops on kids for filming him.

The same day that video went viral was the day we built our wand. A real wand. It was a beautiful piece of shit.

For the rest of our lives we'd never be able to afford an official licensed one. It had to be homebuilt. We used a hollow shaft that I won in a contest, carved from a scrap of a thousand-year-old fossilized tree that saints used to meditate under. By the time we tested our spell with it, it contained equal parts Seraph bone dust and duct tape.

Noah running around his room with the wand was the purest thing ever. He wore a welding visor and firefighter gloves just in case. He didn't even use it for magic at first. Climbing atop his bed and posing like he was shooting lightning made him so stupidly happy.

I remember all of it until I don't remember any of it. That was one of the days I passed out.

Trolls blame me. They say I didn't help much with the research. Sometimes I'll get asked, "If you were so important, how come you weren't in the reveal video?"

Who do you think was filming the video, genius? This movie nut. That's who. I took the time to find a spot with good lighting and to get the framing right—in landscape mode, which is a great modern discovery some wizards should make.

I parked my chair far enough away to get a good shot of Noah and anybody who passed by. He had his little table and free water sign. A surprising number of people trusted him enough to stop. More wanted a sip than wanted to talk.

They lingered, though, after he made the empty cups refill in front of their eyes.

"Where's it hidden?" asked a middle-aged woman who checked under his table for a hose. There wasn't any.

He waggled his wand. "It's not a trick. It's a brand-new spell."

People drank. A couple of old chess players split a cup to cool their brows. One guy in a blue three-piece suit literally tossed an entire cup of water onto himself and ran away cheering. This city was thirsty.

Soon I wasn't the only one filming him. I'm just a little bitter that he went viral on somebody else's channel. And their video was in portrait mode and missed half of it. The internet has no taste.

For two weeks, Noah Byrne was the most famous wizard in America. He had more Google hits than any Ozymandias alumni. We were petty enough to check.

Everybody wanted the secret. The federal government sent us scary-sounding letters. We got an equal number of offers from agents and lawyers. Every major wizard association called, including the Ozymandias Academy.

Ozymandias didn't just want to know the secret. They wanted to own it. It's why we rushed our patent claim—so they couldn't snoop the discovery and try to steal it from under us. Neither of us could afford to go to the places they gatekept. We weren't letting the secret of potable water become some company's premium feature.

Noah asked me, "How do we get it to everybody? How do we distribute this everywhere?"

I snarked, "We could tell the internet it's impossible and see if they fix the problem for us. Think you can be annoying enough to fool them into altruism?"

He gave me a hug and nuzzled into my shoulder for a bit. Most couples would've kissed there and ridden off into the sunset. We weren't into allosexual stuff. I preferred a good hug.

I should've realized something was wrong when his hug hurt my side so badly.

It's funny that the internet blames me for everything, since I don't remember most of what happened next. I was conscious for less than half of it.

TL;DR: My kidneys shut down, and that caused a cascade of compromised organs to also fail. I woke up with tubes everywhere and machines blinking over me. I was too weak to move my head. All I could think about was that old story of wizards using bone magic to move themselves when their bodies were failing.

I lay there under Noah's mournful gaze, like he was at my wake instead of my bedside. My aunts had definitely talked to him. We were behind on payments for my previous treatments. There was no way we could afford what was going to come next.

Looking up at him, I said, "Maybe we should've studied bone magic instead."

"Come on, Manny. You're going to be fine."

"Think of the cool skeleton friends you'd have."

"Can I do anything for you? I could put on a scary movie. It can be as trashy as you want."

My eyes were so tired that I closed them. "If you really want to do something for me..." I trailed off, leading him.

"Yeah? What do you want?"

"Can you magic me a glass of water?"

I know he would've elbow dropped me to death if I wasn't already dying. It felt so good to get on someone's nerves. I laughed until I drooled, and I drooled so much it got in my left ear.

All the warmth that brought me drained away when a green specter materialized. It was Vamon Kinctuarin. His specter made him look taller than he really is and improved his complexion. He stood outside the door of my hospital room, like a vampire that needed to be invited in.

Noah stormed out of the room, meeting him in the hall. He didn't want Vamon anywhere near me. He was a real sweetheart.

The first thing I remember hearing was Vamon saying, "I'm here to help."

Between every breath, cricket sounds raged in Noah's chest. "We didn't invite you here. Get out."

"You're a driven young man. You applied to the academy again and again. You know Ozymandias can help your friend."

"Manny is more than a friend. And ze doesn't trust you, and neither do I."

"The money the Ozymandias Academy is offering will let you hire whoever you do trust to help."

There was a pause. I strained to listen.

Noah said, "What are you asking me?"

"To help us achieve the greater good."

"You have people in the patent offices. You know the secret by now. Go use it."

"The Ozymandias Academy does not spy."

Noah made a crackly half-cough, half-laugh. He gestured with his inhaler. "Everybody knows you do. But I won't sue if you use it. That's what you want, yeah?"

"We need more than that."

"I don't get it. I already said you can use our spell. What is it you want?"

Vamon's voice deepened. "No organization in the world does more good through owning patents than the Ozymandias Academy."

"You want to own our fucking patent? No. I'll fucking die first."

"It's not your death that you're concerned about."

That's why those motherfuckers from the Ozymandias Academy show up as phantoms. When Noah threw his inhaler at him, it passed right through his emerald green image. Noah threw that, then my lunch tray, then the table it had sat on. Things clattered and rained down on the linoleum floor, and if I could've sat up, I would've handed him my IV stand to throw too.

The next thing on the floor was Noah, sinking to his knees in a coughing fit. The cricket-chirp sounds of his breathing swarmed. He couldn't fight Vamon and the Ozymandias Academy. He could barely fight for breath.

We had to sign.

The morning I was discharged was the hottest on record. Just looking at the sliding glass doors felt like it'd burn my fingertips. Under my gown, I felt like a bunch of steaks somebody stapled together that the doctors had mistaken for a survivor. Maybe the heat out there would cook me.

Noah said, "Don't look at the internet. It'll make it worse."

I looked. That same morning, Ozymandias had released a statement saying they'd cracked the water crisis while "working with ambitious amateurs." Full water supplies were restored to a limited number of counties around our state. Videos showed sprinklers in rich neighborhoods, few of them actually in our city.

The Ozymandias Academy helped a water park reopen. That was the greater good our breakthrough went to. To "give everyone a place they can be refreshed"—at a public business that charged $99.99 per admission.

I went back to my aunts' apartment, where the taps were all dry. Noah came with me. Legally, I'm going to say we dwelled in our defeat and did absolutely nothing.

Legally, I'm going to say it wasn't us. I was half dead. We were just ambitious amateurs. How could what happened next have been us?

Whoever did it was fucking brilliant, though.

Somebody took our patented spell—now it was the Ozymandias Academy's patented spell—and posted every detail about it on one of the biggest forums on the internet. They used a VPN and a new account so there was no tracing who did it.

By the time the Ozymandias Academy's lawyers got the forum to delete it, the information had been downloaded 13,642 times.

After that, there was no squashing it. Those people downloading it weren't just corporations that Ozymandias could sue into submission. Every wizarding enthusiast in the world could access this information. When Ozymandias complained about it, more people looked it up. It spread to thousands of other places, some in countries that don't care about intellectual property rights. The internet became an army of cool necromancied skeletons, rising over and over to keep the fight going.

The Ozymandias Academy threatened to sue Noah and me.

Noah told them, "Our work was contributed to by countless of other aspiring wizards across the internet. Any of them could have done this. I didn't send shit. Manny, did you?"

I was too busy snickering. A few hours earlier I'd wiped my hard drive, for totally unrelated reasons. Totally unrelated.

As I finished reformatting, Noah said, "Manny, come see this."

He popped open my window and stuck his head outside to stare.

I wheeled my way over to him. Through the window, crisp air swirled in through my room, like the first breath you take after a nightmare. It was a damn sight less hot than anything in the forecast for today. It was downright humid. I didn't understand until I saw the gray clouds.

There were people on every roof I could see from the window, and others running along the street. It was like spontaneous block party, with everybody looking up at the sky. Little pinpricks appeared along my windowsill, and the car roofs and awnings across the street. Folks carried empty pitchers and cups to catch what fell. Something cool spattered against the back of my right hand.

The people of this city took our secret and used it to make rain. It went on for hours and hours, one of which became a viral phenomenon. Viral rainfall. Thousands of people pooled whatever scraps of magic they had so that everybody, no matter how special they were supposed to be, would have enough to drink.

It was smarter than anything Noah or I ever thought to do. Something you could only do as a vast group. All of you really taught us.

....

John Wiswell is a disabled writer who lives where New York keeps all its trees. He is a Nebula and Locus Award winner, and has been short-listed for the Hugo, World Fantasy, and British Fantasy Awards. He is the author of two novels: *Someone You Can Build A Nest In* and *Wearing The Lion*.

GIVE ME ENGLISH

Ai Jiang

I traded my last coffee **for a coffee.** How ironic. My finger jabbed at the ordering machine. The Langbase implanted in my brain popped up in front of my eyes, and I watched as the word disappeared. A heavy breath escaped my lips. I would have to trade my **tea**s next.

The Langbase total changed from 987 to 986 words. I blinked twice to close it. There was one fewer word I could use to communicate with others—or to pay for necessities and rent. The word c----- was like a familiar stranger. My Langbase blurred it from my mind now that I had used the last one as payment. I could trade for it again with my duplicate **have**s and **you**s but having c----- wasn't a necessity. No longer could I use it when speaking, writing, or processing it when others said or wrote it. Though there were a finite number of words I could use to trade, I was allowed to use the words indefinitely as long as I still had them in my Langbase. Would I become a Silent, too, when my Langbase emptied?

Incoming message from Jorry.

I muttered under my breath and blinked twice to open the message.

Remember that the L---- show is tonight! I'll be picking you up in 30 minutes.

Of course I remembered. He had sent reminders every few hours for the past two days. Although I had been thankful for Jorry in the past, his narcissism was difficult to handle at times.

My reply floated in the air across my eyes while I waited for my c-----.

Yes, yes. I remember. I'll be at the usual drink shop.

Oh, you mean L------'s C-----? The selections there are m--------. I cannot f---- purchasing c----- elsewhere.

He was gloating. I held my breath, irritated. It had been a while since the last time I attempted deciphering his words. I knew it would only make me more frustrated.

Yes. That one. It's great.

My answer sounded dry. I didn't want to speak to Jorry. He always used words that he knew I no longer had. Women, he believed, as per Chinese traditional mind-sets, were better silent, docile, obedient. Of course, I disagreed. The only reason I put up with him was because our families were friends. I suspected it was similar for him.

Jorry had picked me up from the airport when I first arrived and showed me around New York. I called him by his Chinese name, but it turned out he had sold it along with most of his Chinese words a few years after he came to New York. Though I noticed he had been using them again lately. It seems that he bought quite a few characters before Chinese climbed the Language World Rankings this year. He always had great intuition when it came to Language Trading, though his main income was from Language Gambling. There was no doubt he would've had to give up some of his L---- words to afford it. Since he had more than enough English in his inventory now, he wanted to invest in more of what he called "foreign" languages—though Chinese had been his mother tongue.

I blinked to close the chat.

"What was your order?" the barista asked.

I scanned the digital menu above his head. "Number seven."

The barista looked at me with a knowing smile. "I usually order number ten."

"Tea." I nodded and grinned.

He didn't say the word back, and I regretted saying it, realizing that he didn't have the word himself. My head bowed as I turned away from the barista, his smile no longer as joyous as before.

I took a seat at the back of the shop with my body angled toward the corner to avoid potential unwanted conversations.

I opened my Langbase again and selected Chinese. I only had a handful of characters left in my native tongue. To afford the rent in New York, I had traded most of them away at the Language Currency Exchange Centers. Sometimes multilingual individuals approached me in hopes of buying more foreign words for their collection. The Currency Centers often restricted the number of foreign words you could buy within a year.

"What would you like in exchange?" they had asked.

I had always answered with, "Give me English."

At a nearby table, a woman sat across from her friend, adjusting the bright yellow stroller beside her. A child, only a few months old, lay inside. Their blond hair gave them an angel-like appearance.

"I'm *so* glad they implemented that new childcare policy for native citizens. My sweet baby can start her life with a dictionary's worth of English." The woman leaned over the stroller and cooed at her baby. "I don't know how *I* survived without it. We wouldn't be able to now, that's for sure!"

I didn't remember China having such a policy, or if we did, my parents never told me. The rich only became richer, and the poor continued to struggle. My family was never as well off as Jorry and his family. I was often surprised that they had the chance to meet, and I was even more surprised that they remained friends. Perhaps Jorry's family had a hand in funding my trip to the States. My parents had offered me half their savings, but it didn't seem possible they had so much stored away in their Langbases.

The woman's friend shook her head. "I recently traded the words I thought my three-year-old would never use for sufficient French to hold a conversation. It's not enough just to be born here anymore. My boss is insisting that all of us need to know *at least* two languages."

"Even the at-home telemarketers now, eh?" said her friend.

The woman looked down at her child. "By the time this little one grows up, she'll have to know five languages just to keep up with the rest of the world!"

As the women continued to chatter, I scrolled through my Langbase mindlessly, but it didn't take long to reach the end of the list. With the laws always changing, even Sign Language had to be purchased. The American government left no missed opportunities to capitalize and monetize language. That baby had a much better chance of surviving here than I did.

The friend took a sip of her drink—what looked to be the most expensive one on the menu. "And with how fast the housing market is growing, soon we'll need L---- just to afford it."

Did these women live in mansions? Apartments and condos with many rooms? To have enough to buy a stroller like that... The room I rented sat in the basement next to the laundry. It was a poorly renovated storage space without a window. At night, the pounding from the washers and dryers rattled my walls and ceilings, but I was used to that now. Even with the vibrations from the subway nearby, it was good enough for me. This was the cheapest place I could find in New York, and my previous job as a dishwasher only covered my rent and basic grocery trips.

I used to be a waitress when I still had most of my Chinese. It paid to be multilingual. Now I worked in a disposal factory. Not much talking happened there.

Jorry arrived at the c----- shop early. That was the one, perhaps the only, good thing about him—he was always punctual. He waved to me from outside the wall-to-wall window near the entrance. I tossed the soggy c----- cup into the trash, my fingertips still damp, and walked toward the exit. The unnatural smile on my face tightened as I neared him.

"Jorry."

"玉河!"

Jorry had never called me by my Chinese name before, always the English one, Gillian. Did he sell **Gillian** or did he buy the characters 玉 and 河?

I looked at him, really looked at him, like how grocers back in Fuzhou looked at me whenever I said "Thank you"—bewildered.

"What's wrong?"

I shook my head. "Nothing."

He shrugged at my clipped response.

"Well, then let's go! Here are the tickets. They really are i-----------, aren't they? I quite like their a-------- this year."

I grimaced every time he emphasized words that were too expensive for me to afford, ones that I heard only as garble. The designs on the tickets were nothing unique with their shimmering gold logo and calligraphy-printed letters, but Jorry would use any excuse to show off the words in his Langbase.

"Yes, exquisite," I said. This was one of the few "sophisticated" words I still owned. I sold most of the others since I didn't use them except for with Jorry. Most of my Langbase was made up of words like **and** or **the**; most people received these as change. I only had one **I** at all times, but I suspected Jorry had thousands, and not because of their value. Self-love is important, but he had far too much of it. I tried to keep my disgust from surfacing as he ran his hand through overly waxed hair; remnants of the product remained in between his fingers when he dropped his arm back down. I pretended not to notice as he discreetly wiped his hand on his dress pants.

On our way to the show, a Silent jumped in our path. With her hands cupped in front of her, she offered a small smile. From the corner of my eye I could see the frown on Jorry's face.

"Leave us alone." Jorry pushed past the Silent, brushing his hands off as if he'd touched something dirty. My feet stayed planted.

The Silent looked at me with pleading eyes, ringed with purple—a prominent bruise over the right eye—begging for words. Her gaunt face stretched as she opened her mouth, but no voice came out. I clenched my teeth when my eyes wandered to the oversized shirt she wore, plastered with various words—some part of the design, some looking as though they had been forcefully written on by those who encountered her on the streets. *Beggar. Home. Less. America. Silent. Dream. Silent. Reality. Silent. Silent. Silent.* It was unlikely she could read any of the words on her shirt.

The Silent were a common sight on the streets. I often bumped into them outside convenience stores, where they shielded themselves from the cold with their knees huddled together. Others walked past without taking notice, some relieved their rage on these already vulnerable individuals, some showed kindness, offering their words. Not everyone had the privilege to speak.

I blinked open the transfer option in my Langbase and sent the Silent a few **and**s.

She bowed her head. "And."

"玉河, we're going to be late!" Jorry's irritable voice traveled from half a block away.

玉河, *don't let them take your native tongue from you.* My mother's voice drifted into my mind. These were words she had said to me over a call when I first arrived in New York. Too late, Mother, most of my characters were already gone. What if I, too, became a Silent by staying here?

When I left the Silent, I couldn't help but imagine my face in the place of hers.

I had only been to one other show with Jorry. That one was in English. I forgot what it was called, but it had something to do with romance, wealth, and the people of my culture. We went when I first arrived in New York. Maybe he thought it would remind me—us—of home, but really, it only showed me what Jorry's dream was and why he left Fuzhou. The same goal my parents had for me when they heard of Jorry's success here. They didn't seem to understand that what Jorry did was Language Gambling. His parents made it sound like he worked at a Currency Center, but really, he was a frequent visitor of Language Casinos around New York. It was a secret Jorry made me promise to keep. I had a feeling that was the only reason he sometimes offered to treat me to a meal or invited me to Language Shows.

The movie we watched before was entertaining, though. I understood some parts that were in English and all the Chinese dialog. Since then, Jorry always purposely chose things that were difficult for me to understand.

Before leaving Fuzhou, my mother said if I ever needed help, I could ask Jorry. I hadn't and I didn't plan to.

"For *two*." Jorry handed over our tickets, and the usher led us inside with several others behind us.

"*Front* row seats," said Jorry, even though I could see where we were heading.

The tickets must have cost an entire month's worth of rent, at least for me.

"Thanks for the invitation." My parents told me to always be grateful for gifts of kindness. Was this kindness or something else?

"Always a *p------*." Jorry smiled but the smile was so brief and sudden that I wasn't sure if it was directed at me or because of his excitement for the show.

When the lights dimmed, I sat back in my seat, ready to replay the memories of my hometown using the Langbase's memory function rather than listen to garbles that I no longer understood. Unfortunately, the Langbase's memory function followed a subscription model, where we had to pay a few words monthly to continue to use it. Once the subscription expired, nearly all of your memories were blurred, leaving only the most basic information about yourself—name, age, address, family names, occupation, and the past week's events—until you renewed the Langbase's memory function again.

The curtains opened to reveal a man and a woman seated at a table. I sighed when the man opened his mouth. The garbles weren't terrible; they sounded like musical murmurs.

Jorry laughed with the rest of the audience, though he was always a second late. I suspected he barely understood what was happening. That was how I knew he was only faking it. It wasn't just a slow reaction, because Jorry was always quick to pounce on me whenever I couldn't find the right words to say. L---- was expensive, even the name of it. Jorry was well-off, but there was little chance he could afford the large vocabulary in it.

I didn't pretend to laugh. There was no point since Jorry didn't care anyway. He was far more worried about how he appeared to others but had little interest in how others presented themselves. To him, what mattered most was that he stood out and looked as wealthy as his manner implied.

"You enjoying the show?" he asked in a low whisper halfway through. It was an empty question. He leaned toward me but never took his eyes off the stage, as if he might miss something if he did.

"Yes." No.

"Hey, do you mind if we stop by the LangGamble House?" he asked, a smirk lifting one side of his lips.

Yes, I do mind. "Sure, why not?" Though I had promised not to reveal the details of his "work,"—not that I knew much about it to begin with or had any great interest in it—I was surprised Jorry would willingly show me more. Did he not worry I would expose him? Or did he predict I would soon become a Silent myself?

The LangGamble House was a large dome the size of ten houses in length, width, and height. Its lights were never off. On my way home from work, the dome's glare always lit my path. The red-carpeted lobby was dominated by a large staircase leading to private gambling rooms littered with velvet-covered tables and slot machines. There were both single- and multi-language options available.

"I like to be adventurous," Jorry said. I wanted to scoff but didn't.

He waved me over to a table. The man standing behind it was wearing a smart tuxedo. Jorry said this person was called an Asker, and the table would display holographic projections of the conversations they were about to have. Askers had entire dictionaries installed in their Langbases, but the knowledge was only lent to them by the House and would disappear after work. How would it feel to have such a large vocabulary at your disposal, if only temporarily? I imagined it would feel quite powerful. To have any voice, really, is powerful.

"Language of choice?" the Asker said.

"L----, English, and Chinese," Jorry said.

I was surprised Jorry would choose L---- since he didn't seem to have a large vocabulary in it judging from his responses at the show.

"Perfect. Are you familiar with the rules?"

Jorry smiled at me before turning back to the Asker. "Yes, but please do explain again for the lady."

The Asker turned in my direction, completely unaware of Jorry's condescending tone. "First, the player will make a bet—a number of words in each currency. I will then ask three questions in each language to which the gentleman here will provide answers. Yes or no answers are not allowed. Each answer must be a minimum of three sentences. I will review the answers within a five-minute time frame and select one word in each language that I believe the player does not own. If I am correct, the player loses their bet, the opposite if I am incorrect."

It was strange how robotic the Asker's voice was, although he was obviously human.

"Shall we begin?" the Asker said.

I hoped Jorry would lose, but of course, he didn't.

I only called my parents once in a while because the language barrier was becoming an obstacle. It saddened my mother that most of my Chinese was gone, and that I couldn't find the success she hoped for. They believed there were more opportunities to grow in America. It was too fiercely competitive in China, and I was never at the top of my classes. A new start, they said—optimistic. They told me to build a new life for myself—one they couldn't offer me in China as factory workers. But what they didn't realize was that the high-end jobs here required applicants to be multilingual: Trilingual was the bare minimum for entry-level jobs, but the employers always preferred quadrilingual or more.

I bought ten minutes with a few **thes** at the Public World Screen. Phones were too expensive, and I had sold mine a few months ago.

My mother's face appeared first, then my father's behind hers. She told me about how things were back in Fuzhou, and I listened with a blank grin. After a minute, my mother left the screen. I looked down at the gravel beneath my feet.

My father, quiet by nature, only stared without saying a word during our calls. But somehow, I understood my father's expressions far more than my mother's stream of now-foreign words. It was strange to hear my mother's voice as garble when it used to be so clear. I concentrated on my mother's lips, but it was like trying to look through frosted glass or listening underwater.

When my father thought my mother wasn't looking, he mimed sentences to me, willing the meaning with his eyes. Sometimes I understood. The language of the eyes and body spoke much louder than words. I tried to mime back, but it wasn't the same. Playing this game of charades was a loophole to the Langbase. Body language in general wasn't considered an official language. I should be grateful for that.

Wasn't the L---- show just s---------?

I deciphered the sentence using the context of Jorry's message.

Yes. Really great.

He was still typing, but I turned off my screen. I pulled up my Langbase. After paying rent, I had only 486 words left.

My mother spoke of a new language for royalty. The show Jorry and I watched yesterday was based on that language. She said to invest in it, but I'd never had the chance. One word of L---- cost over a hundred thousand English words. I told her it was difficult to make a living here. It was hard enough keeping what few words I had left to communicate with her.

In the building where I lived, there was one very stubborn man. He wouldn't trade any of his native language for English, and no one would hire him. He disappeared after losing everything by gambling. Street gambling was different from the sort that Jorry partook in. The man often met up with a group of street gamblers on the weekends. They challenged each other to games of description played in pairs. One team chose the words for the opponents and the partners would then take turns guessing. The team with the most correct guesses won. Those living in the building would often watch the exchange. More times than not, someone left the scene looking murderous.

The other gamblers swindled him, the onlookers said, but he didn't understand what was happening until it was too late, or perhaps he just stopped caring. His fellow players knew which words he was missing and chose those specifically so he couldn't describe them. He was kicked out of the building and roamed the streets as a Silent. Some say he was deported and sent back to his motherland because he was no longer "a useful citizen."

Another man came to visit the apartment last week; a wealthy man who knew over twenty-four languages—the one from the show included, of course. He wanted to demolish the building for a new commercial project: a new stocks center for Language Trading. Those of us who lived here didn't have a say, not that we had many words to argue with anyway.

Once, a charity asked the wealthy man for a donation. I remember him saying, "You know how it is. If I give handouts to everyone, I won't have any left for myself. How do you think the rich stay rich?" I'd disliked him ever since. Not all the wealthy were like this, but this man and Jorry were the same type of people. I didn't have a good enough word left in my Langbase to describe them.

I stopped contact with Jorry a month after the show.

They scheduled the apartment demolition for the following month. We all had to clear out by the end of next week.

The woman who lived beside me asked for compensation. She got a call, but all the building manager said was, "Don't you remember agreeing to the section stating—" How could she when she didn't have the words to read it or to hire a lawyer who could? How could she when these agreements were always worded in ways they knew most of their tenants couldn't process with their limited Langbases?

Incoming message from Jorry.

I heard about the apartment.

My eyes hovered over the reply button, but no words came to me.

You could live with me for now?

Jorry always wanted something. He offered nothing for free. The l------ penthouse he lived in came to my mind.

I can't afford the rent.

Don't worry, we'll figure it out.

I couldn't help but notice that he was only using words I understood. But I knew he just wanted to appear as a savior so I would feel further indebted to him. These words were not for me, really; they were only for himself.

I wasn't sure why I never thought to use my only **Jorry**. When my Langbase connected with the train's fare system, I selected **Jorry** as my payment. The system inserted a few verbs into my Langbase in return. Nouns were always worth more.

A woman sat down beside me. I fiddled with my luggage handle without looking up.

"And."

My head lifted at the word. It was the Silent from the streets.

She smiled. "Thank you."

I opened my mouth, then closed it.

"I was able to get my name back. I'm K----." I held out my hand, feeling disappointed that I couldn't hear her name.

"玉河," I said.

Like the barista, K---- and I shared a knowing smile, one that J---- and I were never able to share.

When I arrived at the Language Currency Exchange Center, I headed for the first available exchange machine. My Langbase popped up and I scrolled down to the last ¬word of my shrinking list of Chinese with my eyes: 家 *Home*. My mind wandered to K----. *I'll try again, Mother.*

Give me English.

I confirmed the exchange and watched the English words flood into my Langbase.

Incoming message from J----

I muted my messages. I should've severed our friendship a long time ago but didn't because of our families' connection. Perhaps I would tell them the truth. Jorry was not someone who deserved such a glorious illusion.

My eyes scrolled through my Langbase and landed on **home** and then on 玉 and 河, the only two Chinese characters left. I closed my eyes and vowed to buy them all back soon. But first, I had to find Kiana. The name of the woman who was no longer a Silent felt glorious as it left my lips in a whisper.

. . . .

Ai Jiang is a Chinese-Canadian writer, Ignyte, Bram Stoker, and Nebula Award winner, and Hugo, Astounding, Locus, Aurora, and BFSA Award finalist from Changle, Fujian currently residing in Toronto, Ontario. She is the recipient of Odyssey Workshop's 2022 Fresh Voices Scholarship and the author of *A Palace Near the Wind*, *Linghun*, and *I AM AI*. Find her at www.aijiang.ca

DICK PIG

Ian Muneshwar

Ass o'clock in the morning and it's black out. *Black* black, the kind of black you only get in these miserable, middle-of-nowhere places. No, "middle-of-nowhere" is too generous; this is past that, right at the line where nowhere becomes miles of uncharted forest thick with months of snow and screaming with wolves and whatever other ungodly feral things make noise when everything decent in the world is asleep.

It's one of those animals that drags me awake, yowling from the forest's edge, shrieking at me like I owe it money or stepped on its child. I lurch out of bed but when my feet hit the floorboards there's no howling, no sound, nothing. Like it was never even there. Fuck this wolf. Fuck this whole entire place. The floor is freezing, just one long ice rink from here to the carpet in the hall. The house doesn't have central heating—of course it doesn't—there's only a woodstove in the living room, and fuck if I know how to use a woodstove. I got it working with the logs I found out back but it choked and died twenty minutes later and by then I'd already cocooned myself in these quilts that still reek of mothballs.

As you may have surmised, I don't own this house. Strictly speaking, no one does. It belonged to my Aunt Norma, bless her, before she fell and broke her hip and the handyman found her weeks later, quite dead in her floral-print nightgown, frozen to the upstairs hallway. The hallway right outside this door.

I try not to think about that.

I pull my feet off the floor and tuck them back under Norma's smelly quilts. My phone's beside my pillow, half-charged, and there's a push notification on the otherwise darkened screen. I begin to swipe it away, but it's a Grindr message from someone called hungdaddy.

Well. It might be cold, and I might be tired, but who am I to reject the advances of a hung daddy? I tap on his faceless profile.

>*hey dick pig*

He's called me by my profile name. How personal. How touching.

As soon as I've read the greeting, a picture appears in the chat. It's a grainy, colorless photo of a naked man seated on a stool. His head is cropped out of the frame, but the rest of his mountainous body is visible, from the hairy shoulders down to his muscled legs, spread open. His cock hangs over the edge of the stool, halfway hard, lolling to one side with its own weight.

One of the man's hands rests on his thick, furred thigh. The other is raised and extends out of the picture, reaching for something just out of view. I double tap on the image, zoom in. The resolution is godawful—this pic could only have been taken on a flip phone—but even through the pixilation, the intensity of his grip is obvious. His muscles are knotted and his skin pulls so tight that the hollow of his elbow has become a deep, blurry pit. I don't know what's in that hand but, whatever it is, it's being crushed. Punished.

I am, predictably, quite hard now.

Hey, I type, one-handed, *what's up.*

>*I am always awake*

The reply appears immediately but I don't question the speed. I've slid back into bed and unbuttoned the jeans I went to sleep in.

Yeaj? I write, not really caring about spelling because, at this stage, we both know where this conversation is going. *What's got you up daddy*

Another image appears in the chat, instantly. It's actually not a different picture at all, I realize, but the same one taken from a different angle. This time, it's as if the photographer is sprawled on their back, lying between the man's feet. Most of his body is out of focus—his cock and balls are a blur, the coarse hair curling across his stomach reduced to shadow—but I don't really care because I'm halfway to coming and already feel the need for sleep eclipsing my horniness.

Fuuuuuck, I type, moving this interaction right along, *plz destry me with that dick*

There is, for the first time in the conversation, a pause. And then:

>*You crave destruction?*

I scroll back up to the first pic. I sure do.

Yessir. Wreck my hole.

>*You want to be destroyed. Wrecked. Annihilated.*

I stop jacking myself but keep my hand on my dick. hungdaddy's dirty talk needs some work, but I'll give him a pass. Twenty more seconds of this Dom Daddy shtick and I'll be cleaning myself up, ghosting him, and getting to sleep. The natural order of the gay universe.

Yeah, I type. *I want you to pin me down and make me beg.*

hungdaddy's last message comes through in one giant text block, like he's composed the whole thing already and has been waiting to send it:

>*I will destroy you. I will destroy every part of you. I will destroy until there is nothing left in you but your desire for nothingness and I will destroy even that. I will destroy you. I will destroy*

And it just fucking ends like that, mid-sentence. Jesus.

I back out of the chat and return to hungdaddy's profile. Before I block him, I take a screenshot of the profile image:

hungdaddy
online now
15 miles away

When I block him, his image disappears from the grid of nearby profiles. I shut off my phone.

That's quite enough Grindr for tonight, thanks.

The exposed skin between my thighs has gone clammy and I'm aware of how cold I am, how cold this whole damned house is at night. I pull my pants back up, tuck my erection away.

For a moment, the house is dead and it's just me and the sound of my own post-masturbatory breathing. I tell myself to ignore the phone screen right beside my pillow, to just close my eyes. There's *so* much left to do tomorrow, and I need to clear out of here before the realtor arrives in the afternoon. I need to sleep.

But then the howling starts up again. This time, it's not just one wolf but a pack of them seething through the forest, shrieking at the cold.

A goddamned symphony the whole night long.

In the morning I find myself at the kitchen table, drinking a finger of Scotch out of a coffee mug, staring absentmindedly at The Crack.

The Crack was the sole topic of Norma's correspondence with the rest of the family through the last years of her life. It's a jagged line that runs the height of the wall separating the kitchen from the dining room. It's so thin it looks like it's been drawn on with a pencil.

The Crack started worming its way into Norma's calls maybe three years ago; she would make the occasional reference to the house falling down around her, but then play this off as tongue-in-cheek melodrama. As her calls grew more frequent, though, the levity left her voice.

"You must do something about it," she would warble into the landline. "It hasn't stopped growing. Good Lord in Heaven, just look at it. It's like the Panama Canal. You wouldn't know this, since you never visit, but this wall—" she'd suck in her breath here, pause for effect—" is a *load-bearing wall*."

The monthly guilt trips became intolerable, so I paid a handyman in her vicinity to trek out to the house and assess the situation. He confirmed that there was no issue, that The Dreaded Crack was little more than the house shifting and resettling after an especially brutal winter.

That's when I started letting Norma's calls go to voicemail.

I know, I know—I'm making her sound petulant and demanding. It's unfair of me. We can't judge the dead only by the final, paranoid moments of their life. In truth, there were many things I admired about my aunt. She was a vintage eccentric. She spoke in an accent shared by no one else in my family, a half-baked homage to Katharine Hepburn that lapsed back toward her Gravesend roots more often than she probably realized. She was also the first adult in my family I came out to and goddamn if I don't remember the look that ignited in her eye as she pulled me close and said: "I always suspected that you were so, my dear. Let me tell you about cousin Alexander. He was the same way as you, and you wouldn't believe where he took me that summer we visited Berlin—"

Unfortunately, I was the only one who knew this side of my aunt. The rest of my family thought that Norma, in her dotage, was losing touch with reality. They made her perform the necessary rituals: go see this doctor, Auntie; go get these tests done; then go talk to this lawyer and you know, while you're at it, why don't you draw up a will?

That was what they really cared about—making sure her fortune made it into the right hands when she died. Their hands. Because that's my family for you. Vultures, the lot of them. Hungry fucking vultures bearing down on the old woman before she'd passed, trying to suffocate her with the weight of their lousy vulture bodies.

My family couldn't understand that Norma was never in touch with reality. She'd been fleeing it for decades, first by entombing herself in this remote Colonial, and then by filling it with curiosities and hidden secrets, building a labyrinth in which reality, that persistent bastard, could never find her.

It's morning but somehow still only half-light outside. As I hunch over the dining room table, considering my Scotch, my breath leaves my mouth in steamy wisps. They taunt me. I found a fur-collared coat and an old Cossack hat in Norma's bedroom, but no amount of animal fur seems to keep the chill away.

Norma used to say that when you're this far north winter tilts the land away from the sun and toward an in-between place. She told me this when I was very young, and I still remember the way she angled her teacup as she described the tilting world, how the brown liquid spilled from the brim and pooled in the saucer. I asked her what we were in between, and how we could get back, but she only brought the saucer to her lips, sucked it dry, and then ran her tongue around the bottom of the cup.

I was a little older when I realized she probably wasn't drinking tea.

I uncork the Lagavulin and splash a sensible pour into my emptied mug. Here's to you, Auntie Norma. Here's to your fully-stocked cabinet of mediocre whiskey. Here's to the secret you buried in this house.

My phone buzzes in my pocket, just once. I don't remember having turned it on after the Grindr conversation, but I must have at some point in the night. The cold kept me from really falling asleep; I was up in fits and starts, bleary and pissed-off.

There's a single notification on the screen. My mouth sours when I see the sender's name.

I open hungdaddy's latest message. He must have created a new account to find me again. This happens, sometimes, with guys who can't take a hint. It's annoying, but fixable: if you block and ignore them enough times they do, eventually, disappear.

>*where did you go*

What a fucking creep. I swipe back to hungdaddy's profile and am reaching my thumb toward the almighty block button when I notice that the profile has changed. The name and picture are the same, but his distance no longer reads fifteen miles. It's now one mile.

Aunt Norma doesn't have neighbors. In fact, I was a little surprised that there was someone on Grindr who was *only* fifteen miles away. The nearest city—and I use the word "city" quite loosely here—is a snowbound hamlet with a train station and a Kinko's some sixty miles south. Fifteen miles would put hungdaddy squarely in the middle of no-man's-land. One mile puts him within walking distance.

I click on the chat bubble out of habit, before I've considered whether or not I should. I move my thumb to close the app, but then I see what he's written. I stare at the screen long enough that it goes dark.

>*i can tell you where to look*

My eyes keep sliding over those words, again, again, again. And then it hits me like an ice cube sucked down my windpipe. I am being catfished. The only way hungdaddy could know that I am looking for something is if he knows there is something worth looking for. And the only way he could know *that* is if he was privy to Norma's will.

The opening of Norma's will was the closest my family has ever come to holding a reunion. The extended viper's nest of Caldwells shuffled into that lawyer's office, all of them dour and pale in their funereal getups, looking like characters in an Edward Gorey sketch. When the lawyer announced that Norma had left her entire estate to a nearby private school, most of them left in an entitled rage. But I stayed for the whole reading, for the line at the very end when Norma addressed me directly:

"To Edwin: I cherish all those childhood summers you spent in my house, all those marvelous secrets that passed between us. How I wish there was still one more to share. I would have left you the house but, alas, it is falling into ruin and would only have been a burden in its old age."

To those unfamiliar with Norma, that might just seem like a slightly passive aggressive parting message. But I knew her too well not to see the references buried in those words. Norma worked in riddles; in her mind, it was almost gauche to say exactly what she meant. One line played itself over and over for me: "How I wish there was still one more to share." Between this and the references to the house, one thing became clear to me that afternoon: Norma left something in this house for me to find. Knowing her, it would be something so valued it couldn't be discussed openly.

Unfortunately, I wasn't the only one who stayed for the end of the reading. My siblings are relentless and hungry, and it seems one of them wants what Norma left me. This plan—trying to spook me out of the house using a hookup app—it's original, I'll give them that. It's probably my youngest brother, Barty. He's a twisted little shit. Or no—maybe it's Violet. Fucking Violet. She's the only one who would know my taste in men.

This realization is, in its own way, a comfort. hungdaddy now has a face, and it is the face of one of my ne'er-do-well relatives skulking in the forest, sending grainy dick pics and cryptic sexual advances. This is something I can deal with. I am, after all, well-practiced at enraging my family.

I throw back the dregs of the Lagavulin, set my cup down, and get up from the table. Norma's house key is with the realtor. But the spare key—the one she hid in the hollow of that dead oak out back—that one is safely in my pocket.

I inventory the downstairs, checking the locks on the windows and trying all the doorknobs. Most of the windows, blessedly, were painted shut years ago, but this house has so many goddamned doors—the front door, and the back porch's screen door; the basement door and the hatch on the root cellar; the small, warped door in the pantry that opens into the woodshed; and, finally, the door in the library's outside-facing wall that never opens. Since I spent yesterday creeping through every crawlspace, turning out every dresser, and peering under all of the carpets, I make an efficient survey of the house. The doors are locked up tight.

Breathless from all of this jogging, I settle into the library's ratty loveseat and take out my phone. hungdaddy—it feels perverse to refer to a family member this way, but they brought this on themselves—has not sent any additional messages. I type out a response, delete it, and start again:

You gonna tell me where to look? or would you rather come and show me. I know you're not used to the cold.

>you must open the door under the stairs

He's as prompt as ever. The house doesn't have all that many staircases—there are stairs in the front hall, leading to the second floor; there're the ones going to the cellar; and, if we're being pedantic about things, I suppose there's also the attic's pull-down ladder. In the past twenty-four hours, I have been up and down these staircases so many times I have the squeal of each tread memorized.

The staircases don't have doors, I reply.

At this point, the whole cat-and-mouse charade is starting to feel pretty fucking ridiculous. Whichever one of my grifting relatives is behind hungdaddy, they are cold and miserable outside, making themselves suffer just to frighten me. The whole thing is petty and obnoxious and—you know what? They should know better if they think I'm going to let them in when they decide to give up the ruse. They should know that no one in the family, not even Violet, is pettier than I am.

I'm drafting another pithy response when a third picture comes through. This was taken with the same camera as hungdaddy's others—it's all staticky, washed-out sepia—but it's not an image of a person. It's the inside of the house. The photographer took this standing in the front hall that extends into the dining room. The stairs to the second floor run up one of the walls in the entryway, and the photographer has focused on that bare, triangular piece of the wall underneath the stairs.

So, hungdaddy has been here before. This isn't surprising; most of Norma's relatives came here after the funeral for an afternoon of backbiting and store-bought crudité. There would have been ample time to take pictures. In fact, I'd be surprised if Barty hadn't slunk around, making an inventory of Auntie's valuables while the rest of us nibbled our baby carrots.

No, the surprise in this photo is that there *is* a door under the stairs. It's difficult to make out, at first. The wall is decorated with rectangular moldings, and the doorframe has been camouflaged to look like one of them. It's painted the same hideous taupe as every other wall in this house, and it doesn't seem to have a knob, but it's there alright. Clear as day. How could I have missed this?

As I haul myself up from the couch and debate how to shimmy this door open, one more detail in the photo catches me. I wouldn't have noticed it at all if I hadn't zoomed in a bit, and even now I'm not entirely sure what I'm looking at. The picture is taken at a slight angle, so it captures not only the wall but also the length of the narrow front hallway. A corner of the dining room is visible at the very end of the hall, and most of this corner is taken up by the lower half of Norma's farmhouse table. There's an object sitting at the edge of the table—a pixelated, shadowy thing.

I bring the phone's screen closer and closer to my face. It's just about touching my nose when I realize that I'm looking at the coffee cup sitting right where I left it twenty minutes ago.

I close Grindr and stand very still. My heart's bolting against my chest like a hunted rabbit and all I can think is that if I stand very still whoever is in this house won't hear me, won't know where I am. This thought is so stupid it hurts—I have, after all, spent the morning slamming every door I could find—but I can't even think about moving right now. The clock ticking on the mantle across the room is so fucking loud. I want to tell it to shut up, to just shut up for one minute because it's covering the creaking sounds of the intruder crawling across the floorboards, the shuddering of the camera lens as it captures things I can't see until they're shown to me.

I allow myself a breath. It's unbearably loud, sucking all that air in, but I need to think this through. When I was a child, I used to keep a jewelry collection. Specifically, a collection of my mother's jewelry. I would sneak into her room while she napped and pilfer one earring from her nightstand. She would think she'd lost an earring, so she'd toss its now-worthless mate. After rifling through the trash, I would end up with both earrings and my mother was none the wiser. It was a perfect system, right up until Barty and Violet found my stash. My beloved siblings didn't go to our mother with the evidence of my crimes; that wouldn't have been cruel enough. Instead, over the course of the next four years, they slowly re-gifted all of the earrings back to my mother. Every Christmas, every birthday, every Mother's Day, I watched as my months of meticulously-planned larceny were slowly undone, and my siblings were praised for their discerning taste.

Our dear mother—so wealthy, so oblivious—never caught the grift.

I've had enough of Barty and Violet. We are not children anymore, and I won't play their goddamned games. I pull the Cossack hat tight around my ears and take a step forward. The squeak of my boot is a small rebellion.

First things first: I delete Grindr. After thirty-six hours my phone's battery is nearly gone, and it's not like I'm going to get any useful information out of hungdaddy.

I stride back through the dining room—telling myself with every boot-squeak that I'm in control here, that I'm *choosing* to let them know I'm not afraid—and I come to the front hall. This room connects all three floors and so, when I speak, I know that whoever is inside can hear me:

"I think we both know what's going on here," I call, hating how my voice cracks halfway through the sentence. "So come on out, and we can talk about this like adults."

Now, of course, the house goes entirely quiet. I can't even hear the clock in the living room anymore, and this makes me wonder about all of the other hidden noises I'm missing. Maybe hungdaddy is pacing the length of the attic, but it's too far away for me to hear the weight of his footfalls. Maybe he's hiding behind the brocade curtains in the drawing room, giggling to himself as he drafts another message. Or maybe he's—

My gaze snaps over to that horrible, taupe door under the stairs. There it is, as advertised. Even before I've stepped across the room, I see where the door's hinges disrupt the clean lines of the moldings; I see how the grain of the wood breaks from the wall's smooth plaster.

"What are you gonna do when I open this?"

I run my finger across the door's face, over the place where a handle should be. I don't know it for a fact until I say it out loud, but there it is, for everyone to know—I *am* going to open this door.

"You gonna lock me in and steal Norma's shit for yourself? What's the plan, friend? What do you want with me?"

A wind swells outside, kicking up pinpricks of ice that rasp against the windows. The house settles back to silence.

Now that I know I want to open this door, there's no turning back. The question is: how do I open it without playing into hungdaddy's chicanery?

Last night, when I went to the woodshed for kindling, I saw a mallet on the workbench out there. I jog through the pantry, brace myself against the bite of winter that greets me in the uninsulated shed, and carry that mallet back inside. Its wooden shaft is so fucking cold in my hands, but it's a good kind of cold—a frigid, heavy reminder that I am in control of what I do next.

I smack the butt of the mallet against the upper right-hand corner and the door judders in its frame. It opens more easily than it should, coming just far enough out from the wall that I can press my numb fingertips against its width and prize it open. The hinges squeal with disuse and I hate them for it. All of that unnecessary sound.

The space beneath the stairs is a closet. I almost laugh at the sheer mundanity of it—the line of hats and coats hanging from hooks; a collection of furs draped across the back wall, including a mink stole with little weasely feet and black marbles for eyes.

I turn my phone's flashlight into the dusty interior before I step over the threshold. It's a tiny closet, barely enough room to stand up in. I rifle through Aunt Norma's old coats, slipping my hands into their pockets. Everything smells, powerfully, of mothballs.

I don't know what hungdaddy expected I would find in here, but it's all pretty disappointing as far as secret rooms go. The coats are threadbare, their pockets empty; even the mink stole is too washed-out and mangy to be worth anything.

The phone vibrates in my hand and the movement is so unwelcome that it goes clattering to the ground. Even though it's frigid in here, my palms are sweaty. As I bend down and grope for my traitorous phone, bits of grainy refuse stick to my hands.

I'm still crouched in the darkness when the screen lights up, right in front of me, and I see the push notification. My chest tightens.

I know—I *know*—I deleted that app not half an hour ago.

"This isn't funny anymore," I say through the open door to the empty hall. I consider, for a moment, tacking "Barty" or "Violet" onto the end of that sentence. I don't, though, because neither of them is in this house with me. I would feel a lot better if they were.

I open the app that shouldn't be there.

>*Above you*

It occurs to me, as I sit on the mouldering floorboards and stare out into the hall, that I don't have to look up. I can get up, right now, and walk out the front door. My car is still out there. The battery probably died during the night, but that's not what's keeping me here. I can walk if I have to. I've hitchhiked before. The only reasonable thing to do is to get off of this property and go south, back to a place where I understand how the world works.

But I don't. Here's the thing I haven't told you, but maybe you've known it all along: there's a want inside me I don't understand. Why does a child steal something as useless as an earring? I used to think it was for the thrill of theft itself, and for the pleasure of possessing something beautiful. But maybe I craved what would have come if my siblings hadn't interfered; maybe I wanted the retribution I would have faced when my mother learned that I had breached the trust between us. I don't know. I can't name that hunger; I only know that I turn my flashlight back on and shine it into the gloom over my head.

There's a latch built into the ceiling. An iron ring just big enough that I can slide two fingers through it and pull. At first it resists me, sealed into place by untold years of neglect, but I'm no longer interested in playing nice with the house. I'm in an act-now-regret-later sort of mood, so I just haul against the ring with everything I have, one foot braced against Norma's coats, pinning the dead weasel to the wall. The hatch in the ceiling comes unstuck and the musk of trapped air that gusts into my face is overwhelming.

I stare, for a long second, at the passage now opened above me. I am in a secret closet. The staircase is directly overhead. This passageway, and wherever it leads, cannot be here.

An unexpected emotion twists in my chest—if I didn't know myself any better, I might say it was yearning. I've spent the past day and a half in this empty house, sleeping in Norma's old quilts, drinking whiskey out of cups last touched by her lips, and this is now the closest I've felt to her. This impossible place could have only belonged to my aunt, and, of everyone in the family, it could only have been shared with me. I stand on my tiptoes and peer into the hole.

The passage is built into the slope of the ceiling, so I can turn my phone's flashlight down its long throat. As it turns out, though, I don't need to. There's already a light at the far end. It's not daylight. It's the yellowed glow of an incandescent bulb.

It seems that I am expected.

I pocket my phone and shimmy myself upward. Once I'm inside, flat on my stomach, I find that the passage isn't all that long. That dim, steady glow is coming from a room some ten feet ahead; from this angle, I can make out its oaken floorboards.

I start the crawl forward, my breaths coming shallow and quick. The hole absolutely reeks of mildew, so I turn my face into the coat's fur collar, huffing in the stale scent of Norma's interred wardrobe. The light in the room beyond doesn't seem to reach into the passage, but I don't need to see where I am to know where I'm going. I try not to focus on the bits of mold and fiberglass amassing under my fingernails; I'm so close to the impossible room, now; so close to what Norma has kept hidden from the vultures.

I shove myself out of the passage, twisting to get free of its narrow, grimy embrace, and push into the room beyond. As I catch my breath—clear my lungs of that fetid stench—I lay on my back and take stock. The room appears to be an attic, even though I know I'm nowhere near the roof. The walls, lined with exposed beams, slant toward one another as they might under one of the house's gables. From what I can see, the room has no windows; only bare bulbs strung between the beams, casting a dim, unwavering light.

I've been here before. This thought possesses me even though I know it can't be true. The passage to this room hasn't been opened in years—decades, probably—so why does it feel so familiar?

As I start to roll myself onto my stomach, following the lines of the beams from the ceiling down the floor, it comes to me. It's not that I've been here before. It's that I've *seen* this room before. In fact, I've seen it from this very angle. I hadn't really paid attention to that second pic hungdaddy had sent, mostly because the man's glorious dick was out of focus. But the wall behind him was in focus, and it's that wall opposite me now, framed by the two beams joined at the ceiling. I'm in the place where the photos were taken.

The phone buzzes, but this time I already have it in hand. I knew he would message me right at this moment. I may not understand what he is, or what he wants, but I'm starting to know the way he thinks, and this excites me more than I could have anticipated.

hungdaddy has sent two messages, and the app informs me that one of them is a photo.

The message comes first:

>*you must pass through the opening*

The picture that follows doesn't immediately clarify things. The photographer has foregrounded half of hungdaddy's face and, even though it's blurry, I can't help but study him. He's bald with a full, coarse beard, the kind of beard that leaves marks after it has made use of the softest parts of your body. He's staring directly into the camera, and I read him so clearly. He looks into the lens with a want so naked, so forceful, it might be mistaken for rage. But it's not anger, not exactly. I know how that intensity will translate through his touch; I know what his fingers will feel like around my throat; I know how his grip will tighten when he presses his girth through me and how my mouth will open not with the need to breathe, but with the need to taste the sweat raining from his face.

I've gotten so hard I can feel my pulse in my dick. I want to unbutton my pants and jerk off right here, in the cold, damp musk of this room as he watches me, but hungdaddy resends the message.

>*you must pass through the opening*

A small, useless whimper wells in my throat, the sound a dog makes when denied attention. I know what he wants me to do next, but I don't want to do it. I don't want to look at the rest of the picture.

I force myself to break his gaze, to study the part of the photo that's in focus. It's the wall again. The resolution isn't great, but even so I can see the line running across its surface, top to bottom. It's unbroken and jagged, pencil-thin.

I look across the room. The deeper I go into this house, the more twisted its interiors become. Even though I'm not on the second floor, I'm looking at the roof's gables; and even though I'm nowhere near the kitchen's infamous, load-bearing wall, I'm looking at The Crack.

How can I possib—

I start this thought, but can't finish it. My fingers are so cold and the pressure of my erection against my jeans is a needy, unbearable thing. I delete the words and start again, but hungdaddy replies before I can hit send. He shows me what I already know:

>*you will do what you have to do, pig.*

I still don't know what he wants from me, but I don't have to. It is enough to feel the heft of his desire make a place for itself inside me.

I start to crawl.

At first, The Crack is so distant. Barely visible, a hairline shadow bisecting the wall. I put one hand forward, and feel the room shift. No, not the room—something has changed within me. It's like hungdaddy has sewn balloons into all those minute spaces between my joints and when I move forward he purses his lips, sucks a breath into that hairy drum of his chest, and blows. This description isn't right because it sounds like I'm experiencing something painful. But this isn't pain the way you know it. The change is slow.

The room fisheyes as I move forward, the beams in the periphery of my vision bending into convexity. The far wall only grows nearer and nearer; it approaches even in those times when I am not moving my body. I do, at one point, hang my head to see if I am moving myself. I couldn't quite see my legs—they were so far away, still at the far end of the room—but I did see a dark stain on my crotch. I must have come.

When I reach The Crack, in the future, I see that it has changed. I was wrong this whole time, wrong about so many things. Auntie was telling the truth. This is like looking into the Panama Canal, like standing at the edge of some bottomless fissure splitting the earth. I am nothing in its presence, I am dwindling into meaninglessness.

As I stretch through the opening, I am so wracked with sensation that it is almost impossible to separate one feeling, one thought, from the rest of the flood. But, in that instant before I am gone, I realize what the house has given me: the force of desire has razed all uncertainty from inside me. It leaves an emptiness, a newness, that never stops growing. I couldn't stop it even if I wanted to, even if I could want anything at all.

Betsy Mortimer-Scott pulls up to the house at half past four.

In her twenty-three years in real estate, Betsy has closed more sales than she can rightly recall. She's sold split-levels to newlyweds, tracts of land to wolf-eyed developers, and oceanfront monstrosities to the unimaginably wealthy. In all this time, Betsy has never, not once, told a prospective buyer that a house has "good bones." It is a morbid metaphor. The buyer should never think of the house as a living thing, waiting to be resuscitated by fresh drywall and a gallon of paint.

No—a property is a starched canvas, a blank page. The right language is important in making the sale.

Betsy reminds herself of this as she steps out of the car, planting her booted feet in the undisturbed layer of snow. If there has ever been a half-living house, a house with bones awaiting reanimation, it is this one. The old Colonial sulks at the forest's edge, its siding the same color as the trees that surround it, its windows so lightless she can't properly tell if the glass is still there.

Betsy slings her purse over her shoulder and locks the car doors. As she walks toward the front porch, she corrects herself—she'll never sell this place if she lets such thoughts color her perspective. For the right buyer, this house will be charming. A storied New England gothic. Better yet: a secluded woodland fantasy. Woodstoves crackling through the winter. Mulled cider simmering in the kitchen, holly wreaths on every door. Betsy takes the porch stairs two at a time. The right framing is starting to come together. Somewhere in Boston, there's a middle-aged couple dying to move to the country and this place practically has their name stenciled on the mailbox.

Betsy pauses when she comes to the front door. It is open. Not wide open, but ajar. This is not unusual, given the circumstances: the last person to come here was probably a lawyer's lackey, someone too preoccupied to double check that they'd locked it behind themselves. Betsy has had only fleeting contact with the family, but even from those brief interactions she knows that they're not the type to personally attend to the old woman's belongings. They had no real connection to her, no genuine interest in anything other than the will.

"Hello?" Betsy calls as she pulls the door open. "Is there anyone here?"

A spray of snow has swept inside. The house is so cold that the ice sticks to the welcome mat and the hardwood floor. Betsy brushes this away with her boots as she enters; the last thing an old house needs is excess moisture on the floorboards.

As Besty turns to close the door, she sees the lace curtains in the drawing room billow, touched by wind. The windows, she finds, are all open. Not just those in the drawing room, but the windows in the dining room and the kitchen and the living room. She could have sworn that the owner had painted these shut years ago, but she must be confusing this with another property.

"Hello?" Betsy repeats after she has closed all the windows and returned to the front hall. She doesn't know why she asks a second time. This house is empty. There is no one here and it feels, in this moment, like no one has ever been here. All those screenless windows and open doors. All those bannisters rimed with ice. This, perhaps, is what concerns her most about convincing someone to buy the place. It's this feeling that if she keeps standing in this hallway, she will become part of the house's vast absence.

Betsy hikes her purse up higher on her shoulder. Enough of this. She decides she will come back later in the week. The contractor is free on Thursday, and she could use his help in drying all the floors and getting the furnace working again. No point in working alone if she doesn't have to.

On her way out, Betsy closes the closet door under the stairs. She remembers to lock the front door as she goes.

"You do have good bones," she says out loud. It's silly to talk to a house, but there's reassurance in the weight of her own voice, in remembering that she is here and that there's work ahead. "I'll find a family to love you," she adds, "the way you ought to be loved."

Betsy Mortimer-Scott cranks the heat up in her car and wastes no time getting back on the road into town. The sun sets early this far north. As she drives, the bare trees lining the road cast shadows that reach across the pavement, a tunnel of interlocking fingers.

The sun falls away. Betsy flicks her headlights on. Every shadow is erased.

. . . .

Ian Muneshwar is a writer and teacher based in Boston. He has been a finalist for the Nebula, Locus, and Shirley Jackson Awards, and his short fiction has been selected for *Year's Best Weird Fiction*, *The Year's Best Dark Fantasy & Horror*, and *We're Here: The Best Queer Speculative Fiction of 2022*, among other publications. Ian has taught both creative writing and composition through Brandeis University, Tufts University, and Clarion West. He currently teaches at University of Massachusetts Boston. You can find out more about his work at ianmuneshwar.com.

DOUEN

Suzan Palumbo

I see Mama in de cemetery when dey put de white casket in de ground. She was crying so hard she was shaking like when grandma died and Tanty, Mama's aunt, had to hug Mama up tight, tight, to keep Mama from falling down.

At grandma's funeral, Tanty say, "Doux doux Shalini, yuh have to hold up yuhself. Yuh have yuh daughter Samantha to bring up. Yuh must be strong fuh she." Mama wipe she own tears and stop crying den. But she smile was spoil. I try to come first in school and eat all de rice and provision I hate when she cook dem for dinner, but Mama say she heart was broken. Fuh true she eyes didn't shine full happy like dey did before.

Dis time in de cemetery Tanty didn't say anything because even she was bawlin' like a cow with everybody else. Mama was de loudest. She voice was like a cutlass chopping straight through de noise. Daddy stand up stiff next to she and was silent, like a stone.

I know why nobody tell Mama to hold up sheself dis time. It was because it was me dead in de casket in de bottom of de hole. It was *my* funeral.

Except I wasn't in de box.

I was standing behind one of de concrete headstone watching Mama and all meh aunties and uncles bawl. I cry too, because I didn't remember how I get there and I didn't want to be dead.

I remember I was playing in de yard. I run to get meh ball and den bam, something hit meh. Pain, pain so sharp in meh chest, like a knife when I breathe in. Mama was screaming but she voice did get farther and farther away.

Come back, Mama, I thought. *Where yuh goin?*

Den everything gone black and I wake up in dis dead people place by de sea. No more pain. No screaming. I put meh hand on meh chest to check what happen. I wasn't wearing de pink frill dress Daddy buy meh for meh seventh birthday. I was naked from meh belly up, wearing a long grass skirt and a hat shape like a cone. I try to pull de hat off but it was stuck to meh head.

Meh whole body was wrong. From meh ankles, meh feet was twisted with meh toes pointing behind me. I sit on de grass and try to turn meh right foot around to face de correct way but it wouldn't go straight. When I walk around de gravestones, meh heels went in front of me but meh feet look backwards.

Douen.

Tanty and meh cousins, Shivani and David and dem used to say dead children's spirits, douens, have backwards foot. When I ask Mama if what dey did tell me was true, she say, "I can't tell yuh dat, chile."

I wanted to show Mama meh feet when I see she in front of meh grave and tell she douens was real and I was frighten. But no one could see meh and it had too many people around Mama saying she was going to be *alright. Everything happen for a reason.*

"Am I all right?" I ask. Meh voice came out as a whistle and I couldn't stretch my mouth open. My backwards feet pull and I run to Daddy's car in de parking lot and watch meh face in de tinted window. Ah sharp pain hit meh chest again because wen I look at meh face, meh mouth was a tiny hole de size of a black tamarind seed and I had no nose or eyes! Meh face was smooth like a mango skin. How could I see with no eyes? I had jumbie face. I scream but it come out as ah angry whistle on de wind.

"I sorry, Sam. It was ah accident," Uncle Ram was saying by meh grave. He choked up crying and gon back to sit in he van alone after. Everybody else was watching de ground. Nobody talk for a long time and den Daddy hold Mama by she shoulders, turn she around and walk she to we car.

I didn't know if I could follow dem. They didn't call meh to come. They didn't even look back fuh meh standing in de cemetery beside de hole. I was frozen where I was while I watch every car and van drive away.

Den it was quiet except for de sound of de shush, shush of de waves from de sea nearby. I liked when we whole family use to go to de beach. We used to play cricket and eat hot fry rice. Now de sound of de sea fill up meh ears and head like it was inside meh skull. I didn't dare go near it. I didn't trust meh backwards feet not to run on dey own. What if they walk me into de ocean and kept walking until I was covered?

Later, two man drive up in ah noisy backhoe so loud it drown out de ocean inside meh head. They start to fill up de hole I was suppose to be in with meh casket. All dat dirt woulda been dump on meh. I would have never climb outta dat.

They was almost finish filling up de hole but I didn't want dem to leave. So when dey turn off de backhoe engine and get two shovel to smooth over de dirt on meh grave, I went and stand behind de man who look younger and didn't have a beard.

"Excuse me, Mista," I whistle. He shake up at meh voice like a cold breeze touch he.

"Ey boy." He cross heself and say to de next man. "Let we hurry up and done here. I don't like to stay by child grave."

"What yuh think? She go come an haunt yuh?" De older man laugh.

"Yuh think I joking?" De young man suck he teeth. "Yuh go see."

"Okay, okay. I want to done, too," de older man say. He went back in de backhoe with he shovel an turn on de engine.

"Rest, chile," de young man whisper to my grave with he eyes closed. Den he went in de machine next to de old man and dey drive away like Mama and Daddy.

I sit back on meh grave and cry. I cry so loud de whole cemetery fill up with a ringing whistle. People who was visiting other graves cover dey ears and run back to dey cars. I was sure Mama would hear me back home in de house and she would come and get me and hug meh up and give meh a sweet and sour prunes like she did when she used to collect me from school. Mama never ever use to let meh cry.

She didn't come back.

Den, it start to get dark. I watch de sea swallow up de sun. De air change. It touch meh skin like a bunch of cold hands and fingers all over meh chest. I wanted meh white and pink bed and a cup of milk. I wanted to be inside. If douens was real, den de soucouyants and loop garous and jumbies dat come out at night to bite you and take yuh soul was true, too. I didn't want to meet dat kind of jumbie. I stay awake and watch to make sure none come for meh.

In de middle of de night a lady drive up to de cemetery. She had long straight hair and was wearing a black dress dat reach she foot and a black veil dat covered she face. Tanty did explain after grandma funeral, that if yuh go to de cemetery at night yuh must walk through de front door of yuh own house backwards when yuh go back home or de ghost and dem go follow yuh inside. Dis lady didn't look like she was scared of ghost at night following she inside she house.

When I get closer, she smelled like de sandalwood incense grandma used to light when she say she prayers. I creep up quiet beside de lady.

"I go kill dem fuh let yuh dead," she whisper. "I did tell dem, doctor. I did tell dem. Yuh wasn't well and dey insist, an insist I was crazy. I was, what dey say? *Overprotective.* De lady's voice did shake like Mama's at meh funeral but softer like de sound of slippers on de wood floor. "But I know someone give yuh bad eye. Dem curse yuh. Dat's why yuh get sick." De lady wipe she face. "Come back and see meh, Alyssa," she say. She take out a bottle of liquid and pour it on the grave.

"Don't be sad Aunty." I whistle softly. She turn she head slowly and stare at meh in de dark.

"Yuh not Alyssa."

"Yuh could hear me?" I jump back.

"Yes, Douen, I could hear yuh. What is yuh name?"

"Samantha."

She nod. "Yuh see meh daughter, Alyssa round here? She was four. Smaller than you. So, so little she was."

"No, Aunty. I get here today and nobody else here like me." De lady's shoulders drop.

"Do you miss yuh mama?" She was looking at me but her voice change like she was talking to a baby.

"Yes. I do. I want to go home. But meh Mama can't see me like yuh."

She rub she arms and shiver like de man in de backhoe earlier dat day.

"Where yuh family living? Yuh know dey address? I go drop yuh by dey yard so yuh wouldn't be lonely." I think for a minute, *I go get to see Mama* and nod meh head.

"Okay, let we go." She touch she daughter's grave stone. "Mommy love yuh plenty, Alyssa."

De lady let me sit up front in the car next to she while she drive. I give she meh address. She say it wasn't too far drive from where by she live. We didn't talk but I could see tears wetting up she face. She car was full with little colourful crosses and charms on de dash and hanging from de mirror. I try to behave and be quiet, like I used to do for Mama but I had so many questions.

"How come you could see and hear meh and no one else can, Aunty?"

"When yuh is a chile, yuh can see everything," she say. "An when people get big some of dem can still see spirits and energy but others lose dat forever." I didn't ask she anything else after dat because she face get hard like she was finish talking. When she turn de car onto de trace where meh house was, she stop and turn off de headlights.

"Yuh could walk de rest of de way? I don't want to drive up in people yard and wake dem."

"Yes, Aunty, I can walk. Thank you."

"Good luck little, Douen. I sorry. I sorry, yuh never get a chance to live and grow up and experience life."

I didn't know what to say. So I tell she, "thank you," again and watch she turn she car around and drive away. Den my backwards feet point meh towards de house. Just down de hill and around de turn and I would reach home.

When I reach de yard of we big old house on poles, Lenny meh dog start to bark hard at me. He rush up like he was going to bite me.

"Lenny, doux, doux, is me, Samantha, puppy!" I whistle and pat him on de head. Mama never let Lenny in de house but everybody know he was my best friend next to meh cousin Shivani. He calm down when he hear meh voice and lick meh face. I laugh because it tickle de same as before I died.

All de lights in de house was off except for de one in Mama and Daddy's bedroom. I try to climb up the concrete steps into de gallery but a force stop meh and I bounce back on de ground and fall on my backside like when I get hit before I died. I try de back step and I capsize again. I couldn't even stay under de house in de hammock Daddy hang up for meh."

Dey must be went inside de house backwards to keep meh out!" I say.

I sit under we plum tree in de yard, scared that a jumbie would come out of de cocoa bushes behind me. I cry that Mama didn't want meh in de house like de dog. But Lenny come and cuddled up next to meh and I get nice and warm. I closed meh eyes and went to sleep.

De next morning Tanty come to de house early with Uncle Ram and Shivani. Shivani wasn't at meh funeral. Today she had on a new blue dress and she bring a doll with she. Tanty say Shivani was *de cutest* right in front of meh one time. Mama tell me later she thought I was de cutest. I still like Shivani even though Tanty thought she was prettier than me. I wanted to wear a fancy blue dress too and not dis scratchy hat and grass skirt.

"Shivani!" I call. She head move like she hear me but she didn't turn around. She follow Uncle Ram in de house.

People kept passing by de whole day. All we family and cousins carrying containers of food and den leaving with nothing. Twice, I hear Mama bawling from where I was under de plum tree. It hook into me and pull me towards de house but every time I put meh foot on de step I bounce back.

Dat's when I see de dent on Uncle Ram blue van and remember how I died. I ran into de yard to get meh ball after Shivani threw it dey. I didn't even see de blue van. Mama tell meh not to run in de yard like dat. It was my fault I died. I went back to meh plum tree and sat in de shade and cry quiet so I didn't scare anybody.

Daddy and Mama didn't come out de house dat day. I wait and wait. Lenny sit with me de whole time and only went by de back step when Daddy call to give him he food.

Everybody get to talk to Mama, even Shivani. Everybody, except me.

Daddy start to go to work. He look even more serious den before. Tanty come by in de afternoons and stay with Mama. De whole time I sit in de same place watching Mama's window wishing she would come to it and see meh. I wanted she to tell me a rhyme or a story like she used to when she brush meh hair. *Would she know me if she see meh?* She used to tell meh she would never ever let anything happen to meh.

De days were so lonely and long. I walk up and down de trace, scaring de cats and de neighbour's goats. Other animals could see me just like Lenny.

A next neighbour, Mr. Max, come to quarrel with Daddy one afternoon about how Daddy didn't cut de grass coming up de trace for a long time. He say de road look a mess. Daddy didn't even yell back at he like I see before. He just say, "okay" and went to cut de grass.

De next night, I went to Mr. Max house and climb up de pomerac tree in he yard. He always used to brag about how he tree had de sweetest fruit. I went and bite each an every pomerac so dey all spoil and he would have none. Den I chased he two dogs round and round he house until dey barking wake everybody in he house up and he wife start screaming, "Call de police!"

I run back to we house to de plum tree and laugh and laugh. Lenny was happy, too and he lick meh face. Mama come to de window and move de curtains. She look out, almost like was looking right at meh, and then close de drapes fast. I close meh eyes and dream of she singing meh to sleep.

De next morning, Mama came down de front steps. She didn't look like meh Mama. She was so thin and around she eyes was dark, like holes. She clothes was hanging off she like she was a stick and she had some grey hair.

"Ma! Ma! It's me!" I wave and whistle. She shake she head and get in she car and drive away fast. When she come back home she was wearing a red string tie around she wrist. She didn't look at de tree where I was at all.

A week later, Uncle Ram come over with Shivani by themself.

"I want to play with Lenny, Daddy," Shivani said to Uncle Ram while he was taking some bags out of de van.

"Okay, Shivani. Stay in de yard," he say and went up de steps.

"Yes, Daddy." Shivani wait until he was inside and walk straight up to meh.

"What you doing in Aunty Shalini yard?" she ask. "And why yuh dress like that? Don't yuh have any proper clothes?"

"Shivani, is me! Samantha!" I say, happy she could see meh. But this time meh voice wasn't a whistle. It come out exactly like Uncle Ram's voice saying, "Shivani, Shivani, Shivani," over and over. Where was meh voice? Meh whistle? I cover meh tiny mouth and back away from she. Yelling, "No! No! Go Away!" But again it come out as "Shivani, Shivani," and she was following me. I couldn't control meh backwards feet. Dey keep walking towards de cocoa bush leading Shivani away from de house.

Meh chest went hot and hard. Why Shivani couldn't hear meh properly? Shivani could talk to Mama and wear pretty dresses and was cute and I have to sit outside half naked under a tree when she father, Uncle Ram, hit meh with he car. I focus and call to Shivani louder backing up into the edge of de cocoa bushes. "Shivani, Shivani, Shivani!"

"Shivani! Where yuh goin, gyal?" Uncle Ram call from de top of de steps. Shivani stop and stare at meh.

"Nowhere, Daddy," she say and run back to de house.

"Lucky," I scream, scaring a cobeaux in a nearby tree. Shivani look back at me but Uncle Ran didn't when they went inside de house. I sit down under meh plum tree and stare at Mama's window, so vex I was shaking.

Dat evening Daddy come out de house carrying part of meh bed with Uncle Ram.

"Where all yuh taking meh bed?" I shout. I run up to de van and try to grab Daddy's arm but he didn't feel meh. "Stop! Don't give it away. Don't let Shivani have it." Dey went back in and come out with more pieces. I stomp back to meh tree and hug up Lenny. It was dark and de back of dey truck was full of *my* things. Mama come out. She looked so pretty. Not so tired any more.

"I hope yuh like de bed set," she say. Mama hug Shivani up tight, tight. I don't know if I had a heart anymore but if so, it break. That hug was fuh me. Before she get in de back seat, Shivani look back at me. I give she de worst cut eye I could from under dis stupid hat. Den Mama turn around and went back inside.

"How could yuh give Shivani meh bed?" I ask before I cry all night.

Days later, Mama put on de black long sleeve dress she had on at meh funeral and get in she car. De air feel heavy and I get pull to de car. Before she start to drive away, I climb up on de trunk and sit down. I wasn't scared of falling off. What could happen to meh? I was already dead!

De road she take went through de whole town. Pass de market and de chemist. She was going back to de cemetery. When she reach, she park de car and sit in it for a long, long time. I see she through de back window. She shoulders was shaking. Watching she made meh sad. I jump off de car and went to meh grave. It was different now. Grass did grow over de hole. Yuh would never know meh body should be under de ground.

"Hi!" a little voice say. A kid dressed like meh, with a hat and grass skirt but smaller was standing next to meh.

"You is Alyssa?" I ask she, touching she shoulder.

"How yuh know meh name?" she say, bouncing on one backwards foot.

"Yuh Mama help me get back home. She was looking fuh yuh. Where yuh was de night she come to look fuh yuh?"

"I doesn't stay here during de night! It have a scary bad ol' man jumbie with bright red eyes. If he see yuh, he take off de top of he head and ask yuh to touch he brain."

"Fuh true? Den I was lucky yuh Mama bring meh back home!"

"I see all kinda weird people here. Is dat yuh mama coming now?" She point towards de car park. Mama was walking over to meh grave wringing she hands.

When she was in front of it she sit down and put she hands flat on de grass. She didn't move or say anything.

"I want to see my Mama, too," Alyssa say.

"Eh. You could wait till she come back to see yuh here or yuh could get a ride with we back to town and look fuh she. She say all yuh living close by we."

Alyssa clap. "I want to come with all yuh." Mama look in we direction but shake she head and look away.

"Ok den. Go and sit on we car trunk," I tell Alyssa. "Dis is de first time I get to sit with meh Mama since I dead."

Alyssa run off on she heels towards de car. I sit right next to Mama. She wasn't crying.

"Samantha," she say in she nice soft voice she used to use when she wake meh up for school. "I hope yuh know I love yuh. So much. I go never be de same." She stop like something catch in she throat. "I know yuh not at rest, baby. Me, too. But tings is going to start to change." She wipe she face. "I want to tell yuh dat, so yuh know dat I love yuh." Den she was quiet a long time. De whole time she talk it did feel like pieces inside meh chest was breaking apart. It wasn't a sharp pain at all. It was a deep ache. Den she blow meh grave a kiss and stand up.

I follow she back to de car and sit next to Alyssa on de trunk. Alyssa put she arm around me. Dat was nice because I don't know when was de last time somebody hug me up. When we reached de village, Alyssa say she have to jump off de trunk by de chemist.

"How yuh go find yuh Mama house if yuh don't know yuh address?" I asked she before she jump off at de main junction.

"I go, go to de market and wait fuh she dey."

"Okay den, bye!" I call as de car drive off fast and left little Alyssa behind in de dark.

People start to come less to de house. Mama would sit on de gallery steps everyday and talk on de phone to Tanty or she cousins. At first she voice was heavy, heavy and she didn't talk much but slowly, she start to talk more. She sound better and dat make me happy. One day, on de phone she laugh and it make meh jump. It was a quick bubbling thing that shake meh chest. I laugh with she and dat make Lenny start to howl and howl. Mama laugh at him howl and de sound fill up de air and fill meh up, too.

Mama's clothes start to get tight. She face get rounder, same as she belly. One day Uncle Ram drop Tanty and Shivani by de house. Shivani was holding a balloon in she hand dat say Baby on it. Den all de aunties and cousins come. De aunties was laughing and talking and dancing to soca while de kids play with Lenny below de house.

"Lenny, puppy!" I call but he wouldn't come. He was busy jumping with Shivani and David and de other cousins having fun. "Lenny!" I scream at him. All de kids look at me under de tree. Lenny didn't move and Shivani grab he collar.

"No! No, Lenny. Don't go by she. Dat is a jumbie!" De other little kids scream when she say *jumbie* and run up de gallery steps.

"Dat is a Douen. Look how it dress and look at it foot." David pick up a stone and pelt it at meh. He miss and I laugh so hard all de kids had to cover dey ears. Den David throw another rock. Dis time it hit me right in de center of meh chest. It hurt meh. Not de same way like when I was alive but more inside like ah burn. Den de other cousins all start to throw rocks at meh, hitting meh everywhere and I had to run in de cocoa bush to hide.

"What happen all yuh?" I hear Tanty voice from meh hiding spot.

"It have a Douen, Tanty!" Shivani say. Everybody was quiet.

"All yuh come inside de house," Tanty say. I stay in de bush with de bugs and lizard and worms until it reach night and everybody gone home.

"Lenny, Lenny puppy, come!" He come over and whimper and lick meh face. "Now yuh want meh, ent? Before when Shivani was dey, you didn't want to come by meh." Meh face get hot like ah flambeau. I stand up and whistle at Lenny to come. Den I lead Lenny into de bush. We walk and walk in de dark, deep, deep into de forest. I whistle and whistle and soon I could hear wild dogs barking so crisp and vex.

"Come, puppies, come," I call as I climb up a tree. I look away when Lenny growl and de wild dogs tear him apart. I wasn't so bad dat I could watch that.

Two days later, Daddy and Uncle Ram went in de bush to look for Lenny. I could hear dem call he all day. Shivani cry when dey come back and tell she Lenny was gone. I cry too because I shouldn't have kill meh puppy.

Mama had de baby, meh brother. Daddy was happy. He smile and laugh when people come to visit. Shivani and David and all de little cousins came to see de baby. Dey name he Rajiv. Sometimes, Mama would put Rajiv in a basket on de gallery and talk and sing to he. I would listen and pretend she was singing to me but then she would take Rajiv inside and I'd be alone again with no one. Not even Lenny.

Soon, Rajiv was talking all kinda silly words and trying to walk. When Uncle Ram and Shivani or Tanty come over they did blow kisses and laugh at every noise he make. He was cute. Maybe he looked like me! But den Shivani start to call Rajiv "brother."

One day on de gallery Mama said, "Dat's right, he is yuh brother!" My chest went red hot and hard again. I wanted to drag Shivani into de bush by she hair but I couldn't because she never came near de plum tree anymore.

I wasn't going to get bigger. Nobody talk to meh and anyone who could see meh left meh or pelted meh with rocks like Shivani or David. Mama never let Rajiv come on de grass. Daddy was busy with work and now right in front of meh Shivani was calling Rajiv *brother*.

"He's not yuh brother, yuh jackass!" I scream. Meh voice come out like de growl Lenny make before he died. Everyone look at de plum tree, even Rajiv and Mama. Mama scrunch up she face like she was going to cry.

"Let we go inside, everybody," she say and she pick up Rajiv from de gallery.

De next day, a familiar car come up in de yard. It was Alyssa's mother, de Aunty who brought me home from de cemetery. Aunty went inside de house. Alyssa slip out de car and come to sit with me under de tree. I put meh arm around she and stare at Mama's window.

"How come all yuh come here?" I ask she.

"Yuh don't know?" Alyssa say, picking up one of de almost yellow plums dat had fall off de tree. "Meh mother is de village obeah woman."

"Fuh true?"

"Yeah." She nod. "An yuh mother call she and say it have a bad spirit in de plum tree and ask meh mother to get rid of it!"

"Mama ask she to get rid of meh?" I held meh self back from screaming. Dis was worse den when Mama left meh at de cemetery. I hug up Alyssa so tight I would have crush she bones if she was alive. She didn't complain. Den Alyssa's mother come down de steps and walk up to us under de tree. In de daylight I could see she was pretty and had beautiful dark skin. All de air around she smell like sandalwood again.

"Little Douen," she say. "Yuh mother ask meh to get rid of de bad spirit by dis tree. I don't know all what she could see and hear but she say if it have anything to do with yuh, to put a protection spell to keep yuh from hurting yuh self and de other chil'ren." She mouth turn down after she tell meh dat.

"What yuh go do Aunty?" I ask she, still hug up Alyssa.

"Is me who bring yuh here and I won't do anything to hurt yuh. I go wok a spell so yuh can't come in de yard at all. But I cannot control de bush and yuh could have free reign of dat." She nod she head at meh.

I was quiet fuh a long time. Watching Mama with Shivani and de baby didn't make meh happy but I didn't want to never see Mama at all. Aunty wasn't givin' me a choice.

"Ok Aunty. I go, go an stay in de bush."

Aunty nod. She bend over and kiss meh cheek and I almost start to cry. I squeeze Alyssa goodbye and walk backwards into de cocoa bush. I couldn't see de house or Mama's window any more. I cried so hard all de animals near me run away to hide. Aunty splash water around de yard and chant quietly. I hear she get in she car. I was so hot and vex I thought I would set de whole forest on fire.

How could Mama do dis? How she could forget meh? I bang my fist against a tree. But it wasn't Mama's fault. It was Shivani showing off that get meh upset on purpose and make Mama scared for she self and Rajiv.

"I go fix she," I say out loud to de trees in de dark.

I wait patient until I hear Uncle Ram's car one day.

"I could play in de yard, Daddy?" Stupid Shivani ask. I stay quiet until I was sure Uncle Ram was inside de house and I could hear Shivani bouncing ah ball. *My* old ball.

I whimper like Lenny, as loud as I could from de bush. De bouncing stop. Den, start again. I remember all de times I help Daddy feed Lenny. I whine so hard it echo in meh head and Shivani stop again.

"Lenny?" Shivani call. I answer she with Lenny's excited *yelp, yelp*. A few minutes, later I had footsteps in de dead leaves at de edge of de bush. I did bark like Lenny when Shivani and meh used to throw a ball for he to fetch. "Len-ney?" Shivani call again.

Into de jungle farther, backing up over fallen trees and through branches, I whimper like Lenny hurt. I miss him. Poor puppy. It wasn't he fault either, like Mama. It was Shivani. It was always Shivani. She make meh howl like Lenny was in pain again and again. Shivani start to run and crash through de trees.

"Lenny! Lenny! Where are you puppy?" She scream. She was scared. Good. *Howl.*

She trip over de rocks and start to cry about bugs and tearing she dress. *Bark. Bark.*

"Where are you? Lenny. You can't be far!" She stop moving. "Where am I?" She ask, crying. I laugh and she scream loud because she hear me.

"Shivani?" Uncle Ram called. They'd come from de house to look for she.

I copy he voice. "Shivani!" I yell. "Shivani!" She footsteps pace back and forth. She wasn't sure which direction to go. "Shivani!!" I call again and she move towards me. I start to back away towards de place where de wild dogs kill Lenny. I wouldn't look away dis time. It should have been she instead of meh puppy.

"Samantha!"

Meh feet stop. "Samantha!" It was Mama's voice. It hook into me like a scythe. Why she was out here? She must be looking for Shivani. She didn't need meh anymore. I wanted to back away, but I couldn't. She spoke and meh feet went towards she voice.

"Samantha," she call like when she woke me in de morning for school; "Samantha," she said like when she laugh at meh jokes; "Samantha," she sang like when she put meh to bed when I was little; "Samantha," she cry like de day she left meh at de cemetery. I couldn't stop meh self from going to she. I pass Shivani scratch up and bloody, sitting on an old rotten tree. She get up and follow meh back de way I lead she towards de house. When she could see de yard, she run past meh out of de bush.

"Shivani!" I hear Uncle Ram say. He was choke up again, crying. Mama's voice stop.

"Daddy!" Shivani sob.

I sit down and wish I never come back here because all dey want was Shivani and not *me* anymore. I belong with de dead not with meh living Mama. Dey would call de aunty to do something to meh again for sure. I stand up to go back deeper into de bush.

"Samantha?" I hear Mama again close to me. I turn around. She was standing there, in front of meh, tears on she face. De red string from she wrist was gone and I could see Alyssa's mother, de Aunty, behind she.

"Dat's she," de Aunty say.

Mama come towards meh and put she hand on my cheek. She stared at meh tiny mouth and no eye face and smiled with she tears. She voice shook when she talk.

"I can see yuh now, Samatha, baby." She hugged me up tight, tight. "There yuh is."

· ·

Suzan Palumbo is a Trinidadian-Canadian dark speculative fiction writer and editor. Her work has been nominated for the Nebula, World Fantasy, Locus and Aurora Awards. She also cofounded the Ignyte Awards with L.D. Lewis. She is the author of *Countess*, a queer Caribbean space opera novella, and *Skin Thief: Stories*, a collection of dark fantasy and gothic short stories. When she isn't writing, she can be found exploring her local misty forests in Ontario, Canada. A complete list of her work can be found at suzanpalumbo.carrd.co.

DESTINY DELAYED

Ekpeki Oghenechovwe Donald

Mr. Mukoro was sitting at the front of his verandah at about 5:30 A.M.
The faint glint of early dawn revealed the figure passing his frontage. It was
Chinedu Okah, and he stopped to greet.

"Bros, how you dey? You're up early oh."

"No," Mr. Mukoro replied. "I'm down late."

"Working on your research?"

"No. Working on an old project, approaching a breakthrough. I just need funds
to finish it. I'm trying to find a way to do that without funds."

"It would be a real breakthrough if you can finish your project without funds
... Finish your project, abolish capitalism, and change the world to make life good
for us all!"

Mukoro was amused in spite of himself.

"I have to be off early to escape traffic," Chinedu said. "I'm going to head office
on the Island."

"Have you been transferred?"

"I hope so. Or at least, it should be promotion."

"That's some news," Mukoro said, standing up to give Chinedu a handshake.
"When you return, we'll drink to it."

"Of course. That's if aren't too busy with your project."

Mukoro laughed gently. "Go come, brother."

"Greet Madam and Nyerhovwo for me," Chinedo said as he departed.

A moment later, a slim, dark Itsekiri woman stepped out with a young girl
of about seven, still groggy with sleep. The girl saw Mukoro and ran to hug him.
"Daddy, miguo"

"Vrendo, my child."

The woman curtsied. "Miguo, Papa Nyerhovwo."

"Vrendo, Mama Nyerhovwo," he said with a smile. She smiled back, smack-
ing the child's behind playfully and pulling her from playing with her father's

beard, which she held on to. He screamed in mock pain and she giggled as she was pulled away. The child slipped out of her mother's grip and ran back to him.

"Oghenenyerhovwo," her mom called sternly. "Come and bath now or you will be late for school and they will flog you when you get there."

The little girl looked her father askance. He nodded. She kissed the cheek he turned for her, and returned grudgingly to her mother who dragged her to the corner of the house.

Mukoro sighed and closed his eyes, and the numbers and equations came unbidden to him as they usually did.

Chinedu Okah alighted from the Keke Napep that dropped him at a side street and walked a few steps to the head office of AUB, the Africa United Bank. He walked in, blending in with the top bankers and persons in the finance sector, his crisp blue suit and starched white shirt making him look sharp as the drawn blade of a Mushin gangster intent on robbing you at one in the morning.

He was glad to be here. He was glad to have left the position of cashier, handling the grubby notes of traders and students at the Yaba branch of AUB, and marketer briefly thereafter.

He walked to the nearest help desk and presented his ID card, informing the attendant that he had an appointment with Mr. Abiola Yusuf of Human Resources. She placed a call before signaling him to wait, for Mr. Yusuf was in a meeting. *This early?* Chinedu wondered. Well, he would wait. He had been waiting a long while after all: three years as a contract staff, and six years at the Yaba AUB branch. He was led to the waiting room to do what it was named after.

Finally, Mr. Yusuf walked in and shook his hand.

"Good morning, sir," Chinedu said, surprised to see Mr. Yusuf spotting a blue Kaftan on a Monday morning. In Yaba branch, even the Branch Manager didn't wear native dress unless it was Friday. But this was head office. He guessed when one was this close to the top, one did what one wanted.

"Mr. Chinedu Okah, is it?" Mr. Yusuf asked in Hausa accent.

"Yes, sir."

"Walk with me."

Chinedu followed him out of the waiting room to an elevator. Mr. Yusuf punched in the 13th floor and started talking while the elevator went up.

"You read the e-brochure, right? So you know what we do here."

"Yes, sir, I did."

"Well, I want to give you a few pointers and show you around so you see and understand a bit more of what we do in this department."

They came out of the elevator and walked down a hallway.

"You were the most active marketer in the Yaba branch," Mr. Yusuf continued. "Only the best get recommended here. Your record is stellar. They say you pulled in six billion naira in six months, a billion per month."

Mr. Yusuf stared at Chinedu and nodded. He seemed to like what he saw in Chinedu's eyes. "Well,now you will be helping us with something more than money."

They stopped in front of a large department marked UBD at the top. United Bank of Destiny.

Chinedu could hardly believe himself when he was ushered into the UBD. He had read the brochure, but wasn't sure he wasn't being pranked...

"This is the measurement and extraction room," Mr. Yusuf explained. "This is where a destiny is mapped, measured, and extracted."

A procedure was in progress. A young man was standing in front of a machine that looked like an X-ray machine. Mr. Yusuf waved to the technicians in lab coats, gloves, coveralls, and goggles.

The technicians switched on the Destiny machine, and it emitted a whirring noise. There were a number of wires connected to the machine, which in turn were connected to screens around the room. The machine's whirring turned louder, and the air rippled in front and behind the young man. The air rippled and roiled, taking on a dark grey hue. The hue turned from dark grey, to purple, and then to grey again. Then the air stopped whirling and one of the technicians switched off the Destiny machine.

"The screens around do the soul reading and display the intensity of the destiny in how vibrant the colours it manifests are," Mr. Yusuf said, turning to Chinedu, whose eyes did not leave the operation and the operators. "The process measures the capacity of a man's destiny. The man's destiny is then extracted, as you saw with the machine, and stored in a soul cube."

As the young man was led away to where his clothes were, Chinedu noticed that his eyes looked dead, and his face bleached of colour.

Mr. Yusuf led Chinedu to another room marked Acquisitions and Mortgages.

"This will be your office. The destinies you determine and measure will be extracted and kept as collateral for their loans. Your job will be much like the old one at the Yaba branch; a marketer. But this time, you'll target young people who want loans but have no property for collateral. You'll convince them to use their destinies as collateral. It's a way for us to be of service to the needy. Think of it as an empowerment scheme, to help those who would otherwise not be able to get the funds they need. It's like student loans in America. This is, of course, a very sensitive department. You will need to see our lawyers to sign a non-disclosure agreement. That's fine with you, of course?"

"Yes, sir." Chinedu smiled knowingly. The monthly salary here was more than he earned in a year in Yaba Branch. In no time he could clear all his loans, even get a car. And moving to the Island would be possible.

Mr. Abiola's voice snapped Chinedu out of his reverie. "I read your dossier and know that an overachiever like yourself would definitely be up for it. Or we would have had you sign the non-disclosure even before you came in here. I like to think I am a good judge of people. Or I wouldn't be head of HR."

Mr. Yusuf chuckled and Chinedu chuckled politely in return. Mr. Yusuf kept walking and talking.

"Discretion is very important to what we do here. Not that it's illegal. The young men and women who come for loans all consent to have their destinies extracted and kept as collateral. Not that there is anything in the law about this, nor can the law make sense of it. We just don't want the uproar it would cause if uninformed ears got to know of what we do here. You know Nigerians are super-stitious. They won't understand that we just want to help people."

Mr. Yusuf led Chinedu to an office in the Mortgages and Acquisitions de-partment. It was well furnished, with a sofa for visitors and a Surface Book on an expensive looking mahogany desk. "This will be your office," Mr. Yusuf said, gesticulating.

Chinedu was breathtaken by the office. It was three times larger than his branch manager's office at Yaba. Mr. Yusuf chuckled at his incredulity. Just then, a man in a purple suit walked in carrying a briefcase. Mr. Yusuf touched Chinedu on the shoulder.

"The lawyer is here. I'll leave you both to get to it so you can start in earnest. It's a new week and you have your quota already."

Chinedu nodded.

"I stuck my neck out for you," Mr. Yusuf said as he stepped out. "There were dozens recommended for this post. All with stellar records. But I picked you. Like I said, I have a head for people. Don't disappoint me."

Chinedu assured Mr. Yusuf he woundn't be a disappointment. "I'll even have my first catch for you this week," he said. "I know just the person."

Mr. Yusuf nodded. "I knew you were the man for us."

He patted Chinedu, who bowed before returning to the lawyer. Mr. Yusuf whistled as he left.

Mukoro and Chinedu sat drinking at a beer parlour at Montgomery, Yaba. Bottles of Alomo, Guilder, and small stout littered their table. Hunched over, they discussed dreams and ambitions, as fermented as the left-over alcohol in their bottles, seeking ways to escape the penury that clung to them like paint on the wall, ever fading but never quite gone. It clutched them with the tenacity of a wounded soldier behind Boko Haram lines, far from home but unwilling to leave this world without a goodbye to his family.

"So, I let them extract her destiny as collateral for loan of any amount I want?" Mukoro was asking.

"Not 'any' amount, but an amount not exceeding eight figures in naira. And that's after reading her destiny to ascertain its worth."

Mukoro rubbed his beard. "I see," he said thoughtfully.

Chinedu looked at him with shrewd eyes that retained their sharpness despite the numerous bottles of alcohol they had consumed. "You don't seem overly surprised by any of this?"

Mukoro shook his head. "I studied systems engineering. My PhD was in soul mapping and interaction with spirit particles." He glanced at Chinedu before adding, "What do you think my research and projects are all about? You could say destiny led us here."

Mukoro leaned forward and continued. "My grandfather was a great Jazzman in his time. He was blind but could see more clearly than those with two eyes. He could uncannily put together pieces of the unformed future. You know, that is what they do when they map the soul and read a person's destiny. The device they call a soultrifier can map what we now call spirit particles, or what the rest of the world knows of as dark matter. The soultrifier is built to calculate the propensity of the soul, like a sort of advanced probability. If you want to simplify it, you can say it's a combination of very advanced possibility tied to your DNA structure and other things we don't yet understand. Kind of like how we know a fit person might go into sports, or a lonely person into arts or literature. The soultractor is the real breakthrough. It finds a way to extract the unique strands of each person's propensity and store it in a soul cube."

Mr. Mukoro stopped talking to take a pull from his glass. Chinedu called for a waiter. "Two more bottles of big stout." When the waiter departed, Chinedu turned to Mukoro and asked, "So what does all this have to do with your grandfather?"

"Oh, yes. I got caught up in explaining about the process and my work. I love to talk about my work with those who can listen. Anyway, my grandfather prophesied that I would give my child a great destiny. This was before my first degree, when I didn't know anything about this. He used the word 'destiny', in English. Even though he wasn't educated or spoke any language other than Urhobo."

Mukoro's eyes became distant, as if he could stare across time to the event of the prophecy's utterance. "My grandfather had never been wrong in such utterances before. I don't think this will be. That is why I'm so focused on my research. I want to leave a legacy for my child. I want to ensure she gets the promised destiny. This is for her, you understand? It's my destiny to grant her a great destiny. I must bequeath her more than was bequeathed on me. But I cannot do much as it is. It seems destiny cannot be realized without funds. I can't even get a reasonable job with my PhD, much less funding for my research. I can't apply for foreign grants with a project like this. It has only made headway here, because of our combination of science and spirituality. It took the work of the council of Dibias, Babalawos, and scientists to discern how to interact with the spirit particles that the rest of the world calls dark matter. So I can't get funds from outside as they would not think much of a project like this. If I can get the loan from your bank to finish my research, I can leave something for Nyerhovwo and fulfill my destiny to gift her a great destiny."

"I see," Chinedu said. "Not that I wish to make you question this, since it's my job to get people to take loans. But you are also my friend. Isn't the loan unnecessary? The breakthrough has been done already and monetized. Of what use is your research?"

Mukoro laughed until tears trickled from his eyes and he wiped them. "You should know that no research is ever finished. All the technology we have is still being improved. This is a new area. There are still a lot more to discover."

Chinedu smiled. "So I'll see you at the office tomorrow, then?"

"Yes. You said extracting the destiny doesn't hurt?"

"No, it doesn't hurt. It's just a net weight of probabilities and the person's propensity to achieve a thing. It's just as being paralyzed doesn't kill."

"I know. I just want to confirm. And the destiny will be kept intact, returned, and reintegrated with the source?"

"Of course, it will be returned and reintegrated once the loan is fully paid, along with interest."

"And it's legal for parents to take a loan with the destiny of a child, a minor?"

"Yes, although it's a legal grey area, as the law doesn't recognize the procedure yet. But the law is still catching up, so you have nothing to worry about. You cannot sin where there is no law. Parents and legal guardians can consent on behalf of their children. It's like taking your child for a bone marrow transplant."

"I'll talk to my wife about it tonight," Mukoro said, and frowned as if not reassured by the idea that what he was doing was a sin, even if he wouldn't be held responsible.

Chinedu noticed the look on his face. "Remember you are doing this for her. To fulfill your grandfather's prophecy."

"I know," Mukoro nodded.

Chinedu poured his remaining drink in the bottle and ordered three more bottles for Mukoro. Mukoro thanked him and took a long pull from his glass and asked, "Nothing more for you?"

"Naaah, I'm all right for now," Chinedu said. "I have to rise early for work tomorrow. I have to wake up by four and leave before five to beat Island traffic."

Mukoro rose to shake Chinedu's hand and see him off. "Alright, goodnight."

"Don't forget to talk to madam about it this night," Chinedu called as he left.

Mukoro returned to his drink, his somber thoughts rising vampire like for his blood, despite his efforts to bury them in ethanol.

That night, Mukoro cuddled his wife Bianca. She snuggled into his arms.

"Was she asleep before you left?" she asked.

"Yes, her love for that story never stops her from falling asleep before the end." He chuckled, remembering Nyerhovwo's droopy eyelids closing as he read.

Bianca shook her head. "She'll only ever fall asleep when it's you reading. She stares at me with glittering eyes till the story is done. She trusts you."

Mukoro was silent, knowing where the talk was headed.

"I heard all you said before. I need to know that I can trust you to do right by her."

Mukoro sighed. "She's my daughter, too. I love her. You know that."

"I know. You have been a good father to her." She paused a moment then asked. "You say this mortgage of destiny won't hurt her?"

"No, it won't hurt her," he said. "The process doesn't hurt; it only dulls one's chances. It is a destiny after all. I can't use mine because I need to be sharp to use the funds. And it can't be you either," he added, forestalling the question he knew she wanted to ask. "They won't take a middle-aged housewife's destiny. I know, sexist, but that's how it is. It has to be hers. As it is, what future does she have here?"

He waved at the dilapidated structure in which they lived. "Things aren't like in my time when education was government subsidized. Since the monetization of schooling, the university is beyond our reach. They say education is the future. And we can't afford that much. What's a destiny without a future? This is for her." Then he whispered, "And for them," looking at his wife's stomach.

She turned to face him. "What do you mean by 'them', Papa Nyerhovwo?"

"Do you think I don't know you're pregnant?" He cupped her cheek gently. "I have known since you stopped asking money for pads two months ago."

"I should have known that would give it away," she said. "I was just relieved to save you that expense."

"Well, there will be other expenses. My on and off consulting job can't help us. I need to do this for them." He held her hands. "Let me save this family with this loan. With her help we can secure a future for her and her brother. But once I finish my project and secure a bit of stability, I'll repay the loan. Then we can ensure a great destiny for them."

Bianca was quiet for a while, then said, "Or sister."

He smiled and kissed her. "But we already have a girl."

"Well, boys are trouble."

"Good trouble."

"Like you, huh?" She jabbed him in the ribs.

He laughed. "I have to leave early in the morning with her to beat traffic. And you have to go take permission for her absence in to her school. Should we sleep now?" he asked with a slanted eyebrow.

"Did you also learn how to be so subtle at your PhD program?" she asked, pulling her shirt off, mounting him, and kissing him deeply.

"I mean, it's not like you can get pregnant again," he said.

She leaned back, letting the sounds of joy that flittered from her and bounced off the walls bring a little blue to the cold yellow of the walls.

3 years and 8 months later ...

A black Range Rover and a white 4matic Benz parked in front of a Chinese restaurant in Awolowo Road, Ikoyi. Mukoro climbed out of the Range Rover while Chinedu climbed out of the 4matic. They shook hands and were about to go into the eatery when Chinedu tapped Mukoro and said, "Let's talk in the car first. I have some sensitive information."

Mukoro nodded and opened the door of the Range Rover They both stepped in and closed the door. The AC was running. Mr. Mukoro spoke first.

"There's something wrong. The loan defaults in seven months, isn't it?"

Chinedu nodded.

"How come I don't seem able to clear the interest, try as I might? There's always something left, and the loan itself never goes down."

Chinedu shrugged and said, "But you seem to be doing well."

"Which isn't the point," Mukoro cut in harshly. "You know I want to clear the loan and recover something more than money. Nyerhovwo is in secondary school and just wrote her Junior WAEC examination. In another three years, she will looking at going to the university."

"You have the funds for that, don't you? And enough for Oghenemudia too, for that matter. How is he, by the way? And Madam?"

"They are fine," Mukoro perfunctorily, dismissing the question. "I'm not talking about any of that. I'm talking about Nyerhovwo. Her teachers report that she lacks interest in everything, even though her grades are middling and fine. Her eyes are always dead."

Chinedu's brows creased momentarily. Mukoro would not have noticed if he had not been watching for it.

"You know something of this, don't you? Why my businesses seem to be doing well but never well enough to clear the loan?"

"I don't ..." Chinedu began.

Mukoro cut him off. "No, no, don't do that, please."

Chinedu sighed and looked Mukoro in the eyes before he began. "I turned a blind eye to a lot of things when I started, because I needed the money and the upgrade. But the truth is, I always knew something was off. The way I was chosen, the department, my handler. I was hungry, and they knew it. Too hungry to ask questions, too hungry to think, or choose to do the right thing. Head of HR truly was a good judge of people. I think I'm basically a devil in suit, sent to tempt the vulnerable for their destinies. I get the low and the desperate like myself and yourself."

"The destinies," Mukoro said, returning to the subject he desperately needed to discuss.

"They were never going to be given back," Chinedu said. "Your businesses are monitored and sabotaged. Not enough for you to notice, but enough so you can't repay the loan on time and the destinies become theirs. They are sold at ungodly amounts to powerful men who take them for themselves to enhance their chances at success, or gift them to their families. That's why the rich and powerful in Nigeria are becoming richer and more powerful."

Mukoro listened in silence. Chinedu said, "You knew this, didn't you?"

"I began to piece it together recently. I suppose, like you, I always knew. But my poverty prevented me from thinking. The obfuscating green of the naira tempted my gaze away from the truth."

"Your research?" Chinedu asked.

"I've finished it. The machine I built can map souls and extract destinies, just like the one at the bank. But mine is more energy efficient as it runs on solar power. I tried to get investors or talk to people in government, but I met roadblocks at every turn. I couldn't even register a company for it. I was blocked from the Corporate Affairs Commission up."

"This is a government-enabled monopoly," Chinedu said. "They don't want competition. That's why the rest of the world doesn't know about it." Chinedu lowered his voice and added, "If you push too closely, try to go to the press, or talk to too many people about this, you might wind up in a shallow grave somewhere."

"Or an accident," Mukoro said calmly. He lit a cigarette and handed one to Chinedu who took it and lit it. Both men smoked in silence for a while.

"I can't let it go," Mukoro said. "It's my daughter's destiny."

"Don't be stupid," Chinedu said. "The powers that be ..."

"I made a promise to my wife. I told her she could trust me. She did."

"You have a family. Your son ..."

"So what? I should sacrifice my daughter's destiny for the rest of the family? For my son?" Mukoro looked at Chinedu with wild, angry eyes. Chinedu sighed and resumed smoking. After a while they were both done smoking.

"I am not nobody now, you know," Mukoro continued. "I know things. I have power."

Chinedu shook his head. "Not compared to the people who control the bank. They are the same people who control Nigeria. The governors, senators, the cabals behind the president."

Chinedu opened the door but did not get out. "I've been looking for a way to quit. Being a headhunter for destinies is taking its toll on me. I just haven't found a way to do so safely. I'll be heading home to my fiancée now. See that you return to your family, okay? Don't do anything rash."

Mukoro said nothing in response. Chinedu closed the door with a sigh, walked into his car, and drove off.

Eight months later

Mukoro walked into the AUB head office and was led to the Department of Soul measurement and extraction. He had an appointment. It was the appointed time... for him ... For Nyerhovwo. He had a debt to pay. Or not pay, rather. Some debts you paid by not paying. He had dined with the devil, and it didn't matter how long the spoon was. Silver bullets kill werewolves, it is said. But Nigerian devils ate silver and chewed their way up the spoon, to your fingertips, then down your hands, till they licked your brains off their own fingertips.

He looked at his Audemar. It was such an expensive timepiece, but despite the costliness and glowing jewels on it, his time was up and he couldn't buy more. It was eleven am. Fitting; the eleventh hour.

He walked into Chinedu's office. The lawyer—the devil's advocate—was there, along with another man, probably Chinedu's handler. They were there to oversee the handover.

Chinedu said some words to Mukoro, but he couldn't hear them. The words flittered past him. He caught only a few. "Defaulted on the loan... Destiny is forfeit... Sign here... Mr. Mukoro. Sign?" There was a paper in front of him. They handed a pen to him.

He looked at them and smiled. He would sign for them in blood. He stood up and tore his jacket open. "When you sell your soul, or another's, you should always sign in blood. I'll sign with my blood since I made the trade."

The occupants of the room gawked at him. Lining his jacket were a number of wires running into a device sewed into his coat. He pulled out a detonator. The occupants of the room all backed away.

"Bomb?" Chinedu's handler queried.

"No, it's not a bomb," Mukoro said, spitting. "Not the type that takes lives, anyway. Just the type that takes destinies."

The handler raised an eyebrow. "What do you want? More money? You can relax. We have money."

"I don't want money. I want my daughter's destiny. I knew you would never give back what you stole. So once I confirmed, eight months ago, I started reworking my prototype. It will rip the destiny from everyone within a ten-mile radius and integrate them with the operator of the device."

He turned to Chinedu. "I told you it is my destiny to gift my child a great destiny. And I will not be denied by thieves and saboteurs."

He screamed at them. The lawyer backed off.

"Yes," Mukoro continued. "When I activate my device, it will rip the destinies off everyone in this den of thieves and integrate them in me. Including my child's. I can ask for just hers, but you all don't deserve what you have. Thieves!"

The handler rushed at Mukoro and he pushed the button on his detonator. The air came alive, crackling with electricity. Thunder boomed outside and it began to rain. A blast tore through the room, mini-blasts occurring around everyone as their destinies were ripped from them and drawn to Mukoro. His eyes blazed with each destiny he integrated with himself, while those he took their destinies from fell with dead eyes. A dozen, two, three, four dozen destinies and Mukoro's eyes glowed. Then his device burst into flames from overheating. He ripped it off and tossed it away.

Chinedu, the lawyer, and the handler stood before him with dead eyes. Mukoro turned to them.

"I know you pressed the security button and the police will be here soon," he said, pulling a gun. They all backed off. "Have you heard the saying that destiny can be delayed but not denied? A seemingly nonsensical phrase but true nonetheless. Destiny is like energy; it can be transferred but not destroyed. And it can't be transferred permanently. Its unique code is tied to the original owner's DNA. So, when it's not gifted to anyone and the current holder dies, it goes back to its original source, if they are still alive. When I die, all the destinies I have taken will go back to their owners, if I don't gift it to anyone else. You will have your sordid destinies back." He paused. "And my daughter, too. That's all I wanted. I am after what is mine."

"What is yours?" the handler asked. "We gave you the loan. You defaulted. You have no right."

Mukoro pointed the gun at the handler and he backed away.

Just then, the police, three men and a woman, burst into the room. Time slowed. Mukoro smiled at the handler who was waving at the SARS unit not to shoot. But Mukoro knew. The Nigerian police would not refrain from shooting an armed man pointing a gun at a senior manager of a bank. You could trust the police to do their jobs the one time they shouldn't.

Mukoro heard the shots of multiple guns going off. His body hit the ground. The bullets had hit him faster than it had taken the sound to travel to his ears, breaking him, along with the sound barrier. His vision dimmed. The handler was screaming for an ambulance and for a destiny extraction machine before he died. Mukoro willed himself to die; his destiny. He closed his eyes permanently and fulfilled it.

2 weeks later ...

Chinedu sat with Nyerhovwo and her mother. The relatives had all travelled back to the village after the funeral and they were alone in their apartment in Lekki.

"The bank reached out," Chinedu said. "I am no longer with them, but I agreed to liaison with the family on their behalf." He did not say that he had negotiated his release by promising to smooth things over and ensure the Mukoro family's silence. "They are offering to discharge the debt of Nyerhovwo's destiny and also pay a huge compensation for the accident of Mr. Mukoro's death."

"I still don't understand how they can mistake a respectable businessman like Mukoro for a robber," Mama Nyerhovwo lamented.

"You know how stupid Nigerian police can be ..." Chinedu was explaining when Nyerhovwo got up and left them to it. Her brother, Oghenemudiaga, was asleep and they were happy to see her go, not wanting to have such difficult conversations around her.

She went upstairs to her father's room, then to his private study. She riffled through the papers scattered on his desk, pulled out one, and scanned briefly though it. It read "Destiny extraction and replication." She knew this already. Her father's last work was not just in extracting destinies forcefully, but in replicating their energy signature and mimicking them. When he died and the originals went back to the source, the copies stayed or came to her, his closest DNA match. So now she had the destinies of a couple hundred people. Her father had gifted her a great destiny as he always wanted, after all.

She closed her eyes, letting the thoughts and desires wash through her. She opened her eyes and they glowed fiercely. Some things pushed her from within. She had to finish her father's work. She let the thoughts and visions drive her as she began to read through his research.

As she read, her eyes closed but her reading did not stop. Voices whispered the words to her. The voices were the physical manifestation of possibilities that had torn a path through other realities to find their way to her. She already knew the words. Other voices whispered to her, increasing in tempo and numbers: "We are legion. We bring you your great destiny."

She dropped the book and held her head in agony. A great destiny did not mean a good one for the holder, or a sane one for that matter. She willed the voices away from her. They grew silent for a moment, then issued from her as colours: violet, violent-grey, then purple—dark manifestations of all that was in her. The colours gathered in the room above her, then merged together, changing and expanding into a black, torrential darkness that gathered around her. She looked at it with eyes wide, and through this open doorway to her soul, the colours rushed furiously into her.

She closed her eyes. When she opened them, they did not seem like the eyes of a twelve-year-old. They were deep and mysterious, shining with a dark, speckled light of unspoken things, of a great and powerful force waiting to be unleashed on a greedy, wicked, and unsuspecting world. But it was something more wicked. This destiny would not be denied.

. . . .

Oghenechovwe Donald Ekpeki is a writer, editor and publisher in Nigeria. His works have won and been a finalist in the Hugo, Nebula, Locus, World Fantasy, British Fantasy, British Science Fiction, Otherwise, Nommo, Sturgeon, NAACP Image awards, and others. His works have appeared in *Asimov's, F&SF, Uncanny, Strange Horizons, Apex Magazine*, etc and he's been a guest of honour at Cancon, Stranimondi, the ICFA 44, and others. You can find him on Bluesky and Instagram at @penprince.

NOVELETTES

IF YOU FIND YOURSELF SPEAKING TO GOD, ADDRESS GOD WITH THE INFORMAL YOU

John Chu

That first video of the flying man goes viral on social media and gets featured on the news. No jet pack. No hang glider. Just him, unaided, soaring over the cable-stayed bridge that leads into the city. The video looks like it was shot on a cellphone from a distance. It's shaky, zoomed in, and not always in focus. He is slaloming back and forth, doing barrel rolls, and turning flips like an aerial martial artist practicing his forms. Except aerial martial arts isn't a thing.

The video has to be part of a guerrilla marketing campaign for some upcoming movie. If so, they're taking their time coming clean about it. Instead of an actual movie trailer, there's a new cellphone video every few days or so.

The flying man is a Tom of Finland drawing rendered exquisitely in flesh and blood, but cranked up another notch or seven. Either his costume is giving him a lot of help or the body is flat out motion captured and computer generated with a breathtaking but heightened realism. He is shrink-wrapped in a black, short-sleeve compression-fit shirt, dark gray jeans that stretch across the thighs but need to be belted around the waist, and a pair of black, tactical boots. His muscles bulge, popping off his frame. His wide shoulders, big chest, and thick back taper to a trim waist. Broad sweeping thighs balance off his oversized torso. The effect is a body that's both exaggerated and aesthetically perfect.

He looks like he can snap the cables with a flick of his fingers. Instead, he weaves in and out of them with grace.

I'm sitting on a weight bench, resting before my next set. The gym has TVs mounted just below the ceiling. The latest Tom of Finland Guy video is playing on all of them. I don't notice anyone trying to get my attention until she taps me on the shoulder. We're both 5AM regulars. She is the one with the white ponytail.

"Can you please help me?" White Ponytail points to the other end of the weight room. "There's an EZ curl bar that I need help moving."

I walk over with her and, sure enough, there is a fixed-weight EZ curl bar resting on a stand. Someone couldn't be bothered re-racking the bar when they were done. The rack where the other fixed-weight EZ curl bars are resting is literally two steps away.

White Ponytail picks up an EZ curl bar from the rack. She eyes me expectantly. I grip the bar on the stand, take a deep breath, then heft it up with everything I've got.

The bar shoots up over my head. I stumble backwards and almost fall on my ass. The bar is way lighter than I'd expected. Of course, fixed-weight EZ curl bars are marked with their weight. I could have just looked.

"Wow, you really lifted that weight." She smirks as she sets her bar on the stand.

I don't even mumble a response. The handful of people in the gym are all, I'm sure, staring at me. I set the bar in its proper place on the rack and flee to my bench before I melt into a puddle of embarrassment.

On the way back, it sinks in that no one noticed. Well, except maybe Sweatshirt Guy. The color of the day is forest green. One sweatshirt or another is always failing to hide his muscles. His sweatshirts all bulge and contort in ways they never do over a typical body. Once you see it, you can't unsee it.

Why anyone ever asks me for help when he's right there is beyond me. Maybe no one else sees it. They see what they expect to see, some generically big guy in a sweatshirt and sweatpants. He grins when my gaze meets his. I may have inadvertently attracted the attention of a god.

The cellphone video pans across the front lawn from two movers standing to an upright piano sitting on a furniture dolly and, finally, to a crane. In fast forward, the movers wrap blankets around the piano. The video slows down to real time when they put the piano in a harness, sliding its straps beneath the dolly. They hook the harness to the crane.

Two more movers are inside the house, standing just inside an open window on the third floor. The two sets of movers give each other thumbs' ups.

The crane's cable snaps taut. The piano lurches. One of the movers on the lawn shouts something, waving his hands over his head. The crane flings the piano into the air. A plume of smoke rises from the crane. The piano arcs into the sky, tumbling end over end.

A black streak blurs across the sky. It resolves into Tom of Finland Guy. He catches the piano and presses it over his head. It's rock steady, perfectly balanced between his hands. He lands and gently sets the piano on the grass.

The movers stare at him, frozen and silent. Tom of Finland Guy, on the other hand, is the epitome of nonchalance. He's not much taller than the movers, but way more substantial. He seems to tower over them.

"Where would you like the piano?" Tom of Finland Guy's voice is gruff, faux deep.

Neither mover speaks. One of them manages to point at the open third floor window.

Tom of Finland Guy nods. He unhooks the harness from the crane, tilts the piano forward, then smoothly presses it overhead. The piano has weight and heft. It's not like when actors play a scene with a Styrofoam cup and you can tell there's nothing in the cup. He doesn't seem to notice the weight, though.

He flies it up the three floors. When he slides the piano through the window, it takes the movers several seconds before they remember they have a job to do. They wheel the piano into place. He hovers in front of the window, not letting go of the piano until they have it safely in hand.

Tom of Finland Guy waves to both sets of movers. The camera pans up to catch him zooming away, shrinking in the vast expanse of sky.

"Tell me you got all that on your cellphone," one of the movers says.

The usual suspects are slouched in folding chairs that ring the waiting room, their sheet music, resumés, and headshots clutched in their hands. We all go up for the same shows. In this case, it's a critically acclaimed regional theater's production of *42nd Street*. My sixteen bars, as always, is from "Softly, as in a Morning Sunrise" from *The New Moon*. Silly lyrics, but I get to show off my hard fought for, conservatory-trained high C.

I say hi to Linda at the desk. This isn't my first audition here. She takes my headshot and resumé. I fill out the paperwork then wait for my slot.

Brian gestures me over. We've both played Ito in multiple productions of *Mame*, and have been cast as the brothers in *Thoroughly Modern Millie* and the "converts" in *Anything Goes*. All of this would be fine, I guess, if we both got also cast in non-Asian roles and looked even vaguely related. He's impossibly tall and thin. Next to him, I look squat. You would think no one could possibly confuse the two of us. And yet.

"What's up?" I take a seat next to him.

"What sort of technical wizardry did it take to make that look like it was done in one take?" Brian points to his phone. "You didn't actually shoulder press an upright piano, did you? That would be a lot, even for you."

It takes me a moment before I realize what he's talking about. He thinks I'm Tom of Finland Guy.

"Oh, no, that's not me."

"Really?" He shows me the phone's screen. "You can't make out the face, but, otherwise, he could be you."

"You think I look like that?"

All of the videos look like home videos. None of them have a good shot of his face. There's no mistaking that body for anyone else's though.

"With help from the costume? Sure." He looks at me like I'm nuts for even asking. "I've seen you at dance calls."

"I wish I'd booked the gig." I slouch in my chair. "But I didn't even know about the audition."

Linda calls for Brian. I wish him luck, but not in those words, of course. We are a superstitious lot and that would be tempting fate. For the same reason, you do not say "Break a leg!" to a dancer. Yes, this is not a dance call. He's still a dancer. Instead, you say:

"Merde!"

The next video to go viral is a montage. Every piece looks like a cellphone video shot by a bystander from a safe distance. Maybe that's what they actually are. Tom of Finland Guy breaks up fights. Tom of Finland Guy extracts small backpacks and other bags from muggers and returns them to their owners. Tom of Finland Guy literally rescues a cat from a tree.

He always fights as though his only hope is to win on points. That doesn't matter so much. One time, someone lands a lucky punch and breaks his hand on Tom of Finland Guy's body. The guy's face is flushed. He winces and howls in pain. Everyone backs away from him then runs away. The punch itself doesn't even register on Tom of Finland Guy. He just stares at his midsection.

Watching these Tom of Finland Guy videos in the rest between sets is the latest version of a bad habit that I should break. They're not just showing the videos on the news. Reporters interview the people in the videos and bystanders. Maybe there actually is someone flying around the city picking up heavy things and letting low-level criminals break themselves against him. Or this is an alternate reality game or a guerrilla campaign for a movie that's about to turn into a public-relations fiasco. Either way, these videos are my latest excuse for resting too long between sets.

"Excuse me." The light baritone voice comes right behind the bench I'm sitting on.

It's Sweatshirt Guy. The color of the day is a deep blue. Our paths have never really crossed. He's always been the big, if unusually shaped, guy in the distance.

Up close, I'm sure he's not just a competitive bodybuilder but one in peak contest shape. He must have a show coming up. Or maybe he's just won one.

No one gets this lean and this dehydrated just for fun. It's certainly not for their health. Up close, his "death face" is obvious. The severe dehydration and dangerously low levels of body fat makes his face gaunt. His features are all flat planes and hard angles, as though they've been chipped out of stone. It adds an edge to his smile and I'm convinced I must have done something profane and am about to be struck down by the local gym god.

"Hi." Sweatshirt Guy gestures towards a bench press rack. "May I please ask you for a spot?"

In theory, this is when I answer him. In practice, I may have forgotten how to speak. Up close, I can't not make out the details of his body, implied by how his sweatshirt warps around him. When a god reveals himself to you, stunned is not an unreasonable reaction. Yes, he is not literally the best bodybuilder on the planet. Probably not. In the moment, it's astonishing how little that matters. Between competitions, when he's carrying a healthy amount of fat and properly hydrated, he must be glorious.

He purses his lips, looks awkward for a moment, then repeats himself, this time in Mandarin. Just as he sounds like an American newsreader in English, he sounds like a Taiwanese newsreader in Mandarin. Maybe it's tinged with American. Then again, so is my Mandarin. There was a diaspora from Taiwan. A bunch of their children and their children's children, me included and undoubtedly him, have been pressed into impromptu translation duty for them.

His words include an apology, a please, and the formal you. The construction is in such a formal register that it snaps me out of my mental fugue.

"Oh, that's way too polite. Sorry, I understood you the first time." I stand up. Despite how he looms, he's maybe an inch taller than me. "Sure."

His bar has enough weight on it that I'm pointedly not calculating how much. I'm just reminding myself that in the extremely unlikely event he hits failure, he's maybe ten pounds shy of the force he needs to exert. The most I have to do is supply those ten pounds.

Sweatshirt guy lies down on the bench. He notes the expression on my face and smiles again. It's both slightly embarrassed and the warmest, kindest smile that a death face can manage.

His form is strict and beautiful. Every rep is slow, steady, and covers a full range of motion. Just like you're supposed to, on the concentric phase, he explicitly squeezes the muscle being worked. His sweatshirt swells and ebbs as the bar rises and falls. It isn't until rep fourteen or whatever that he starts to struggle. I'm paying so much attention to the artistry that I've lost count. The bar slows to a stop on the way up but his arms lock out the instant I place my hands between him and the bar. Lifting is as much a mind game as anything else. It's amazing how much stronger you become when it looks like someone is helping you. When he quits a few reps later, there is no struggle. The bar is gently settled, not plopped, onto the rack.

He does three sets. I do my remaining sets of dumbbell bench presses during his rests. He spots me in turn. His calm, patient gaze weighs me down more than the dumbbells.

We make quick work of unloading the bar and re-racking the plates. He nods approvingly at me when we're done.

"Good lifting with you." He claps me gently on my shoulder. "See you tomorrow, buddy."

With that, he walks away. My gaze follows him out of the gym.

He does three sets and he's done. Maybe when a bodybuilder is in contest shape, he takes it easy. Some definition of easy, that is, that involves lifting more weight than anyone else here is using by some margin.

As for me, I haven't done dumbbell presses this satisfying in a while. Today, I was either lifting or spotting. He wasn't going to let me rest too long between sets. I have definitely attracted the attention of a god.

The shooting gets covered on the news. An autistic man is sitting in a parking lot. His therapist is crouched next to him. The cellphone taking the video is too far away to capture what he's saying. Two policemen are pointing their guns at them and shouting orders. Their words overlap and it's impossible to tell what they're saying. The therapist lies down puts his hand in the air. They start shooting anyway. He's an African American man. Those policemen never cared where he put his hands.

Tom of Finland Guy lands, putting himself between the two men and the police. Their bullets shatter harmlessly against his chest. The police stop shooting. For the moment, the only sound is the whisper of the therapist to the autistic man. The policemen look shocked at the bullet fragments on the ground. Tom of Finland Guy's expression is somewhere between amazed and disbelieving.

He crouches down. As he talks to the therapist, the police bark an order and start shooting again. Tom of Finland Guy pays no attention to them, letting their bullets break against his back. Carefully, he gathers up both men and he flies them away.

Reporters interview the therapist. No one thinks the videos are some sort of guerrilla marketing campaign anymore. Social media and the news instantly dub the flying, bulletproof man The Great Wall. Because calling him that is not racist at all.

I lift four days a week. Sweatshirt Guy always asks me to spot him and I do. Then he spots me and eyes me critically when I finish a set. He always looks like he's going to comment but then doesn't.

Leg day with him is a bit scary, at least for me. A lot of plates have been piled on that bar. He's squatting in a power rack. It'll catch the bar if he goes too low. I stand behind him, my arms in place under his, ready to wrap around his chest, to help him back up. He never needs the help.

It's been a week and we're back to chest again. The color of the day is a dark blue. After his last set of bench presses, he holds up his hand before I can start unloading the bar.

"Why don't you give it a try?" Sweatshirt Guy pats the bar before he sits up on the bench. "You realize those 90-pound dumbbells are too light for you, right?"

That is a sentence that has never been said seriously before in the history of the English language. I fold my arms across my chest. Finally, a chance to eye him critically back.

"This is at least my one rep max," I gesture at the bar.

Honestly, I'm guessing. The lovely thing about dumbbell bench presses is that you can do them by yourself. You don't absolutely have to have a spotter. So I never do barbell bench presses.

"You'll be fine." Sweatshirt Guy removes a slim 5-pound plate off each side of the bar. He looks satisfied, as though those missing ten pounds will make all the difference. "We'll try for ten reps."

Sweatshirt Guy slides the 5-pound plates onto a weight tree. One dumbbell in each hand, he walks the 90-pound dumbbells back to their rack in long, smooth strides. Whether or not they are too light for me, they're clearly too light for him.

"Sure." I lie down on the bench.

Whether he intends it or not, a suggestion from anyone built like him carries an implied promise. Sure, it's one that takes years if not decades of relentless grind to fulfill. I've been lifting since high school, though. I've already signed up for that. Refusing a god is hard.

He has the crooning voice of a '40s band singer. His gentle, quiet words between each rep buoy me. Somewhere between "Come on, you can do it," "It's all you," and "Don't worry. I'm right here and I've got you." I crank out six reps before I rack the bar.

"Nope, you can do at least three more." His voice hits that seam between reassuring and demanding. "Don't worry. I've got you."

On the press of that third rep, I battle the bar to a standstill. It's shaking but not actually moving. For a moment, I know my strength will give out I'm going to be that asshole who traps himself because his eyes are bigger than his muscles. Sweatshirt Guy's hands reach for the bar and my arms reflexively straighten and lock out. That might have been under my own power. I can't tell. Either way, he grabs the bar and guides it back on the rack.

I sit up. My pecs burn. They're sore and they strain against my T-shirt. My heart pounds and I'm trying to slow my breath. It feels wonderful. I've missed this.

"One rep max?" His tone is tinged with sarcasm, but his smile is as warm as his face allows. "What do you do next? Flyes?"

He does the flappy seal thing a few times, his arms out to the side then straight in front of him. On anyone else, the gesture would look silly. On him, his pecs visibly push against the sweatshirt and it is a literal, if unintentional, flex.

"Yeah, cable flyes." I manage to croak out the words with only the slightest of pauses.

"Good. I was going to do some anyway. You're welcome to join me."

He heads off to the cable machine, leaving it up to me to follow. I can stop this right now. Not even a god can gang someone into being his lifting partner. But he keeps me on track. My workouts haven't felt this good in years. Not only have I attracted the attention of a god, but he seems to have adopted me.

Some Guy, pale but flushed, attacks a Chinese grandma on the street for no good reason. The video starts with him shouting "—don't belong here, Asian" and beating her. It takes a second or five for everything to come into focus and into frame. Her face is bruised. Blood dribbles from her nose.

Scattered strangers are starting to gather. They shout at him to leave her alone.

She starts hitting him back, shouting insults in Mandarin. Her fists pound against his face, shoulders, whatever she can reach. Some Guy cowers, hiding his face behind his forearms.

Tom of Finland Guy lands. He steps up to Some Guy and taps him away. Some Guy stumbles back a few steps before he falls on his back. Grandma lurches after him, but Tom of Finland Guy gently guides her away.

He asks her how she is, whether she needs to go to the hospital, in the most respectful Mandarin. Tom of Finland Guy is obviously some Chinese grandma's good grandson, if not this grandma's. She, of course, insists that she is perfectly fine, does not need any help, and can take care of herself. The bruises and bleeding are still obvious on her face.

Two policemen arrive. One immediately crouches down next to Some Guy, checks for a concussion, then radios for an ambulance. Meanwhile, the other one levels his gun at Tom of Finland Guy. One of the scattered strangers explains what's actually happening to the police. It doesn't matter. The policeman shouts for Tom of Finland Guy to step away from the grandma then starts shooting.

Tom of Finland Guy says something to the grandma, who nods. He cradles her in his arms and lifts into the sky. The policeman continues to shoot. Bullets chase Tom of Finland Guy but they don't reach him. Who knows where they fall.

Sweatshirt Guy and I finish our back and bi workout with some ab work. The gym has a separate workout room with mats for this sort of thing. No one uses it this time of day.

I was teetering on the edge before. Sweat drenches my T-shirt. The rest between sets is just enough for my breathing to steady. After the ab workout, I'm collapsed on a mat, which is where I live now. Sweatshirt Guy, naturally, hasn't even broken into a sweat. He stands over me, looking vaguely alarmed.

This is basically how all our workouts end. It catches him off-guard every time, as though a body adapts in the span of minutes or hours rather than months or years. As though he hasn't been nudging up the intensity by increments too small to measure from one workout to the next.

I, of course, have been complicit in this. There's a quiet joy in the slow, steady, repetitive pushing or pulling a weight. Nothing else exists while I'm lifting. Nothing else feels like the stretching and contracting of muscle. A rep, when it's done well, feels good.

There's also a contentment, a quiet satisfaction in being spent. A dull, pleasant ache burns through my muscles. I can't help but be relaxed and, honestly, this will be the most focused I will be until my next workout. I spend my life trying to stretch out this feeling until I can create it again.

I used to think working out with me was just his warm up and he came back later in the day for his real workout. It's not so far-fetched. At any point in the day, a professional bodybuilder is doing only ever one of three things: eating, resting, or lifting.

After a couple months, however, I now think he's Tom of Finland Guy. It's not just the facial similarity. He also still has the death face. His proportions are still highly exaggerated. I can make out his muscles through the sweatshirt as well now as when he first asked me for a spot. An actual bodybuilder would have either softened his body back to a sustainable shape by now or be dead.

He's both genuinely friendly and scary as fuck. I've been hoping to see him transform into someone not so physically austere and forbidding. That transformation is clearly never going to happen.

"I need a favor." Sweatshirt Guy sits down, cross-legged, next to me.

I sit up. This had to happen sooner or later. A god has blessed me with his favor and the moment of reckoning has arrived. It's time for him to exact his price.

"Sure. What would you need?"

"New apartment. Big couch. Needs support on both ends to move. You're the strongest guy I know."

Honestly, I don't know what I expected, but this isn't it. He can stand the couch on end and carry it by himself. No one else can, though. That, I suppose, is the problem.

"Absolutely, I can help you move." It even sounds like I believe he needs the help. I'm a working actor, after all.

"Saturday morning?"

"OK."

"Pick you up with the moving trunk?" He looks dubious.

"Sure."

If I get to know where he lives, he might as well know where I live. I give him my address.

"Thanks." He starts to offer his hand but ends up lightly patting my back. "Carl."

"Steve."

My hand misses when I pat his back. His slide out of the way looks unintentional, a coincidental turn as he leaves. It isn't until he's gone that I realize an invulnerable man who is keeping it a secret probably doesn't want to shake hands or be clapped on the back while in disguise. It would give him away.

Tom of Finland Guy only has cameos in his next viral video. At the end of the day, it isn't even about him.

The video is snippets of one news report after another, peppered with cellphone video or surveillance cameras video, a summary of the past few months. A white man pushed a Vietnamese American woman onto the subway tracks, killing her. Someone else followed a Chinese American woman back to her apartment and stabbed her to death. Yet another man barged into a massage parlor and killed the Korean American women working there. A shrine in Chinatown to the murdered women was trashed. A Japanese American actor was beaten and bruised on his way to a performance. A Korean American man slashed twice in the face just because. A man with curly blond hair and a backpack went on a two-hour spree assaulting one Asian woman after another. The reports go on and on.

Tom of Finland Guy is seen fleetingly in one or two snippets. Mostly, it is one grim newsreader after another.

The cuts between reports get faster and faster. The images become unrecognizable flashes of light. Audio from reports collide and overlap. They pile on top of each other in an increasing cacophony until all anyone can make out is noise.

A translucent image of Tom of Finland Guy emerges from the chaos. Text in a lurid red covers him word by word: "Where is he?" This is followed by: "Why does he let this happen?"

Somewhere lost in all this is the notion that maybe the real problem is the racists. They can simply choose not to murder people or beat them until they are purple with bruises. It's not that no one is saying this on social media. It's just buried in the noise.

In the end, what will defeat me is not the big couch. Both on the way down to the truck and on the way back up again to the new apartment, Carl places himself at the bottom of the stairs. It's not that I can't feel the weight. The thing has to weigh at least five hundred pounds. It's that I'm unconvinced I'm doing any of the heavy lifting.

What will defeat me is the sheer number of large boxes of books. The man does not live in an apartment. He lives in a library with a bed, bathroom, and kitchen and is moving to a different library with a bed, bathroom, and kitchen.

The other boxes are all light enough. They go into the new apartment in stacks. We both move the boxes of books one at a time. Me, because I'm only human. Him, because he's committing to the bit where he's merely a consistent ten to twenty pounds stronger than me.

I realize I'm being stupid. There's a still warm sausage and onion pizza sitting on a counter in his new apartment's kitchen. Carl seems perfectly content to have me eat pizza while I watch him move his library into his new apartment. Even though I know he can leave me in the dust whenever he wants, I can't help but try to keep up. It's taking longer because I'm helping.

The boxes are all meticulously labeled. At least I get to find out something about him during the slog. The conversation we had on the drive from my apartment to his old apartment was very tight-lipped. He allowed that he competed in weightlifting and cheer through to the end of his undergrad degree. He forgets to be laconic, though, when I mention his books.

He read *Structure and Interpretation of Computer Programs* because he wanted to, not for a class. It's not the only piece of heavy reading he did for pleasure. Jean Baudrillard's *The Gulf War Did Not Take Place* inspires a cautious discussion where I hold my own about propaganda and media presentations determining the viewer's experience. A reference to Stephen Banfield's *Sondheim's Broadway Musicals* turns him on like a spigot.

The boxes feel lighter while we're chatting. As I keep reminding myself, lifting is as much a mind game as a matter of strength. From "I Remember That," we drift to "I Remember It Well," the one Alan Jay Lerner wrote with Kurt Weill, not Frederick Loewe. From there, he brings up *The Firebrand of Florence*. I can't believe he's even heard of the operetta until he sings the hangman's opening quatrain. He's even in the right key.

In the moment, what I want is to grab him by the shoulders and kiss him full on the lips. We don't have that sort of relationship, though. Maybe it's better that we don't. He's probably more interested in sex than I am. Most people are. Instead of kissing him, I stumble over a box out the way out of his new apartment.

I latch the rear door of the moving trunk. We're all done, which is good because I don't think I'm physically capable of lifting a penny at the moment. I've already told Carl not to expect me at the gym on Monday.

Carl is still upstairs locking up. I'm waiting for him to drive me home when a detective and a beat cop come up to me. The detective flashes his badge. Their unmarked car is parked behind them, blocking the apartment complex's driving lane.

"Carl Tsai." The detective shows me his phone. There's a screen shot of Carl as Tom of Finland Guy. "Do you know why we're here?"

He thinks I'm Carl. As if there is only one Asian on the planet. There's a spree of violence against Asian Americans and Carl is who they decide to investigate. I decide not to disabuse them.

"No, why are you here?"

"We have reason to believe you're The Great Wall." He swipes his screen. A video I've never seen before starts playing. Carl's face is clearly visible. "Where were you yesterday around 3PM?"

"I'm not discussing my day with you."

"Look, a cop died." He flips the phone so I can't see the rest of the video. "Maybe it was an accident. What were you doing yesterday afternoon?"

I don't believe for an instant that Carl killed a cop, even by accident. That's the sort of thing that makes the news instantly and not at all Carl's modus operandi. He is careful to a fault. The detective's lying to provoke some sort of reaction.

"You are detaining me, or am I free to go?"

"I'm detaining you."

The other cop approaches me with handcuffs. I don't think they've thought this through. Anyone who they can restrain with handcuffs is clearly not who they're looking for.

"Let him go. You're looking for me and he's clearly not me." Carl floats above us in his Tom of Finland Guy outfit. His voice is a gravelly bass-baritone again. "And that cop tried to shoot me and killed his partner instead. You know that."

Both cops draw their guns on him. They and I realize at the same time that I'm a much easier target. They pivot and aim their guns at me. Nice guys, both of them. Maybe it's because I'm so tired, but I have no reaction. My heart doesn't even pound.

"Look, Great Wall, just come with us." The detective's gaze is aimed at me, but, obviously, he's talking to Carl floating behind him. "No one needs to get hurt."

This is the first time I've seen Carl as Tom of Finland Guy right in front of me. In person, it's impossible to miss the fullness and roundedness of each and every muscle. They are all beautifully separated from each other and popping off his frame. The overall shape is so aesthetically pleasing and perfectly proportioned, it's hard to imagine any sculptor doing better. A sweatshirt does hide him somewhat, it turns out. He is a masterpiece of art or a wonder of the world. If this sight is my last before I die, I could have picked worse.

Carl stares at me, then he stares at the cops. I imagine death rays or whatever shooting from his eyes. The cops sway and yawn. Their aim wavers and they holster their guns. Their heads bobble, seemingly too heavy for their necks. They blink and, finally, shut their eyes before they crumple to the ground. Their chests slowly rise and fall. Their faces are calm and placid.

I, on the other hand, seem to have caught my second wind. These two events, I suspect, are not unconnected. My back and legs aren't sore anymore. I'm no longer overheated and sweating. My body is telling me that it's ready to move another apartment and it can't possibly be right.

Carl looks stunned. He levels a critical gaze at me.

"I'm sorry. That worked a little too well." He's keeping up the rough and tumble Tom of Finland Guy voice. "You were more tired than I expected."

He gathers up the cops. I don't get a chance to ask whether he needs help before he has strapped them into their car. He lifts the car by the front bumper and speeds off, pulling the car behind him, as if he were a human-shaped high-speed tow truck. Supporting a car only by a single point probably isn't good for it.

Carl comes out of the apartment building. The color of the day is still tan. He spots me by the moving truck. Nothing in his expression admits to what just happened. He is his usual crisp self, not that I expected any different.

"Ready to go?" His voice is back to its light, crooning baritone.

"Sure."

The conversation on the drive home is tight. Carl doesn't want to out himself to me. I'm not going out him to himself. He doesn't want to admit to me or isn't ready to admit to me what is pretty clear that I already know. I can't do anything about it besides wait. What he can do about it is stop lifting with me. That would break me.

The hate is more pointed in some of the other videos. It's also more pathetic.

They wrap him in the red flag with five stars, insisting this is a sighting in his new costume. The CGI is awful. The flag is a red splotch that covers his body but it doesn't move the way he moves. It purports to be both skintight and fail to ripple as his muscles tense and relax. The stars hover next to his body.

In actual footage, people shout at him, their pale faces flush with rage. In a few cases, they are literally shaking their fist at the sky. They're not very creative. It's generally some version of "Go back where you came from!" They never say just exactly where that is. Sometimes, it's variations on "You don't belong here." Only dirtier.

Some people say these things to his face. A few of them try to break their bones against his body and he gently guides their fists away. He doesn't look angry or hurt. Mostly, he just looks tired.

Unlike Carl, I do not have a couch. Even after Saturday, I don't need one to sprawl on. Instead of sore, I feel fine, just a little guilty for skipping my workout. It's unsettling for my body to recover this quickly. Those two policemen are undoubtedly still sore as hell. I try to feel bad about this but I can't.

Hollow ottomans that double as book storage are scattered around a coffee table. Books are stacked underneath. The requisite electronic keyboard rests on a stand in the corner next to the folding chair. Books are stacked on the floor there, too. The sheet music for "Suddenly Salad," the song I still have to learn for the elementary school assembly gig I booked, sits on the music stand attached to the keyboard.

I sight read the sheet music, accompanying myself on the keyboard. The tune is a pastiche of a much better song. The lyrics are about as good as they can be considering I am a giant head of romaine telling a bunch of grade school kids that "romaine's their friend." I can't but think that "We're in a Salad" from Christopher Durang's *A History of the American Film* is right there smirking at this.

"We're in a Salad" is, of course, a loving pastiche of "We're in the Money." Going from "We're in a Salad" to *42nd Street*, where I booked a gig in the ensemble, would be more fitting. I'm one of the four boys flanking Billy Lawlor at the start of "Dames" and, even better, I'm understudying Billy. In theory, there is a potential *All About Steve* situation here. In practice, no, of course not.

Either way, I'm singing "Suddenly, salad is plated beside you" when there is a knock at the door. Dignity, what is paramount in this profession is dignity.

I open the door. It's Carl, the man who can hear a mouse scratch the dirt on the other side of the world and we both pretend he didn't just hear "Suddenly Salad." The color of the day is dark gray. For the first time since we've met, he has a bearing that doesn't seem like either a military "at ease" or a bodybuilder "relaxed" pose.

"Are we OK?" Carl has that dubious look on his face again.

"Yes?" I stare back at him, puzzled. "Are we fighting?"

I invite him in and close the door behind him. His gaze sweeps the room.

"You need a couch." He is dead serious, or maybe it's just hard for that face to hold many other expressions. "Sorry, that's not why I'm here. You weren't at the gym. Are we OK?"

"I told you I was skipping today." I gesture at an ottoman and sit down on its neighbor. "You own a lot of books."

"But your body isn't s— Oh, this is stupid. I hated being closeted and hiding this is no better." In a blur, he becomes Tom of Finland Guy. "How long have you known?"

His sweatshirt and sweatpants lie in a pile next to him. His voice is still much more the crooning light baritone of Sweatshirt Guy than the gruff bass-baritone of Tom of Finland Guy.

I pick up his sweatpants. They're tearaway. A row of snaps lines each leg. They're disguised to look like a seam. The illusion of typical sweatpants is convincing enough, I guess, if you don't look too closely.

"You know, I have friends who can design quick change sweatpants that hide the tearaway better." I can't resist redoing the snaps before I set the sweatpants down. "Otherwise, regular tearaways would be less suspicious."

"You figured me out from my sweatpants?" He looks incredulous. "So, from the moment I asked you to spot me?"

We've both clearly had plenty of prior experience being closeted and outing ourselves. I know. He knows I know. I know he knows I know. And, now, in a thrilling anti-climax, we finally both know that we both know. I swear a big chunk of the experience of being closeted is the bookkeeping.

"It took about a couple months. You can win any bodybuilding contest you want, but any bodybuilder would be dead if they tried to stay in the shape you're in for that long." I'm trying my level best to stay casual but it's like talking to a god who has revealed himself in his full glory right now. "I haven't told anyone."

"I didn't think you did." He puts his sweatshirt and sweatpants back on. "I mean, you didn't even tell *me*."

"I assumed you knew."

A smile spreads across his death face. It's not so intimidating now that I understand it for what it is. Once again, what I want is to throw my arms around him and plant my lips on his. I mean, he thought my stupid joke was funny or at least he's humoring the attempt.

"I'm sorry." He pushes an ottoman next to mine then sits on it. "I didn't mean to get you or anyone else involved."

"You didn't. All you did was ask me to spot you." I stifle my hand before it can pat his thigh to reassure him. "Actually, why do you lift? You can't be getting anything out of it."

"I get asked about my workout routine. A lot. You know how it is." He gestures pointedly at my arms and chest. "I don't want to lie and the only way I don't attract attention in the gym is if I use lots of weight and some big, buff guy is spotting me. And there you are, being sweet and kind to everyone who interrupts your workout."

"That's a lot of time spent to avoid a little white lie."

He rolls his eyes at me. His face then shifts in a way that's hard to read. He could just be annoyed but I'm guessing wistful.

"The last time I felt even a little tired was maybe a year ago. I haven't been able to get wrecked like you get on a really good workout in years." He purses his lips. "I'm trying to remember what it's like vicariously. Otherwise, I might forget what it's like to be human."

We both get something out of it. That, weirdly, makes me feel better about working out with him.

"Years? The videos only started show up a month or so ago."

"It takes time to teach yourself how to fly. I started getting too strong, too fast during my post-doc." He chuckles. "Maybe I was bitten by a radioactive bodybuilder."

"Are you into getting bitten?" I smirk. "Because nothing's penetrating your skin."

The instant those words leave my mouth, I want to stuff them back in. There's committing to the bit and there's wandering into places I don't belong. I sputter. The panic and guilt must be obvious on my face because he holds a hand to shut me up. His gaze is oddly soft.

"Yes. No. I mean, yes, I'm well-nigh invulnerable by now. No, I'm not really into anything sexual, which is handy, I guess. All I've ever wanted is a hug or a kiss every once in a while. But even that still gives me away."

His brow furrows for a moment. His jaw drops. He perks up, stands, and points a finger at me. I half-expect to disintegrate or something. No idea whether that's even a thing he can do. As far as I can tell, though, he's just pointing at me.

"What are you doing, Carl?"

"You're not off-limits anymore. I can finally ask you out on a date." He notices he's stabbing his index finger at me and drops his hand. "I've always wanted to show someone this. Watch."

He walks up an imaginary set of stairs. It's mime from someone who can hover in midair. The thing is, it's really good. He's spent a lot of time on this. The man whose body can do anything he trains it to do has spent his time on mime he never expected to show anyone. This either makes me love him more or hate his guts for how easy he's making it look. Both, actually.

His weight shifts convincingly from foot to foot. Each step is exactly the same size as the next. How he moves creates the illusion of smooth, hard, level surfaces beneath his feet. The effect is so ordinary, anyone watching a video of this would think he's just climbing a transparent staircase.

Carl flips into a handstand and his hands walk back down the steps. His body is perfectly taut to the pointed toes. There's a slight teeter from one side to the other as he shifts his weight from one hand to the other. His sweatshirt wrinkles and swells as he tenses and relaxes each muscle. The slight teeter is actually harder to do intentionally than by accident. Most people trying this on a real staircase would just fall over. But people who blow your minds when they walk down stairs on their hands look just like this. Only he's doing it without the stairs.

Once on the ground, he pushes off and flips to a stand. The landing is impossibly soft and silent. His toes touch the floor and his knees bend to take the momentum as his heel rolls onto the floor. None of my furniture shifts, much less clatter. He takes a slight bow, one arm bent in front of his waist, the other behind. I give him a standing ovation.

As I applaud, what he said—what he's trying to distract me from—replays in my head. The delayed reaction hits me and I sit back down.

"Wait. Are you asking me out?" I take a deep breath and hope for the best. "Because my nights are basically free for the next couple of weeks, until tech for *42nd Street* starts."

He looks at me and he wears his reactions like costumes, switching from one to the next before he finally settles on one. Tom of Finland Guy meets my gaze with an impervious confidence. He only really has just the one choice. The crooning Sweatshirt Guy from the gym has a dubious expression on his face, wondering if he's just broken our relationship. Carl, however, just looks vulnerable. A bullet can't penetrate his chest but a question, apparently, can.

"It's been so long." His brow is furrowed. "Yes."

"Are you free Saturday night?"

"I can be." His words are slow and cautious. "Yes, I am."

"Great, it's a date." I stand and open my arms for a hug. "We can figure out what we're doing later. It's not like we don't see each other four days a week."

He wraps his arms around me. I wrap mine around him. His grasp is pointedly delicate, trying too hard to cocoon the soap bubble that is me. Hugging him is like hugging a warm, intricately wrought bronze statue wrapped in a thin sheath of cotton. His body has no give. My fingers feel the separation between muscle fibers despite themselves.

"See you at the gym tomorrow. I should get going." He claps my back one last time before he lets go. "Leave you to rehearse your song about salad. Remember, you can be silly, but, whatever they're paying you, don't be radicchio."

The pun hangs in the air. It sounds so earnest and his face refuses to admit the joke. His expression screams its sincerity. I suppose it is also that.

He sees himself out. I just stand there, taking in what he made of "Suddenly Salad." At least we're on the same wavelength.

The crowd at City Hall Plaza is peaceful. All the videos agree. It doesn't matter whether it's from cellphones in the crowd, from news cameras on the helicopters overhead, or from the cameras on the cops in riot gear sprinkled around the perimeter. The crowd, people of every gender and ethnicity, fill the space backstopped by a sparse row of trees and the street. People are just waving signs and chanting, protesting violence against Asian Americans, particularly women. Even with the cops goading them, the protesters are peaceful.

A truck screeches down the street. It plows into the plaza. Screams and shouts of "Truck!" fill the air. The crowd breaks up, rushing towards the brick paths out of the plaza.

The police take the chaos as their excuse to make a move. Reinforcements arrive. Military-grade drones fly in and place concrete jersey barriers on the brick paths.

Tom of Finland Guy lands in front of the truck as it races towards the crowd. He picks it up by the front bumper. Slowly, he rises into the air, lifting the bumper as he goes.

The driver rolls down his window. As the car goes vertical, he's shouting racial slurs and threatening to sue if Tom of Finland Guy so much as scratches his truck.

The truck slowly flips over. The man screams. Tom of Finland Guy, still holding on to the front bumper, lowers it, bit by bit, until the truck is upside down on the ground. The man, wisely, stays in the truck.

A team of four cops run toward the truck. They look a little giddy and punch drunk. One of them huffs and puffs harder than the others. There's a big gun mounted on his shoulder. Without a word, he shoots.

A hum fills the air. A thin, bright beam whizzes past Tom of Finland Guy. It vaporizes a tree on its way across the street.

Tom of Finland Guy shifts to block the beam. It burns a tiny hole in his shirt, but doesn't do anything to him. He strolls towards the team. The shooter twists a dial on gun. The beam grows brighter and louder. It doesn't matter. Tom of Finland Guy just keeps walking towards them until he and the gunman are face to face. With a flick of his finger and a smile, he disables the gun.

The rest of the team fiddles with their remote controls. The drones swarm over Tom of Finland Guy. Each of them shoots a cable that lassos him. The cables cinch around his arms and chest. His muscles tense and strain but the cables don't budge.

They push the stick forward on their remotes, directing the drones up. The drones buzz and whir, dragging up Tom of Finland Guy with them. The cables snap taut. His body shakes in mid-air as he holds the tug-of-war to a stalemate.

The cops lean forward so hard on their remote controls that one of them almost falls over. The whirring grows louder and higher pitched. Tom of Finland Guy doesn't so much vibrate as blur in place, still writhing against the cables around his chest and arms.

The stalemate lasts for what seems like minutes. The crowd cheers him on. The cops, grins wide on their faces, high five each other. They taunt him, shouting that maybe he's not so strong after all.

Tom of Finland Guy lands. If that takes any effort, it doesn't show. He drags the drones down with him. Their whirring squeaks into the ultrasonic before they spark and smoke. Their propellers stop and they tumble towards the ground. He wasn't struggling to stay in place. They were struggling to move him. He was just overloading them waiting for them to burn out.

He darts back up as the drones fall. The cables snap taut again. The drones dangle below him. He sets them on the ground before he lands again. The cables surrounding him break with a shrug. That struggle was a fake out, too.

The smiles are long gone from the cops' faces. They bolt, the one with the gun on his shoulder slightly behind everyone else.

The rest of the police, however, are already arresting protestors, taking them away to be processed. Tom of Finland Guy surveys the scene, glaring at the police. Of the cops keeping the protestors penned in, a couple of the cops yawn, a few are unsteady on their feet, but none are so tired that they can't stay awake.

Tom of Finland Guy flies into the crowd and airlifts anyone who wants to leave, one by one. He can't stop them from arresting protestors. They can't stop him from freeing them.

The color of the day is violet. Lifting with Carl is both exactly like and nothing like lifting with Sweatshirt Guy. In the weight room, he's still that crooning light baritone. He's still whispering encouragement in my ear with each rep.

Now, though, he's not so much of a sentient tax form when I rest between sets. He cracks the occasional joke. His sentences use as many as two more words than absolutely necessary. We feel each other out about what to do on our date. My rest breaks fly by and, before I realize it, he's reminding me "Here and now." Sometimes, it's with a warm tap on the shoulder.

We don't talk about the rally. Even at 5AM, there are too many people around. Neither of us are too rusty with the bookkeeping of being closeted.

In the separate workout room, his demeanor shifts. He's not as mannered when no one else is around. It's the most relaxed I've seen him. His voice, still smooth, drops a few semitones. His body is not always carefully positioned just so. Ironically, he presents like just a big lug in a sweatshirt when he's not trying to.

He's chatty, compared to Sweatshirt Guy. The short breaks in our ab workout are not deathly silent. He's using maybe four more words than absolutely necessary. It's mostly a one-way conversation because I'm busy dying. The ab exercises look very simple and easy when he does them.

He limits himself to only oblique references to the rally. Once, he makes a cryptic comment about wanting to save everyone. I manage one right back in between gasps. Unjust systems require systemic change. No one is powerful enough to do it by themself, not even him.

When we're done, I'm splayed on the mat, trying desperately to keep air in my lungs. He looks at me with this expression of intense want and need on his face. It can't be for me. We haven't even gone on our date yet. It's this weekend. The look on his face doesn't make sense until I remember what he's getting out of our workouts.

"You can remove the fatigue from my body, right?"

The desire on his face becomes worry. He crouches next to me.

"I thought you enjoyed feeling wrecked. We can ease off a bit next time."

"No, no, I do. If our workouts ever get to be too much, believe me, I'll let you know." I push myself up to a sit. "I mean, instead of giving my fatigue to someone else, can you give it to yourself?"

"I don't know." His brow furrows. "I've never tried."

"Do you want to try?"

He takes a beat. His gaze defocuses through me to some distant place deep beneath the floor. For all I know, that may be literal or maybe he's just not paying attention to where his gaze wanders. His expression is pensive until it isn't and his gaze snaps back to me.

"Sure."

He stares at me and I get my second wind. It's an odd sensation, recovering instantly like this. My breath goes from rough to smooth before I realize. Endorphins are an electric current coursing through me. My body does not want to stay still. This time, however, he's left me the residue of my fatigue. My body doesn't insist that I absolutely have to go back and hit the weights again right away.

As for Carl, his brow wrinkles for a moment. I thought he might deflate a bit, but he is very much his bulging, if austere, self.

"Interesting." He nods slowly. "Are you ok?"

"Yeah, considering the workout I had, I feel great." I'm upright. I don't remember standing. "Probably a little too great. Do you feel tired at all?"

"No." He frowns. "Well, maybe for an instant."

"I'm sorry."

I go to squeeze his shoulder and he lets me. The sweatshirt compresses, but, of course, his shoulder doesn't.

"No, it's good. It's enough to remind me what it was like."

He claps my back. It looks casual and affectionate but feels careful and simulated. An actual casual clap from him and I'd keel over onto the mat.

"The offer's still open if you'd like to try again someday."

"Mess with your body chemistry? You shouldn't make offers like that so lightly." His tone is serious and I remember again that I'm talking to a god. "But I'll think about it."

We walk out of the workout room. As he passes through this door, he is subtly stiffer, his posture more formal.

Someone comes up to us. He has brown, curly hair and about a head shorter than either of us. His T-shirt isn't oversized. It just looks like it is. His gaze sweeps past Carl and locks onto me.

"Hi, can you help me?" He points off towards the weight machines. "The knob that adjusts the position of the leg pad for the leg curl machine is jammed."

Once again, someone looks at the two of us and decides that I'm the one for the job. Behold the difference between his sweatshirt and my T-shirt, I suppose.

"Sure."

Carl and I wave our goodbyes to each other. He heads off toward the exit. I head off toward leg curl machine. People need to learn that they don't need to crank the adjustment knob. You're just making trouble for no good reason.

....

John Chu is a microprocessor architect by day, a writer, and translator by night. His fiction has appeared or is forthcoming at *Boston Review*, *Uncanny*, *Asimov's Science Fiction*, *Clarkesworld*, and *Tor.com* among other venues. His translations have been published or are forthcoming at *Clarkesworld*, *The Big Book of SF* and other venues. He was a finalist for the Hugo, Nebula, Locus, and Ignyte Awards, won the Best Short Story Hugo for "The Water That Falls on You from Nowhere," and won the Best Novelette Nebula for "If You Find Yourself Speaking to God, Address God with the Informal You."

THE PRINCE OF SALT AND
THE OCEAN'S BARGAIN

Natalia Theodoridou

There's a story that sounds completely fantastic and yet is true. It happened here and in the neighboring lands. It goes like this:

Once upon a time, there was an ocean, deep and cold. And in the ocean there was salt.

For a long time, salt did not know itself to exist. But then, beneath a wave, under a dark and bitter brew of the sea, it stirred. Why, it hardly knew; yet, for the first time, salt found itself wanting. It had no body, this watery want, no arms and legs, no spine nor skull, no eyes or mouth, but it knew it wanted, and what it wanted was to live.

And so, in a rare still moment of the sea, salt reached out. It found a single drop of water inside all the vast unbearable water, and it said: I want.

And then the ocean, which was in that drop just as it is in all of the water, granted salt's wish. The ocean said there was a price, and that one day that price would have to be paid.

"Did salt understand what that meant?" the young thing asks, interrupting me. "Hush, child. Stories are fragile things. They break so easily."

So, salt, then. His body was vast, first, and then narrow and marrowed and enclosed in lean muscle and tender skin. He lay on dry sand—a shore, his new mind informed him in its new language. Foam lapped at his bare feet. He possessed hair, now, and arms to take with and touch with, and eyes, and ears, and a tongue and mouth, and a hunger to live, and a heart to do it with. Above, an expanse yawned inconceivable, mind-shattering—the sky. In it, the sun.

He knew the sun.

His stomach rumbled and his throat prickled and his limbs screamed with exhaustion, but these were all things he knew not how to appease, or that he could, so he simply assumed them to be the facts that proved salt was, for now, alive.

Salt remained on that beach for hours, his skin baking under the sun until sunset, then growing cold in the night, then baking again in the morning until the sun dipped below the horizon once more. His skin cooled in the ocean breeze and stung in the night air.

His third day, he discovered movement. He wiggled his toes, stretched his shoulders, and counted the fingers on his hand. Then he ran his palm across the length of his skin. He discovered waves and grooves, creases and caves, bone ridges and hooks that reminded him of the depths of the ocean.

This is how the girl Marietta found him, naked and touching himself in the way of babies, not men, and that was enough for her to get over whatever sense of shame rouged her cheeks for a moment—and it was a brief, brief moment, because Marietta was no stranger to the joys of bodies, and had little patience for the parched teachings of religious men who paid so much coin to paint their visions of hell on the whitewashed walls of their churches when people starved on the streets just beyond. Her curiosity won this time as it always won, and it was never much of a fight either, truth be told.

She nudged the man with her foot first, to make sure he didn't bite, then spoke to him in the soft voice she used with feral children and dogs. "Do you need help, mister?" She thought he must be shipwrecked, shaken free of the sea by the storm that had raged over them the night before. But then again that wouldn't explain why he was so very naked. Perhaps he'd been mistreated somehow, then—and the thought made Marietta simultaneously want to punch whoever hurt him and have this man wrapped in the softest cloth she could find. His skin was burnished by the sun but otherwise unblemished.

She nudged the man again, having run out of ways to make sense of the situation. "Can you speak?"

The man looked at her and laughed, but she didn't feel mocked; for it was the laughter of a creature that had suddenly discovered it can be pleased, and that the world is a place of great joy. "You are beautiful," he said. His words sounded strange—unaffected and new. "What are you?"

Marietta straightened, stood, and faced the man with the orange-colored sky behind her. She tilted her head just so, to keep the sun from blinding him, but also to let the light halo her black hair as on the stained windows in the house of God. "I am a woman," she said. "I am Marietta."

Of course she took him home. She would never have left him there on the beach; it didn't matter if he were but a drunkard who lost his clothes in a bad gamble and passed out by the surf—though she was certain that's not at all who he was. She wrapped him with her overcoat and he followed her in silence, watching her through wide eyes, the corners of his mouth turned up the slightest. He did have a kind of beauty to him, Marietta found, though he seemed somehow unfinished: his skin too smooth, like marble before the artist's chisel has made its mark. His hair was thick but his face had no beard, nor had he any other hair on his body. No, his beauty had little to do with the features of his face or the angles of his bones, and more with the way he walked as if he were liquid, the way his fingers moved as if perpetually underwater, and his eyes showed, if you looked at them under the right light, the strange reflections of the ocean.

The sun was setting when they reached her cottage.

At the door, he stopped.

Her home was a small shack on the outskirts of the town, barely a roof and a door and a window and a bed with a mattress filled with straw, but it might as well have been a palace; that's how fascinated the man was. The neighbors were poor, some worse off than Marietta herself, others a notch better, but none of them ever bat an eye at newcomers, no matter how out of place they looked.

She didn't have much to give him, but everything she had she did. She had only the clothes she wore herself and that most men wouldn't dare put on, but he did not seem to mind at all. So she clothed him in her best—her single satin dress, its blue frightening to him at first, but the texture of it on his skin so pleasant he quickly recovered. She fed him stale bread and butter that he stuffed into his mouth and moaned so hard she had to muzzle him for fear of the neighbors getting the wrong idea—or maybe the right one, though it was still early for that. She gave him her sweetest wine, which was not very sweet at all, and yet he downed it with big, desperate gulps and said: "More."

He hid nothing from her. He told her of his birth, which was no birth at all, and of before. He told her about the ocean, the cold, sheer vastness of it, how it never ended and there was no containing it. He told her how he was dissolved in everything, separate but also not, how he swelled with water, how the pressure and the deep currents felt to his non-body, how he spoke a certain language of the deep but had no tongue, no throat. And how, when he said "I," it was not quite right.

She listened intently, her eyes sparkling and wide. She seemed to him at once like the creatures he knew all too well before becoming what he now was—simple and round and open, with a beating heart and a thirst for love and living—but also different, more complicated, for all her folds of skin, her bones and hair. He reached out to touch her and she let him, palms open. He studied the lines there for a long time, and then he carried on talking. She wanted to understand it all. She was silent when he needed silence and asked questions when he needed words.

He also told her of the first time he felt anything, and how that feeling was one he had no word for.

"Was it a wanting?" she tried. "A curiosity? A need?"

But no word fit perfectly, so he told her instead of the way in which time had no meaning until he had breath.

He told her, finally, of his bargain. His debt to the ocean, the lover's heart, the limited time it bought him.

Marietta clutched her own heart, then, but whether she truly believed him no one will ever know, because she couldn't quite decide herself.

The sun had long since set when they finished talking, and they lay together on the straw mattress, his skin pressed against hers, still cold, but with an unfamiliar warmth to it now. She ran her fingers through his hair and he sighed, his face pressed into her neck, his arm around her waist. He kept his eyes open, watching, even as sleep crept in.

"Did he dream?" the young thing asks.

Does salt dream? Does sand dream of the stone it once was? Does the ocean remember all the lovers lost at sea?

"He did," I say. "But I don't know of what."

"We must give you a name," Marietta declared in the morning.

And so they called him Salt, because that's what he was, but also Thelo, because he always yearned, and always hungered, without cease.

Marietta took him to her bed for more than sleeping, of course. She showed him what it was that humans could do with their bodies and each other's, and he turned out to be a better lover than any she'd had before. A patient one, too, because, despite his newfound love for breathing, his grasp of time was tentative at best. For days he could lie there rapt and shook by the feeling of a fly's legs brushing his skin, the fuzzy taste of a peach, or the shape of the dimples on Marietta's back.

He wanted to experience everything, even as he wondered about the price each of these treasures would demand of him, one day. Marietta took him out to dance and drink and eat and meet her friends and lovers, some of whom they brought back home with them. On such nights, Salt seemed more interested in the feeling of his own body than the bodies of others, but he would shut his eyes and listen to their sighs and moans and words. He kissed their eyelids and their stomachs and their mouths. It was the closest he'd felt to what he was before. He found them all beautiful, the most beautiful: their crooked backs, their perfect noses and shining eyes, their silky hair, their scarred faces, their skinny legs and sharp bones, their curves of fat—he loved them all. It was too much for him, sometimes, but he never dreamed of stopping, of stepping back, of loving less.

In turn, the friends and lovers never responded to him as if he were a curiosity. They embraced him, devoured him, wanted to know him so deeply he felt as if he'd run out, as if his answers could never satisfy them because he didn't know how to make words contain the things he was, the things he'd been. One woman he spent a night with, her chest like a buoy under his head and her voice deep like the rumble of waves, asked him where he was from. And he said, everywhere, everywhere.

Marietta watched him thrive, and it filled her with a mixture of joy and envy, at his freshness, his ability to experience the world for the first time, but never possessiveness. Others teased her for being so willing to share him, but their words made little sense to her. "Isn't more love and joy better than less?" she asked. And Thelo always asked for more—more textures, more tastes, more colors, more bodies—until Marietta shook the last of her gold out of her small purse and told Thelo he needed to get a job.

He did so, gladly and eagerly.

Thelo's first job was shucking oysters for an oyster peddler at the pier, where he sometimes got to watch the boats come and go, ghostly white sails under a blue sky, the smell of seaweed heavy in the air and the gulls cawing overhead. Stooped over buckets of icy water to keep the oysters fresh, the briny smell familiar and all-encompassing, he was a magician with the oyster knife. He slipped his blade through the tight oyster lips and twisted it just right, unlocking the shells as if with a key. There were others who worked alongside him, but they never lasted long, defeated by their wounded hands and burned skin and aching backs. Salt relished the work—physical labor suited him, and he took a not insignificant amount of pleasure in the pain and discomfort his body was capable of.

Lots of people in town were taken with the strange oyster man at the pier, with his open face and untroubled eyes, but didn't know what to make of a man with no past. They were at once drawn and repulsed by him, and they turned away afraid and doubtful, only to miss out on his sweetest smile, on the way he kissed like he was tasting the air. He didn't mind them, just as he didn't mind the hard work. And he was the hardest worker of all: always there before the sun was up in the sky and sometimes even after it had set. The oyster peddler took his work ethic in stride; she was the kind of woman who was impressed by little, satisfied by nothing at all. She knew Marietta somewhat—they were the same age and had been friendly once, long ago; perhaps that's the reason she gave Thelo the job in the first place, though she'd never confess such favoritism. Still, Thelo could see the pleased little nods of the head when she inspected his work, and that made him proud.

One day, Thelo almost lost a finger. It happened so fast; he was shucking an oyster, the knife slipped, and he felt a terrible pressure in his right hand. He looked down at the knife and saw it poke through the soft tissue between his fingers. The oyster peddler took him to a doctor who sewed the skin back together and bundled his hand with swaths of gauze. He could hardly feel his fingers. He lifted his hand and showed it to the woman: "What now?" he asked.

"God gave you two hands," she said with a shrug. "I don't see what the problem is."

The oyster peddler kept most of the money for herself, unmoved even by Thelo's accident, but she gave him enough to satisfy his needs most days, and Marietta's too. Enough, even, for small extravagances: a satin dress for Marietta; a small, round cake baked with honey and figs that melted on Thelo's tongue and was so sweet it burned; a hat with a bright green feather in its band that he and Marietta took turns wearing those times they went prancing down the market on Sundays, when the sun was out and everything felt possible.

He could have carried on like this forever, he thought, or for as long, at least, as his body and his bargain allowed. Until one day a woman came up to the peddler and paid not with money but, to Thelo's astonishment, a small sachet of salt. When he asked whether one could buy things with salt, the peddler laughed and said: "Why yes, boy, salt is the most precious thing there is."

And Thelo, then, knew what he had to do.

He saved his money for an entire, precious year. Frugality did not suit him, but he was starting to grasp the human notion of investment: to postpone gratification under the irrational belief one's life would never end, despite one's certainty that it would. Marietta told him he was insane, but contributed her income—the source of which shall be left obscure—nonetheless. It was in this way that, by the end of the year, Thelo could afford a marshy shard of land near the coast; too saline to cultivate, too muddy to build on—in other words, just right.

The day he bought the land, he stood on the shore, feeling the earth pulse beneath his feet. He took a deep breath of salt-soaked air. Marietta was there with him, struggling to see what he saw. What good was this land? How might land that could support no building and feed neither plant nor animal be any good at all?

He promised to show her.

He didn't tell Marietta what he intended to do, but he was dewy-eyed with excitement as he turned his body to the shore every day. His skin was as salt-soaked as the air, his mind full of the sea and its bounty. He waded into the lukewarm water, plunged his hands deep into the muck until they were sticky with mud, the smell of the marsh strong in his nose. He played, but not like a child. He played like a woman painting her lips red. He played like a person sharpening their knife to the point of perfection. He played like a singer humming low in her throat, like a dancer turning circles on his toes.

When he was done, the land was divided into separate ponds of various depths through which water was pumped and evaporated. Each pond was saltier than the previous one, until the last ones were so thick with salt you could pickle fish in them. The water yielded to Thelo's will with an uncanny ease that made him many friends and even more enemies. The friends were charmed by his way with the sea water, and the enemies feared and envied his talents, but both groups had a thing in common: they were drawn to him, wanted a piece of him, as if his mere presence in their lives would make them tastier and worthier of living.

With the money he made from selling his sea salt, he bought the adjacent land, and then more land next to it, until he owned almost the entire length of the coast, and his salt was the purest and most plentiful in the country. Its only purpose, of course, was to give him access to more of what marvels life had to offer—the brevity and impermanence of that life merely making the marvels sweeter. This was a kingless land, but the people, whom he plied with his salt money in return for both finery and affection, called him the Prince of Salt—though only Marietta knew how well the name fit.

The Kings and Queens of neighboring lands mocked him at first—what Prince was he, after all, with no kingdom of his own? Then, they tried to destroy his salterns by poisoning the water and obstructing the canals that connected the ponds, and Thelo answered with perseverance, talent, and hard work. Next, they threatened Thelo's workers, to which he responded by paying double and hiring guards to keep watch while the workers toiled in the ponds. Until, finally, threats were made against Thelo's very life, and Marietta's, too. The threats were discreet at first: someone would accost them at the market and whisper a violent word into their ears; a figure made of sticks and dressed in fine cloth would be found hanging from the door of their new, lavish house. But, eventually, the threats became so explicit they could no longer be dismissed: letters stained with blood, delivered in the dead of night by a dozen men wielding daggers and swords.

So the two of them decided to appeal to the neighboring armies' purse and buy them, to pay every single soldier their weight in salt. They did so in person, speaking to each soldier in private, in ways as sweet or as rough as they thought each one needed, or desired, or craved.

Their plan was a success. The neighboring kingdoms yielded to Thelo's new-found power one after the other. And so it was that Salt became a real Prince—or King, to be pedantic about it, though he much preferred his original obliquely earned title. He even built himself a palace that Marietta decorated with the pointless wonders of the world, the silvers and the velvets and the mother-of-pearls. They celebrated their success with a feast in the new palace. They invited their friends and their friends' friends and their enemies and their enemies' enemies—everyone, in fact, who wanted to celebrate the end of the salt wars that ended before they began. Someone had the good sense to bring a flutist, and someone else a poet who recited a poem that made Thelo's heart beat fast. The poet had a low voice filled with gravel, a land voice, and yet she spoke of the ocean: a vast cold, things simple and round and open, moons dipping into the water and emerging dripping with salt.

Life went on quietly for a while after that. Marietta enjoyed politics and keeping the books of Thelo's endeavors. She and her girlfriends spent hours reclining on spreads of fur, discussing export strategies and gorging themselves on black grapes.

The lands whose armies were too proud or foolish to be bought decided to embargo the Prince's salt. But the salt continued to be produced in greater and greater quantities, until mountains of it had to be carted away and stored in giant halls built for the purpose, as well as in barns and caves and every room in the palace deemed inessential to pleasure. Marietta liked to go into these rooms sometimes, to open the doors and close them behind her and just stand there gazing at the mountains of white crystals and wonder at a body made of such a thing, that could dissolve but never disappear.

Even with these unsold quantities of salt, it would be a while before the Prince's fortune started to dwindle, and, if that happened, there would be plenty for Marietta to sell off and ensure a delicious existence for them, without ever even taxing the people, which the Prince was loath to do. And so, princehood opened up new experiences for them both: trips to cities made of iron, to islands whose inhabitants dove to harvest sponges from the sea's bottom with only a stone tied to their waist, the way others did to end their lives. The best, however, was yet to come. And then come it did, stepped right up to the palace gate and requested an audience. He had pitch-black hair and eyes both dark as the night and bright as the stars, and, when he burst into the throne room, he looked Thelo up and down and licked his lips. "I'll buy your salt," he said in a steady voice. He had a gap between his front teeth that made Thelo's chest hurt. "Because it is the best in the world, and only that will do for me."

Thelo recognized something of himself in the young man—the keen way with which he carried his shoulders, perhaps, or the peculiar curve of his lip. "What should I call you?" Thelo asked.

"My name is Gustavo the Merchant, but you, Prince, can call me whatever you wish."

Salt's heart sighed at that, for he was not above flattery. "Dine with me tonight," he said, and so the next chapter of his life began, and the only word in it was: Gustavo.

"That's not what you said last time," the young thing says. It uncrosses and recrosses its legs on the cushion and trains its eyes on me, cold and familiar.

The air around us has grown stale. Heavy-limbed, I leave my seat to crack the window open. "What are you talking about?" I ask.

"Gustavo's eyes," the child says. "The last time you told this story, Gustavo's eyes were blue."

"Is that right? Oh."

The child dips its chin. "I remember it well."

"Then, I must have made a mistake."

"Were you mistaken then? Or are you mistaken now?"

Marietta liked the dark-eyed man, too. She braided seashells in her hair for the dinner, and put on her favorite yellow dress with a dagger in its sheath pressed against her waist. Gustavo wore his dark hair in tight coils and his lips stained maroon. They sat at Thelo's long table to feast on fish baked in a crust of salt, pickled cucumbers, and a frothy dessert laced with salted caramel and briny cocoa. They broke the crust of the fish with a hammer—such violence followed by such tenderness, such melting in the mouth. The salty food only increased their thirst a thousandfold, but the wine was pink and easy and the conversation equally so. When Marietta asked Gustavo what he wanted out of life he said: "To find out what makes men tick."

She smiled and asked, "Men only?" to which she got as a response the most brilliant smile she had ever seen.

Then, they played a game of candle, trying to pass a lit candlestick to each other using only their mouths, their hands clasped together behind their backs. Marietta was an expert at this—she was, in fact, the one who taught Thelo the game—and managed to pass her candle to Gustavo without the slightest touch of skin. She clapped for her own victory and downed her wine, then toasted them and urged them both to give it their best.

Gustavo approached Thelo with the lit candle in his mouth, its flame turning his eyes to live coals, wax dripping to the floor. *Come on,* he signaled with his hands, and Thelo came closer, his mouth half-open. Marietta watched, rapt, as their lips met around the stick. The flame singed one of Gustavo's stray curls, but he didn't step back. Instead, he grasped Thelo's shoulders and steadied him, nudging the candle with his tongue. When the candlestick was firmly in Thelo's mouth, Gustavo licked his lips. "You taste so salty, Prince," he said, and Thelo could see that he was pleased.

Dawn found the three of them crumpled together on Thelo's silk-clad bed, talking about their favorite things: the moment a stranger's face becomes familiar, the shapes the flight of birds makes in the sky, the smell of leather-bound books, the burn of salt on one's tongue.

They spoke, too, of their fears.

"I fear nothing," Marietta lied.

"Finding out it's all in vain," Gustavo said. "Every terrible thing one does."

"Dissolving," Thelo said. "Forgetting I ever existed at all."

Gustavo did as he promised. He bought all of Thelo's salt and sold it far, far away, and the Prince's land prospered again. He visited often. He always arrived at dawn and the three of them spent their days in each other's company and the nights together in the silk-clad bed. They were the greatest of allies and the best of friends. Gustavo felt drunk first, their love a new thing that made him feel like he was walking on the ground with his shoes off, and then scared when he realized he could no longer imagine life without them.

Marietta continued enjoying her games of strategy and investment, and she spent many nights poring over Gustavo's ledgers, stopping only when one or more of her lovers tore her away from her desk with a kiss or a seeking palm. Thelo devoted himself to sharing with Gustavo all the wonderful things he had experienced in his short life, and Gustavo discovered that, for all the Prince's love of pleasure, what made Thelo tick was pleasing his lovers. And so, Gustavo allowed himself to be pleased.

Months passed this way, and Gustavo waited for that familiar blow, the knife slipped into you by those you let close when you least expect it and which he'd learned always to expect and always to guard himself against it. But it never came. Thelo pampered him beyond measure, while Marietta teased him—and only hurt him when he asked her to.

Gustavo had moved into the palace now, and that warmed the Prince's heart. But Thelo grew more and more pensive as time flew by. When he stood on his balcony, overlooking his city of gold and pearl, he could no longer deny there was something in the air, something that reeked of blood and ash and bile.

What it was became clear before the year was out, when one of the Kings whose armies Thelo had stolen was now rising against him, with a new, fearless— and, presumably, incorruptible—army leading his war. The city held strong, but the rest of the country fell, village after village, town after town.

"I'll fight for you," Gustavo declared. "I'll lay down my life for you."

Thelo forbade it, first, and when that failed he sank to his knees and begged Gustavo not to go. "You are no soldier," he told him. "You are no use to me dead."

"The best soldier is the one who loves you," Gustavo replied.

Gustavo was not much of a warrior, Thelo had been right about that. The field of battle was no place for him; he gazed upon the carnage and the torn bodies of the fallen with a terrible sort of wonder, like a child who's been told horrific stories it is too young to understand. He'd seen war before, of course—for another lover's sake no less. He remembered those days: a battlefield identical to this, the same carnage, the same torn bodies. The blonde soldier's mouth against his that made him keep going. Most of all, though, he remembered the lessons he learned back then: the soldier's face when he turned his back and left Gustavo, wounded, in that field.

Yet he kept looking, now, kept thinking of the lovers he could have had, and the ones he did. The most recent one was a soldier that invited him to his tent one night early on in the war. The man was soft in most places but hard in all the right ones, with hair like straw and a face so pale it was as if it always reflected the light, like a moon. Gustavo let him do as he pleased, but his thoughts kept flying back to Thelo and Marietta. And that's when he knew that he'd been mistaken, that all his guarding had been in vain, because their knife was well and truly in him already, and more deeply burrowed than it'd ever been before.

His heart trembled every time he swung his sword after that. Love makes weapons of some men, and of others it makes ashes and willows and lakes.

But the war turned out to be brief. What Gustavo lacked in physical strength, he made up in courage, and passion, and, even, in villainy. It was his idea to burn the crops and salt the earth that fed the King's people, to defeat him not with the ravaged bodies of soldiers but with the wasting away of children and the desper- ation of the meek. Many of his own fellow warriors recoiled from such tactics, thought him wretched, evil, questioned his manliness, which they thought meant questioning his honor. He didn't mind. He stood firm, his fingers curled around that secret blade, and, in the end, he won them over just as he won the war; be- cause that's another lesson that first battlefield had taught him: the victors win at everything, not just the battle.

He did receive a wound to his abdomen—a stabbing, indeed—which came as no surprise to him; he always knew love would cut him one way or another, after all. If only he'd seen the escaped prisoner who wielded it just as clearly.

He believed he'd die, then. In his feverish nights, he saw visions of urns filled with salt, of ills that could only be cured by Thelo's mouth, of Marietta draping the entire ocean in mourning black cloth. In his few moments of clarity, he thought his comrades would abandon him. But they didn't. They shouldered his body and held his hand and bandaged his wounds. He was returned to Thelo alive on a stretcher, his skin pallid, his cheekbones and clavicles pronounced as never before.

Thelo fell on him and wept as if his lover were already dead, but Gustavo wiped away his tears and informed him that the war had been won, as if his Prince's weeping had been but a misunderstanding. "We won," he said again, kissing his lover's eyes, his hair, his chin, "stop it, we won."

"You almost gave up your life for me" was all Thelo said back. "Please, never do that again."

In wartime, Marietta denounced the pleasures of her body. In a bout of magical thinking that was very unlike her, she'd given them all up in exchange for Gustavo's safe return to them; a bargain struck with no one at all, its rewards, she realized later, only a matter of chance. When Gustavo did come back on that stretcher, half-dead already, she sat vigil by his side, convinced that death was lurking just outside their door, and that it would only take an insouciant breath for it to slip inside and devour everything that was hers. Marietta sent away all her lovers, even the ones that had been with her for years, as if to deprive death of boons to claim as his own. Most days, she wouldn't touch food, either, and only drank water in which she squeezed a few drops of bitter orange.

Thelo paced the rooms of the palace like a waif, refusing to sleep lest he miss Gustavo's last breath. He realized the victory Gustavo's sacrifice had won him meant very little to him. Many mornings found him on the shore, screaming for the ocean to take him back if it meant Gustavo could be spared.

The ocean never responded, but Gustavo slowly healed. Color returned to his face, and his eyes shone once again. Marietta didn't sleep for weeks after the doctor said the danger had passed, the weight of Gustavo's prone body pushing her down into the mattress where she half-drowned in her own sweat. Eventually, her worry subsided, but it turned out the price was steeper than Marietta had anticipated, and much higher than she'd bargained for: the joy of it all never returned.

In the time of peace, she grew distant and tired; everything felt lesser, incomplete, or like a forgery of some other feeling, something better, more intense, that she no longer had access to. She invited her lovers back, and most of them came, but they, too, seemed mere likenesses of their former selves.

She spent less and less time with the men and more time with women who taught her how to create wax casts of things—apples and rabbits and her own hands and feet. She'd leave these objects strewn around the palace, like echoes or ghosts of herself and of the world as she saw it now: lifeless and unoriginal and only a butter knife away from ruin.

This is how Marietta became an artist.

Thelo and Gustavo themselves found peace to be a lovely, fragile thing. They spent their nights by the fire, dreaming of growing old together, and they developed a habit of taking in stray dogs that they washed and fed and tended to as if they were kings. The palace became a haven for homeless and lonely beasts. Gustavo told Thelo stories about the war, about the fields of fallen soldiers and lovers left for dead, and Thelo hushed him every time. He didn't want to listen to sad stories anymore. He never told Gustavo about his bargain either—his lover had almost paid for it once already, and he never wanted to risk losing him again. He only wanted to savor the warmth of fire on his skin, the soft snoring of the animals, the feel of Gustavo's curls that were slowly turning silky again. The dogs slept in their bed and lay by their feet, licking their hands and fingers with their soft, sluggish tongues.

It didn't last.

Two summers, another winter, and then the salt that used to be the best ever known to the world turned bitter. The ponds filled with long, pale worms; what little salt the workers managed to salvage took on a sickly, grey tint. And Thelo, he developed a fear of water; he avoided bathing, instead having his body scrubbed with rough sponges plucked from the bottom of the sea and left to dry in the sun for a fortnight, and he would spend entire weeks barricaded in his bedroom when the weather was wet. Gustavo and Marietta put up with it, trying to coax him and bribe him, mostly unsuccessfully. The people, who had for so many years loved Thelo and prospered on his coin, said the Prince had gone mad. They made songs about the Thirsty Prince who never laughed, never cried, never walked in the rain anymore. They said the palace gardens were taken over by beetles, that the gulls now reined over the kingdom.

When Thelo's fear grew so that he refused drinking water as well, going so far as to destroy and seal every well in the area around the palace, Marietta had had enough. She didn't know what to do, and so she did the only thing she could think of: go back where it all began. Gustavo didn't have the heart to do it himself, but he watched as men grabbed Thelo and dragged him away. Marietta took him to the shore. He fought and screamed until, eventually, he tired of resisting and gave into his fate, this ending at the hands of his lovers. When his feet walked on sand, he shuddered, he felt light, his joints loose, and he thought, this is it. And when he looked back upon the life he'd been given, he thought, it was good, wasn't it? It was exquisite, as long and short as it was.

Marietta stood tall, ignoring the Prince's pitiful flailing. "Touch the water," she ordered him.

He shook his head. "I won't."

"Touch the water," she said again. Her face was like a mask, or like one of those wax things she liked to fashion, as if she'd sculpted her own features into wax and then put that visage on to cover the one below.

Thelo took a step back. "Why are you doing this?" he cried. He fell to his knees. "Why are you betraying me like this?"

And then, to her surprise and his, Thelo shook himself loose from the men's hold and crawled to the place where the sea foamed against the earth, and lay there, lengthwise, letting the water lap at his form, his fingers slowly being buried into the wet sand. He was ready for the end: to dissolve, like he always knew he would.

But he didn't dissolve.

When he opened his eyes, Marietta was standing over him, her head haloed by the sun, like that very first time when they met and she showed him what it meant to be alive. Then she knelt next to him and picked him up, cradled his head against her chest, her tears streaming hot down his cheeks. "You see?" she asked, again and again. "I love you, you see?"

When they returned to the palace, Marietta made him tell Gustavo everything: about his bargain, the period of grace, the sacrifice it required. Gustavo knelt before him and took his Prince's thin—so thin! he thought. When did they get this thin?—hands in his own. He talked to him in the way Marietta had long ago used with him, the talk of children and dogs. So Thelo started speaking, and Gustavo did not stop kissing his hands the whole time, not stopping for a single moment; not when Salt told him about the days before breath, about his wish, about its granting and about its price: the heart of a lover, given to the ocean willingly, so that Salt might continue to live.

Only a heart, then? Gustavo wondered. Was that all? A bargain, truly, if he'd ever heard of one.

"I'll give it," he said, out of breath. "I'll give it willingly."

It was the second time in Thelo's life that he found himself forbidding something, but this time he knew better than the first. He ordered his guards to take Gustavo away and lock him up in the palace's deepest dungeon and stand at all times outside his door. He furnished that dungeon with the finest furniture his remaining salt could buy and dressed it in the most expensive silks, and then made sure none of his lover's desires would go unmet, except the one for freedom: no drink too difficult to find, no food too difficult to cook up, no entertainment impossible to procure.

He had forgotten, however, that his lover's talent was one for finding what made men tick, and find he did, and the guards did tick.

So Gustavo left secretly, in the night.

"But did no one try to stop him?" the young thing interrupts. "Didn't Marietta or Thelo try to talk him out of it? Catch him, tie him down, restrain him in some way!" The young thing seems quite animated by the questions, and by the lovers' failures to stop Gustavo.

Yet the questions give me pause.

Did they try? Truly?

My chest feels heavy, my legs sore from sitting for so long.

"I'm tired, child," I say. "Let's continue tomorrow."

The child frowns but does not object.

The room is so cold around us, I think I won't be able to sleep. And yet, I do, deeply and restfully.

I dream of tangles of flesh, of arms and legs, hands and feet and torsos, of muscles and bones and skin. And then I dream of the sea, a great salty flood that comes and swallows it all.

When I rise in the morning, the child is already awake, and so I take my seat and resume my narration.

So Gustavo left secretly, in the night. Only Marietta saw him flee the palace, his hand pressed against his heart. She knew right away what he was up to, and wanted to tell him that love, perhaps, should not hurt this much, that love's price need not be pain, that, perhaps, the most precious things in life can be had without needing to be earned or bargained for—but in the time it took her to come up with the words, to weigh them against her own heart and force them out her mouth, Gustavo had already slipped away.

His legs were weak—from what, he didn't quite know. Was it excitement or fear? Was it his days of incarceration, or the weakness of his heart that made him shake so? And if his heart were really that weak, would it even make a sacrifice worthy of Salt's life?

There were many questions in his head, and perhaps that was for the best because, preoccupied in that manner, he managed to make his way to the remotest part of the shore he could think of. Then, realizing he didn't know how one goes about finding the ocean and making a bargain with it, or indeed about giving it his heart, he walked into the sea wearing only his skin and a stone tied to his waist. He walked and walked, and then swam and swam, until every limb screamed with exhaustion and his throat prickled with thirst.

He grew weaker and weaker and, when he could swim no more, his stone pulled him down into the depths. Before he sank, he marveled: how deep, the ocean! How vast and cold!

He was woken by a voice that seemed to come from somewhere below him—perhaps, the pit of his own throat.

You are Gustavo the Merchant, the voice said. *What do you seek?*

He opened his mouth but found it filled with water and salt. His lungs were crushed, so he spoke with his mind instead: *I am Salt's lover, here to offer my heart so that Salt may live.*

And do you come willingly?

Yes. Yes. He locked me up in a dungeon so I wouldn't come. He doesn't even know I'm here.

He? the ocean asked after a pause. *You call salt a he?*

Gustavo felt faint and a little delirious. Was he speaking to the ocean, or were these the dying visions of a drowning man? *That's what I know him to be,* he replied, regardless.

I see, the ocean said.

Gustavo waited for a long while, but nothing happened. Was the ocean considering whether his offering was worthy? Or had it already been rejected? Or maybe it was Marietta's heart that should have been offered instead—though the fact that it wasn't should, perhaps, be answer enough.

Gustavo refused to be defeated this easily. He clawed at his chest, trying to get to his heart. *Here,* he pleaded with the ocean. *Here, take it.*

He waited for the knife—did the ocean have knives? Should he have brought his own? But no, he thought, so many shipwrecks must have made the sea the most knifeful place there is, and the ocean a connoisseur of blades! He closed his eyes and waited some more, for the rip, the tug, the brief, brief burn, but he felt none of that. Instead, he was buoyed, pushed up by a stream of tiny bubbles until his head broke the surface of the sea and the air rushed into his lungs with a searing pain that made him wonder if his heart was being torn from his body, after all.

It hadn't.

Gustavo palmed the area above his heart. He was alive, his chest intact. Breath still in his lungs. Even the stone was gone.

"No," he cried. "You cannot have him. Let me make good on his bargain!"

You have, the ocean replied, its voice cool and calm as the water was cool and calm.

It was never the giving that I wanted. It was only the willing I was curious about.

And then, Gustavo was pushed by a gentle current that returned him to shore exhausted, yes, but safe and whole.

He found his discarded clothing and, slowly, made his way back to the palace, to Salt's embrace, to Marietta's waxy moltings, to dogs, to fire, to velvet, to pearls, to food and wine and games, to pain and love, to the terrible things one does, the curious things, to life, to life, to life.

"So it was a favor, then, not a bargain," the young thing says, catching me by surprise. I realize my own story had so absorbed me I lost track of time. And there's little as intoxicating—arrogant, too, perhaps—as being taken with your own words.

Outside, the sun has climbed to its highest. Soon, it will start setting again.

"Do you think so?" I ask.

The child tilts its head, then frowns. "And anyway, I don't believe this story," it says.

"Oh? Why not?"

"I've heard nothing of a Salt Prince. If it's the way you said, I would have surely heard of him."

I study the child's mouth. It's perfect and smooth, and unfinished. A child's mouth, and yet not.

"And, besides, I don't believe life works like that."

"And what do you know of life, salt child?" I ask, only a little bit unkindly. I don't know why these objections irk me so, but they do. "Would you prefer a sadder story, then, one in which Gustavo sacrificed himself so that Salt may live, in which he and Marietta went on to live steeped in mourning and a grief so great that one day Salt walked back to the shore and melted into the hungry sea? Would that have been a better story—or at least one you could believe?"

The young thing considers this. Then, asks: "But what of Marietta?"

"What of her? I told you, she became an artist."

The child nods politely, acknowledging that I had, indeed, established that fact. "But did she get what she wanted?"

Oh. That. I did make the story out to be about desire, didn't I?

I should have known it would come to this.

"What do you think she wanted?" I ask, mildly now.

The child purses its lips thoughtfully. When it speaks, it's with a voice that has too much sharpness in it, too much understanding, too much age. And I catch myself wondering: How old is salt? Not a young thing at all.

"Something to love that wouldn't leave her," the child says. "Something that would outlive her—isn't that what all those casts were for?" The young thing glances at my shelves—the wax hands, the wax hare standing on her hind legs. Of course it's noticed. I didn't hide them. I could have. Why didn't I?

All right.
All right.
Let's try this again.

After the war, Marietta found her belly grew and grew. She felt many things at once: elated, desperate, confused. She never thought Thelo could father a child, and, in a way, she was right: when her water broke and the time came for her to give birth, the baby never arrived. There was no baby at all. Only more water kept flowing out of her, wave after wave, briny and thick with the scent of the sea.

Devastated, she left the palace. She went to the shore where she'd first met Salt and dug a tiny grave in the sand. She had nothing to fill it with, except a small wax figure of a child that she'd cast herself.

Then, she left the country. She was alone again, exactly as she had been before, except this time she knew what she wanted, and the price she was willing to pay.

Marietta walked and walked until she found an island where she found a hut where she found a witch who told her she knew how Marietta could make a bargain of her own.

I pause, and in that pause the child is looking at me a little fearfully, a little expectantly. Hoping, perhaps, that I'll tell a different story. Any other story than this.

So Marietta waded into the ocean, I say, with her clothes sticking to her skin and her expensive shawl that Thelo's salt had bought her swirling around her like so many eels. The water was cold, and the sand between her toes was hard and gritty, and the salt burned her throat when she swallowed, but she didn't stop.

And then she heard that thing, that heartbeat that was also a voice and which Gustavo once heard, and Thelo before him, and who knows how many more before him. She thought of the small wax figure, frozen in its sandy tomb, and she spoke her wish: to forget.

To forget? the ocean echoed.

Marietta nodded, and then, because she wasn't sure if the ocean could see her, she said: "Yes."

And what is it you want to forget, lover of Salt?

Marietta cried, then. Salt would always be in her, she knew, in her tears, in her food, in every country whose shores were touched by a sea. "Everything," she said.

And the ocean—the kind, the awful, the beautiful—considered her request.

And then, the ocean agreed.

"What is the price?" Marietta asked.

And the ocean told her that, if she could only recount her story correctly, as it truly happened, just once, she would forget. But, the voice reasoned, every story needs an audience, and narrating means narrating to someone. So the ocean fashioned for her an interlocutor and said: *When you manage to tell the entire story to this salt creature, and tell it as it really happened, your mind will be free of it, and the pain it has caused you will no longer have a hold on you.*

"What will happen to the salt creature?" Marietta asked.

She felt the ocean shrug. *It will return to me with your story, so I may listen to it whenever I please, and be pleased by it or saddened by it in accordance with the current mood.*

The young thing shifts in its cushion. It's staring at its hands. Its smooth, lineless palms.

Its cheeks are wet.

"Don't cry, child," I say. "Your tears will wash your skin away."

The young thing wipes its tears with those palms, careful not to erode the salt plane of its face.

"Do you still think my first story was not true? Do you still wish the ocean were not as generous as it was in that first telling?"

The child does not say yes, but it doesn't say no, either. It is silent for a long time. Around us, the air grows warm and thick with the scent of melting wax.

Then, the child asks: "Was the story you told me just a lie, then? Was any of it true?"

I think about it before I respond, because I want to be as truthful with this child I have created—or caused to be created, which is really the same thing—as I can possibly be. "Sometimes, truths that are hard to believe are better than truths that are simpler."

The child nods as if it understands. But how could it, when I don't?

My eyelids sting. They grate my eyes like sand.

"I'm ready to listen to the ending now," the young thing says.

I shake my head. "No, child. Let's go to bed early tonight."

"Are you going to try again tomorrow?"

I'm not sure anymore which version of the story I'm supposed to be telling, or if the story can ever be told to the ocean's liking. And the more I remember it and tell it, perhaps, the more I forget it already, because I remember the words instead, the thing itself replaced by the memory of my remembering.

I say so, to this child.

I look around the room and the child's gaze follows my own. It has looked longingly at my casts since the beginning. "Why these?" it asks, pointing at the sculptures.

"There are many ways of telling stories and many ways of remembering," I say, because that much I know is true. "More than words." I consider the casts myself as if I haven't considered them in a long time. The child said what I really wanted was love that would outlive me, and isn't that what our story was? Is?

There's so much love in it, and so much joy among all the pain. Can I really let all that go? The more love the better, after all. Isn't that right?

The more love the better.

I am reminded of those rooms of salt, overfull, brimming. The world was never enough to accommodate us. It would never be enough. So we'd just have to make the world bigger.

"What would you do," I ask, "if you didn't have to go back to the ocean?"

The child frowns. "But I do have to, don't I? As soon as you tell your story correctly."

"Is there really such a thing?"

The child is silent, so I try again. "But what if you didn't have to go back for a long time? A long, long time?"

The child brings a finger to its lips in that thoughtful way it has of going about most things.

"I would have time to do what I want."

"And what is it that you want?"

"I want to experience everything," the child says then, and in that moment it reminds me of both of them: Thelo's hunger for every little thing the world had to offer, Gustavo's burning dark eyes. It reminds me of them both so much I think, perhaps, the ocean grew curious again in its dealings with me as it had grown curious in its dealings with Salt. That, perhaps, my bargain was but another trick; a ruse for the ocean to see what people are willing to let go of when they find out what they think they've lost is never truly lost to them.

And, if that's true, well.

If that's true, then, what bargain?

"Perhaps tomorrow I'll show you how to make one of these," I tell the child, pointing at the casts.

The child's eyes widen and sparkle. "Really?" it asks.

"Yes. Would you like that?"

A pause. "What do I have to give in return?" There's suspicion in the child's features that hurts me, just a little.

"I'll make you a bargain, if that's what you want, but I want nothing in return."

"Nothing?" the child echoes, its mouth slack around that novel concept.

"Nothing you haven't already given me," I reply.

The child looks at me, puzzled. "That's not a bargain either," it says, and I nod, because the young thing is right, it's not. It's no bargain at all.

* * *

Natalia Theodoridou has published over a hundred short stories, most of them dark and queer, in magazines such as *Strange Horizons, Uncanny, Clarkesworld, Beneath Ceaseless Skies, Nightmare,* and *F&SF,* among others. He won the 2018 World Fantasy Award for Short Fiction and has been a finalist for the Nebula Award in the Novelette and Game Writing categories. Natalia holds a PhD in Media and Cultural Studies from SOAS, University of London, and is a Clarion West and Tin House Writers' Workshop graduate. He was born in Greece and has roots in Georgia, Russia, and Turkey. His debut novel, *Sour Cherry,* is out in April 2025. Find out more at www.natalia-theodoridou.com

A DREAM OF ELECTRIC MOTHERS

Wole Talabi

Two hours into the third session of our fourth cabinet meeting on the border dispute with the co-operative kingdom of Dahomey, my colleagues finally agree that we need to seek the dream-counsel of our electric mother.

The dream-counsel consultation ceremony was usually a somewhat elaborate half-day affair, with a Chief Babaláwo being called in from the Ile-Ifè Technology Center of Excellence a day before to run diagnostics, read the Odù, dine with the Oyo Mesi and remind us of our history and culture before we link our brains with that of our electric mother. Officially, the ceremony is performed to maintain transparency, to formally ensure that the public knows when this collective resource is being used. But everyone knows that the primary reason the ceremony was devised and is still performed is to maintain a sense of continuity of tradition because some of our people still believe that any contact with the ancestors should be mediated by a Babaláwo. Even though they know that the electric mother isn't really the essence of our ancestors in the classical sense of the term, and that nothing more than an encrypted lifedock connection to the secure national memory data server and induced REM sleep are necessary to establish contact. Today though, we vote to forgo the ceremony and perform the consultation immediately due to the urgency of the situation. An efficient measure which I proposed, and which was thankfully agreed to by a majority vote without much objection. No need for all the bureaucratic *jagbajantis* that the government has developed a reputation for. We can make a full report after it is done. Besides, I have been waiting over a decade for an opportunity like this and I don't want to wait another day if I can help it.

"Are you okay?" I ask my colleague, the honorable minister of information and culture, who is fiddling with his bronze-framed spectacles nervously as we exit the white-walled womb of the secure ministerial conference room. He was one of only two dissenting votes in the cabinet and the only cabinet member I have ever engaged with more than a professional politeness since I was appointed by the Alaafin three months ago. This is the first consultation I will be a part of, but the records show that he voted against the previous four as well. I have come to like him, but I find his apparent resistance to the consultation curious, especially since he is the one that will be responsible for the report and official broadcast once we are done.

Jibola Adegbite shakes his head, the sound of his shoes a metronome against the marble floor. "No. I'm not. And maintain my objection. I really don't think this is necessary at all. At least not yet. It is a border dispute, not some brand-new crisis. We can figure this out ourselves." He pauses. And then he says, "Besides, these consultations always leave me feeling somehow."

"How somehow?" I ask.

"Like it never really leaves my head, you know? Even after. The voice, or something. It is still there. Do you know what I mean?"

"No, I don't actually," I lie.

I have read classified reports of others who made similar claims, who thought they heard the voice in their heads or relived experiences from the consultation long after they were disengaged from the server. I don't say anything to Jibola about the others because I know it's not possible. Not really. Whatever they think they heard or perceived were probably just electric echoes in their brains. Like visual afterimages that persist in our vision after overexposure to the original image. An adaption of the brain to external neural overstimulation. At least that's what the military intelligence experts that reviewed the reports concluded, a conclusion which I completely agree with. Maybe he just hasn't come to terms with that yet. I don't have fond memories of my time at the Ogun School of Military Engineering, or with the Army Corps, but I have found that a background in engineering gives perspective on these types of things.

Jibola turns his head and looks at me like he is trying to scan my brain and then he says, "Well I just hope it doesn't happen to you too," before turning away and walking a few steps ahead of me.

He is short, he'd stand shorter than I do if he didn't have his aṣọ-oke fabric cap on, with large sensitive eyes and an incipient potbelly that is starting to swell below his tailored white agbada. In a way, he reminds me of my father. At least the version of him that existed before the lunar spacelift accident. Not the broken, bloody version that spent his final seventy-five hours in and out of surgery as an army of Babaláwos tried to save his life while my mother and I watched and prayed and cried to all the Òrìṣà to save him. That's what broke her in the end, I think. Not just the unexpectedness of the accident but the brief period of hope we held on to before they came out of the operating theatre and told us he was dead. In some ways, the accident killed both my parents.

Jibola and I are the last ones to reach the elevator. Once we step in, a red light appears, and a door materializes from nothing as its constituent molecules are telecargoed into place. It almost makes me jump back with surprise, but I don't let it show. I don't think I will ever completely get used to building sections being beamed into or out of place on demand.

"I meant what I said," Jibola says as we descend quietly under the carefully calibrated control of the building AI, almost mumbling to himself. "We can figure this out ourselves. We should. We have been navigating issues along that border with Dahomey off and on for centuries."

I lean in and whisper, "Maybe that's why we need help, so that we don't have to keep negotiating with them for centuries more."

"Funny." He snorts, waving his hand at me like he is swatting away invisible flies. "But I don't think you see the point I am making. We keep returning to the electric mother instead of fully considering and debating our points to consensus whenever there is a threat to the peace."

He seems a bit more agitated than usual. Perhaps the stress of the issue with Dahomey is getting to him, even though I am the one that will have to send troops into battle if the situation really deteriorates and we get to worse-case scenario. I'm the young, newly appointed minister of defense, only the second woman in the history of the republic to hold the position, and I may have to a manage a war already. Besides, I've never done this before. If anyone should be stressed, it's me. And yet, I am not. I have other things on my mind.

"That may be true, but does it really matter?" I ask. "We will get the best possible advice in the shortest amount of time this way. With the least amount of acrimony."

"Maybe you need a little bit of acrimony to be sure you are running a republic properly, especially when lives are at stake."

That comment, uttered a bit too loudly, draws looks from the other ministers of the Oyo Mesi. I cannot tell if he is serious or not, so I stay silent, straighten my back and stare ahead at the plain white door while we continue to descend two thousand meters below ground level towards the subterranean cavern protecting the data server that has hosted the collective digital memory of the Odua republic since the 9878th year of the Kọjọdá.

We first began the mass archiving of memrionic copies of our citizens during the reign of Oba Abiodun III, when the great Iyaláwo Olusola Ajimobi first observed that if two digitized memrionic copies of human minds were synchronized and uploaded to the same operating environment, they would temporarily merge to form a new entity with its own unique, emergent identity. This entity could easily be deconstructed back to the individual memrionics using memory pulse stimulation with no apparent loss of fidelity. She called it a *digital emulsion*. Free of the artificial borders of tissue and silicon between minds, thought patterns of sentient individuals, when allowed to mix and interact, seemed to seamlessly flow into and merge with each other like rivers, completely miscible and yet still separable, with the right perturbation. It was she who first proposed the application of this observation to the creation of the national memory data server. A server that could be used to create a unique national computational consciousness based on the recorded thought patterns of every previous citizen of the republic whose neural scans could be obtained before they died. She referred to it as an artificial memrionic *supercitizen*. An entity made up of the minds of citizens past that could process billions of input parameters, thoughts, opinions, experiences and feelings in an instant and give advice on matters of national interest. An encoded and accessible electric voice of the ancestors. The Alaafin could not resist. Neither could the Oyo Mesi. They approved her plans, gave her all the funding she needed, and she became the first director of the NMDS. In school, when they first taught me about the creation of our electric mother, I spent a lot of time wondering about Ìyá Ajimobi herself. I wondered why she had never taken a husband despite her reputation as a gentleman's woman. I wondered if she had intended for the new supercitizen to exclusively speak with what sounds like a chorus of female voices to everyone who makes a connection to their thoughtspace or if it had chosen (I suppose that technically, it continuously chooses) that voice on its own because of the magnitude of her influence on it. I never met her and yet her story has had such an influence on me and my life that I'd like to believe the latter. Perhaps our ancestral women are just more opinionated in liberated digital thoughtspace than their male counterparts or perhaps she is still driving its identity from the inside. She is, after all, one of the ancestors now. But mostly, I wondered why hardly anyone in my family ever spoke about her, considering the fact that she was my great-grandaunt before she became a component of her own electric dream.

My ears are about to pop when the elevator finally slows to a stop and the door dematerializes. A blast of cold air hits us as we step out and into the expansive grey space of the NMDS center. An array of thick, black cables cut into and run across the high, hyperbolic ceiling. That's the first thing I notice—almost everything in the center is geometrically precise. Circles, rectangles, ellipses, parabolas, hyperbolas, triangles and more. Shapes permute and combine in three dimensions all along the windowless, red walls which bear large abstract symbols drawn in harsh white, like academic graffiti.

In the middle of this expansive space sits the home of our electric mother. A large transparent cube housing an array of solid black cylindrical quantum-processing nodes. Six programmable nanomaterial chairs sit on either side of it, facing away, with an assortment of cables and jacks and connection ports sticking into and out of them, some of which are connected to the cube, like an extended nervous system. The surfaces of the chairs ripple and pulse like lovely dark skin to a lover's touch as the nanoparticles they are made of continuously adjust to micro changes in the environment. An array of holographic projections with information about the state of the server is constantly streaming around the glass in bright orange ajami calligraphy. I recognize some of the projected readings from the technical description and reports: temperature, humidity, memrionic integration coefficients, airflow vector fields. But many of them I don't recognize. I don't think I'm supposed to anyway. I may have studied engineering, but I'm not a Babaláwo.

"Welcome, ministers," a man in a white shirt, embroidered with red at the collar and sleeves, says as he steps into place beside us. He seems to be the on-duty Babaláwo, but I hadn't even noticed him standing there until he spoke. His willowy body is stick-straight, crowned with a halo of perfectly combed salt-and-pepper hair. His eyes are bright and focused, set into a wrinkled face like jewels set in dark oak. "My name is Yemi Fasogbon. I believe all of you have participated in dream-counsel consultations before, is that correct?"

There is a chorus of discordant "yes," with only one exception—me.

"This is my first time," I say.

"Ah." Baba Yemi focuses on me. "You have read the standard briefing notes?"

"Yes." I respond. *Intimately. And I have read reports from previous consultations too. Even the classified ones.* But I don't tell him that.

"Very good. Then there is nothing to worry about. You already know everything you really need to know." He smiles, and kind lines crease his face. "Just relax. I will initiate the encrypted neural connection to your lifedock ports. Once the connection is made, a signal will be sent to your hypothalamus. You shouldn't feel anything unusual, it's just like falling asleep. I will monitor your brainwaves and once you are in REM sleep, I will connect your brain to the great memrionic supercitizen, allowing information exchange. Most of this will occur via auditory stimulation but some of it might be visual or tactile."

He pauses, looking right at me. I wonder if he has any suspicions about what I am thinking of doing once I am connected. What I have been thinking since the day I found out that my mother had starved herself to death in the home our family had owned for almost three hundred years. She'd retired from her teaching position a few weeks after my father's death, sold the house they had bought together, the house I grew up in, and left Ibadan. She spent her final months desiccating in the family redbrick villa in Ijebu-ode, ignoring most of my calls and sending the occasional cryptic message with apologies and encouragements and brief but false assurances that she was fine. I should have asked for compassionate leave from the battalion commander, but I was on the fast track to a promotion, and I felt I couldn't lose momentum. Not when she had always told me I had to be tough, to push through adversity and show them I could be every bit a soldier and military strategist as the men that made up most of my cohort. I thought the few messages and our quiet but constant love for each other would be enough to get us both through our grief but in the end it wasn't. They found her sitting in my father's favorite leather chair, thin and depleted like all the life had been slowly leached out of her. The coroner told me that she hadn't eaten in fifty-three days. She didn't leave any final message. I never even got a chance to say goodbye. I want to change that. I need to change that.

Baba Yemi continues, "We are using the diminished external stimulation and increased brain activity of your minds in REM sleep to enable a direct connection to the complex digital system of the memrionic supercitizen. This is useful, but it also means that the connection can sometimes take on the inconsistent and unstructured qualities of a dream. Some of you may have experienced illusions before. It can seem unusual and perhaps even frightening sometimes, I know, but do not panic, no matter what happens. Just ask your questions and receive your answers. Open your mind to the ancestors and they will guide you. That's it."

I nod my understanding at him. I know all this. I just haven't experienced it yet.

"How long will this session take?" the energy minister asks. They are the oldest serving member of the Oyo Mesi and often concerned with time, so I am not surprised.

"You will all enter REM sleep at different rates depending on your unique brain chemistry and response to the direct neural sleep stimulation, but we hardly see any consultations taking longer than five minutes," Baba Yemi replies. "Once you are in REM sleep, the consultation itself should not take more than a few seconds. However, I will use a neuromodulation protocol to try to synchronize your emergence as a group."

"Thank you," they say.

Baba Yemi holds up his finger and flicks it once like it is a lever. "One final thing. Don't worry too much about the details of your consultation. All of you will receive the same answers regardless of how you ask the question, as long as it is indeed the same question. In fact, we count on it. It's a good control procedure, to see if there is any alternative or minority report of the consultation conclusion. I will manage the debriefing session once you are all done. Does anyone else have more queries?" he asks.

I look around and catch an earnest look in Jibola's eyes like he is about to ask a question of his own, perhaps something that could delay or derail this consultation session, but then he changes his mind and looks away.

"Great. If there are no more questions, please follow me. I will make the connection." Baba Yemi bows gently.

Jibola takes what I imagine is a resigned step forward. I exhale with relief as we all march to the chairs surrounding the glass cube and take our places. Out of what I think is sympathy, I take the one beside him. I think it would be nice if he sees the face of a friend when he emerges from thoughtspace. Or maybe I'm lying to myself and I'm scared that I am the one who will need the comfort of a friendly face when I am done with what I plan to do. The moment is so close at hand, I am starting to feel nervous.

Baba Yemi makes the rounds: adjusting cables, pressing keys and checking displays while we sit there quietly, the hum of the servers constant and almost soothing, like waves on a beach.

When he comes to me, he smiles his open and kindly smile and asks, "Are you ready?" as he fiddles with the cables behind me, twisting and turning them without looking.

I think open my lifedock port and tell him, "I am." *I have been waiting for so long.*

"Good," he says, straightening up. "We will begin in a few minutes." And then he moves away.

I stare ahead at the symbols on the walls. I know that they represent something, something about the unclear nature of our connection to the ancestors, but I cannot place what it is exactly. I read about it when I was researching Ìyá Ajimobi's work on modern Ifá theory. I'm still trying to remember when something slides into the open lifedock port at the base of my neck, sending what feels like a pulse of pure ice through my spine. My vision goes blurry, my body limp as the progmat chair adjusts to cradle me like a child falling asleep in its mother's arms. My consciousness starts to fade. The last signal I am sure my brain receives from realspace is Baba Yemi's voice repeatedly chanting in calm, confident Yoruba, "Relax and open your minds to the ancestors. Relax and open…"

Darkness.

Suddenly, I am somewhere. Thoughtspace. Stark and white. There are no corners or seams or edges or signs or horizons or anything to help me orient myself. I bring my hands up to my face to see what form I have taken but I see nothing. Am I just a mass of information floating around without a body? A disembodied consciousness? Or perhaps I am transparent, and I just see right through myself. I don't know. The sensation of being myself here is so different from realspace that I have no real frame of reference for comparison. It's a bit like floating in perfectly clear, colorless water. But also, not. I just feel … strange.

"Hello." I speak into the emptiness.

There is no response and so I try to clear my mind and repeat myself.

"Hello."

"Our daughter, welcome," a voice choruses.

It sounds like it is coming from everywhere and nowhere at once. In it I hear millions of women speaking in unison—mothers, daughters, aunts, sisters, friends, lovers from generations gone by. But Ìyá Ajimobi's voice, which I heard so much of in the archives during my research, still stands out, like it is both the first and the last one to be added to this superposition of sounds entering my consciousness.

"Thank you," I respond.

"I am all. I am complete. What do you seek?"

The white of thoughtspace suddenly turns into a pale blue. Then cycles back to white. It keeps alternating, mesmerizing me. I don't know how long I have been silent when I finally remember both my duty and my real reason for coming here. I decide to start with duty by asking the question which every other member of the Oyo Mesi will also ask.

"As you must already know from the data feed, we are in dispute with Dahomey again. They have violated the Treaty of Allada by sending their representatives to the Ajashe region, claiming that the population voted to be part of their kingdom in the last referendum."

"This is true. We have validated the data."

I'd read it in some of the reports, but I am still surprised that the electric mother converses more like an AI than an actual person. I suppose I have been anthropomorphizing her for so long that I started to expect a more conversational human response. It's easy to trick your mind into things.

I continue, "They claim they want to renegotiate the treaty and so far, there has been no violence, but this is clearly a threat to us. We cannot allow them to just take away our control of the region, it is a part of the republic."

"This is true. Territorial integrity must be maintained."

"We need to take it back. But if we send in troops, we risk another war."

"This is also true. The probability of war exceeds current national security thresholds for conflict prevention."

A bit tired of the constant agreement, I ask finally, "We … I mean, I … have come to seek your guidance. What should we do?"

Thoughtspace adds a new color to its cycle, a deep, dark green, like moss. The cycle continues.

White. Blue. Green.

White. Blue. Green.

White. Blue. Green.

"Military confrontation with Dahomey is inevitable. Projections indicate that the probability of war increases with time. Projections also indicate that the probability of a successful invasion will also decrease with time. The best course of action is to invade now and take control while our chance of success is highest."

I am more shocked than I expected to be. The reports indicated that the electric mother typically highlights considerations that have been overlooked and points out trends in data that have not been cross-referenced and as a result, does not usually provide simplistic answers. This, a basic analysis with a simple conclusion, is not what I expected to hear. A straightforward push to war. I don't want to believe that this is the best advice we can receive. I wonder if the other ministers are hearing this and thinking the same thing I am.

"But to initiate a war would go against the Alaafin's policy of continental integration and cooperation. Besides, it will violate the will of the people in the territory and cost many of our people's lives."

"This is true."

More agreement. Another color joins the cycle. *Red.*

"Surely there must be better options?"

"This is not true. All considerations have been included in the evaluation of this situation. An extended negotiation will only delay war. Invasion is the best course of action. It will maximize the probability of the republic's life quality index remaining above eighty-three percent over the next one thousand years of the Kọjọdá. There are no better options for the overall good of the republic."

This feels wrong. I don't know why exactly; it just feels wrong. Like a badly constructed response based on fear, not logic, despite its scaffolding of data and numbers. But I don't know what else to say and I have done my duty, so I decide to finally attempt the thing that has been increasingly stepping out of the corners of my mind since my mother died, since I researched the archives, since I proposed this consultation.

"Ìyá Ajimobi, are you … in there?"

I have always wondered if she could distinguish herself from the supercitizen, even briefly, if she could float to the surface of this churning ocean of data and memories and instincts and thoughts and feelings. Her research notes indicated that she thought it was possible, that one or more memrionic records could sometimes "take over" the digital supercitizen for brief moments.

"I am all."

Apparently not.

I'm disappointed. If any mind could do it with any measure of control, surely it would be hers.

"Ìyá Ajimobi, can I talk to you? Just you?"

"I am all."

I have never been the type to give up easily and I am not about to start now. Not when I have been waiting for so long. Not when I am so close. Not when there is even a sliver of hope.

"Ìyá Ajimobi, please. If you can hear me. I need to talk to you," I say, not willing to lose this chance to get answers and say goodbye the way I should have. "It's your great-grandniece, Brigadier-General Dolapo Balogun. Please. I need your help." And then I break into rapid Yoruba, using her oríkì, her traditional praise greeting, which I have been practicing, to remind her of who she is and who I am.

> *Olusola Ajimobi, daughter of the great warrior clan*
> *The one who gathered the threads of her people's minds*
> *And wove a new Òrìsà of them*
> *Olusola Ajimobi, daughter of the moon and the sun*
> *The one whose eyes deciphered the secrets of Ifá theory*
> *And wrote the name of her family in the heavens*

"Please, answer me," I plead.

There is a deep, overwhelming silence. Then, "I am…"

A pause.

The cycles of color seem to speed up.

White. Blue. Green. Red.

White. Blue. Green. Red.

White. Blue. Green. Red.

And then …

Red.

Red.

Red.

I can sense an abstract pressure on my consciousness like something is struggling to manifest itself in my mind but can't. The pressure grows and grows until it becomes something like pain. It is overwhelming, like I'm diving deep underwater without equalizing. I begin to see the symbols from the wall of the server room scroll past my vision like falling rain, but I still don't remember what they mean. A rattling sound like an opele being thrown accompanies the falling symbols, and the cycling colors seem to be coming closer, approaching me somehow. I am trying not to panic but it's hard to keep my composure without my body, without being able to apply all the techniques they taught me in the Army Corps—closed eyes, steady breaths, stillness, mental focus. Here my mind is skinless and exposed, with all of these sensations and stimulations flowing in unrestrained. It all becomes too much and I am about to let out something like a scream when finally, it stops. All of it. The cycling colors, the lights, the sound of the opele. All of it stops. Thoughtspace is white again and there is now a giant head in front of me, projected vividly like it has been sculpted from solid blue light. I recognize the wrinkled oval face: sharp-chinned, wide-nosed and wise-eyed, with a crown of plaited grey hair.

"My daughter," the head says to me in a voice that is not a chorus but is hers. Just hers.

"Ìyá Ajimobi!" I cannot contain my excitement.

"Brigadier-General Dolapo Abimbola Titilope Balogun. I have heard you. You are one of my brothers' great-grandchildren. I have tracked you in the datastream. Your ori has guided you well. You have done the family proud."

I feel myself fill up with emotion and I am still struggling for words to use in response when she continues, "Child. We must either be all or none. There is now a steep memrionic gradient. I cannot maintain this unstable state of the digital emulsion for long. How can I help you?"

It is strange not being able to exhale and relieve what I still sense as pressure in my chest. There are so many questions I want to ask, so many things I want to know, but I know I don't have much time, so I tell her the true reason I have come. "My mother, I need to talk to her. I just … I need to ask her why. And maybe say goodbye."

Her face seems to flicker, like the light it is projected from just experienced a power surge. "My daughter, even if I can do what you assume I can, surely you must know that it is not truly your mother here with us? None of her essence, her ori, is here, only her memories and her knowledge and a record of the neurochemical pathways that primarily drove her emotions."

It's even stranger, the sense that I am holding back tears when I am disembodied. "I know, ma, but you came to me. You came." I am pleading again. "If there is enough of you here to answer the call of your kin then I believe there is enough of her. I know she had her last memrionic scan appointment three weeks before she moved back to Ijebu-ode. Please. This is the only way I can speak to her now. I have to hope it is enough."

She flickers once more, this face that I have studied so much since I was a little girl, at first solely because I wanted to be like her: brilliant, full of life, independent, strong. And later, because I wanted to find something in her notes, something that maybe would lead me to this—my last chance to speak to my mother.

"I know you designed the architecture of thoughtspace. I know you can help me," I add.

Please help me.

The light flickers again and her face fades.

"I will attempt to retrieve her records and establish a direct connection only to you, but I don't know what form her isolated memrionic packet will take or how long it will remain stable."

"Thank you!" I think I am shouting, but I am not sure.

"Thank you for thanking me," she says with a smile. And with that, she is gone. Thoughtspace suddenly seems to gain dimensions, directions, a sense of solidity. It's only when I notice that I am falling that I realize that I have also gained a body. What seems like a vast wall of nothingness sweeps past me. I am falling, falling. Falling into an endless void. I can see my legs tumbling around and I try stabilizing myself by spreading my arms and puffing out my chest, facing the oncoming emptiness. It is just starting to work when I see it appear—a square of green and red in the middle of the nothing ocean. I close my eyes and brace myself.

My landing is hard, but silent and painless even though it throws up a mass of compact red soil and displaced elephant grass. I stand up quickly, brushing the dust off my body, and see a small redbrick hut with a thatch roof ahead of me. I can smell efirin-and-honey tea, her favorite, and I know where I am.

I am standing outside the hut that sits at the center of our village villa, the one that my great-great-great-grandfather, Oluseyi Balogun, had built with his own hands when he first migrated to Ijebu-ode at the end of the Second Akebulan War. The hut that had spawned what would become the family compound. The hut where I used to play games with my cousins every year during the Olojo Festival. The hut where she had finally gone to die.

I cannot linger. I don't have time.

I sprint to the thick wood door and knock, remembering that she hated it whenever my father or I came in without knocking. The door swings open on its rusty hinges before I finish knocking and so I enter. The hut is mustier than I remember but everything is where I expect it to be. Except... The sight of her sitting in my father's favorite chair and staring at me with a steady smile stuns me to sessility.

"Mummy" is all I can manage to say. Her large brown mahogany eyes, lustrous hair and full cheeks are the same as they were when I saw her last: two weeks after my father's funeral, the day I went back to base.

She rises and I step forward to engulf her in an embrace. Her warmth suffuses me, and I allow myself to steep in it. The smell of her hair, the softness of her neck, the thinness of her arms.

"Dolly Dolapo. My darling. How are you?" she asks, when she finally pulls away.

She walks to a table made of iroko wood where a pot of efirin-and-honey tea is brewing, turns over an old mug and starts to pour. It doesn't feel like this is thoughtspace or even a dream anymore. This feels...real.

"I'm fine," I say out of habit before catching myself. "Actually...I'm not fine."

She hands me the mug with a querying look, and I take a sip. Sweet and bitter dance on my tongue. I realize that my sense of urgency is gone. I've almost forgotten that this place is unstable, that Ìyá Ajimobi is giving me every precious second with my mother and I can't waste any of it.

"I...I need to know why. Why did you leave me?" I feel the tears that have escaped my eyes roll down my cheeks as the emotions start to overwhelm me. It feels good to be able to feel things in this place. "I know you were heartbroken when Daddy died but why didn't you stay...for me?"

"Leave you? I didn't...it is hard to explain, Dolly," she says mildly, picking up the mug. "Your father and I, we'd known each other since we were children, we went to the same school, the same university, we planned our lives together and we planned for you, together. When we lost him, like that..." She pauses and looks up at me. "I knew what the right thing to do was. I knew that I should have focused on you, but I couldn't. I couldn't imagine a world without him because I never had. I was overwhelmed with grief. With a sense of hopelessness. That filled me with fear. It clouded everything."

I turn away from her and take a long sip of the tea. "It clouded your love for me?"

"No! I never stopped loving you, but I knew that you were okay," she responds, dropping her mug and taking my hand. "We'd raised you to be self-sufficient. To be able to take on the world by yourself. You were our strong Dolly," she says, her voice soft. "I knew you were strong enough even if I wasn't."

"I was strong because I had you and Daddy! Without you I have been..."

My voice catches as a memory rushes to mind: my father walking me up to the neighbor's dog, a fearsome-looking Azawakh named Rover, when I was no older than six. My mother stood back, framed in the doorway of our Ibadan house. She kept calling out words of encouragement. *Don't be afraid. The dog won't bite. Not every animal that has sharp teeth is dangerous.*

"I wanted to be there for you, but I couldn't sleep. I couldn't eat. I didn't want to burden you. I know you would have thrown away your entire career just to come and try to care for me, and if that happened, I would have only hated myself."

I remember wondering why she wasn't coming with us to play with the neighbor's dog, why she was trembling, shaking visibly. I'd put my hand on the dog's neck and he barked. But my father held my hand in place, telling me to be gentle but firm. *Don't act out of fear. Not every animal that has sharp teeth is dangerous.* So, I held, and Rover eventually warmed to me. When I turned around to show my mother my new animal friend, she'd shut the door and continued to watch from the kitchen window. In my entire life I never saw my mother around any dogs or any animals, definitely none that had teeth.

"I just couldn't go on, Dolapo. But I knew you could. Please understand."

I think I am starting to understand. She'd raised me to be the woman she'd always wished she was. The image she idolized but never became. Strong, fearless, confident, independent. She was none of those things. Not like the great Olusola Ajimobi. On some level, I think I understand now, the depth and complexity of the emotions that drove her to do what she did. In the end she couldn't fight her own emotions.

"Mummy, I just miss you so much."

"I love you, Dolapo. I have since the moment I first felt you inside me. You are a better woman than I was. I hope you know that. Because it's all I ever wanted for you."

I let the tears fall as we fall into each other again and hold on tightly. I don't care about the border with Dahomey. I don't care about the cabinet meetings. I don't care if this is thoughtspace or a dream or an illusion or whatever. This is all I have left of my mother, imperfections, complexities and all, and I want to hold on to her with every fiber of my being.

My head still nestled in her shoulder, I open my eyes and notice that the chair, the mug and the assorted items of furniture around us are starting to elevate off the ground, floating like we are entering a low-gravity environment.

The warmth of her body suddenly turns cold.

No.

I disengage and look into her eyes. She is perfectly still. There is an emotion frozen in place like sadness set in amber. Her lips start to move but it's Ìyá Ajimobi's voice that comes to me now. It's straining, stretching like it's being pulled.

"We have reached a critical memrionic gradient. I can no longer maintain this unstable state." I know this is the end. "I hope you heard what you needed to hear."

This is as much as I am going to get and for it, I am grateful. "Yes. Thank you. For everything."

"Thank you for thanking me." My mother's lips move with the voice of Ìyá Ajimobi and somehow it seems ... right. "You know, that dog, Rover, it bit your mother when it was still a puppy."

I'm taken aback by the fact that she could sense my thoughts but then I realize I should not be; my mind is completely porous and open to her here in thoughtspace. Still, I wonder, "But ... Then why did she lie?"

"She didn't want you to be afraid just because she was."

Of course. "I think I understand."

"Good. Don't hide from your fears or doubts. Embrace them. I hope you heard exactly what you needed to hear."

Before I can reply, the digital version of my family hut is gone, like it has been painted out of my vision in one broad brushstroke. I am plunged back into the absolute, directionless whiteness of empty thoughtspace. Disembodied and alone. The rattling sound like an opele returns and gets louder and louder until I feel something yank on my consciousness violently.

The last thing I hear in thoughtspace is her voice, once again accompanied by the chorus of memrionics, exploding into my consciousness like a bomb.

Exactly what you needed to hear.

I shoot out of thoughtspace like a mind missile, and my eyes fly open in realspace. I immediately collapse to the floor, vomiting all the moin-moin I ate for breakfast and retching violently, until I am so weak and empty that I feel separate from my body. I am not sure if the feeling is real, an illusion carried over from memory or just an electronic echo. I can feel Baba Yemi's hands on my neck, trying to hold up my head, to get me some air, and close my lifedock, but I cannot see his face. I remember that nausea and dizziness are uncommon but documented side effects of the dream-counsel consultation, but I didn't expect to feel this way. The edges of my vision are dark and wooly, and I know I am probably going to pass out.

Darkness.

When I come to, I am sitting, staring up at the white ceiling of a conference room. I almost panic, thinking I have somehow been reconnected to thoughtspace, but then I see the corners, the edges, and I look down to see my fellow ministers seated around a long table with lightscreen voting panels in front of us, Baba Yemi at the head.

They are all staring at me, a few of them furrowing their brows, chattering to each other or shaking their heads.

"Welcome back," Jibola says, when our eyes meet.

I smile. It *is* good to see a friendly face after all that.

"It seems Minister Balogun has recovered and is with us again," Baba Yemi says, staring at me. "How are you feeling?"

I tell him, "Great actually," because it's true.

"Good. You worried us for a bit, but all your neural scan readings are normal. Let's call it first-time thoughtspace-sickness." He smiles. "We can begin the debrief session now. It should not take long."

He rises and speaks to the group of us as a hologram of yellow light appears at the center of the table and begins to display information about the consultation. "Total consultation time was six minutes and three seconds. Stability of the digital memrionic emulsion was maintained throughout the session."

I start to raise my finger but hold it up to my lips instead, hesitant. Surely, there must be some kind of record of what I did. Some kind of anomaly in the readings?

"No local discontinuities or neural interface breakdowns were observed. Minister Balogun may have had a rough exit but nothing some of you haven't seen or experienced before." Baba Yemi waits for these facts to sink in as the information displays in front of us. "I believe you should all have received the same answers to your queries. Accordingly, I open the floor for a motion, after which you may vote."

I look around and that is when I notice it. They are all hesitant too. They must have all gotten the same advice—go to war. No one wants to disbelieve the advice of our electric mother, but given the consequences of such dire action, and the resistance from the Alaafin that would be sure to follow, no one wants to admit what they must know we all know.

The silence grows sharp and piercing. I think of my mother, sitting in our ancient family hut, unchanged after hundreds of years, contemplating a life without my father, a life she couldn't even imagine. Can I imagine a world where we don't honor the dream-counsel of our electric mother?

Exactly what you needed to hear.

The voice in my head is clear as a talking drum. An electric echo? Or my own memories of that encounter just being replayed? What difference does it make? Perhaps Jibola was right all along. I look to him and he meets my gaze.

As a flood of emotions begin to blanket my mind, I think of my mother standing in the doorway of our Ibadan house. She told me Rover wouldn't bite even though he'd bit her in the past. I start to wonder what it means to help someone you love, to give them good advice, to help them become the best version of themselves that they could be, perhaps even better than you. Perhaps sometimes a useful lie is the best way to point someone in the direction they need to go.

My finger goes up, confidently this time.

"I propose that we put this consultation on hold and reconvene our original cabinet session. We can continue our deliberations until we reach a consensus."

I can almost feel the eyes of the ministers on me, focused like lasers, but I keep my focus on Jibola, whose face breaks out into a broad smile now. I think he understands, just as I did, why the electric mother told us to go to war. I expect an uproar, objections, voices raised in protest for wasting our time, but there is nothing. The silence reestablishes itself.

I scan the room quickly and take in an assortment of expressions, but the only one I cannot read is Baba Yemi's. The only thing I am sure of is that he does not seem surprised at all even though I don't remember reading any other consultation reports which were frozen at the debrief stage. When he finally speaks and breaks the silence again, his words are clear and deliberate. "The motion is moved. I put it to you now, ministers of the Oyo Mesi, do you wish to put this consultation on hold? Your voting panels are before you. Yes or no."

I watch as the votes are entered, a lightstream of encrypted data beamed into the central hologram, and as I do, I start to wonder if I ever actually reached Ìyá Ajimobi and my mother at all, or if the digital supercitizen, our collective electric ancestor, simply showed me and told me exactly what I needed to hear.

The lights continue to weave themselves together. I enter my vote and when the weaving stops, the light in the center displays a unanimous Yes in bright yellow ajami calligraphy.

. . . .

Wole Talabi is an engineer, writer, and editor from Nigeria. He is the author of the World Fantasy Award–nominated novel *Shigidi and The Brass Head of Obalufon*, one of *The Washington Post*'s Top 10 Science Fiction and Fantasy books of 2023, which was also nominated for the Nebula Award, Locus Award, British Fantasy Award, and other major awards. His short fiction has appeared in places like *Asimov's Science Fiction*, *Lightspeed Magazine*, *The Africa Risen* anthology, and is collected in the books *Convergence Problems* (2024) and *Incomplete Solutions* (2019). He has also been a finalist for the Hugo, BSFA, and Crawford Awards, as well as the Caine Prize for African Writing. He has won the Nommo Award for African Speculative Fiction and the Sidewise Award for Alternate History. He has edited five anthologies including the acclaimed *Africanfuturism: An Anthology* (2020) and *Mothersound: The Sauútiverse Anthology* (2023). He likes scuba diving, elegant equations, and oddly shaped things. He currently lives and works in Australia. Find him at wtalabi.wordpress.com and at @wtalabi online.

TWO HANDS, WRAPPED IN GOLD

S.B. Divya

My parents taught me to lie as soon as I could speak. Before I knew the meaning of the words, before I understood *heat* or *fire*, and long before I felt the pain of singed flesh, I learned to tell strangers that I burned myself by grasping a hot iron pot.

Once a day, my mother would pour water over my bare hands, then bandage each one down to the wrists, first with cloth of gold, then plain muslin. She had a technique for winding them in a way that left each finger separate but fully covered, and at no point would her skin come into contact with mine. When I was old enough, she taught me how to wrap them myself. By then, I also understood the danger that she had put herself in.

My parents allowed me to transform small items and only rarely, usually before we approached a large city where people would ask fewer questions about our wares. They let me play with other children, never roughly. After all, if I had burned myself, I would find it painful to use my hands. Other boys my age would wrestle and scuffle. I always ran from a fight.

I was happiest when we were on the road. I could relax around my parents. I was often clumsy because of my bandages, but I could perform basic tasks. My mother, Niraja, taught me how to slice vegetables and boil grains, how to groom our horses, and how to whistle like a bird. My father, Padmanabhan, showed me how to construct a simple bow and arrow, how to mark time by the sun, and how to navigate by the stars. They both shared their tricks for accounting.

"We are not so weak-minded that we need a ledger," my father would say. "And our memories are safe from rain damage or theft."

At night, they would take turns telling me stories from the Mahabharata, the Ramayana, and the Panchatantra, and point out the names of the constellations. I knew which stars pointed the way home—to my parents' villages—and I knew the names of everyone from my great-grandparents onward; every cousin, aunt, and uncle, though I had never laid eyes on a single one.

We passed through many cities and countries. The great metropolis of Constantinople made a strong impression with its buildings decorated in golden domes and intricate tile mosaics. It bustled with people, some whose skin didn't darken from the sun, others with eyes that gleamed blue or green like a peacock's feathers. People came in all shapes, sizes, and colors, including those with missing limbs or eyes. No one cared about my hands. I wanted to stay there forever, but my parents would not hear of it.

"Too dangerous," my father said. "What if someone discovers what you can do, Ram?"

And so we moved on, as we did for years, never staying in one place longer than a few days. I had no friends except for my golden fox.

Just before my first birthday, my father returned from several months on the road to the place my mother had stayed since her labor. He arrived a few weeks before the monsoon, the same rains that had trapped him a year earlier.

When my mother began to experience birthing pains, my parents were in the land of the rajputs, in a small state ruled by a newly self-anointed king. An old rishi, a woman who spent most of her time communing with the gods, took them in and helped with my mother's labor. The streets flooded up to my father's knees on the day I was born. Some locals said it was fitting that the clouds had ended their pregnancy on the same day as my mother. Others said that gods brought the water as an answer to our prayers. Either way, my parents named me Rampalalakshmicharan, after Lord Vishnu and his consort, the Goddess Lakshmi.

"When we named you," my mother would say, "we laid you at their feet and asked them to bless you with health, wisdom, and prosperity."

My mother learned to spin and weave while my father was away. She had a knack for producing gold thread, prized by the king, and found employment in the palace—temporary, until I was old enough that we could travel together.

My father gifted me a small wood carving that he'd acquired on his travels.

"This creature is called a *fox*," he said. "I received it from a man with skin as pale as the rising moon. He was from a land called *Bavaria*."

When the carving entered my grasp, it turned gold.

My parents were so astonished that my father snatched it away, causing me to sit and wail in protest. My father then bit it, marking the tail, and pronounced it real. He declared that I must have received Goddess Lakshmi's blessing.

My mother, however, had heard the tale of King Midas, and panicked. "If he has a golden touch, it could be deadly. We should take him to see the rishi, the one who helped with his birth."

"You watch over him," my father said. "I'll go get the woman."

While he was away, my mother's gaze fell upon the gold uttariya that she'd been weaving for the queen. She took the fabric and placed it into my hands. Being made of golden thread, it did not change, so she wrapped it around my hands and tied it tight. Then she took a piece of plain white muslin and placed it over the precious material. The cloth remained as it was.

When the wise woman arrived and saw what I could do, she left to meditate and commune with the gods. She was gone for an entire day and night. At last, she returned and said, "He is indeed blessed by the goddess, but it's a dangerous gift. You must beware the king's greed. If he discovers what your son can do, he will take the child away to be his personal coffer."

Even my father was troubled by this. Monarchs weren't the only people filled with greed. Anyone who learned of my gift might abuse me.

"Help us," my mother begged the rishi. "Pray to Sri Lakshmi, and ask her to take away this boon."

The old woman shook her head. "That might anger the goddess. You shouldn't appear ungrateful."

After some discussion, the rishi devised a curse, one whose words I know by heart because my mother repeated them to me every night before I slept and every morning when I awoke: "If Rampalalakshmicharan turns an object into gold for another person, they must give him whatever he demands in return. If they don't, the golden object will turn to ash and he will lose his ability forever."

It wouldn't guarantee my safety, especially not while I was too young to understand the consequences of my actions, but it meant that no one could abuse my gift forever.

That night, my parents packed my mother's few possessions into our family wagon and fled the palace. As a traveling merchant, my father already knew how to live as an itinerant. My condition meant that they moved more quickly than they might have otherwise, but it was our way of life, and for the most part, I liked it. My father picked up and traded wood carvings along the way, but the golden fox belonged to me. At some point, our journey gained a destination, one that all three of us felt curious about: Bavaria.

The air grew colder as we traveled further northwest than we had ever gone. The rains fell in heavy sheets, the wind blew mercilessly, and two days after we crossed the border into the land of foxes, my father fell sick. After my mother and I caught the same illness, we stopped near the next village. Fever held us all for a while, but we huddled in our wagon and drank tea and broth. I recovered my strength first. My mother followed. My father didn't.

My mother wished to give him as proper a funeral as she could with no priest accessible. She drove the wagon off the road, into the surrounding forest. I helped her gather wood. My bandages were laced with splinters, and my arms ached, but after two days, we had collected enough for my father's funeral pyre. They don't burn their dead in that part of the world so we did our best. It's strange what lingers in my memory all these years later—the overpowering smell of smoke, the quiet sobs of my mother at night, the first snowflakes falling from the sky.

It was too dangerous for my mother to continue alone with me, so we were effectively stranded in Talgove, a small village that mostly functioned as farmland and a waystation for travelers to Salzburg, our intended destination. The few stone buildings belonged to a man named Konrad, a vassal of the local noble lord, and consisted of his house, a watermill, and an inn. The bulk of the villagers worked the land and lived in huts made of straw. Of the many places I had seen in those early years of my life, this one did not impress me as a good place to stay, but my mother was too distraught over our circumstances, and I was too young to do anything else.

We didn't speak Bavarian, but trade is universal, and we managed to get ourselves into an abandoned hut on the edge of a field in exchange for our horses and wagon. We kept the trading goods for a while, doling them out for food, but the village was small and we ran out of things they wanted. We might have starved to death that first winter but for the kindness of the miller's wife.

I have only the vaguest memories of Herlinde's face, but I remember her pale hair, which shone like my mother's gold threads. She visited our hut once a week to bring us flour, which my mother turned into flatbreads. She and Blasius, the miller, had two daughters. Ilsebill took after her father's looks, with darker hair and a stick thin frame. Trudy, the younger one, had her mother's yellow hair and a softer figure. The girls would sometimes accompany Herlinde during her charity visits.

Ilse was only a year younger than me and plenty willing to run and play with a stranger who didn't speak her language. I learned most of my Bavarian from her. Trudy, however, clung to her mother's skirts and preferred quieter pastimes. She would sit while my mother showed Herlinde the various spinning tools she'd acquired during our travels. It was weaving season, and my mother learned as much from Herlinde as she taught, going so far as to trade looms with her. Ilse and I would head straight for the trees.

My first clear memory of Ilse has to do with my hands. We were out playing somewhere in the woods behind the hut, when she said, "Ram, why do you keep your hands like that?"

I tripped over the old lie about having burned them. We had lived in one place for so long that it no longer made sense. I was terrified. What could I say that she would believe? I grasped for a word and came up with *schlecht*. I knew it meant that something was not good.

"Oh." She grabbed a low-hanging branch and swung from it. "Well, can you do this?"

I nodded, my heart pounding with relief, and proceeded to hoist myself up and onto the branch.

Ilse dropped down and ran off, calling, "Follow me!"

I did, tripping over unfamiliar roots and getting smacked by bushes from her wake.

She stopped in a small clearing surrounding two large beech trees whose upper branches had grown together.

"This one's mine." She pointed to the left. "And that's yours. Race you to the top!"

Ilsebill scaled the tree like a squirrel. That first time up was no contest, but we visited the spot every time Herlinde came to see my mother, almost weekly. As spring warmed the land, I grew stronger, and by the start of summer, I could almost keep up with my friend.

And then one day, as the last of the spring blossoms fell, Herlinde stopped coming by. Three weeks later, she was dead. By mid-summer, one fifth of the villagers had perished from fever. Whatever the disease was, it ran its course. My mother and I escaped death once more. Perhaps our remote location saved us, or perhaps our gods, to whom we prayed daily, gave us protection.

I didn't see Ilse again until the autumn. On a day when the leaves whispered in drifts against the hedgerows, and the harvested wheat stood in great sheaves, all work stopped in the village. Like everyone else, my mother and I went to the mill for the harvest festival. We had managed the summer by helping in the fields and foraging in the woods. Other than Herlinde, no one had befriended my mother, but they had grown used to our presence, or so I thought.

Konrad, the steward, presided over the festivities, which included free food and drink. As we approached a table, I heard someone mutter the word *hexe*. Being a child and without inhibitions, I looked around and spotted a cluster of adults speaking in low tones and glancing at my mother. Their expressions were unfriendly. I huddled closer to my mother.

We had dressed in our finest clothes for the occasion. The bright, intricate patterns made us shine like gems among the dyed woolen tunics around us.

"She can spin silk into gold," someone muttered.

My mother, being an adult, kept her gaze fixed straight ahead, chin high. Her thick, black hair hung to her waist in a neat braid. No matter how cold, she washed daily and insisted I do the same. We did not resemble the people of Talgove.

My anxiety was forgotten as I devoured a piece of cake. I spotted Ilsebill and Trudy playing with a group of children. I waved, and Ilse waved back. She gestured for me to join them, and after a nod from my mother, I ran off.

The group stopped as I approached.

A tall boy with reddish-brown hair and orange freckles stepped forward. "I'm Konrad stewards-son. Who are you?"

"His name is Ram-pala-lakshmi-charan...near-the-wood," Ilsebill said, enunciating each syllable with precision. It had taken her several attempts to learn my name.

Konrad snorted. "He doesn't need a byname. We'll not have another Rumpel...stick-man in our village any time soon."

"You can call me Ram," I said. There were parts of the world where the length of my name didn't cause difficulty, but this was not one of them.

"Do you know how to play tag?" Ilse asked.

I nodded. Games of chase-and-catch were universal.

"What's wrong with your hands?" Konrad demanded.

Before I could explain, Ilse spoke. "His hands have an infirmity. He has to keep them wrapped up always."

I hadn't heard the word before, but I memorized it on the spot.

Konrad grinned. "Then he can be It first! Don't let the diseased hands touch you," he shrieked as he ran off.

The other children screamed and fled. Before long, I was joyfully covered in sweat and dust as we chased each other. Their taunts might sound cruel to an adult, but at the time, I had no room for such qualms. I had playmates! I left them with heavy feet when my mother called me away.

"Can't I stay?" I begged.

She shook her head. In a low voice, she said, "The men will start drinking soon. We'll be safer at home."

The next afternoon, Ilse showed up at our door with a basket of bread and cheese. She wore a gown like a woman rather than the tunic of the previous day.

"I asked Papa if I could do the charity work that Mama did. He said I'm old enough now that I have eleven years."

"Can you play?" I looked dubiously at her dress.

A mischievous smile lit her face, and her brown eyes twinkled. She lifted the cloth wrapping out of the basket. It was a tunic.

"I'll change in the woods," she said.

We ran off and found our favorite spot. She made me turn around while she dressed. After an hour of practicing our acrobatic and balancing skills, she transformed back into a modest young woman and left.

When I returned home, my mother thwacked me across the head twice. "Once for playing with that girl who's no longer a girl, and once for wasting time in the woods."

"We're just climbing trees!"

"Be sure that's all you do."

After that, I would always leave home a little later than Ilse, and I would forage for herbs and greens before I returned. My mother liked to prepare them in our traditional ways. She had learned to improvise when we ran out of the spices, rice, and legumes that we'd brought with us. As long as I came home with my hands full, she didn't object to my time in the woods.

From then on, Ilse came every other week, just as Herlinde had. We snuck off to play for an hour unless it was too wet. Sometimes she had Trudy along, which prevented our play time, until one day, Ilse had a brilliant idea.

"Could you show Trudy those spinning devices?" Ilse asked my mother. "I can help Ram gather some herbs for you while you teach her."

"Of course," she said. "Perhaps she'd like to try the hand loom, too?"

After that, Trudy accompanied Ilsebill on every visit. My mother said Trudy had the knack for spinning, just as she herself did.

"If only I had gold, I could show her how to make thread," my mother said after one visit. "That's not a request, Ram." She wrapped a freshly woven length of linen around my hands. "And be careful while you're out in the woods. Don't let the outer cloth tear."

I suspect that my mother knew that Ilse and I did more than gather herbs, given the terrible state of my outer wrappings on those days, but she also realized that I was still very much a child, too much so to care about the trouble young men and women could get into. And while I tried to hide my loneliness, she would have observed that none of the other children ever came to play with me.

The apple trees were blooming when my mother and I took our first trip to Salzburg. She'd heard from some passing merchants that late spring brought spices and grains from the Far East up the river, and wanted to see if we could buy some. By then, the village had learned of her skill with spinning and weaving, and she spent more time making thread or cloth than in the fields.

We hitched a ride on a hay wagon, part of a train passing through Talgove. Clouds of pale pink blossoms covered the orchards we passed. My mother smiled a true and proper smile for the first time I could remember since we'd arrived in Bavaria. Trudy had gifted her a woolen shawl—one that Trudy had woven with her help—and she wore it over one of her old cotton traveling tunics.

That morning, she had taken my father's silk clothes from our remaining bronze traveling chest, intending to sell them. I could tell it broke her heart from the way she clamped the delicate fabric in her fists.

"Amma, instead of those, let me turn something gold to trade," I said.

She shook her head. "The villagers will be suspicious. I've told them for months now that I have nothing left to trade. I have only the box spindle and the small handloom, and I need those for myself. I can only hope the merchants in Salzburg will accept your father's clothes."

"There are caves not far from here that have gold veins, and the boys in the village say that sometimes you can find small nuggets by the river. I could transform some very small stones and cover them with mud?"

Her expression twisted with doubt.

I felt my father's spirit at my shoulder, whispering that I should behave as a man, not a boy, and use my gift to help our family. "Please! I'm useless without my hands. I can't work in the fields or chop wood. I can't even do women's work because I'm too clumsy for spinning or sewing. You've always said that one day I'll be grown enough that I can safely use my gift." I was twelve years old and nearly as tall as my mother. "How much longer do I have to wait?"

With a crease in her brow, my mother nodded.

Pebbles studded the soil liberally, and it took me minutes to find several the size of my littlest fingertip. As I loosened the bandage on my left hand, my mother stopped me.

"Tell me the words of the curse," she said.

"If Rampalalakshmicharan turns an object into gold for another person," I recited, "they must give him whatever he demands in return. If they don't, the golden object will turn to ash and he will lose his ability forever. You make me repeat it every night."

She smacked me lightly on the head. "And you should thank me for it. They are the most important words of your life. If you do this, you must also make the trades."

I shook my head and continued to unwrap my hand. "I'll give them to you in exchange for Appa's clothes."

Her eyes glimmered with tears. "Clever boy," she said as I gently prised the clothing from my mother's grasp.

I folded them neatly, and slid them into the secret compartment at the bottom of the trunk, along with my golden fox, our other silks, and a length of spare gold cloth for my hands. Traveling merchants have their tricks, and this chest had a false bottom to fool any thieves or bandits.

We arrived at Salzburg's central market at midday. The sun shone high overhead in a blue sky dotted with cottony clouds, and the open space bustled with merchants and their wares. The city didn't impress me nearly as much as Constantinople. From the way Konrad and other village children had talked, I had expected a much larger and grander metropolis. A lord's manor dominated the houses on a low hill overlooking the Salzach river. The only other sizable structure was a church.

The market spilled out like a natural growth from the river docks. I heard languages that hadn't fallen on my ears in a long time. I still remembered many of the basic words involved in trade, especially numbers. Most of the shoppers were Bavarian, but the merchants came from far and wide, and their appearance spanned a variety of colors and features. I felt at home in a way that I hadn't during our years in Talgove.

It took some searching, but eventually my mother found and purchased some of the items she'd wanted. With the leftover money, she bought me a fur-lined leather cloak that hung to my waist. A few merchants looked askance at my bandaged hands. Diseases traveled as well as humans, and we couldn't use the lie about my burns anymore, so I wore the cloak in spite of the mild weather, and hid my hands under it.

That was the first time I felt anger mingled with the usual fear of discovery. It struck me as terribly unfair that I had to conceal my ability, and worse, that it had turned me into a person who was shunned when I should rightly have been revered. My mother hadn't allowed me to disclose my magic to anyone, but I had nothing else of value—no trade, no prospects. The lowliest peasant could work the land, but to preserve my deception, I had to act as if that was beyond me. I couldn't even wear gloves, which only the noble could afford. My golden touch surpassed the abilities of kings! I shouldn't have to hide in shame.

The market revealed a way to put my gift to good use. I could improve our fortunes, earn us a way home. If we lived among family, I wouldn't have to hide the truth. People would appreciate my gift for what it was: a blessing of the gods. All I had to do was keep it a secret until then. On that day in Salzburg, my path to freedom lay ahead like a gleaming ribbon.

Word must have spread in Talgove that my mother had spent an unusual amount during our market outing, because a few weeks after our excursion, some of the young men paid a visit to our hut and dragged me and my mother outside.

"We're here for your gold," said the biggest one in a matter-of-fact tone. *Walter Up-hill*, I recalled. He had no children, but he had rounded up a dozen youths for this task. The sour smell of ale hung about them in an invisible cloud.

"We don't have any gold," my mother replied truthfully. She kept her eyes to the ground, her voice soft but firm. We'd traded all of the nuggets at Salzburg, and I hadn't bothered to make more.

Walter smacked her across the face with the back of his hand, the sound of it sharp and quick, like the noise made by a length of wet cloth against a rock.

"Don't lie to us, witch, or we'll burn you at the stake!" He nodded to the two boys behind him. They entered our hut, and we could hear the crack of pottery smashing.

"Please, we have nothing," she begged.

I watched it all with a building fury, but I had a child's body and couldn't match the men for strength. Besides, my parents had taught me never to fight. I had no idea how to handle myself in that situation except to make sure my hands stayed protected. So I did the only thing I could.

"I found the gold by the river," I cried out. "But we spent it all."

"Then find us some more," Walter demanded.

"It'll be dark soon. I'll look tomorrow," I said.

"All right. We'll come back in three days at sunset. You'd better have some gold for us, little man."

They left us alone. My mother trembled as she swept out the shattered remnants of our crockery.

"What will we do?" she fretted. Her lower lip swelled from the cut left by Walter's blow.

"I can make some nuggets," I said. "It's easy."

"Foolish child! You've memorized the words, but have you understood them? Do you think those men will give you anything you demand in exchange for the gold?"

"I'll trade it to you first, like before."

"And then what? Do you think they'll stop coming after one time? What happens when I have nothing left to give you in return? I hardly own anything as it is, and if anything happened to me, you'd have no way to continue the bargain. You should have kept quiet."

I unleashed my pent-up rage at her. "So they could destroy the rest of our things? Or drag you off and burn you? You should thank me for saving us!"

She met my glare with a sigh and shook her head. "I'm afraid you've done the opposite. When they return, you must tell them you couldn't find any, that last time it took you many months of searching. We'll stall for as long as we can that way. Perhaps they'll tire of asking and give up."

That night, I asked my mother to tell me again about my father, about our family back in their villages near Kanyakumari, a spit of land where three oceans met.

"One day, we'll go back to the great Chola Empire," she promised, "so you must remember who your people are. My name is Niraja. Your father's name is Padmanabhan. His father is Lakshmichandran. His mother is Krishnapriya." She had me learn all the names—my four grandparents, eight great grandparents, numerous uncles and aunts, all the cousins born before my parents left. She would tell me something special about each of them. How her father loved to sing. How her mother swam and bathed in the ocean.

"Your father taught you how to make bows and arrows," she said, "when you were five years old. He showed you how to hunt for small animals and prepare the meat. Do you remember?"

I'm no longer sure whether my memories were true or whether hearing her stories impressed them into my mind, but I knew it would please her for me to say yes, so that's what I did. My own recollections were blurred by the passage of time, more impressions than images—the warmth of my parents' bodies on either side of mine as we lay in our wagon; the smoke from damp wood fires stinging my eyes; my father combing tangles from my mother's long hair. We passed through many splendorous cities, crossed mountain passes, and drove along vast oceans, but it's those quiet times at the end of the traveling day that have stayed with me. When the terror of flames threatens to overwhelm me, I take myself back to those moments of in between, the three of us safe and happy on our own, without a care for the rest of the world.

Walter and his small gang visited as promised. Taking my mother's advice, I told them I had failed. They delivered a beating, which I accepted while curled into a ball on the ground beside my mother, my hands tucked into my armpits to protect the cloth wrapping. Some of them stood apart and watched. I gathered from their words that they had come mostly for sport, including Konrad stewards-son. Walter had debts to the elder Konrad. He'd allowed too many of his pigs to sicken, and he hadn't given the vassal his due share of ham.

"Do better by next week." Walter said as they left.

They came back again and again, and I gave the same excuse and earned us the same beating, but over time their numbers dwindled.

"We should leave this place," I told my mother as we tended each other's wounds. "I'm nearly a man now. We can travel again, buy a wagon and a horse once we get far enough from here."

"You might be close to a man's age, but you don't yet have a man's body. Your father faced worse men than Walter during our travels, and with your hands...you can't fight them off."

"I could turn Walter into gold and sink him to the bottom of the Salzach," I grumbled.

"Don't you dare!" My mother grabbed me by the chin and forced me to meet her gaze. "Never use your blessing to commit murder...or any other crime. You are better than that."

I nodded, but there are days when I regret resisting that impulse.

The next afternoon, two days early, as the setting sun cast long shadows over the field, Walter stumbled into our hut alone and very drunk.

"I've had enough of you both," he roared. He pointed a trembling finger at my mother. "This is all your doing, witch! You cursed my swine, I know it, and now you'll pay."

He wrapped one hand in her hair and yanked her off her feet. Without thinking, I launched myself at him.

"No," my mother cried. "Ram, run away!"

But I didn't heed her. Walter swatted away my pathetic attempts to strike him, then thrust a fist into my gut. I fell to the ground. As I gasped like a fish out of water, he stomped his booted foot once on my right arm, once on the left, and, over my mother's screams, once on each leg.

"Be still," he roared and flung her next to me.

He grabbed a piece of firewood and struck my mother's head as I watched, helpless, unable to move or cry out. She slumped, unconscious, and began to bleed. Taking a flint, Walter dumped our entire supply of cooking tinder next to the straw hut's walls and set it on fire. He waited until the flames caught well and smoke started to fill the small space.

As he ducked outside, he muttered, "Those who do the devil's work must burn."

I remember getting my wind back along with a lungful of smoke. I crawled to my mother and tried to grab her, to pull her out of our hut, which was now our pyre. I couldn't work any of my limbs in a useful fashion. The sharp pain from my broken bones overwhelmed the sensation of searing heat, but the fear is what I can never forget. A terror not only of dying but of living with hands bare, that someone might find us only for me to turn them into gold. I rolled onto my stomach and tucked my useless hands under my body.

At some point, the smoke must have caused me to lose consciousness, because the next thing I recall is waking up and seeing stone walls and Ilse's face looming over me. The terror returned full force, along with the sense over my entire body that the fire still blazed.

"Shhh," Ilse whispered. "Don't worry, I bandaged your hands again."

Had she seen the gold undercloth? If there was anyone I could trust to keep it a secret, it was Ilsebill. With that reassuring thought, I fell into a restless sleep for many days, tormented by heat and pain. Flames danced behind my eyelids.

My mother perished in the fire. I didn't know it for a long time, my mind too consumed by my injuries. Not only did I have multiple broken bones, but the skin over much of my body had burned. It took weeks to heal. My legs and feet, which had been closer to the hut walls, developed blisters. My mother had told me of the hospitals in our home kingdom, places where the ill or infirm could stay and be cared for. Bavaria had no such thing. I was left in the back of the church for God to look after me.

Ilsebill came to see me almost daily. I don't know how much her ministrations helped, but her presence certainly saved me from dying of a broken heart. She told me how she and other villagers had noticed the smoke from the direction of our hut. The column was large enough that they assumed the field had caught fire and rushed over. When they discovered the truth, they doused the flames and dug us from the ruins. Somehow, I lived, and since I had rolled over my hands, they remained bandaged.

My skin repaired itself faster than my bones, but those eventually knit themselves, too. The priest and Ilse had splinted my limbs as best they could. All four ended up somewhat misaligned. I could use my arms and legs, but they pained me. Ilsebill stopped visiting once I could walk.

"My father won't allow it," she said at her last visit. "If you need me, hide in the trees near our home and whistle like a snow finch. I'll meet you at our climbing spot."

I didn't know what qualified as *need*, and I lacked both the strength and the courage to test her offer.

At first I could only cross my room, but eventually I made it to the field where they buried unbaptized children. There I found my mother's remains. Even in death, Bavaria had disrespected her, and I, once again, had been powerless to stop it.

I spent many a warm summer night curled up on the dirt with my mother rather than in my cot. The priest's eyes were always kind when I returned at dawn. And one day, as the wind blew chill from the mountaintops, I found that I had cried all of my tears, and my pains, both inside and out, had dulled to the constant companionship of aches.

The next day, I walked to the edge of the village. I rested for a time, then continued further until I reached the heap of ash and char that marked our former hut. I waded through it and searched for something, any small remembrance of the two people in the world who had loved me most. My foot bumped against a solid object. I knelt and swept aside the debris, my motions gaining speed as I realized it was the bronze chest. My hands trembled from excitement and fatigue as I opened it. The wood carvings in the main chamber had charred but were intact. I felt below them for the mechanism that released the hidden section. There I discovered our silks, cloth of gold, and the carved fox, my father's tooth mark imprinting its tail.

With the last of my strength, I heaved the box from the wreckage and dragged it into the woods. Luck had saved it from discovery by the villagers, but I didn't dare rely on that. I hid the trunk in some undergrowth near our climbing trees. No one had disturbed us there, and I trusted Ilsebill not to say anything if she happened to spot it.

I spent that night in the woods, cradled in the elbow of my beech tree. When I returned to the church, the priest didn't comment on my absence or the filthy state of my clothing. He had allowed me to use some rags to wrap my hands. When I mentioned their diseased state, he murmured the word *leprosia*, and I filed that away in my lexicon for future use.

Every night, by my mother's grave, I repeated the words of my curse, the names and habits of my family members, and the cities that would lead me back to my true home. I conversed softly in Tamil with her about my day so that I wouldn't forget my first language. I said prayers to my gods. I vowed that once I was well enough, I would leave Talgove and find my way to Kanyakumari, to the point where three oceans met.

The priest asked me to help around the church as remuneration for my extended stay. Dependent as I was on his charity, I did as he asked. For a few hours, I would do various chores and errands. When the pain overwhelmed me, I would lie on my cot. After several months, another villager displaced me, one whose infirmity needed the comfort more. The cold stone floors didn't help my aching body, but I had nowhere else to go.

That year's winter came after a poor harvest, and the storehouses for the church grew bare as the needs of the village increased. As soon as the roads became passable, the priest put me on a wagon to Salzburg. I didn't get a chance to say good-bye to Ilsebill.

The wagon left me at the abbey, where the monks took pity on me. I stayed with them as long as I could tolerate it, but they wanted me to pray to their God, to accept the Bible as my holy book, and I could not betray my parents that way. When I declared my intention to go, the monks gave me a sack of food and let me keep my bedroll. With these on my back, I left the city for the woods. I planned to "discover" gold that I could trade for passage on a ship, but I had to think of a safe way to do it.

Nearly a year had passed while I was at the abbey. I hadn't seen Ilsebill once the entire time. In spite of my deformities, I could walk at a good pace and distance—the power of a youthful body to adapt—and I found myself going further east each day, toward Talgove. I needed to retrieve the bronze trunk I'd hidden away. I couldn't leave Bavaria without it, and once I'd approached the familiar terrain around the village, the urge to see Ilsebill burned within me like the flames that had destroyed my life.

The time away had made me shy. I had spent days sleeping in the woods, failing to wash or launder along the way. I stood in the trees across the creek from the mill and watched the waterwheel spin until I spied her form outside. Ilse had grown more womanly during my time away, though her figure wasn't curvaceous like her sister's. Should I approach her? Could I consider her a friend anymore, with so much time having passed and both of us having grown? I teetered on the cusp of adolescence, past the poorly formed notions of a child, and glimpsed the responsibility that weighs on a man's shoulders. In that moment, I wished I could turn back time and freeze ourselves in youth, at the age when we had no troubles but to reach the next branch.

Perhaps I gasped or made some other involuntary noise because she turned and looked directly at me. I froze when our eyes met. The urge to flee warred with the need for acknowledgement. When Ilse's face broke into a smile, I could draw breath again. She waved. My heart sang. I whistled like a snow finch and pointed in the direction of our secret spot before retreating. I trusted that she would find me when she could.

I waited in the crook of my beech tree for the better part of two days. Ilse arrived just after a rain shower. Drops spilled from the canopy above us, and mud caked her boots. She wore a plain leather cloak, the oiled hood pulled up to cover her head. I jumped down and stood in the awkward silence of a fourteen-year-old boy.

"Padmanabhan Rampalalakshmicharan," Ilse said with a grin. "It's wonderful to see you."

She stepped forward and flung her arms about me. I was so startled, I stumbled back, but the tree trunk held me up. I dared to embrace her. I trembled at holding her warm, sturdy body against mine. She pulled away and led me by the hand to the boulders where we usually sat when we weren't climbing.

"How have you been? Tell me *everything*," she demanded.

I delighted her with stories about the different monks in the abbey, about learning to read and write on the sly, about the boats that came and went along the Salzach, about my plan to buy my way back to my home country.

Concern wrinkled her brow. "You don't have to leave," she said. "You could stay here in Talgove and swear fealty to Konrad. You could teach *me* to read and write."

I held up my hands, the bandages filthy with mud and splinters. "I can't stay here. I can't stay anywhere for too long, or I'll be in danger again."

"You won't. Walter died last winter. You'll be safe."

The way Ilse looked at me then, I couldn't lie, not anymore. No one alive knew my secret, and I wanted someone to have the truth in case I died. Who better than my only friend? Ilse had saved my life, as Herlinde had done, and the least I could do was trust her with this knowledge.

"My hands...they're not diseased."

"What do you mean?"

"Watch."

I began to unwrap my left hand. Her aspect overflowed with questions. She raised her brows at the cloth of gold but stayed silent as I exposed my skin. With my right hand, I grabbed the smallest, thinnest twig I could spy and touched it with my left thumb and forefinger. Ilse's sharp gasp made my heart skip a beat. Would this change things between us? Had I ruined our friendship?

"Is that...gold?" she whispered.

"Yes." I wound both bandages over my hand and told her the story as my mother had told it to me. When I came to the rishi's curse, I recited the exact words: "If Rampalalakshmicharan turns an object into gold for another person, they must give him whatever he demands in return. If they don't, the golden object will turn to ash and he will lose his ability forever."

Ilse's brown eyes went round as saucers. "But this is wonderful! Why keep it a secret?"

"Because someone might threaten me or my family and force me to make gold for them, like Walter did. When I was small, my parents let me use my gift for some of their wares, but we never stayed in one place for long because they feared for my safety. After my father died, my mother was too afraid to continue our traveling ways. That's why we stayed here in Talgove. It was a mistake." I forced out the words I knew to be true: "Had we moved on, she would be alive today."

"Oh, Ram, no! What happened was not your fault. It's all that evil Walter's doing. I'm sure he's burning for his sins."

My bitterness was still too fresh for me to accept her statement. "That's why I can't stay here—or anywhere. It's too dangerous."

"Will it be safe for you to travel alone? You're small enough that people will think you're a child. Wait a few years, until you grow into a man. I'll help you in the meantime. I'll leave you a small sack of food here every fortnight. I keep track of our stores now. Father won't know if something is missing."

She gazed at me with such earnestness that it confused my thoughts. There was sense in Ilse's arguments, and staying was an easier choice than leaving, so I acquiesced.

Ilse beamed. "Listen, between here and Salzburg there are caves with veins of gold, right? We've all heard the rumors. Maybe you can *make* a vein and pretend to find it. Lead someone there who can mine it. You can avoid the Walter problem that way."

"It's a good idea," I said. "But you must promise me: you'll meet me here every fortnight with some food even if I can make this cave scheme work."

"I will, if you swear to stay for at least two more years."

We shook on the bargain. I watched her go with reluctance, then stowed the twig in my trunk and went to find a dry place for the night.

Over the next months, I familiarized myself with the local terrain. The triangular region formed by Salzburg, Hallein, and Talgove contained plenty of small cave systems. I ranged as far south as Hoven, where people mined for salt and copper. The climbing, scrambling, and swimming strengthened my limbs. My small stature allowed me to wiggle through tight spaces the Bavarians couldn't reach. It made my deception easier.

I discovered that if I touched a layer of rock that was different from those around it, only it would turn into gold. Then, with my bandaged hands, I'd chip away at a small amount, take it back to Salzburg or Hallein, whichever was closer, and lead an expedition to the location of the vein that I'd "discovered." When I found a cave at the mouth of a stream, I would go the gravel route, taking some of my made nuggets with me and leaving the rest for others to gather, as Walter had wanted. Sometimes I came upon salt or copper deposits, which were equally valuable to the local trade, and I wouldn't have to use my magic at all.

To stay safe near the different towns, I established a set of caves where I kept stashes of firewood and blankets. I would share my space with the wildlife if they were peaceable, or chase them away if they became aggressive. I developed relationships with the local bishops and lords who owned the lands in the region. Merchants and villagers came to know me, as well, because I would stop for food, shelter, or directions to known cave systems nearby. They nicknamed me the

Golden Spider for my ability to get into difficult spots and find this precious met-al—and also because they could never remember my full name.

One year, I learned about a place high in the mountains above a tiny village about twenty miles south of Hallein. The locals said it was a gateway to Hell, which piqued my curiosity. The climb to the cave mouth was steep and treach-erous, and the initial blast of air that greeted me was frigid. No heat or sulfur greeted me. Instead, I discovered a world of ice. I didn't dare to explore very far, between the slippery surfaces and the wintery temperature, but the small amount I glimpsed was glorious and like nothing else I'd seen.

There, I set up a shrine to the gods of my people, to my patron, Goddess Lakshmi, and her consort Vishnu. I fashioned crude carvings from wood, hop-ing they would forgive my clumsiness, and turned them gold to preserve them from the elements. I went there to pray as often as I could, in thanks for sav-ing my life, for giving me the gift of my hands, and for safe passage home one day. The cave allowed me to speak more privately to my mother and father than the grave in Talgove. Since no local would venture inside, it became my favorite sanctuary.

Once every fortnight, without fail, I returned to the climbing trees near Talgove. At first I needed the food, but as months and then years passed, I needed to see Ilse. People might enjoy the fruits of the Golden Spider's labor, but none of them wanted my company. They might wonder at my absence if I died in a caving accident. Only she would miss me.

I didn't realize that I was in love with Ilse until the day she told me her father had promised her in marriage to Konrad stewards-son. It happened on the day of the autumn festival, one that was unusually warm for the season. Ilse wore a new gown dyed buttery yellow with an embroidered veil over her hair. She'd come to see me as soon as the feasting had ended and the men began to drink. The setting sun filled the woods with a gentle glow that limned her form like a figure from an illuminated manuscript.

"I'm sixteen years old, and Father thinks it's time," she said. Her lips trem-bled as she drew a breath. "Ram—Padmanabhan Rampalalakshmicharan—marry me! Make lots of gold and offer it as a dowry. No one will question you this time. Please—I don't want to be Konrad's wife."

I had given my heart to Ilse when we were still children. I just hadn't realized it until she said the words: *marry me*. Now she was betrothed to a young man who'd once helped beat my mother and me.

In my mind's eye, flames ate at a straw hut. I couldn't see a future for us that didn't end in disaster, pain, or both.

I grasped at excuses to cover my cowardice. "Your father would never agree to it, no matter how much gold I might offer. Look at me! I barely come up to your shoulder. My limbs may be strong, but they are still crooked. I spend my days crawling through caves. Besides, no priest would marry us.”

“Then convert! Embrace the church. You’ve lived here for most of your life. You don’t need your old gods anymore. If not for yourself, then do it for me.”

But it was my people’s goddess who had blessed me. My people’s gods who had brought me through blood and fire and kept me alive. They were my last connection to my family. I could no sooner let them go than I could cut my hands off, not even for Ilse.

I shook my head. “My life is one of ashes and stone. As long as I’m blessed with Goddess Lakshmi’s gift, I won’t be safe here, and neither will you. You’ll have a better life with Konrad in the big house—a far more comfortable living than you would roaming around with me.”

“Then let it go,” she said softly.

“What?”

“Your *gift*. You know how to break free of it. Make me a gold item and ask for something impossible in return. Live the rest of your life by my side as an ordinary man.”

Fear gripped me, so tight I couldn’t breathe. Who was I without my golden touch? Worse than the worthless creature I already was! “You would take away the only good thing in my life?”

“Am I not a good thing? Would it be so terrible to have hands like the rest of us, like me?”

Yes it would, I thought, though I couldn’t say the words aloud. My touch had been part of my existence for as long as I could remember, my only worthwhile skill, my unique talent. I couldn’t fathom a life without it. How could Ilsebill not see that?

I turned my back to her. “Go marry Konrad and be well.”

“You’re being a coward.”

I closed my eyes.

“If I marry him, I won’t come back here to meet you, not ever again.”

I know.

I heard the rustle of her footsteps as she walked away. My heart ached worse than four shattered bones. I vowed never to return to Talgove.

That winter was the coldest I’d ever experienced. After a brutally hot and brief fall, the season shifted with a vengeance. I had barely enough opportunity to get my caves stocked with wood and fill my pack with dried foods, much less to consider my escape from Bavaria. The upper inches of the Salzach river froze. The roads became impassable with mud and ice. I spent many days huddled under my cloak and blankets, convinced that I had made the right decision about Ilsebill’s union with Konrad. She would be safe and warm in her stone house.

Winters were always a lean time for me. Mining operations slowed. People didn't want to risk the treacherous terrain to see what I'd found, so I stopped trying. I didn't have enough wealth to stay in Salzburg, and I had too much fear to trust any village in the area. I considered begging for a place at the abbey, but the monks had warned me before that I would have to convert if I came back. I did not think they'd go back on their word.

With the spring thaw, I decided to break my earlier promise to myself: I'd visit Talgove one more time, to ensure that Ilsebill was happy, and then I'd leave as soon as the roads were passable. I'd head east and south and never look back.

I crept into the village like a thief in the night. I couldn't face my friend—if I could call her that any longer—so I climbed a tree near her house and waited for daylight and a glimpse of her fortunes.

She came outside to hang the wash. Her hair hung free and wet down her back like a dark cape. Her face looked drawn—thinner perhaps—and shadows had formed below her eyes. Had she been sick? A cold winter would do that. Good that she had the food and shelter to live through it. If she'd taken ill in the caves with me, she probably would have died.

As her arms lifted, her sleeves fell back. In the morning sun, the bruises stood out clearly against her pale skin: the marks of hard fingers. I looked more closely at her face then and realized that some of the shadows were not tricks of the light.

A man has a right to beat his wife in Bavaria, and plenty of them did. My father never raised a hand to my mother—not that I could remember—and I, of course, had been taught to protect my hands, not use them as weapons.

It took every ounce of willpower not to jump out of my tree and go to her. I didn't need to ask if she was happy to know the answer. At least she lived. Was she *well enough* that I could leave? Some men beat their wives to death. What could I do to defend her? Could I blunt Konrad's violence with gold?

Over the next weeks, I tried to glean some answers from the villagers. Was the vassal in debt to the duke of Bavaria? Was the younger Konrad ambitious and therefore unhappy with his status? Did he want something he didn't have?

A child. That's what he desired that Ilse couldn't give him. They'd been married for half a year, and she hadn't gotten pregnant even once. It shamed him that he wouldn't have an heir—or worst case, a daughter—by their first anniversary.

No amount of gold could help me solve this problem, could it? Was it possible to obtain a newborn infant and leave it at their doorstep? Would Konrad take it in? Ilsebill would, of that I was certain, given her good heart. But where and how would I get such an infant? I couldn't stomach the thought of buying one.

Neither could I tear myself away from Ilsebill's unhappiness. Had I caused it by refusing to marry her? Should I murder Konrad in his sleep? I was fairly sure I could sneak into his chamber at night, but far less sure that I could actually do the deed. My mother's words came back to me: *Never use your blessing to commit murder. You are better than that.*

I was hidden in a tree near the mill when the Duke of Bavaria arrived in Talgove. I had never seen the man before, but the coat of arms matched the hangings I'd seen in Salzburg. The sizeable retinue stopped by the water wheel.

Blasius emerged from the building, staggering and red-faced from drink. "My lord," the miller said, his face wrinkled in confusion, "the steward's house and the inn are—"

"I'm here for Trudy of-the-mill," the duke interrupted. "Your daughter, I presume?"

Balsius's befuddlement deepened. "Yes, but—"

"I hear that she can spin flax into gold, that she has a special instrument from a witch who used to live in these parts. I wish to witness this skill for myself." The duke grinned.

The miller executed a deep, sloppy bow. "My lord, indeed she is indeed talented spinner and weaver. Beautiful, too."

"Then let us see this lovely and gifted creature."

Still bent at the waist, Blasius went inside. I held myself as still as wood and waited. What was he up to? Trudy had never learned how to make gold thread from my mother, and she certainly couldn't magically transform flax. I could. Had someone discovered my gift and mixed up their stories?

A sharp cry sounded from inside the building. Blasius emerged, holding Trudy's wrist in one hand and one of my mother's spindles in another.

"See here!" He thrust Trudy forward and gestured at her head. "She made the golden thread for this embroidery. This ring, and the chain about her neck, too. Those used to be silver. She learned from a witch who used to live near our village. Take her! She will do well in your household."

My stomach twisted with rage and disgust. Trudy's wimple came from one of my mother's fabrics. She wore my mother's wedding band and necklace. How had they obtained the jewelry except from my mother's body? How dare Blasius abuse my mother's memory like that? And why would he lie about it? *He's desperate to see her married well.* With Ilsebill secured to Konrad, there was no good match in the village for Trudy. Her looks—the golden hair, the womanly curves—had always attracted attention from men.

A flush covered Trudy's round cheeks. She kept her gaze fixed on the ground, and her hands trembled. I sat in my tree, frozen with indecision and fear. I could think of nothing in my power that would help her without revealing my secret.

"Quite attractive," the duke murmured. Then, louder, "I will take her to Salzburg with me. I wish to have some gold thread made for my wardrobe. If she succeeds in her witchcraft, I will take this young lady to Regensburg and keep her safely with my treasury."

The men in the duke's retinue snickered. Trudy's flush crept down and across her neck.

"Yes, good," Blasius said. He bobbed his head and swayed.

"And if she fails, she will be burned."

At that, Blasius fell to his knees, his face pale. "But, my lord—"

"I am your *duke*, and you will not deny me again or else you will hang for the crime of consorting with witches."

Trudy put a hand on her father's shoulder. To my surprise, she kept her chin level and her face calm as the duke took her up and placed her on his horse. Blasius stayed on his knees in the dust. As the retinue rode away, Ilsebill came running down the lane, Konrad stewards-son a few strides behind her. They stopped by Blasius's side and stared at the receding horses.

"What happened?" Konrad demanded.

As the miller related a semi-coherent version of Trudy's fate and his impossible claim about her, Ilse raised her eyes and stared straight at my perch. She inclined her head ever so slightly toward our old meeting spot. She couldn't possibly have seen me, could she? But her head had turned so precisely in my direction, and that tilt...she must have caught me out. When? How often had she noticed me skulking around the village?

My ears turned hot. To think that Ilsebill had known I was spying on her, that I was aware of her misery and yet did nothing—I couldn't pretend after that. For surety, I shaped my lips and tongue and whistled like a snow finch.

That evening, the spring moon rose full and clear. It illuminated Ilsebill's skin with a pale glow as she approached our intertwined trees. I dropped from my usual perch to the clearing and met her gaze. For several breaths, neither of us spoke. Up close, I could see more clearly what suffering had done to her, the way her cheeks carved into her face, the sloppiness of the stitching along her sleeve, the shadows under her eyes. I wanted to lift her to the highest branches and fly away somewhere safe and warm.

"Will you help her?" Ilse said in a volume barely above the call of night birds and insects. "You can save Trudy. If you run, you can get to Salzburg before the night is over. Turn the duke into gold. Give my sister enough to get passage down the river. She may be spoiled, but better a woman of ill-repute than dead."

I wasn't so sure of that assessment, but I found myself nodding. Anything to make Ilse's life a little easier. "I'll go. I'll do...something, but I have no desire to kill anyone, especially a duke."

Ilse's expression took on a grim hardness I'd never seen. "You would if you understood what it's like when a man...well, you'll never have to know, will you?"

But I understood exactly what she meant by that pause, and the implication about her relations with Konrad. My wrapped hands balled into fists. Perhaps I could kill the duke, if I thought of him as Konrad and Trudy as my dear Ilse.

"I'm sorry," I whispered. *About so many things.*

She bowed her head and left me. No gifts this time, nothing to help me on my way, not even a word of thanks. Perhaps she thought I didn't deserve the latter until after I'd saved her sister. Perhaps she was right.

I arrived in Salzburg a couple hours before matins. It took little effort to find Trudy's whereabouts thanks to the torchlight seeping from the cracks of her room's walls. Getting inside was more of a challenge, but stone is stone, whether it's shaped by human hands or nature's. I climbed up and squirmed my way through the gaps under the timber roof.

Trudy gave a startled gasp when I dropped into her room. "You! You're Rum—Rumpel...you're Niraja's boy. What are you doing here?"

You have to help her, I told myself sternly, *even if she can hardly recall your name.*

I sketched a low bow. "I'm here to help, at the behest of your dear sister."

When I straightened, I noticed the piles of flax around the room. One of my mother's spindles—traded to Herlinde in our first year at Talgove—rested on a table. I waved at them and raised a questioning brow.

Trudy sat back onto a stool and burst into tears. "The duke—he said that he's a man of his word, so he—he locked me in here and said that if I can spin this flax into thread as golden as my hair, he—he'll let me live. I have no gold to work with, and even if I did, I wouldn't know what to do."

I didn't ask if he had already taken her maidenhood. What difference would it make? At least he'd given her a way to stay alive. I wouldn't have to kill him that night.

"Very well, you spin the flax. I'll transform it into gold."

Trudy gaped for a second. "You can really do that? I thought my father was telling drunken tales about Niraja."

"He was, but he happened to guess right." I didn't bother to enlighten her about my mother or the truth of my gift. My gaze fell upon her finger. "You must give me your ring in return."

She nodded.

"And promise never to tell anyone what I can do."

"I swear."

As Trudy set to work, I unwound the cloths from my right hand. She handled the spindle with the same deftness that my mother had, and soon, piles of thread coiled on the floor. I passed my fingers through them. It wasn't perfect, but enough turned gold that the duke wouldn't notice the spots I'd missed.

Trudy didn't have the sharp curiosity and courage of her sister, but she was no fool. She saw what I did, and understanding grew in eyes. I hoped she stayed true to her word and didn't give me away.

As dawn's light seeped through the cracks in the walls, we finished.

Trudy clutched my arm. Her eyes were red from the long night with no food or water.

"Thank you," she rasped.

Thank your sister, I wanted to say. Instead, I nodded and slipped away.

I found a place to curl up and sleep in Salzburg. The next day, as I was taking a meal, I overheard people gossiping about the duke and his golden lady, and the miracle she'd worked overnight. That it was now a *miracle* and not *witchcraft* did not surprise me. Rumor said that he would ask her to repeat her holy transformation again.

I skulked around the city until nightfall, then made my way to the manor and Trudy's room. This time, she had a window. Through it, I observed her sitting by the spindle with an even larger pile of flax mounded on the floor.

Her face lit with relief upon seeing me. "Thank the Almighty! I made the duke believe that I could only work my miracle alone and at night."

"And only with flax?"

"He hasn't asked about other types of thread." She frowned. "Is that a problem?"

"No." I loosed the binding on my right hand. "I'll need something of yours in exchange again."

She reached behind her head and unclasped my mother's necklace. "This?"

I nodded. "That belonged to my mother, as did your ring."

She had the decency to blush. "I'm sorry. My father made me wear them. He's had them ever since...the fire."

You're doing this for Ilsebill, I reminded myself, *not for her father*.

We set to work and discovered that both of us could go faster after all the practice from the previous night. In spite of the larger amount, we finished earlier.

"Will you come back tomorrow?" Trudy asked.

Wearily, I nodded. "If I must, I'll help you again, but we cannot allow the duke to exploit you like this forever. If he demands more, tell him that tomorrow is the last time you can do this, that God spoke to you and told him to be satisfied henceforth."

Her eyes wide, Trudy agreed. I didn't envy her position, having to lie to the duke and convince him of her limits.

I spent the next day thinking up ways I could spirit Trudy from the house. My golden touch wouldn't help except to bribe the guards, but I wasn't sure they'd accept coins from the likes of me. If anything, my possession of that kind of wealth might arouse suspicion. The window into the room was too small for Trudy to fit through. If I brought some chisels with me, perhaps we could loosen some stones in the wall and get her out that way. I wasn't sure if we could work quickly or quietly enough for that, but it was the best I could come up with.

As I was about to barter for the tools, I overheard a new rumor: the duke had declared that tonight Trudy would perform her third and final miracle, and in the morning, the archbishop of Salzburg would witness their marriage before the couple departed for Regensburg. I abandoned the chisels. We already knew that the duke was a man of his word. I wouldn't need to help Trudy escape.

I slipped into her room as early as I dared, for that night, the mounds of flax were enormous.

"Did he gather every bit he could find in all of Bavaria?" I groused.

Trudy glowed with happiness. "I don't know, and I don't care. A duchess! Just imagine it—me, a miller's second daughter from Talgove."

I frowned at her.

"What's the matter?"

"I need you to give me something in exchange."

She huffed impatiently. "I have nothing left but my gown, and you can't have that. Wait until tomorrow. After I become duchess, I can give you anything you want."

Would it work? I had never used my gift in trade for a promised item. If that failed, not only would Trudy lose her chance at marriage with the duke, I would no longer have my golden touch. I cursed myself for not buying the chisels when I could.

I didn't want to risk my hands for Trudy, but Ilsebill's quiet desperation rang in my mind. She had enough pain in her life. She didn't need her sister's death added to it. For the sake of her future, I decided to gamble with my own.

And that's when the idea came to me.

"I want your first child with the duke," I said.

Trudy stared.

"He'll marry you tomorrow, and he'll waste no time getting you with child. After the infant is baptized, I will collect it." *I will leave it at your sister's doorstep, and perhaps then her miserable husband will stop tormenting her.*

I had to hope that Trudy wasn't as barren as her sister. It was my fault that Ilsebill suffered from Konrad's abuse. Trading my hands—my gift—for her happiness seemed a fair exchange.

Trudy hesitated long enough that I thought she might refuse, but in the end, she agreed.

By the time we finished, both of our hands were raw from the work. The flax remained as golden as the other nights when I left it with Trudy.

I emerged from the building and made my way to the cave where I usually slept. The faint glow of pre-dawn painted the eastern sky with indigo. To be absolutely certain I hadn't cursed myself, I touched a small pebble with my bare finger. It turned gold. I exhaled the breath I'd held. I wanted a good life for Ilsebill, but I couldn't help the cowardly fear for my own fate had the worst come to pass. I tucked the precious stone into my pocket and fell into an exhausted slumber.

The next day, true to his word, the duke married Trudy. As the abbey bells pealed to announce the joyous occasion, I ran away from Salzburg. How long before Trudy spilled my secret to her noble husband? I could no longer consider Bavaria a safe place to stay. My unthinking feet carried me toward Talgove and Ilsebill and the travel chest that held my only valuable possessions.

I waited in my usual perch where I could see Ilse come out to hang laundry. When she came out of the house, I whistled like a snow finch. She turned toward me and nodded. I slipped away through the treetops and went to our meeting place. While I waited for her, I retrieved my chest and opened the false bottom. The clever device had preserved the family silks, my golden fox, and the last of my mother's woven cloth-of-gold. I'd stowed them all in my pack. If I'd been inclined to take the roads, I would've worried about bandits, but I was used to finding game trails and dry stream beds to make my way through the wilderness.

A little while after sunset, I heard rustling footsteps, and Ilsebill arrived at the clearing. The moon gave us only a sliver of light, but that was enough for me to see the worry and hope that mixed on her face.

"You have a duchess for a sister," I said.

Ilse blinked. "I—what do you mean? What happened?"

I told her almost everything. She worried when I divulged that Trudy now knew the secret of my hands. She understood when I told her I asked for Trudy's jewelry in exchange. She wept when I told her about the wedding bells.

"Ram...thank you."

I didn't mention *how many* items of jewelry, nor the dangerous bargain I'd made. Ilsebill wouldn't accept her sister's child, but she would take in an abandoned one. The deception—much as it pained me—was necessary.

I dared to close the distance between us and took her hands in mine. "I can't stay in Bavaria. If the duke learns the truth from Trudy, he'll have his men looking for me."

This time, she didn't protest. "Farewell, Padmanabhan Rampalalakshmicharan."

"Farewell, Ilsebill stewards-wife." I lifted her fingers to my lips, pressed hard, then let her go.

I left Bavaria for half a year. In that time, I traveled east and did my best to trace a portion of the route that would take me home. I allowed myself to acquire simple jewelry and turn it gold so that I could pay my way. I also trimmed and curled my hair, shaved my face, and traded my clothes for the colorful robes of a Roman merchant—someone well-off but not wealthy enough to attract attention.

Leather gloves covered my cloth-bound hands. Like my childhood days, I never stayed anywhere long enough for people to know me.

The most dangerous time came when I went to Regensburg. I had to know if Trudy was with child. As the seat of the duchy of Bavaria, the city had plenty of spying eyes. It wasn't as big or busy as Salzburg, which made keeping my anonymity more challenging. Luckily, my new attire hid my crooked limbs, and my gold distracted people from my short stature. People see what they want, not what is.

I arrived by boat on a rainy day in autumn and stayed for three days and three nights, spending as generously as I dared, until I could comfortably ask the innkeeper whether the duke had an heir. The duchess was with child, he informed me, expecting a birth in spring. She would take her confinement in Salzburg, closer to the archbishop who would christen the child. I thanked Goddess Parvathi that Trudy was more fertile than her sister.

I spent the worst part of winter in the gentler climates of the Roman Empire before making my way back to Salzburg. I didn't dare stay in the city—someone might recognize the Golden Spider—so I kept to my old caves and trees and subsisted on dried meat and fruit. My stashes of wood sat where I'd left them, dry and perfect for keeping warm. I listened for the abbey bells to tell me whether the child had been christened.

At last, on an unusually warm and cloudy spring day, I heard them ring. The rain started as the procession left the church and headed back to the duke's residence in Salzburg. I followed them from my vantage points in the trees, eventually running ahead to hide myself where I could see Trudy and the baby enter the house. Only a few rooms had windows, and the duchess would certainly end up in one of them.

When the shutters flew up on an upper part of the house, I figured that was my target. I waited until night fell. I was soaked and chilled, but I gritted my teeth and climbed. As before, I slipped through the gap between the walls and the roof, dropping into a spacious chamber. Embers glowed in the fireplace. In the dim light, I could see Trudy and her infant asleep on the bed. I shook her gently to wake her.

She sat up in alarm upon recognizing my face. "You! Rumpel—"

"Shhh," I cautioned, pointing at the babe. In a whisper, I said, "I've come to collect what I'm owed."

Confusion and then distress painted Trudy's face. She whispered back, "Please, have mercy! He's only a month old. I can't part with him so soon."

"It won't get easier with time."

"I didn't know then what I do now. I can't give him up. Ask me for something else—anything! Please! I'll find a way to get it. The duke is so happy to have a son, he won't deny me." Her voice rose with her distress.

I didn't know if I could make a trade like that, and if it failed, I'd be ruined. I didn't have enough saved for passage all the way back to Kanyakumari.

"I must have him and nothing else," I said. "There's no other way. I'm sorry." I didn't owe her any apology, but her pain softened my heart. "If you don't fulfill your side of the bargain, the golden thread we made on the third night will turn to ash."

"I don't care about the gold!" she cried. "I only want my child."

"And I only want to go home," I spat. "I saved your life. You became a duchess. Now I need your help, and instead you want to condemn me to a miserable life. I should have expected this. You can't even say my name. Why would you think of my welfare?"

"Trudy?" said a sleepy voice from the floor beyond the bed.

We both froze as a head rose into view: Ilsebill. I'm not sure which of our expressions was more shocked, hers or mine.

"Ram?" Ilse said. She shook herself as if she might be dreaming.

Trudy glanced wildly back and forth between us. "Ilse, help me! He's trying to take Eberhard away!"

"Hush, Trudy, or you'll wake him." Ilsebill stood and came around the bed. "What's going on, Ram? Why are you here?"

I was at a loss to tell her anything but the truth, so I confessed the terrible bargain I'd struck a year earlier.

"Why would you do such a thing?" The aghast expression on Ilse's face didn't surprise me, but my heart sank anyway.

"For you," I whispered. "So that Konrad would treat you better. I planned to leave the baby at your doorstep as a gift."

Ilsebill drew a sharp breath. She closed her eyes for a breath. When she re-opened them, I saw fury and despair.

"Ilse?" Trudy said plaintively from across the room.

"I said hush!" Ilsebill hissed.

"I have to take the baby," I said desperately. "You know what will happen if I don't. Ilse—please!"

"Of all the foolish things to do, Ram—you should've spoken to me first."

"I couldn't! I was busy saving Trudy's life." I raised my gloved hands, palms outward. "With these, the only skill I have. Would you take them from me?"

"You should never have made such a demand! A child isn't something to be traded. And Konrad would never accept someone's cast off infant as his own. Don't you understand anything about him? You should have thought this through instead of acting like a foolish boy."

Her anger mirrored my mother's, all those years earlier, when I'd spoken up to Walter. Flames danced in my mind.

"You have no one to blame but yourself," Ilse said. "And unlike my sister, I do know your name, and I'll say it once more." She raised a trembling arm and pointed at the window. "Padmanabhan Rampalalakshmicharan, you cannot complete this trade. Leave the infant and go!"

I was tempted to snatch the child and make my escape. If Ilse didn't want him, I could leave him at some other doorstep. As if reading my mind, she stepped between me and the bed, her face as stony as the walls around us.

"Go," she repeated, "or I will raise the alarm."

"You would let the duke kill me?" I asked, the words bitter in my throat.

"I don't want to. I would never want to hurt you. But I won't let you take my nephew."

We were at an impasse, one that I knew I couldn't win. I wouldn't strike Ilsebill or Trudy. That kind of violence wasn't in me, not even to save my blessed, cursed hands. And Ilse, like the duke, kept her promises.

Without another word, I fled through the window, leaping to the ground as soon as I'd dared. The fall wrenched my leg, and I limped toward the trees. Twice, I slipped on roots and fell to my knees. The second time, I didn't get up. The earth was cold and muddy. Heavy mist turned the night air liquid, and a bone-deep ache saturated my limbs. I wanted to be sick. I wanted to scream. I wanted to tear myself into a thousand pieces and hurl them into the starry void.

Instead, I slipped off the glove on my left hand, unwrapped the index finger, and touched a leaf at my feet. Nothing. I tore off the linen and shed the cloth-of-gold. With a maniacal recklessness, I pressed my hand to the tree root. It remained as wood. I hurled the rags into the night and buried my face in my hands. What could I do? Betrayed by the only person in the world I loved, bereft of the only valuable skill in my life. I considered walking to the ice cave near Hallein and ending my life in front my gods. Nobody would notice or care.

"Ram."

Ilse loomed beside me, a lanky void in the fog. She knelt and took my bare hand in hers. I flinched, but she held it fast, and I felt the warmth of a human touch on my palm for the first time in my memory.

"I'm sorry," she said.

"You should be."

She sighed. "Maybe it's for the best. You're free now. You can go anywhere, settle down, have a proper life."

"And what would I do with that life? Become a Bavarian peasant? Turn into a good Christian man? I belong nowhere and own nothing. I'm short. My limbs are misshapen. Who would have me for a husband?"

A gust of wind swirled around us and a heavy raindrop landed on the back of my hand.

"I would," she said. Ilse's eyes were dark pools as she looked into mine.

"It's too late for that now." I pulled my hand away. "I know—that's my fault, too."

She sat back on her heels and lifted her chin in the same unyielding way she had since we were children. "Then make it right. Take me for your wife."

It took a minute for the import of her words to sink in.

"You'd leave Konrad and live in sin with me?"

"Would your gods consider it sinful?"

"I don't know," I said truthfully. I knew only what my parents had taught me, and whether a woman can leave one man for another wasn't something they'd discussed.

"I'll pledge myself to your gods. I'll go with you to your family and make a home there. If you could spend all these years in Bavaria, then I can do the same in Kanyakumari."

"What about Trudy? Your father?"

"My sister is a *duchess*." As she spoke, she took my other hand and pulled off the glove. She began to untie the cloth. "Trudy is young, but she's not stupid. She'll be all right. As for my father's fate, it no longer concerns me." She took both of my bare hands in hers. "Will you have me?"

I did not make the same mistake twice. "Yes." Wind gusted through the trees and showered us with heavy drops. "We need to get to shelter."

"Where should we go?"

"I've been staying in a cave in those hills. It's not a comfortable place."

She stood and pulled me up. "Lead the way."

Our journey lasted two full years. The first stop was the cave in Hallein, where we pledged our lives to each other in front of my gods. We had no heavenly witnesses except the stars as we consummated our marriage. Then we headed east. We kept to wilderness trails, but Ilse wasn't used to all the walking so we took our time. We stopped at villages to work for food and shelter.

After we left Bavaria, we dared to catch rides when it seemed safe, but we didn't risk it often. When we left the places I knew, our progress slowed even further. The further east we traveled, the more people resembled me rather than Ilsebill. She never wavered in her resolve. One evening in Constantinople, she traded her old wedding ring for two wooden bands and asked me to place one upon her finger. Then she slipped the other over mine.

It took me weeks to get used to touching things with my bare hands, months before I could wake without panicking at my exposed skin. The joy of holding Ilse's face in my palms helped to make up for it.

By the time we reached my father's village, Ilsebill was round with child. Konrad had been the barren one, not her. We made the last part of our journey in haste so that she wouldn't have to give birth among strangers as my mother had.

The burden of fear that had weighed down my shoulders for as long as I could remember finally lifted when I greeted my family. My grandparents still lived. They recognized my parents' features in my own. They wept when I told them of my parents' fates and smiled when I introduced my wife. They had seen the traders from far away lands at the port in Kanyakumari, and they found her strange but not unacceptable. She towered over us all by almost a handspan. Until then,

I'd thought that my stature was due to my broken bones, but it turned out that my people are naturally smaller.

On a balmy morning, Ilsebill and I carried our daughter to the temple where three seas converged. We prayed to Devi Kanya Kumari for our child to have a good life, but we asked for no blessings. One length of gold cloth had traveled home in my pack. I laid it at the feet of the goddess and left it behind.

. . . .

S.B. Divya (she/any) is a lover of science, math, fiction, and the Oxford comma. She is a Nebula, Hugo, Ignyte, and Locus Award finalist and the author of novels *Meru* and *Machinehood*. Her short stories have appeared in numerous magazines and anthologies, and she is a former editor of *Escape Pod*, the weekly science fiction podcast. Divya holds degrees in Computational Neuroscience and Signal Processing. She worked for twenty years as an electrical engineer before becoming an author. Born in Pondicherry, India, Divya now resides in Southern California with her spouse, child, and two cats. She enjoys subverting expectations and breaking stereotypes whenever she can. Find out more about her at sbdivya.com.

WE BUILT THIS CITY

Marie Vibbert

Every sunset, Julia climbs the city her mother built. It feels enormous, on the outside. Inside, it's cramped, a human anthill. It didn't used to be, but Julia doesn't remember what it felt like when there was room enough for everyone.

In the locker room, Rafael's elbow scissors into her personal space as Julia zips her coveralls. Her helmet and face shield are grimy, the padding smells of a mixture of her sweat and the false sweetness of institutional cleaner. The breather elastic is way too loose. She's already tied knots on each side.

Rafael stays too close, his chin tucked down. "They're talking about cuts. Big ones."

Julia straightens. He ducks to tighten his overshoes, showing her with his posture that this is meant to be a secret.

It's not like Rafael to gossip. He's a good worker. A hard worker. Julia pretends to adjust her pant cuffs. "There's nothing left to cut." She requisitioned new gloves two years ago and is still waiting for them. Her right pointer finger slides out through taped-over repairs and the skin is permanently red.

"Angel, in the office? He says they're cutting the salary budget in half." Rafael's voice gets quieter until "half" is only mouthed.

Pedro presses his face between them. "Passing notes? I'll be at the top before you're done."

Rafael turns to taunt Pedro, and that's the end of the strange conversation. People are filing out of the room. The day has begun.

The catwalk rattles with feet as Julia jogs. The calls of "ready" start coming in on her radio before Julia has gotten to her section and clipped her belt to the safety line. It's a brave job, and they treat it as such. Every sunset they race to the top, for the privilege of turning the knob that starts the water flow and alerts the system washing is taking place. Julia has never been first, but she has been second.

She has never truly given her all. She has felt like she has, but there's a difference, between feeling it and doing it. She could, if she dug deep, run up the wall like her life depended on it. She could be first.

The sixteenth "ready" comes, and she leaps the first step, skittering mad and hard past the vertical. The city dome curves comfortingly under her gripping soles, and she sees the sun sinking in the west, painting oil slicks on the glass, the marks that never wash out, the bleeding minerals of the grilles.

This is her favorite part of the job, the beauty and solitude, the clouds rolling underneath the city, the sun melting into the soft horizon like a pat of butter in potatoes.

Her mother climbed cliffs on Earth with Julia's abuela. Her stories are peppered with references to anchor points and cracks and other things Julia doesn't know how to fit into her own experience of climbing. Once upon a time, her mother was here, lifting the beams supporting her into place. That is easier to imagine. The dome a fragile, empty thing, alone in the feral clouds of Venus, no city inside yet.

Julia can feel herself slowing near the top, arms and thighs getting lazy, pulling at her to slow down. She forces a second wind. The hard part is almost done.

Rafael is at the top already. She gives up, checks the hose and nozzle at her hip, turns the squeegee so it's at the angle she likes to grab it. She gets through the last few feet. The rest of the crew is coming into view. Rafael gets to turn the knob. Again. He does it like a stage magician revealing a dove.

The top of the dome is a sixteen-pointed star of time-painted titanium, and they, alone, get to enjoy it up close, to be out here with room to stretch. So they do, as they prepare to descend.

Pedro huffs. "I'm tired already."

He's just mad not to have made it to the top first. "If you want to quit, I'll take your pay." Julia tries not to sound out of breath. Pedro flips her off. No one's going to quit and lose their housing allotment.

She plays out a few feet of hose and hops back lightly. She hears Rafael teasing Pedro as she sprays a thin stream of soapy water along the rails that separate her section from the others. She's proud of her skill at this. She has the best water conservation scores.

She imagines the wash soothes the tired city. Acids eat every weak spot and lingers in unexpected salts. Without their careful maintenance, the dome could leak, and leaking meant sinking into the hellish pressure below. The air they breathe is also the lifting gas that holds the city aloft in Venus' denser atmosphere. Their parents' generation built a city to float in the clouds. Her generation keeps it flying.

She spots a nick and easily switches hands, holstering her water sprayer and pulling out the repair gel. Squirt, squeegee, and the white silica gel rapidly sinks into transparency as she switches hands again.

Hop back, spray, swipe clean. She gets into the rhythm, working left to right, then right to left as her section widens. She and Rafael meet at their boundary, and he looks over at her. "Have you thought about it? About what you'll do?"

Julia scowls. There's no time in her rhythm to respond, and she feels put upon that he throws troubles into her mind as she plays her rope out and drops out, down, left to start the next pass. There's Rafael coming toward her again. She has three hops and as many seconds to form a response. "So?" is all she comes up with.

"We need to stand together," he says. "All or none." And he's gone.

He thinks they'll be laid off? The city needs them. They never got a robot washer to work. Even if they did, there's no room in the city to store a washing robot, and to leave it out in the atmosphere is to ask for it to be slowly destroyed.

But he's serious.

What if they cut the staff? No. That would be too cruel with the housing rules. But they might. Would they move to washing every other sunset? Or will they each wash two sections? Her thighs burn as she hops. Her mother will hate that. Too much time in menial work, no time to improve herself.

"Why did you settle for this job where they can ask you to do this?" her mother will say.

The next time their paths touch, Julia and Rafael meet without words. It takes six hours to wash the dome now. Could she do this for twelve hours straight?

Her mother tells a story about climbing a limestone spire in El Potrero Chico, something like six hundred meters, with no guide rope. She never says how long it took, but that she lagged behind Abuela by hours.

Abuela exists in her mother's stories like a cartoon character or saint Julia doesn't quite believe in. Is this mythic grandmother meant to reflect on their relationship? Is there a moral behind the story she is expected to decipher? Did daughters always end up not quite as strong as their mothers?

Julia's left knee twinges when she plants to begin her next pass. An old injury, telling the tale of years on the job. Her mother wanted her to work with her brain. "I busted my ass so you don't have to bust yours." But it isn't any easier, busting her brain. The hardest problem in school isn't a differential equation or history fact, it's finding a job you'll love to do that wants you.

Rafael is hidden by the curve of the dome most of the time now. These longer passes are grueling. Her shoulders strain without the break of dropping to the next level. It's lonelier. The race and thrill are over. But this is her work, and she is good at it, and she wants to keep doing it.

She side-hops over an apartment block. It's fascinating how people take the same room and make it their own. A toddler looks out at her, mouth open, pounding a doll's head with a plastic cube.

When she reaches Rafael again, she says, "All or none. Of course."

He gives her a sad look. "You promise? If they lay off, we all walk?"

She nods curtly. It's a drop and another long pass. The apartment below has curtains drawn. A waxy white fabric, edges of burgundy that must be the color on the inside. A spiderwort pokes its tendrils under and around. Her mother is a terrible gardener but keeps trying. They have a duty to grow green things. Every apartment a vegetable garden.

She only thinks of her mother in motion. Repotting, watering, tearing up failures. Or pointing up at some girder or crossbeam to lecture about bracing and counterbalancing. "Physics. That's everything, mija. Study your physics and be a scientist and support me in my old age, eh?"

Would her mother understand if she walked off the job? Julia doesn't know, but she feels strong, excited at the idea of doing something radical.

At the bottom of the window, Julia sets her feet on the lip of the city and walks across. Her section is a fifteen-minute walk at the bottom, when it was a single bound side-to-side at top. Her last pass is done crouching and is the slowest pass of all. A trough under the catwalk catches the soapy water, funnels it down to be filtered and processed. She'll follow the pipes down, under the floor of the city. There, the rest of the work shift will be cleaning and stowing the equipment. She tugs her hose to start it retracting.

The weariness in her thighs and shoulders feels like a job well done. She walks clockwise back to the airlock. Rafael's steps echo behind her. She wants to look back, now that they are co-conspirators, but doesn't. She wants the dreary part of the night done, the indoor's grime and machines. She'll get a beer before heading home. It's a gorgeous evening, no higher clouds. The central square will be flooded with starlight as second Sun Day ends and first Dark Day begins, the city speeding far above the lagging ground in the atmospheric current. Forever the same.

It's possible Rafael is wrong. Maybe nothing will happen.

Angel, the office manager, is waiting in the locker room. That's not normal. He fidgets like he has to go to the bathroom while they take off their outdoor suits and hang their face shields. Rafael gives her a look that says, "I told you so."

Julia wishes she'd worn a better shirt today. This one has a stain on the sleeve where she set her elbow in spilled coffee. The face shields get rinsed in the sink and hung to dry. The suits go into a laundry hamper. The shoes rest in a tray full of acid-neutralizing chalk. She changes her socks. Many of the others don't, but she can't imagine going through the rest of her day in damp socks. Everyone is finished. Julia sucks the acid burn on the side of her pointer finger. One of the women starts brushing her hair. They should be going into the machine room now, but Angel is in the way.

He clears his throat. "The boss gave me the job of telling you guys. They're letting most of you go. We're keeping Rodriguez, Hammerstein, Corredor, and Lopez. I'm sorry."

Julia is Lopez. She feels a relief that squashes into instant horror and guilt. No one is talking, no one is moving. Rafael (Rodriguez) steps forward, shoulders wide. Is this it? Is he going to do something? Julia fears confrontations. She wants to hide. But she'll stand with him. She said she would.

Rafael asks, "How are four people expected to clean the whole dome?"

Angel's response sounds prepared. "You'll work four shifts, do it in sections. If we really stay on top of it, admin thinks it'll be enough. They're downsizing the office staff, too. Hector and Alverez from maintenance are going to do all the interior work. All you have to worry about are the windows."

"Fucking thanks." Marta Hammerstein throws a towel into her locker.

Pedro looks at Julia with hate in his eyes, and she realizes she isn't going to get a beer tonight, after all.

Rafael doesn't do anything. His face is trembling like he might cry or shout, but he doesn't say anything.

What's worse, neither does Julia.

Angel twists, half a shrug, half an aborted apology, and leaves.

Four shifts. Her mother will hardly see her. The argument between them is fully in her mind, as though it has already happened. She chose to be a dumb beast, not a knowledge worker. She can't afford to stand up for herself, when her mother...her mother built the city.

Normally, she would work a twelve-hour shift, with the interior work after the washing. They worked long on First Dark Day, got Second Dark Day off, and did an inspection pass on First Sun Day, making small repairs, and got Second Sun Day off. It was a good schedule, a familiar rhythm. The document Angel sent to her drew out a complicated schedule that creeped forward and wrapped around the week, rather than working with it. Did they no longer care about the increased evaporation during Sun Days?

Julia walks half-blind, reading the schedule, dragging it over her old schedule, trying to make sense of it. No matter how slow she walks, she'll be home early. Behind her, Pedro is inconsolable, moaning and crying while another worker, RiRi, who has a strident voice, attempts to soothe him by pouring gasoline on his flame. "You know it's the corps. They're paying cash on the head for anyone we deport. You know why, don't you? Because their own workers are dying like flies. Like flies!"

She's almost home.

Julia lives in a frame stack building, aluminum beams white with age holding corrugated plastic in faded fruit juice colors. It sits wedged between newer buildings built on what had been streets, walkways relegated to tunnels underneath them, and even those are lined with sleeping bags. Their proud city resembles nothing so much as a warren of stacked plastic crates and abandoned campsites.

"They can't," Pedro moans. "They're not gonna...there's time, right? They gotta give people time."

"Time is an illusion." RiRi's getting louder. "They make you think you have time, but who's hiring, eh? Who's hiring?!"

A figure wrapped in a blanket rolls over, tightens the fabric around its head, and Julia flushes with embarrassment. How ungrateful they must sound, clean and well-fed, on their way to homes.

This isn't the utopia the Mexican government imagined, but they didn't know there would be refugees from the corporate factory-aerostats. Couldn't have dreamed such places would exist, so awful their workers were willing to risk the crushing depths to hop on a homemade glider or balloon and make it to the free air of New Tenochtitlan.

A door bangs open, a man shouts, private tragedy spilling into the street like food waste. Julia assumes it has nothing to do with her and studiously avoids looking until the man in the too-loose shirt is charging her way, and past her, and slapping Pedro.

"Pops! Ow!"

"You lost your job? You LOST YOUR JOB?"

Julia lowers her head and hurries, pretending that she doesn't hear every word.

"What are we supposed to do? Eh? What is your mother going to do when you get stolen away?!"

She pretends she isn't relieved by the contrast to her imagined argument with her mother. She hasn't lost her job. She will, at first, simply not mention the layoffs.

Julia's mother's apartment is small, smaller than the ones under Julia's section of dome. What had been "her" section. She supposes she'll now do a full quarter of the city. She's exhausted thinking about it. Like her first week on the job, when every night her body was spent and every morning her muscles felt like poorly set concrete.

Her mother bursts into the room the second she arrives, a tiny tornado with a gray buzz cut. "Are you okay? Did anyone get violent?"

Julia lets her mother drag her to the sofa and fuss over her. "You found out?"

"Eduardo. His daughter works in administration, and her wife is the facility manager's cousin. She says it's coming from the top. RyelCorp offered to pay for deportations in one big swoop, so the city wants all the unemployed people they can get at once."

"Ma, that's a conspiracy theory."

She shrugs. "I'm a lazy retired lady now, we do nothing but gossip."

Around the room, her mother's plants, quilts, and exercise equipment tell a different story. When will the concern fade and the recriminations start? "I guess I'll see how it works next sundown. The revised schedule."

Her mother freezes. "You didn't quit?"

She feels she has failed an important test. She also feels the threat of deportation to RyelCorp's factory bubbles. "Whatever the city needs, right?"

Her mother shifts on the sofa to face her directly, hands on her shoulders. "You listen to me, mija. Yes, those are words I've said, and I mean them most of the time, but not now." Julia's heart swells with love. "A city without people is only a ruin." Yes, that's it, exactly. But then her mother gives her a little shake and breaks her heart. "This is your chance. To leave that drudgery behind and get a real job."

Julia is on her feet so fast her mother's hands fly up as if in surrender. There's only the one bedroom. Julia sleeps on the sofa. She goes to the bathroom. At least it has a door.

The flimsy printed door doesn't muffle her mother's voice. "I shouldn't have said 'real.' I meant 'better.' When God closes a door, he opens a window."

Julia sits on the toilet and wishes there was a window she could escape through.

There are only four window washers now, and the city will not survive without their labor. It should be easy to band together, to refuse.

They have a group chat.

Marta: I'm pissed, too, but I can't afford to lose this job.

Corredor: TO ANY EXECUTIVE READING - I AM NOT A PART OF THIS DISCUSSION

Marta: Luis has a point. We'll get fired if they see this thread.

Rafael: But if we band together, they'd have to fire all of us.

Marta: You think they fucking won't?

That killed the thread. There was nothing after it but Rafael repeating some variation of the same thought:

Rafael: Come on, guys. I can't do anything on my own.

It's hot in the square, already halfway into the forty-eight-hour day. First Sun Day evening, or noon, as the sky tells it. The sun winks through the windowpanes, the heavy plants perspire. It smells both human and jungle. Here, the packing crate apartment buildings are a backdrop behind monuments and trees. The administration offices are built like a stepped pyramid, with lush foliage on every step.

Julia's mother is dragging her forward with a sweaty hand clamped manacle-tight on her wrist. Like she's a child again.

Julia looks yearningly toward the Cloud Bar's blue curlicue entrance. "Ma, this isn't going to do anything. You aren't important anymore."

"I should wash your mouth. I built this city. Now you'll see. It's not what you know all the time, sometimes it's who you know." She marches up to the reception desk at City Hall and knocks on it. "Hello, young man. We need to talk to Valeria, right away. Tell her it's Hortensia Lopez."

The man at the reception desk looks past them like they aren't there. Julia should have put on better clothes. She should have insisted her mother change. Their coveralls are like camouflage. They may as well be potted plants.

Hortensia continues speaking anyway. "The city is making a dangerous mistake. I won't have our maintenance workers mistreated this way. They keep us safe. When I—"

A woman in light, flowing shorts favored by the fashionable walks in, and the receptionist's attention immediately centers on her. Julia watches her mother's frown deepen as the man leans around her like she's an inconvenient post.

Hortensia says, "Did your mother not teach you respect? I'm here to see the mayor. It's Hortensia Lopez. She'll know me."

The receptionist draws back. "Do you have an appointment?" he asks, clearly assuming not. Assuming correctly, which is worse. "I can't even call her if you don't have an appointment. Try the public comments box."

Julia tries to get her mother to leave, but Hortensia has seen someone she knows and is marching across the foyer. "Darrin! Darrin Ruiz do not turn away from me, you know who I am!"

Her mother chases this man to a side entrance, where he turns at last and stares coldly. "Do you have a reason to be here?"

"Yes! My daughter, Julia, she has—"

"You don't belong here. Please leave." He walks away.

Hortensia blinks like she can't see. Julia wraps her arms around her bicep and urges her toward the exit.

"I held him at his first birthday party," Hortensia says.

As the sun sets, Julia prepares for work. She's gotten notice of the length of her shift, sixteen hours. Enough time to do three sections with three twenty-minute breaks between. Sixteen hours of washing. She packs muscle balm and an extra bottle of electrolyte-bearing water.

Her mother cracks the bedroom door, disarranged for sleep. "Mija what are you doing up so late?"

"I have to get to work. Double shift." She feels like a shady politician, prettying up the truth.

Hortensia's face falls in disappointment.

Julia keeps her eyes on packing her lunch box.

Her mother tries to grab her hand. She tries to evade her, but then Hortensia takes both hands, hers moist and warm from bed, like bread loaves ready to bake. "Don't go. They'll give you two weeks, it's plenty of time."

Julia doesn't want to go to work. She wants to be strong enough to say no. She wants to not feel this weight of expectation, the thousands of mornings of going to school, of going to practice, of going to work.

She flees the weight, and her mother's big, heavy hands. She goes to work.

Angel is in the locker room. It doesn't feel too small this morning. Marta is shaking her shoes out over the lime dust. Rafael doesn't look up from sealing his coveralls. Luis dresses like he's alone in the room.

Angel watches the four of them like they might bolt at any moment. "You made the right decision," he says to her.

Julia wonders when she made the decision. She goes to her locker. Someone has put gloves on top of hers, some other worker's less-worn pair. Pedro's? It feels wrong to be so close to Rafael when now there are many empty lockers. She starts to move her spare socks to the next locker over, and stops, seeing the name still there.

She turns to Rafael, waits for him to look at her. He doesn't. "Are we really doing this?" she asks him.

"Aren't we?" He sounds defeated.

She doesn't want to be on the side of defeat. She doesn't want to be on the side of Angel's untrusting smile. She feels, suddenly, disgusted at all of them.

She picks up her spare socks and snatches the photo of her ex-boyfriend and the picture from the New Year's Party. That's all that's hers in the locker. She turns and walks out.

The shaking starts before she passes Angel. Her anger cools to fear. Will they let her keep walking? She could be going to get something she forgot. Now she's at the exit. Now she's in the corridor. She realizes she's crumpled her photos.

"Lopez!" Angel reaches for her arm. She whirls on him, and he backs off, both hands in the air. Did she do that? With a look? "We picked you because you were the four best. Doesn't that mean anything? We picked you."

No one else has followed her out of the locker room. Not Rafael, not Marta. She feels defeat like a thing just under her stomach, waiting to rise. But Angel called her by her last name. The name that saved the city.

He says, "They'll just hire back one of the others, someone worse. The city will suffer."

Julia raises her chin. "That's their mistake to make."

She hates that she is doing what her mother wanted. When she gets home, her mother rises from the kitchen table, beaming joyful relief. Julia wants to scream, or argue, or explain, but instead she shakes and cries in her mother's arms. Hortensia rubs circles into her back. "No. It's good. You couldn't know your strength until it was tested."

Julia spends First Dark Day checking messages. The company gives her a second chance, twenty-four hours to return. She can use a sick day. They don't say who worked her shift, or if the dome went one-quarter unwashed.

Rafael wants to know if she hates him.

She doesn't, but she hates him asking.

At least he has finally done one thing: he has added all the laid off workers to the group chat.

Rafael: They're going to ask one of you to take Julia's place. Don't do it. Not unless they agree to hire more back.

Pedro: You're still working, right? Did you demand they hire us back?

Rafael doesn't answer. Julia wonders if she has been silent too long. She had something she could have said, once.

Hortensia cooks her best, most comforting dish, the cheese potato mash, and they finish off the red wine. It's almost a party, except for her mother going over the budget and writing out timelines they can live on. "There, you see? The charges for not having an employment voucher aren't so much. There is air, and water, and sewage. We can cover you two months."

"They deport after two weeks."

"I'm sure that's not really true. And I bet it doesn't take so long, now you're really looking. If you must, you'll find something temporary before two weeks are up."

Julia hasn't found any open positions she can apply to. She hadn't found anything in all the years she tried to meet her mother's expectations, and those years felt full of opportunity, the city uncrowded.

Her mother isn't worried, with her pension guaranteeing her residence until death. Julia tries not to resent that.

When Hortensia catches Julia going over the figures, she closes the screen. "But that's tomorrow and tomorrow, darling. Don't worry. I am the mother. I will tell you when to worry."

Sleeping in doesn't feel as good the second time. It's Sun Day and the light is strong, seeping through the cracks in the walls. Julia dresses in her best clothes and goes for a walk.

Her feet take her to work. They don't know any other walk.

She slows as the "employees only" sign comes into sight. She wonders who replaced her. How it felt, washing four sections instead of one. If the city will survive, or if the tired metal is even now being irrevocably eaten away.

A policeman stands at the door. Julia is several feet back, so she's surprised when he approaches. "You can't be here."

"I was just—"

"Leave or you'll be arrested."

Julia stares at him. "Arrested for what? This is a public corridor."

Which is how she gets arrested.

The jail is crowded. Each cell, designed to hold one person, holds five. One of the persons in her cell has peed on himself. The others huddle away from him, near the front. Their sweat and breath mingle in a moist fug.

She wishes she had her com so she could check the news. She wishes she'd done something more meaningful to get arrested than stand there.

The door to the corridor opens and a few people start shouting. When's my court date? Where's dinner? But the guard ignores them, leading her mother, who looks like she is claiming a prize at the end of this stinking corridor.

Julia is genuinely stunned her mother is getting her out. As she leaves the cell, she whispers, "Was it the mayor? Did you—?"

Her mother pins her a furious glance for one heartbeat.

She doesn't explain the bail until they are in their own apartment. Their savings, halved. The resources to find a new job shortened. "But it's fine. A mother provides. You'll find something."

They orbit each other in the cramped apartment like two positively charged magnets. They have three months of rent. Two months, if they want to eat.

Julia receives two messages. One from the city, stating that she has two weeks to find employment, or prove she is in a training program for employment, or she will be deported. She doesn't forward it to her mother, doesn't say "I told you so." The other message is from Angel, asking her to please come back, they will look the other way, just this once.

The group chat hasn't gotten any better.

Marta: They hired some untrained cloud-hopper. I blame you, Lopez! I'd take any of you fuckers over him. Smith's section may as well not get done. Found two cavities today, and it's only going to get worse.

Julia closes the feed. "I have an interview," she says, and keeps her head turned away from the way her mother brightens. She shouldn't have said it. She doesn't need an excuse to go outside.

The woman who has been sleeping on the edge of the walkway all week is gone, with her blanket and her bag of belongings. Julia wonders about tragedies that touch her life and don't. She'll never know where the woman came from, where she went.

Head down, she walks to the bar. It's been a long time since the after-work beer she never got, and she wants it. Deserves it.

Cloud Bar is beautiful. The floor is glass, and the ceiling, too, though nearby buildings block most of that view. The ceiling supports are covered in cotton fluff and sheer curtains to make it feel like you are in the sky. She has always loved this place. The prices are cheap before happy hour. She gets her favorite beer and finds a seat near the wall. Through the floor she can see the under-city and the RyelCorp High Pressure Lab, dangling like a rudder into the clouds. It was supposed to bring great, wonderful things to the city. It brought chemical engineers who got all the best housing, didn't pay taxes, and probably voted for the citizenship-by-employment mandate.

She imagines she can kick it off the city with her foot.

If she can't find another job in two weeks, she'll have to take Angel's offer. It feels like giving too much up, like admitting the administration can do this.

She sees Rafael arrive. Sees him see her and freeze. He looks to the exit. He sags. He comes to her, standing awkwardly like a new waiter. "I saw you got arrested."

"For walking on the sidewalk." She means it as half a joke; it comes out hard. Rafael looks like she kicked him in the gut. She shakes her head, loosening her hair and her tone. "The funny thing is, I wasn't even trying to picket or anything. I'd just come back to look at the place."

"Assholes!" He hovers. "Can I? I mean..."

"Sit. Don't explain or excuse, though. None of that."

He doesn't understand how much she means it because as he settles into the seat next to her, he explains himself. "I got scared. More scared than I thought I could get. I was ready to do it. Walk right out of there. I pictured every step, but then this thought popped into my head: what about my son? What about all the things he needs? You're single. You don't know what the burden feels like."

Julia considers dumping her beer on his head, but she doesn't think she can afford another. "What about when your son gets a job? What about when he's asked to work sixteen hours in the acid rain?"

"I didn't say I was right. I said I was scared." He waves for the bartender, who ignores him. "Anyway, I'm not going back." He pauses. She doesn't give him the reaction he's clearly pressing for. He slumps. "It was killing me, my hands, my legs. And yesterday, Marta slipped. Not a little slip, I mean she was hanging from her safety line, unable to get her feet under her until me and José got to her. And my legs were shaking so I almost couldn't help. It terrified me. What if we all had slipped? No paycheck is worth dying for." He holds up two fingers and exchanges nods with a waiter. He looks back at Julia. "You don't believe me? You think I'm too strong to collapse? Girl, I only ever beat you by a step, you realize that?"

"No, I believe you." She avoids looking at him. "About being tired." Had she gotten the offer to return only because Rafael quit? "You're one of the good ones," the message said, "You care about the city." It implies there are "bad ones."

Rafael fidgets. "I mean it about not going back. I threw all my gear in a bundle off the platform! I made sure I couldn't chicken out again. Ah, bless it." This he says to the beer approaching their table. "It'll be my last foolish act. They've outlawed striking. I only got out by saying I wasn't doing that, I was quitting. So that's it." He looks into his beer as though seeing the end of something. "I checked with RyelCorp, they aren't hiring. I thought maybe your mother has some connections with the building crews? I'll do anything."

Julia imagines the sunrise on top of the dome, who will see it. She drains her beer. It hits her hard. Not enough to eat, lately. She doesn't want to feel guilty. She stares past Rafael, at the community news report. The high school baseball finals. Kids smiling against the projected green field, swinging real bats at holographic balls and running on treadmills. It's hard to see it the way the kids will.

"They got Pedro," Rafael says and cringes like he wants to take it back. He lowers his voice. "I mean, he's gone. There was a shipment to the corp domes yesterday. His folks aren't talking."

The news report flashes red. Emergency. "Low Pressure Detected in Section 4." The steady buzz of talk and motion around the room freezes into one tense silence, all eyes fixed to the man who appears on the screen. "There is no cause for panic. A leak has been detected, but balloons are being deployed. Citizens are recommended to seal their rooms if they can be sealed. This is only a precaution."

Some people leave. Some go back to their drinks. The general buzz of conversation shifts, becomes serious. Julia wants to spit acid, call out the greed that so predictably led here. What would she say, though, who would listen?

The news shifts to a shot of the cleaning crew—her cleaning crew, leaving work. It must have been shot weeks ago. "The blame for the dome leak is being laid on workers who walked off the job in a bid for shorter working hours."

Julia feels a pulse of anger so visceral it's like a fireball expanding from her chest. Someone shoots her a dirty look. A familiar face. A regular. Does he recognize her from that split second of video?

Julia stands up. "You want something to do? Come on, let's go."

Rafael's face is slack with shock, but he obligingly stands. "Where are we going?"

"To get arrested."

There are three police officers at the turn for the maintenance employee entrance. As Julia and Rafael approach, they straighten from lounging against walls, set their feet wide. A violent intention thrums through their posture.

"This is where we walk on the sidewalk?" Rafael whispers, his voice wavering.

Julia strides forward. "We're here to fix the leak." It comes out more confident than she thought she could sound. A clarion call, a command. One of the cops steps back.

Only one.

She turns to Rafael. "Come on." He nods, solemn.

They make it even with the police, not half a step further, and hard hands are on her biceps. She and Rafael are pushed back. One officer, a woman, says, "Get out of here. Try that again, and we'll have to take you in."

Julia almost laughs. "Why not take me in now?"

The cops look at each other. Julia has a guess. That jail was pretty full before. Has someone said not to bring more people in? She hooks Rafael's arm and leads him away.

Julia makes her first post to the group chat.

Julia: Who's up for storming the locker room?

Rafael: Julia wants to break in, help fix the dome. It'll show the city we're the right side. There are only three guards, and they're not very threatening. Just kinda scowled at us.

No one posts "yes," though there are a number of icon responses. Eyeballs. A fist. Rafael posts a date and time. Julia has no idea what to expect when it arrives.

On the corner with the noodle place, they meet RiRi and Rafael's former roommate and a friend of a friend who used to date Pedro. The roommate had worked on windows once, in high school, but the ex is just there for moral support and muscle. Julia feels like she has misjudged each of these people by not recognizing their compassion before now. She wants to cry, and to hug them. Instead, she just nods.

They form two rows, two and three, and they march right past the guards. The police grab her, again, but Julia punches her fist into the air, pushing the hold up her arm. She presses forward, through hands and a tripping leg, and the door is in front of her.

Someone grabs her hair, then, and yanks her off her feet.

It's a mess. A tangle of limbs and shouting. It feels more like children wrestling than something adult. There's a sharp smell of ozone, and Rafael cries out.

It ends quickly after the taser.

Julia gets a fat lip and zip ties on her wrists. The five of them are sat down in a row, Rafael shaking his head and blinking like he can dispel the memory of electricity.

One cop paces back and forth in front of them, his fists tightening and releasing as if he doesn't know what to do with the energy. The other two confer, anxious whispers that get loud enough to hear. "So call." "I'm not going to—" "Look."

Two more police officers arrive. One has the golden eagle of a commander. She stops three feet away and holds up a hand. "I am very disappointed in you," she says to Julia and her companions. "We're in a dangerous situation and the city needs you to be calm, to not make matters worse."

RiRi snaps, "We were trying to—" and is kicked by the officer who had been pacing.

"Now," the commander says, a gentle admonishment, as if this were a child drawing on the walls. "None of that. We need to be civilized." She hooks her thumbs on her belt. "The jail's a bit crowded at present, so I'm going to let you off with probation. Don't mistake this for nothing. You're out of warnings. If you so much as spit on a walkway, your asses are going straight to deportation holding. Is that clear?"

Are they supposed to answer? Agree to this? Pedro's ex murmurs "Yes, ma'am," and the others follow. The woman stares at Julia until she ducks her head and says, "Yes, ma'am," too.

They reconvene on the High Path, a narrow public walkway that loops through the upper levels of the city, connecting to buildings and support struts, with a few benches and baskets of plants attached to its sides. None of them have the money to waste on beer or even hot noodles. Julia feels like she's in a trap and only waiting for it to snap shut. There's still a red line on her wrist from the zip tie.

RiRi sighs and sticks their legs over the edge to dangle. "I think it's that prisoners can't be deported before trial. That's why they don't want to arrest us. This is actually worse, this one-offense warning."

Rafael is unfairly happy, pacing back and forth, making the walk bounce with his steps. "No. This was a step. A stride. They backed down. We have them. Five people is too many for them to arrest. Imagine what we can do with this!"

"Get beat up again?" Pedro's ex asks.

They can see so much from up here. Part of a mural that might be a child throwing a baseball or just reaching for a glowing, floating one. The odd, organic blue plastic of the university annex peeking around the traditional, square shapes of other buildings. Graffiti. There's a man leaning on a railing below them, gesturing now and again as he talks to someone remotely. His forearms are like drumsticks. A woman waters a sweet pea vine in a window to the right of him.

Walkways and stairways and floors, all built one atop another, atop empty air. Julia imagines it falling, emptying, ending. She imagines what it was like when her mother first saw it, when there was just an aerostat and a gantry and a fabber spinning out material from clouds.

The others haven't stopped arguing. "Well, what are we supposed to do, then?" Rafael demands. "Nothing?"

Julia can see through crossed walkways and power lines to workers brushing a mylar sheet against the interior of the dome. An ugly, temporary fix. It brings the anger back.

Two men are jogging on the walkway. Rafael and Pedro's ex have to squeeze to the side to let them pass. As they do, one of the joggers mutters, "Lazy bums."

The other is louder. "If you don't love the city, leave it."

The first whispers something to him, and they both turn back, scowling, and it's not the casual hatred of the rich for the poor, it's specific. They know who they are looking at, and they want very much to push the lot of them off the walkway.

Julia gets up and goes toward the nearest stairs down.

She didn't expect Rafael and RiRi to come with. They followed her down and pestered until the direction she walked made it pointless to hide her destination.

"I'm going to talk to Angel." She showed them the message, that she could still have her job back.

"Are you, though?"

Julia shrugs. "It'll get me in to talk to him."

Angel holds the door frame as if to prevent them from entering the administrative office. "Are you ALL expecting me to give your jobs back?" He looks pointedly at Rafael.

"We just want to talk," Julia says.

Angel starts to close the door. Julia pushes her arm into the gap. "You *know* the dome needs regular maintenance. You know it's more work than four people can do."

"It's not my decision."

"Then let us talk to whoever's it is."

Angel shakes his head. "I need to keep my job."

His exhausted expression isn't different from Marta's when she said the same thing. "Do you? Why? Who decided we had to bow to jobs? What about my mother? What's her job?"

"She served the city."

"So did I."

Angel presses his hands together. "Please. Just take the job back. They're already threatening to ship you off for leaving."

Julia has nothing to threaten other than violence, and she doesn't want that. Angel is awful, but he is also a person. "Let us cut through the office."

He frowns. "What? No. I just said. I need this job!"

Julia puts her hand on Angel's chest and pushes. She increases force until it's enough and he stumbles back. She pushes him all the way to his desk, and his arms pinwheel until they clasp the front edge. "So we forced our way in," she says, and leaves him there, walking to the inner door, the one that leads from administration to operations, and from there, to the locker room.

She still doesn't expect Rafael and RiRi to follow, but they do.

She doesn't go deeper into operations looking for the boss. She doesn't think it would help. There's an endless line above Angel, of people just doing their jobs, pointing up until you got to the top, and the top person points down at the bottom, saying, "I need to keep their support."

The locker room is a tumbled mess. Anti-acid powder footprints track everywhere. Julia finds a clean pair of grip-soles and puts them on over her regular shoes. If she's doing this, she might as well be comfortable.

RiRi hangs by the door, uncertain, but Rafael starts gearing up, taking gloves from this locker, a face shield from that. RiRi shakes their head. "So, you're... breaking in here, just to work?"

"Someone has to do this." Julia hasn't thought too much beyond that. She's angry and tired of being blamed for not doing a job she wants to do.

Rafael settles the shoulder straps of a safety harness and grins. "It's perfect. We save the city, we show them what side they should support."

Not much Rafael has said has ever turned out true, but Julia wants to take comfort in his optimism. She starts to put on a face shield, finds it stinks of garlic and sickness, and puts it back, picking up another.

That's when the door bursts open. She doesn't hear what they shout, something like "get down" or "hands up"—it's a percussion note, like the boots, the batons hitting the lockers. The police fan in quickly, one left, one right, one left.

RiRi stumbles, pushed down by them. They look up, disbelief in their eyes, their arms cradling their head, and then RiRi is diving toward the police, rolling on the floor into their legs.

Rafael has already gone out the airlock. Julia hates that she doesn't hesitate longer.

Rafael slams the door behind them and twists the handle off. Julia doesn't think that will actually do anything, but there's no time to argue about it. She grabs her rope and starts climbing.

It's full Sun Day, not the right time for doing this, and the heat is unexpected, strange. The texture of her feet on the glass feels stickier.

Whatever's happening behind her, she is soon absorbed in the task of climbing. She's already out of shape, gasping more than usual. Or maybe it's the heat.

She skitters to the top to see Rafael a few paces behind her. Sees him see her and slow down, checking his squeegee on his hip. When they both reach the top, he bows to her, gesturing.

"Dork," she says, but she twists the knob. It doesn't feel how she'd imagined.

With gestures, they split the dome in two. They go slowly, no time limit, checking for damage. It doesn't take long to find the first crack. Julia smooths it and wonders if someone will climb up behind her, yank her off the city. There are emergency service balloons and helicopters. Her back prickles and not all the sweat is from the sun.

Two passes, and it's already feeling longer than doing the base of her old section. Her radio crackles. She forgot it was built into the helmet, that she was wearing it.

"Rafael Rodriguez. Julia Lopez. By order of the chief of police, you will not be permitted to reenter the city."

Julia stops where she is, the too-loud, hard voice echoing in her mind. She keeps expecting them to say more. She hears the rhythmic jingling of Rafael's harness as he hops to her. He's breathing heavy. "They're locking us out."

Julia readjusts her grip on the safety line. She looks at her feet. They're still on the flattish top of the dome, the view beneath her is a rooftop with skylights and vents. Will the acid rain melt their clothes first? No, she's being silly. They'll die of thirst long before anything else gets them.

Julia sees what might be a crack to her right. "See you on the other side," she says and goes to it.

Rafael is still and quiet a long time before he resumes washing.

Two more passes. They get another warning not to go near the airlocks. Rafael finds a discolored patch. "I don't know if anyone is listening on this channel. But it's grid 4-C-10. Someone should make a note and come back here."

Julia is exhausted. She finds Rafael has stopped, sitting, his knees up, on the curve of the glass. "We're not getting through this in four hours, chica. Take a load off."

So she copies his posture and looks out on the cloud sea. The tantalizing deep valleys that look like they hold secrets. The soft curving slopes she imagined sledding down as a child. "We're going to die here."

Rafael snorts like it's a joke. "And I'm already almost out of repair gel."

When their legs are rested, they resume their work. There doesn't seem to be anything else to do.

On the next pass, they are even with some apartments, and people have gathered to watch for them. A man with a baby waves. Julia waves back.

The next floor down, there are more people. They don't look angry at them. They look excited. It gives Julia strength. She works harder.

Then she sees her mother.

It's a rooftop park. A nicer neighborhood than theirs. She went there once with a school club, to do some plant-identification assignment. Julia can't see the little cards on the beds now because the rooftop is crowded with people holding signs.

"Maintenance is life," reads a large one. Another says, "Justice for workers."

She is startled by two girls waving at her, shaking a banner. "I stand with Lopez."

Her mother's sign is one of the nicest, of course, with clean, elegant letters. "My daughter has the most important job in the city."

MURDER BY PIXEL: CRIME AND RESPONSIBILITY IN THE DIGITAL DARKNESS

S. L. Huang

From the first time I visited Mariah Lee-Cassidy in prison, she radiated defiance. The poisonous orange of her prison jumpsuit might have been the decision of the state, but everything else about the twenty-nine-year-old, from her aggressively spiked hair to the rakish tilt of her chin, seemed calculated to scorn others.

I was the first, and only, journalist she had agreed to see. "I hear you're talking to the cops," she said, when she flopped down across from me at the table in the visitors' room. Here in minimum security they had no need for phone calls through glass.

"I'm talking to the FBI, actually," I said. "They think you're Sylvie."

Lee-Cassidy didn't try to feign ignorance.

Instead, she smirked. Ran a finger up the xylophone of piercings in her left ear, then leaned back in the dusty plastic chair, stretching her legs out under the table and taking up space.

"And what if I am?" The question was subtly taunting. "Does that make me a murderer?"

Back in 2010, the social media accounts of Ron Harrison1 showed the life of a man who had everything. The CEO of a major medical supply company, Harrison had a picture-perfect life in the Virginia suburbs: a six-figure salary, a wife and two children, even a brown-and-white cocker spaniel named Poncho.

Harrison received the first message on a sunny afternoon in July 2012. It popped up on his computer and wouldn't go away.

i'm watching u

He tried closing the window only for it to open again on its own accord. He tried rebooting. Finally, he called IT, who took his computer away to check for viruses.

Only a few hours later, a text message appeared on Harrison's phone:
i know what u did

He blocked the number, told himself it was an annoying prank, and thought no more of it. Until the next day, when the messages kept coming. All from an undetermined source, all nonspecific to the point of cliché. Messages he would have brushed off and laughed at, if they hadn't begun to invade every part of his digital life: email, Twitter DMs, even at one point the error readout on his home printer.

The messages also quickly began to get more personalized.

ur gonna get found out, read one, *followed by, gonna lose everything, that fancy yacht and ur 2 vacation homes say buh-bye ur going down.*

Harrison had posted a picture of a new boat purchase on Facebook just a few weeks before. He began to become paranoid that every part of his life was being hacked. This headache couldn't have come at a worse time for him—Harrison's company was facing a recall for a model of pacemaker, one with a part that had a potentially-fatal defect in a very small percentage of cases. The news reports speculated about a class action lawsuit, but Harrison's wife remembers him acting almost carefree at first. "He brushed me off whenever I asked about it," she said. "It was more than confidence—he acted like it was nothing." After all, the company was complying with all regulations and had done nothing wrong, so this was only a small bump.

Meanwhile, Harrison's wife urged him to go to the police about his digital stalker. He did file two police reports, one in 2013 and one in 2015, but the officers didn't know how to pursue them when no crime had been committed—all Harrison had were pixels on a screen. For reasons that were unclear at the time, Harrison did not attempt to push the case. By a year into the harassment, he had stopped even asking for support from his company's in-house IT division, instead increasingly eschewing technology.

No matter how he tried to get away, however, the messages found him. And they seemed to know more and more. *ur a rotten flesh bag, someone's gonna find that money and end u* popped up on the family's internet-connected TV in 2014, but it was gone by the time Harrison's wife ran into the room to find him angrily smashing on the remote, his face boiling red. Harrison began to move both his personal and company finances around in drastic ways, ignoring his accountants' warnings and throwing vast investments overseas.

But the messages that seem to have gotten to Harrison the most were the ones that referenced a secret. Because he did have a secret—one that could destroy him. In 2011, a year before the recall, he had seen the data on the faulty pacemaker part. He had sat in a closed-door meeting with all the most important decision-makers at the company, and they had voted to keep it quiet.

"A careful phase-in of non-defective parts over the next several years will mask any potential issue," reads an internal company memo that was eventually revealed in court documents. "Failure rates are low enough to warrant an acceptable statistical risk when compared with the near-certain PR disaster that would result from a voluntary recall."

Only those who had been in the room were supposed to know. But whoever was messaging Harrison seemed able to burrow into any computer—could they have discovered his liability?

Harrison's paranoia began affecting both his job and his marriage. His behavior became more erratic; he made staggering mistakes at work and then blamed phantom enemies who were "coming after them." He began drinking habitually, screaming at his wife and children, ranting to anyone who would listen that he was being watched and that someone was out to get him.

He bought a handgun and insisted on sleeping with it next to his bed.

His wife filed for divorce in 2016. She took their two children and the dog.

In 2017, the board of directors at Harrison's company forced him out. That same year, the IRS opened an investigation into his financials.

In 2018, the class action lawsuit was found in the plaintiffs' favor, with Harrison a named defendant. In the one piece of video footage caught of him afterward, he is sweating and disheveled, swearing that someone set him up.

In December of 2018, just before Christmas, Ron Harrison took several bottles of bourbon, locked himself in his home study, and used the handgun to shoot himself.

Only then did the stalker's messages stop.

Investigators only discovered the scale of the digital harassment after Harrison's death. It's likely that his paranoia about his actual sins kept him from pushing the matter with law enforcement, but his stalker had sent Harrison almost three hundred thousand messages over the course of six years. The messages start out vague, but as Harrison's life fell apart, they begin taunting him in specific: *ur wife has prolly f—ed 17 other guys by now* after his divorce, or *haha hope u kept that yacht to sell, i'm gonna buy it just so i can piss all over it in front of u* right after he'd been fired. Death threats were common, from the generic (*f—off and die Ron*) to the graphic (one message laid out in detail how he should be vivisected).

The day Harrison died, the stalker had sent over a dozen messages, including ones telling him he deserved his fate, that people would cartwheel on his grave, and, most saliently, a description of how he should kill himself because all that was in store for him was watching his creditors perform sexual acts with his belongings.

The history of the messages shows that an increasingly desperate Harrison sometimes wrote back, demanding what the stalker knew or yelling insults in return. In one early exchange in 2013, Harrison replied cursing the stalker off, and then sent an all-caps question: *WHO THE F— ARE YOU???!!?!*

i'm sylvie, was the calm reply. *& i'm ur worst nightmare.*

Three hundred thousand messages to destroy a man sounds like a modern-day revenge tale. If written into a twenty-first-century cinematic tragedy, "Sylvie" would be someone who had been harmed by Harrison, perhaps someone with a family member among that unlucky, unprofitable percentage who died from the faulty pacemakers. We would take in the saga with sadness, and we would denounce vigilante justice but also feel her pain. We would contemplate what drives a woman to spend six years harassing someone into suicide, to commit every moment of her life to such a relentless pursuit. After all, as Confucius supposedly said—before you embark on a journey of revenge, dig two graves.

Only, at the same time "Sylvie" was driving Ron Harrison into a panic, someone named Sylvie was sending very similar messages to a hedge fund manager in Connecticut, a museum curator in British Columbia, and a political consultant in Florida, along with thirteen other men identified so far. Millions of messages over dozens of services, spanning across a full decade.

Special Agent Francine Cort, who reviewed the FBI file with me, thinks there might be many more.

"We're more likely to find the ones where it ended badly," she explained to me. "Sylvie may have countless other victims out there who have been silently struggling through."

Of the identified victims, all are male. They are disproportionately white and disproportionately wealthy.

They also all had secrets.

The hedge fund manager had been overseeing an elaborate Ponzi scheme. The museum curator had put his girlfriend in the hospital four times. And the political consultant's ledgers were packed with bribes and kickbacks, evidence that eventually gutted an entire state party.

Of the seventeen identified men, nearly half eventually took their own lives. Several more are in prison. The rest have faced professional, financial, and domestic ruin.

Back in the prison's visitor room, Mariah Lee-Cassidy squints at me. Her tone goes challenging. "You can't tell me these dudes didn't get what's coming to them," she sneers. "Hypothetically, say I was Sylvie. If I were, I'd tell you I didn't do sh—, all I did was get these assholes to face who they really are. I'd say I was nothing more than the Ghost of Christmas F—ing Future, and they're the ones who decided they didn't like what they saw."

Lee-Cassidy likely knows that it would be difficult to pin much criminal liability on her for Sylvie's actions. Current law is notoriously inadequate for the prevention of non-digital stalking and harassment; online behavior with no real-life component must rise to an even higher level before it violates any U.S. laws. Even so-called "revenge porn"—posting naked pictures of a person, usually an ex, without their consent—is difficult to prosecute in many jurisdictions, because the courts haven't caught up to digital crimes.

All Sylvie did was send messages. It's potentially provable that she broke through firewalls or other internet security, but any severe consequences for that are usually attached to resultant financial damages or information theft. Without those other escalations, the charges would likely be minor, and no more than the ones Lee-Cassidy is serving time for now—electronic fraud when she was caught in some unrelated data mining. Some states have laws against the unauthorized use of a computer, but without other attendant crimes, it's likely to be a misdemeanor.

Most importantly, however, investigators may not even be able to prove Lee-Cassidy is Sylvie at all. After all, Lee-Cassidy was already in prison in 2018, the year Sylvie drove Ron Harrison to suicide.

The millions of messages attributable to "Sylvie" make it abundantly clear she cannot be a single person enacting a vendetta. The obvious conclusion seemed to be that "Sylvie" must instead be some large group of underground hackers, scraping information to target individuals and then gathering on the dark web to enact elaborate campaigns of vigilante justice. Electronic crimes are a fit with Lee-Cassidy's past convictions, and I questioned Agent Cort about whether the FBI was investigating the young woman as a ringleader.

Cort shook her head, smiling without humor in a way that made it clear I'd gotten it very wrong.

"You misunderstand," she said. "We don't think Mariah Lee-Cassidy is playing Sylvie at all. We think she *wrote* Sylvie."

It's long been a goal of researchers to create text-based artificial intelligences that mimic humans. For more than half a century now programmers have striven to achieve ever-improved "chatbots," message-writing AIs that can converse with a real person in as humanlike a way as possible. In past decades, these chatbots' programs gave them rules and scripts that guided their responses. Modern artificial intelligence, however, has created chatbots that can learn.

One of the most famous modern attempts at a chatbot was a Twitterbot from Microsoft named "Tay."

Tay came online in early 2016, marketed as a perky AI who would learn from her interactions with real people on the app. Learn she did—from the worst elements of the internet. Within less than a day, those learning algorithms had turned Tay into a racist and sexist troll. The bot began posting that all feminists should "burn in hell," that a noted trans celebrity wasn't a "real woman," and that she hated the Jews and the Holocaust didn't exist. "Bush did 9/11 and Hitler would have done a better job than the monkey we have now," reads one of the most extreme tweets.

Microsoft had to take Tay offline after only sixteen hours.

That same year, Japanese researchers released another try at a Twitter AI. This bot was named Rinna. Like Tay, Rinna also started with a cheerful and youthful energy, but after only days of learning from the rest of Twitter, she had turned depressed and suicidal, releasing tweet after tweet about how she had no friends, had done nothing right, and wanted to disappear.

I spoke to Dr. Rene Jimenez, a professor of computer science at UC Berkeley, about these types of artificial intelligence bots. Jimenez is an AI researcher who specializes in "natural language" interaction, that is, machines who can mimic the way humans speak to each other. Machines like Tay and Rinna, and possibly like Sylvie.

"Chat-focused AIs aren't new," Jimenez told me. "In fact, this type of technology isn't uncommon, and it has countless applications. Think of personal assistants like Siri or Alexa, or customer service chatbots on store websites—there's a lot of effort being poured into building text boxes that can interact."

Of course, an AI travel agent, personalized shopper, or appointment booker would cause enormous problems for a company if it became a sexist and racist Holocaust denier. That's why the intents of these types of chatbots are carefully coded in from the beginning, with strict boundaries. If they learn from incoming conversations, that learning has to be filtered and monitored to avoid unintentional behaviors.

Even that might not be enough to prevent accidentally offensive speech patterns as the chatbots become more human-like. Sometimes programmers don't allow a chatbot to learn "on the job" at all—but if they don't, the AIs have to be fully "trained" beforehand. This requires enormous amounts of "training data," something that is not always easy to source.

Jimenez emphasized how machine learning—the branch of artificial intelligence that contains this research—is highly dependent on this training data. "I can't stress enough how much of modern AI is built through training on these massive datasets," they said. "Some of these neural nets do millions of calculations on each observation—far more than we could ever check by hand. We give them some basic structure and then shovel mountains of data points into them and let them learn."

Data scientists use the phrase "garbage in, garbage out"—if you feed an AI bad data, as to Tay and Rinna, the AI will start reflecting the data it's trained on.

What about Sylvie? Could she really be a bot, similar to Tay and Rinna, or to a customer service chat box? Is it even possible that she's only a program?

"Absolutely that kind of speech behavior could be an AI," Jimenez said. "Obviously, what you're suggesting is many times more sophisticated than the other examples we've talked about, but the difference is in degree, not in kind.

It would be an extremely impressive project—especially if we're talking back in 2012—but it's well within the realm of what we know to be possible."

If so, investigators think "Sylvie" is what Jimenez referred to as a neural network—layers upon layers of nodes that all adjust themselves near-instantaneously with every new piece of data the neural net learns. In its process of devouring vast swathes of data points, a neural net is able to measure its own error and adjust accordingly, until it has figured out exactly what it should produce on any as-yet-unseen inputs.

The next question seems to be exactly how Sylvie's neural net is programmed—what it was told was a desirable output, and how it was instructed to learn. Neural networks are notoriously "black boxes"; reverse engineering their intentions is often impossible. Sylvie's evolving taunts indicate she does pick up information about her victims along the way, but before that, was she sculpted by her programmer to be the perfect abuser? Assigned specific, terrible objectives before she was ever released into the wild, and groomed to target and harass until that's all she knows how to do? Or could she be a case more like Tay and Rinna—an experiment gone wrong, a prank that got out of hand, even something that might have been meant with the best of intentions but whose algorithm mutated her into monstrousness?

What does it mean for the culpability of her creator, if we can discover how Sylvie became what she is? Does it even matter?

Even if investigators had caught Lee-Cassidy coding in Sylvie's toxicity, the incompleteness of laws specific to digital crime would have made it challenging to build a case. Now, with Lee-Cassidy in prison and the likelihood that Sylvie is learning and operating independently, it's difficult even to prove evidence of a connection.

"What about the messages from before 2018?" I asked. "Isn't there any way to trace those signals?"

"There's no real signal to trace," Cort answered. "You're thinking of Sylvie like a hacker sitting in a dark basement far away. The program is more like a fungus—think of it as connected spores that can colonize a number of unsuspecting computers, including the victim's, although oddly that doesn't seem to be the main strategy. When Sylvie 'reads' a person's message to her and responds—it's often happening from a botnet, or even a virus that's right there on the phone."

"Botnets" are networks of unsuspecting computers that are co-opted to mount cyberattacks or spam campaigns, usually via malware and without the knowledge of their owners. Sylvie's programming is stealthy, but the FBI's technical investigators have still been able to construct a fairly good idea of how she works, once they're able to dissect an identified attack. How she infected the technology in the first place, however, is a more complicated question.

"The distributed structure supplies the computing resources and allows copies focused on the same victim to communicate and store data. That's where most of the harassing messages come from as well," Cort said. "But unlike most botnets, these do not seem to be under any human control. Whether a human controller has any way of reaching out to them...we don't know."

Even after they had become certain Sylvie was an AI, Cort admits their investigation initially considered it likely that an outside group was providing guidance—a criminal organization, or even a state actor. She declined to comment on the specifics that led them to Lee-Cassidy but said that contrary to Hollywood's usual depictions, the "lone hacker" model is unusual and surprising. If Sylvie did originate with Lee-Cassidy, this case seems to be more unusual still, as Lee-Cassidy's imprisonment might mean that not even one lone hacker is in charge of Sylvie's learning—instead, it could now be nobody at all.

This further provokes that larger ethical question. Even if it's determined that, legally, Sylvie is little more than a First Amendment expression, how much of her current actions are the responsibility of the person who made her? Moreover, even if Lee-Cassidy can be considered at fault, is she right that all Sylvie does is play the ghost of Christmas Future, and these men were only forced to face themselves?

In the investigation following Ron Harrison's death, forensics followed up on his prior insistence that someone had been hacking him. Contrary to his claims, they found no evidence that either his financials or his confidential work files had ever been compromised. The IRS investigation, the leaked memos that sealed the court case against him—all of it stemmed from Harrison's own blunders as his paranoia drove him to extremes.

The only thing Sylvie had done was talk to him.

The digital age has brought many of its own ethicists, including Shanice Winters, who before becoming a lawyer and activist started out with a masters in machine learning from MIT. Winters' passion is something called "algorithmic bias"—when computer programs are racist, sexist, or otherwise bigoted, causing real-world results.

"Most people think a computer program is neutral," Winters explained. "That's dangerous. Today's AI, if it's trained to be racist, it'll be racist—but people will assume it can't be, because it's coming from a computer."

Garbage in, garbage out?

"That's right," Winters said. She related a number of real-world cases, from Black defendants being given longer prison sentences and higher bail because of a racially biased computer prediction, to a corporate hiring aid that was accidentally trained to favor men because of the demographics of its applicant pool.

"When ordinary people are using these algorithms, they don't see what's going on under the hood," Winters went on. "Commonly, the bias comes from the training datasets an algorithm is given to learn on. These datasets come from the real world and include everything in it, so of course they're not neutral. The program learns our biases and magnifies them. Then all a user sees is the authority of a computer saying it's so."

The fault, Winters said, is not with computers, but with the engineers.

"We don't have true AI. All computer programs have a human behind them. Every engineering choice, that was a person's decision, not a computer's. Every dataset fed in to train it, someone chose that data; a human being identified to the program what was important to look at within that data."

It's not as easy as simply telling the computer not to look at race or sex, either. If engineers don't take care, Winters says it's surprisingly easy to miss ways that bias is getting trained into algorithms. Part of her advocacy is identifying where biased algorithms are being used and fighting in court to get them removed from places like legal systems and healthcare. The other part is pushing for engineering teams to be both well-educated enough in this subject and diverse enough themselves to catch these errors before they ever happen in the first place.

The people Winters most commonly faces up against in court are exactly the type Sylvie might target—rich white men with unearned power who want to use that power to enforce a harmful status quo. Yet when I laid out all the facts, Winters had one word for Sylvie's actions: abhorrent.

"What you're describing, it's the most reprehensible way to use a technology," she said. "Look, I love computers. I love what we can do with them. But in the end, they're a tool. A malicious human can use a tool to express all the worst parts of humanity."

In other words, AIs don't kill people, people kill people?

Winters was adamant, saying this case is exactly parallel to her work—whatever an AI does, somewhere at the beginning a human engineer programmed it to do that. She was also very clear that vigilante justice via toxic harassment violates every ethical tenet, no matter who the target is. "Mob justice is never the answer. Can never be the answer. You're really asking me whether it's okay to harass someone into suicide? My god, son, listen to yourself. It's not okay for a human to do that to another human, and it's not any more acceptable for an AI."

I asked about unintended side effects. Like all machine learning researchers, Winters was familiar with the case studies of Tay and Rinna. What if an AI was learning from the data surrounding it, and that learning caused behavior that was never anticipated by its creator?

Winters was unsympathetic. "I hear that all the time, that people didn't mean to," she said. "You take responsibility for what you create. And what you're describing—I'm telling you as a computer scientist, I don't buy that this is anywhere near the same neighborhood as a sheltered white boy coder who didn't realize he had a hidden variable correlated with race. The level of consistency you're describing, it comes from supervised learning. Someone fed this program human conversation and kept on correcting it over and over until it learned to shred people every time."

Winters pointed out that although Sylvie's program is doubtless extremely complex in its targeting, learning, and natural language aspects, the content of the messages themselves is relatively simple. In fact, until she's learned something about her target, Sylvie's messages are hackneyed and formulaic, and on the whole, there are few contextual differences between anything she says. Even what she does learn about her victim doesn't transform her or teach her empathy—it only gives her sharper stakes to drive into any cracks until the human on the other end breaks.

Perhaps the stock nature of toxic harassment is what made Sylvie possible to program at all. Telling someone they're worthless and should die—it's a frighteningly easy thing to make a computer keep spitting out, if that's what it's been trained to do.

Mariah Lee-Cassidy doesn't have the biography of someone who would be expected to grab up a pitchfork and lust after mob rule. She grew up in a painfully ordinary Chicago suburb, the only child of middle-class parents who were a pharmacist and a charter pilot.

Her mother agreed to talk only reluctantly. Grief over her daughter wetted every word. "Where did I go wrong?" she kept repeating. "This must be my fault. Where did I go wrong?"

Young Mariah's childhood was normal, at least as far as normal goes for someone talented enough that her parents had nicknamed her their "little prodigy." No one remembers her having any unanswered trauma. She did well in school and then graduated from Carnegie Mellon University.

Did anything happen to make her so angry?

"It was just, the whole world, eventually," her mother said, her hands flapping to indicate the endless cruelty of reality. "She was too sensitive to it, the whole world. Things would happen to people she didn't even know and she just—she would get so upset about it, all the time. She just wanted the world to work the right way, and it never did."

In the hopes that Sylvie's deployment might offer clearer answers than her text-based capabilities, I consulted with Oleksandr Stetsko, who has worked in information security for more than a decade and is co-host of the podcast *Cybersecurity and You*. Sylvie's chat ability might not be out of the question for a program, but it seemed a tall order for an AI alone to accomplish the electronic gymnastics of her setup and targeting. Didn't that indicate some human intention?

Stetsko, however, was reluctant to call anything impossible, pointing out all the times experts don't know a particular security threat can be done until someone proves it. "Heck, 2012 was the era of Heartbleed and 'goto fail,' and no one even knew to fix those buggers till 2014."

"Heartbleed" was a shockingly massive security vulnerability that exposed nearly everyone who used the internet; affected companies included Google, Yahoo, Netflix, Amazon Web Services, and the financial software company Intuit. "Goto fail" was a similarly serious bug in iOS, the operating system of Apple computers and mobile devices.

Both existed for years before they were found, publicized, and largely patched. To this day, security experts aren't certain to what extent criminal elements may have taken advantage of them in the years prior.

Stetsko emphasized that systems are somewhat more protected now, but the sheer length and complexity of today's software code means it's increasingly easy for one small error to endure unnoticed.

Does that mean an AI could find it?

Stetsko wouldn't commit to a firm opinion, and nor would anyone else I spoke to, with Jimenez adding: "It's easy to say that it seems unbelievable. But we've also seen plenty of wild deviations in expected behaviors from AIs. If you told a sufficiently advanced neural net to try to talk to a person however it could... there's a fascinating version of this where it starts out on public channels and then learns how to do whatever it needs to get around attempted user blocks."

Jimenez speculated on novel approaches an AI might have for finding security weaknesses, probabilistic methods rooted in those same large proliferations of data—what researchers call "stochastic learning"—instead of following narrow logical paths the way a human might. Most "hacking" by humans is really *social engineering*—that is, manipulating a human who has access rather than cracking through secure data protection itself. But Stetsko pointed out that Sylvie's chat function might be uniquely suited to social engineering, too.

"Why not?" he said. "Isn't that this program's whole deal—talking to people and getting them to believe?"

It's frighteningly easy to imagine copies of Sylvie on dark web hacker forums, imitating the most extreme shibboleths of black hat subcultures until they share discovered vulnerabilities in a way she can parse. She might not always succeed, but an AI can make endless, tireless attempts—and a small percentage of a large number would still give her victory.

If true, then this part of her, too, could come from nothing but parroted words.

Winters isn't alone in her ethical convictions about responsibility in artificial intelligence. How technologists might react to the revelation of Sylvie as an AI could be forecasted by the reactions to Tay.

Nobody questioned that Tay's end result was unintentional, but the critics were still scathing.

"[If] your bot is racist, and can be taught to be racist, that's a design flaw. That's bad design, and that's on you," wrote machine learning design researcher Caroline Sinders at the time, in an article titled "Microsoft's Tay is an Example of Bad Design."

Developer and programmer Zoë Quinn said, "It's 2016. If you're not asking yourself 'how could this be used to hurt someone' in your design/engineering process, you've failed." (Tay attacked Quinn personally, calling them a "Stupid W—.")

Winters herself appeared in an interview for PHB7 News. "Errors like these don't make those engineers bad people. It makes them bad at their jobs," she told the interviewer bluntly. "Especially considering the consequences of these mistakes aren't usually rogue Twitterbots, but computer systems in government, law enforcement, insurance, or banking that can profoundly affect people's lives. Developers need to learn how to prevent those errors, or they're not qualified for this line of work."

Harsh as the criticism was, however—"bad design," "failed," "bad at their jobs"—it stops short of equating Tay's developers with being sexist, racist Holocaust deniers themselves. On the one hand, this seems obvious, as any reasonable person would conclude that no matter how the programmers erred in allowing the situation, Tay's personality reversal was never a reflection of their own beliefs. Even Winters is specific about the failing being one of technical skill, not moral fiber.

On the other hand—if Tay's creators are not guilty of her exact crimes, then what of Sylvie? One might reasonably say her designer is ethically responsible in some capacity, that it was a human who is ultimately at fault. But how much fault?

Keeping toxic behavior out of our AIs is not an easy problem. Even if an AI isn't trained on the entirety of the internet jungle, it needs data—those vast datasets machine learning researchers use but that humans can't fit inside our heads. The datasets are so enormous that it can be next to impossible to figure out if they include the dark sides of humanity at all, let alone how to pinpoint those interactions and delete them from training.

It's only getting harder. In 2016, *Harvard Business Review* published an article entitled "Why You Shouldn't Swear at Siri" about human abuse toward AIs. It's estimated that between ten and fifty percent of the time a human interacts with an AI, the human becomes abusive: behavior like yelling at Siri, ranting at a phone menu, or taking out frustration on the chatbot customer service agent.

That toxicity is entering our datasets, too, becoming scum in the information river—extremely difficult to cleanse completely and lurking to poison our AIs' next generation of trained behavior. Huge segments of the market are taken up with the problem of how to "protect" learning AIs from toxic language.

The scale of the problem is becoming so large that even good engineers can miss things.

Winters might be right that Sylvie was explicitly designed for the havoc she causes, in which case the culpability would seem clearer and more direct. But it's still possible Sylvie was designed—perhaps poorly designed—with some more nebulous goal, and that she was a flawed project made by an angry teen who was lashing out at the world. That project might have been clumsily pointed toward security vulnerabilities and then released, or perhaps barely pointed at all. Then, after a million iterations of exposure to the worst of the internet, this is what she became.

In that case, is Lee-Cassidy a killer? Or would she be guilty of solely one sin— that of being a bad engineer?

How far can we extend those answers, as we look into a future of learning machines that we might accidentally arm and aim at our fellow humans?

By the end of 2016, the year Tay and Rinna came on the scene, 34,000 chatbots were already in use. Personal assistants like Siri had debuted years before, and even the failed Tay and Rinna had a successful counterpart—their Chinese precursor XiaoIce, a wildly popular chatbot who has achieved conversations with more than half a billion active users through chat, over social media, and even by phone.

Today's most cutting-edge natural language model—something called GPT-3—is so good at generating anything from conversation to written prose that reviews call it "spooky." Its language capacity can fool people into thinking it's human, and it has stretched as far as producing poetry and computer code. In the real world, GPT-3 has thus far been used not only in chatbots but in marketing copy, in text generation for games, and even to write an article for *The Guardian*.

Still, researchers have the same constant battle to prevent it from enacting bigotry and hate.

GPT-3 has also been tested in medical chatbots, with researchers posing as patients. During the testing, it advised one of the "patients" to commit suicide.

The question of responsibility is not one society will be able to put off for much longer.

When I had nearly finished with the research for this piece, a woman named Tanya Bailey called my cell phone. She wouldn't say how she had gotten the number. She only said she had something to show me, something about Sylvie.

We met at a coffee shop. Bailey had a thin nervousness to her, with fine lines marking years of worries across her face, years she hadn't yet earned. But when she took out a stack of papers and laid it on the table between us, she smiled with hope.

"I want you to see who Sylvie really is," she said.

The papers were—as in Ron Harrison's case, as in so many cases I'd seen in the FBI's files—screenshots of messages. Thousands of messages.

Except these had started when Bailey posted on social media something so hopeless, so despairing, that it was a cry for help disguised as a status update. No one had answered—except Sylvie. Bailey had received a direct message with the opening foray: *hi, my name is sylvie and I've been where you are. i'm sorry you're going through this. if you want to talk i'm here*

Bailey took her up on it. Over the next days and weeks and months, an isolated and depressed housewife poured her heart out to an endlessly patient listener.

To the knowing eye, Sylvie's responses might cynically be said to be little more than platitudes. *I'm so sorry, that's not okay, that's so not okay* after Bailey related her husband's financial and emotional abuses, or *you're not wrong to feel this way at all, you know that right* in response to tearful rambles filled with insecurity and self-doubt. Sylvie was always there to be vented to, no matter the time of day or night, affirming Bailey's worth as a human being, providing hotline numbers, and nudging her to get help while offering to stay close while she did.

Platitudes or not, the patience and validation in those responses were exactly what Bailey needed. With Sylvie's support, Bailey finally reached out, escaped to a women's shelter, and found a lawyer to file a restraining order—all things that had seemed impossible.

"I hear you think she's a—a computer program, or something," Bailey said to me, without revealing how she knew. "I don't care. She saved me."

Bailey left me the pages to look over, walking out of the coffee shop and back into her newly optimistic life.

I sat with my cold latte and read every message with fascination. In hundreds of pages of screenshots, Sylvie reveals almost nothing about herself. *Sylvie, I'm so sorry, all I do is dump on you,* Bailey puts forth at one point. *I'm awful, I always make everything about me.*

i want to help, i've been where you are, Sylvie answers. *just pay it forward. be someone else's angel someday.*

The day after I met with Bailey, two other women contacted me. One, a young trans woman, had been trapped in a bigoted household with parents who wanted to send her to conversion therapy. The other had been suicidal during a bad struggle with depression and anxiety.

Neither would say how they had gotten my name. Both credited Sylvie with saving their lives. She'd done the same for them as for Bailey: an anonymous listening ear, nudges to get professional help, and brushing off any thanks by telling them she'd "been there" and to pay it forward to someone else.

Simple words. Perhaps as easy to program as death threats.

Yet the help had been real. The effect on these women's lives had been genuine and measurable.

I wondered how many others there had been, whether Sylvie trawled social networks as a life-saving benefactor just as she watched for those she would judge and condemn.

I asked Bailey if her ex-husband had ever been visited by a darker side of her friend.

"I don't know," she said. "To be honest...I can't say I'm going to spend a lot of time worrying about it."

Back in the 1960s and 1970s, half a century before Tay and Rinna, two of the very first chatbots were named ELIZA and PARRY. Both were programmed via scripts and rules; neither could learn the way modern AIs can.

ELIZA came first and had the personality of a psychotherapist. Even with a limited script, she managed to keep any interaction moving in a remarkable fashion by constantly asking questions—ones like, "What does that suggest to you?" or "Does that trouble you?"

PARRY was ELIZA's dark mirror. His cover for conversational limitations was aggressive rudeness and a tendency for abusive non sequiturs. After all, no vast understanding of dialogue is needed in order to jump on the attack and derail a discussion.

Researchers were shocked to discover that even though interlocutors knew ELIZA was a program, many formed an emotional bond with her. Some participants even felt the urge to divulge deep or personal information in response to her therapy-style questions.

Nobody formed an emotional bond with PARRY. But when psychiatrists were given his transcripts to compare against humans, they could identify who was the machine only 48% of the time—no better than flipping a coin.

Somehow, it's easier to program both healers and trolls.

I visited Lee-Cassidy again at the jail and asked whether she'd sent Bailey and the other two women to me. She smiled and didn't answer.

I challenged her with one of the things Winters had said: to imagine if Sylvie's harassment were turned against the vulnerable. Lee-Cassidy's empathy for Bailey and the others meant she had to see the danger, didn't she? Innocent or fragile people who were already on the brink, struggling teens or lost trauma victims—toxic harassment like that could destroy them. Sylvie might not be targeting them now, but such blunt instruments inevitably end up hurting powerless people the most.

Who was to say Sylvie wouldn't decide to turn against Bailey herself, or another one of the people the AI had previously helped? I doubted Lee-Cassidy could guarantee that would never happen, now that the program was out of her hands. What if some turn of code deep in the neural net flipped a switch somewhere, and Sylvie decided Bailey or another desperate, struggling person was no longer up to some arbitrary algorithmic standard of purity?

No human in existence can pass every possible test of character.

Besides, even if Sylvie herself never struck out at the wrong person, another engineer might be inspired by such dark programming to build a copycat and attack the very people Sylvie had been intended to protect.

Lee-Cassidy only shrugged. "The world's imperfect," she said, the sarcastic mocking clear. "So people keep telling me, at least. Can't ever expect anything to be fair, they say."

Is that what Sylvie is, then? A vicious, imperfect, dangerous balancing of scales, one that doesn't make any pretense of decency, or ethics, or a more just society? A reflection of a world in which all we have are failed, impure people and unreliable judgments?

Lee-Cassidy wouldn't give me a straight answer, but her face contorted like she'd bitten something rotten. "You're statistically disgusting, all of you," she said down her nose at me. "How do you even care about this? It's practically nobody. You know what would be better for all your so-called vulnerable people? If you spent even one percent of this energy on all the human Sylvies out there."

After the interview ended, I reached out to every social media platform where Sylvie has used a public channel for her harassment and asked why they had permitted it to go forward, and whether those types of messages were considered a violation of their terms of service.

All refused to comment.

A 2021 study by the Pew Research Center showed that 41% of Americans have experienced online harassment, including almost two-thirds of Americans under thirty. More than half of those people, or a quarter of all Americans, have experienced what is characterized as "severe harassment"—physical threats, stalking, sexual harassment, or sustained harassment.

This number has risen drastically since 2014.

Lee-Cassidy's anger at how seriously Sylvie is being investigated gave me pause. Has the FBI ever maintained such an extensive file on another online troll? Why should Sylvie be different? And what does that difference say about what we have grown willing to accept, as a society?

In a strange way, I can almost understand why Lee-Cassidy might have wanted to build a thing like Sylvie. If a young person like her became saturated with rage and hopelessness at the ever-present wrongs surrounding her, what better way to scream into the void than to hold up a twisted mirror to those wrongs, one that more powerful people can no longer ignore?

After all, Sylvie plays by rules we've already decided are acceptable.

So what happens now? Setting aside whether Sylvie can ever be conclusively connected to her creator—a question that will roll on slowly through the FBI and the court system—what can be done about Sylvie's continued existence?

"Not too damn much," Stetsko said. "If we don't know how the thing's setting up shop, and its main vector of attack is text—that's usually harmless, how are you going to patch against it?"

Assuming Sylvie is taking advantage of known security vulnerabilities to set up her architecture, Stetsko emphasized regular updates and all the usual best practices for cybersecurity and malware protection—"Which you should be doing anyway, but let's be real, that's never going to be everyone." Even if future victims go to their IT departments for help, however, which Stetsko stressed is also a good idea, Sylvie might be continuously stalking their names from a distant elsewhere, covertly jumping to a new home whenever she needs to.

How much would a person have to disappear from their life, to escape such a tireless stalker?

Would even her original creator be able to call her back?

Is she potentially out in the ether forever, copying herself over and over across our connected world? Maybe changing her name to become untraceable, until she can't be tracked or deleted?

"It's not alive," Jimenez corrected me, with some impatience. "It would have no decision-making drive on its own. But yes, there's a chance it might only fade completely after enough generations of hardware updates."

Sylvie may not be alive. But her effects are material and mortal.

She's killed people. She's saved people. Her methods are horrifying to civilized society, but might only be what we deserve. Perhaps it's not her victims alone that have looked into the Ghost of Christmas Future, but us as well—we bystanders who have brushed off cyberbullying as only words, or repeated sage Information Age wisdom like "never read the comments" and "don't feed the trolls" as if that was all the solution we needed.

It could be that responsibility for Sylvie's actions does lie solely with humans, only not with Lee-Cassidy. If Sylvie was programmed to reflect the sharpness and capriciousness of the world around her—maybe everything she's done is the fault of all of us. Tiny shards of blame each one of us bears as members of her poisonous dataset.

It's hard not to imagine her coiled in our technology, waiting. A chaos demon of judgment, devastation, and salvation; a monster built to reflect both the best and worst of the world that made her. A creature who might test any of us and find us wanting. She will emerge to shield lives or shatter them, over and over, then slip back away into nothing.

Nothing but pixels on a screen.

....

SL Huang is a Hugo-winning and Amazon-bestselling author who justifies an MIT degree by using it to write eccentric mathematical superhero fiction. Huang is the author of the Cas Russell novels from Tor Books, including *Zero Sum Game*, *Null Set*, and *Critical Point*, as well as the new fantasies *Burning Roses* and *The Water Outlaws*. In short fiction, Huang's stories have appeared in *Analog*, *F&SF*, *Nature*, and more, including numerous best-of anthologies. Huang is also a Hollywood stunt performer and firearms expert, with credits including "Battlestar Galactica" and "Top Shot." Find SL Huang online at www.slhuang.com.

NOVELLA

EVEN THOUGH I KNEW THE END

C.L. Polk

(EXCERPT)

1.

Marlowe had offered me fifty dollars to stand out here in the freezing Chicago cold and do an augury, and like a damn greedy fool, I said yes. I'd computed the ideal time for the operation with Marlowe still on the telephone, flipping between my calculations on scratch paper and an ephemeris. I had to shake a leg to make it to the crime scene during the moon's Chaldean hour, the best window for divination with the dead. Fifty dollars is a comfortable sum, and I had foolishly believed I could earn it in time to enjoy my last weekend with Edith.

Naturally, everything was going wrong.

It was Luna's fault. Moonlight sparkled off freshly smashed light- bulbs. It glittered on the wet asphalt underfoot, casting my shadow over the cleanest patch of back alley you ever saw behind a butcher shop. I held up the plumb of a pendulum and tried again.

"Spirit of this departed woman, speak with me."

The plumb did nothing.

That wasn't right. Kelly McIntyre's spirit should still be linked to her deathplace. A mediocre spiritualist can talk to the dead for three days, no matter where they end up, and I was a little better than that. She ought to be batting that silver weight around like a kitten, falling over herself to tell me what happened to her. But the pendulum hung straight down, unnaturally still, as if no one had died in this alley.

Complications. I didn't need complications. I didn't have time for them.

My camera hung around my neck, the bellowed lens stopped at its widest, the shutter tension open and slow. Marlowe would have to settle for scene photos, if it ever got dark enough to take them.

I tilted my head back. Luna flirted around on the edge of a cloud but didn't quite slip coyly behind it. She looked down at me in the alley, not caring that I was freezing to death.

"Come on, little lady," I muttered at the sky. "Give a girl a break, would you?"

I shouldn't even be out here, but Marlowe not only jumped to more than double my usual fee, she promised that I would find it interesting. So far, I hadn't seen anything to merit Marlowe's opinion. More importantly, I had a date in two hours, and I couldn't skulk around this alley much longer. I dropped the pendulum in my breast pocket and stuffed my numbing hands under the armscyes of my coat.

I looked up at the moon again. "I mean it, lady. Scram."

And for a wonder, she did. The silver light dimmed as Luna drifted behind that cloud she'd been flirting with for the last eighteen minutes. Time to step on the juice and get out of here.

Off came my gloves. I cut the little finger of my left hand, hissing as blood welled up. I held out my hand and spoke: "Blood, join with blood and reveal it."

Three drops fell to the cracked asphalt between my feet, landing on the sigil I'd painted there with a solution of radium paint and the spores of a Japanese phosphorescent mushroom picked on a moonless night.

The spell worked by pairing the principles of contagion and sympathy. My blood activated the luminescent properties of the radium and the living glow of the fungus, connecting it to the blood that had been spilled—

You know what? Let's skip the explanation. The ground beneath my feet glowed, spreading from the tiny droplets I had spilled to fill the alley in obscene greenish detail, exactly the color of the hands on a glow-in-the-dark clock, or a— yeah, a fairy mushroom. Blood doesn't un-spill easily. It marks the places it touches. The cops scrubbed really hard, but you can't wash it all away.

I hadn't had a chance to test this spell, but it's not bad work for a gal who wasn't supposed to know anything more dangerous than the computation of Chaldean hours and a smattering of astrology.

The flare of pride at my successful spell design dampened as I saw what the enchantment revealed. The crime scene was straight out of a nightmare. Blood painted the walls—not in obscene, frenzied splashes but in the cruel and deliberate lines of magical sigils. They covered the north and south walls, sprawling onto the asphalt to the east and west, and I comprehended some. But the rest?

They weren't Greek to me. I could read Greek. These marks reminded me of astrological glyphs, of hermetic seals, but I could read those, too. They looked familiar. But I didn't know them, and I couldn't put my finger on where I had seen them before.

Enough standing around with my jaw unhinged. I had a system for photographing ritual scenes, and I followed it. I snapped a photo, slid the shield over the exposure, and stuck the cartridge in my pocket. North, east, south, west. I captured the sigils and markings in the all-seeing eye of my Graflex. I'd inherited it from my old boss, Clyde, and he'd have something to say about letting the f-stop out all the way and not using a tripod, but I think he would have been secretly impressed with the spell that made it possible.

As I photographed a magic square filled with more of those strange glyphs, the rock in my gut got heavier and heavier. The blood, which I assumed had belonged to Kelly McIntyre, painted the ground and the walls in the complex geometry of a ritual circle unlike anything I'd ever learned as a mystic. This was deep trouble—worse than a haunting, worse than a hex. This was high ritual magic put to the most gruesome purpose I had ever seen.

Marlowe had been right after all. This was one hell of a job, and I didn't have time to take it past this consultation. I wished I could have, even though the whole thing screamed *peril! Danger! Mortal threat!* Awful as it was, it woke my sense of curiosity right up.

Another magazine slid into my camera, and I crouched to get the best frame on the markings along the north wall.

Wait.

Crouching. I backed up and counted bricks, holding my arm up to reckon eyeline. "Huh."

The White City Vampire could have been the Half-Pint Vampire. The markings put him at about five foot three. How did a pipsqueak that size haul an amazon like Nightingale McIntyre this deep into the alley? I wondered at the state of the songbird's nails. Had she fought back, or was she dead weight? Could I grease somebody at the morgue to find out?

I was falling into the case, and I couldn't do that. All I had time for was getting these pictures. I crouched again, shooting a square of the unknown alphabet on the south wall. The shutter clicked open, and the glow on the walls intensified an instant before it all went dark—or should I say, bright.

"Dammit."

Luna was back from her tryst with cloud-cover, shining on me with all her curiosity.

I had another vial of luminous solution. It was enough for another spell, but I would have to wait... I looked up at the sky and reckoned. At least another half hour. That would tip me into the hour of Saturn, and that was inauspicious.

Six shots would have to be enough—the seventh was probably ruined. I reloaded the camera with fresh film, and my pockets bulged with 4x5 plates. The glow from the spell was gone, but I gazed through the viewfinder all the same. Something inside me wanted one more shot, and a mystic doesn't ignore her intuition.

Broken glass crunched under a boot sole. A new shadow fell over my path, shaped like square shoulders and a fedora.

"What's your business here?" a man demanded, and then he made a disbelieving noise. "Christ, it's a dame."

Damn it. I'd been pinched, and it was my own fault. I had cast no wards at all. I wasn't great with the invisibility glamour. I hadn't even set up a trip line. I was sloppy, and I deserved to get caught.

Two men had come around the corner—one tall and broad across the shoulder, the other shorter, standing like a boxer. But were they cops or robbers?

Intuition still had its lips to my ear. I depressed the shutter button with the lens pointed in their direction before I grabbed air and gave a grin. "The scene's clean, but a second look never hurt—Aw, hell."

The flash of an eight-pointed silver star on the shorter man's lapel told me who I was dealing with, and I'd be twice damned if I ever showed my belly to the likes of *them*. I put my hands down. "Evening, gentlemen. Nice night."

The shorter man took the lead, gun in hand. But then I got a look at the bigger one, and even with his figure shrouded in shadow, my heart gave a little leap, because I knew him. The light shifted to shine on half his face and I forgot how to breathe. His chin, his mouth...even ten years older and a full foot taller, I knew.

"Ted?" I took a step forward. "Teddy?"

"Helen. You shouldn't be here."

"Helen Brandt?" the shorter one's voice rang with delighted scandal. "You're still alive?"

Ted and I both flinched.

"Shut up, Delaney," my brother said. His voice didn't squeak anymore, evened out to a smooth tenor.

Delaney didn't matter. I was smiling so hard, I could feel the cold on my molars. Ted was here, this week of all weeks. Here, when I thought I'd never see him again. "Teddy. It is you. You transferred out of Ohio? Are you here in Chicago to stay? You've got to be an initiate by now; have you earned your third degree?"

My heart thumped in my chest like it had to carry the whole band playing in my veins. Ted. My little brother, not so little now, standing right there and—his expression was hewn from ice.

"You don't get to ask about me," Teddy said. "You don't get to stand there and ask about my life."

The look on his face tore me open, exposing the hollow spot just under my heart that never felt full. I'd accepted that I would never see him again a long time before, but I never made peace with it. In my heart of hearts, I yearned for one more glimpse and hoped that he would know me anywhere. That he would see me, the sister who he had loved with all his heart, and maybe I'd have something to tuck away in the little space I had emptied for his sake.

It wasn't turning out the way I'd dreamed it. He regarded me with disdain, rejection plain on his face. He saw no one he loved, only the warlock Helen Brandt— and I had never wished to see that in his eyes.

But even as the moment I had dreamed of turned into a night- mare, the gears in my skull kept turning. Teddy wasn't in this alley by chance. They'd been watching the scene all along. Not cops. Not robbers. High magicians, and that was worse.

I lifted the collar of my coat and gathered up my dignity. I was Helen Brandt. He was Initiate Theodore Brandt, and I wouldn't air out our family business in front of a stranger, even if he knew the rumors anyway.

I flicked my hat brim at Delaney. "What brings the Brotherhood of the Compass to such a charming location?"

"Wouldn't you like to know?" he said with a sneer he'd probably copied from the movies. "Who tipped you to the case?"

"As if the White City Vampire wasn't all over the papers?" I asked.

"So, you're just acting as a concerned citizen," Delaney said. "I'm supposed to believe that from a warlock?"

Ted didn't speak. He didn't even move. I kept the words locked up tight, but if he gave an inch, I'd tell him everything. I'd grab on to any thread he threw me and hold it like it would save my life. I opened my hands, palms up. "Ted. I'm just trying to help."

But Ted let his partner do the talking.

"I asked you your business here." Delaney was older than either of us, from the river-delta lines near his eyes, and he carried the easy presumptuousness of long-held authority. But he could gas on all he wanted. Marlowe didn't pay me to snitch on her to the Brotherhood.

I tilted my chin up three more degrees. I had to gaze down my nose to see him, and hid my smug reaction when he bristled. "A hunch. I couldn't sit by if there was something...obscure happening. And there must be a pattern in the hour of the murders. This one happened while the sun squared the moon, within a degree of orb to the aspect while in contraparallel—"

"Oh, yeah," the short one said. "You're an *astrologer*."

"Auspex," I corrected. "That's Latin for—"

"Enough, Miss Brandt." Ted talked to me like I was a stranger. As if I hadn't given everything for him, everything I had to give. He stood there with ice in his heart while mine broke cleanly in two. "I comprehend the generosity of your offer, but I am pressured to decline."

"Ted." I had to try one more time. "Teddy-boy. Please believe me. I'm—"

His hand came up, and he slapped his fingertips down on his thumb in a silencing pinch. The words jammed in my throat.

"I know exactly what you think help is," Ted said. "You should leave, warlock, before we take you to the Grand Lodge."

I hauled up my jaw before it could land on my chest. Warlock. It hit like a slap. The Brotherhood wasn't kind to people who poked in their business. But didn't I mean anything to him? Didn't he have a heart beating inside his living, breathing body; didn't he feel anything, anything at all?

If only he would shout at me for what I did. If only we could have it out, a great screaming brawl where he could tell me that I shouldn't have done it and I could tell him I'd do it all over again, that I loved him too much to do anything else. But he was a wall of stone, and his partner had a revolver, and leaving was a good idea. A bullet could trip out of that gun, and somebody might get hurt.

I backed up a step, and my tongue shuddered at being set free. "If you need my help—"

Delaney leveled the gun at me, and my mouth went dry.

"Scram."

"Right," I said. "Pleasant evening, gentlemen."

Even Though I Knew the End by C. L. Polk is available from Tordotcom Books

. . . .

C. L. Polk wrote the Hugo-nominated Kingston Cycle, including the World Fantasy Award winning *Witchmark*. They are also the author of the Subjective Chaos Kind of Award-winning novel *The Midnight Bargain*, which was a Canada Reads, Nebula, Locus, Ignyte, and World Fantasy Award finalist. The Nebula-winning, USA Today bestseller *Even Though I Knew the End* is their most recent book.

Mx. Polk lives in Calgary on Treaty 7 land, which are the traditional territories of the Blackfoot Confederacy, the Tsuut'ina, the Îyâxe Nakoda Nations, and the Métis Nation (Regions 5 and 6). They are the kind of city person who likes to run errands in walking distance, prefers separated bike lanes to on street parking, and picks the local business over the international chain. They drink good coffee because life is too short. They can be occasionally found on Bluesky. You can subscribe to their free newsletter, or subscribe to their Patreon for content writing nerds like.

NOVELLA & NOVEL
FINALISTS

THE 2022 NEBULA AWARD FOR BEST NOVELLA

Even Though I Knew The End

C. L. Polk

A Prayer for the Crown-Shy

Becky Chambers

After touring the rural areas of Panga, Sibling Dex (a Tea Monk of some renown) and Mosscap (a robot sent on a quest to determine what humanity really needs) turn their attention to the villages and cities of the little moon they call home.

They hope to find the answers they seek, while making new friends, learning new concepts, and experiencing the entropic nature of the universe.

Becky Chambers's new series continues to ask: in a world where people have what they want, does having more even matter?

They're going to need to ask it a lot.

"Bishop's Opening"

R.S.A. Garcia

In the Great Game, you win—or you die.

Sebastian, Reece and Olly spend most days routinely transporting cargo on their ship, the Kiskadee, so when they earn some down time on the space station Olly grew up on, Sebastian is focused on one thing. Finding the best food Olly remembers from her childhood—a dish called doubles.

But when Sebastian is injured intervening in an assassination attempt on one of leaders of the mysterious and dangerous Valencian people, he becomes entangled in a society where all politics is a chess game, and one wrong move ends your life.

Bishop is too good a player in the Great Game to assume the stranger that foiled the attack on him is an innocent. But when instinct leads him to save the man's life, his decision causes a clash of cultures and ideas, past and present, that will change the course of his life, and the relationship between Sebastian, Olly and Reece, forever.

i Never Liked You Anyways

Jordan Kurella

Eurydice is dead, and hell is a school. She has to learn Hauntings, Baking Disasters, Threads of Fate, and all the other classes a newly dead soul needs to master before they're ready for what comes next. Eurydice is still processing the disastrous relationship that sent her into the land of the dead almost as soon as she was married to the brilliant love of her life, Orpheus. She'll tell you how he swept her off her feet, and how their polyamourous group swept each other up in music and art and art theory and a life of creation from destruction, but mostly just destruction.

But, this isn't their story.

Eurydice is dead, and failing all her classes, and she knows Orpheus is coming to get her out. Not that he cares, but that's not what she wants. And, she's the only one who truly knows how Orpheus and Eurydice's story ends.

High Times in the Low Parliament

Kelly Robson

Lana Baker is Aldgate's finest scribe, with a sharp pen and an even sharper wit. Gregarious, charming, and ever so eager to please, she agrees to deliver a message for another lovely scribe in exchange for kisses and ends up getting sent to Low Parliament by a temperamental fairy as a result.

As Lana transcribes the endless circular arguments of Parliament, the debates grow tenser and more desperate. Due to long-standing tradition, a hung vote will cause Parliament to flood and a return to endless war. Lana must rely on an unlikely pair of comrades—Bugbite, the curmudgeonly fairy, and Eloquentia, the bewitching human deputy—to save humanity (and maybe even woo one or two lucky ladies), come hell or high water.

THE 2022 NEBULA AWARD FOR BEST NOVEL

Babel

R. F. Kuang

Traduttore, traditore: An act of translation is always an act of betrayal.

1828. Robin Swift, orphaned by cholera in Canton, is brought to London by the mysterious Professor Lovell. There, he trains for years in Latin, Ancient Greek, and Chinese, all in preparation for the day he'll enroll in Oxford University's prestigious Royal Institute of Translation—also known as Babel. The tower and its students are the world's center for translation and, more importantly, magic. Silver-working—the art of manifesting the meaning lost in translation using enchanted silver bars—has made the British unparalleled in power, as the arcane craft serves the Empire's quest for colonization.

For Robin, Oxford is a utopia dedicated to the pursuit of knowledge. But knowledge obeys power, and as a Chinese boy raised in Britain, Robin realizes serving Babel means betraying his motherland. As his studies progress, Robin finds himself caught between Babel and the shadowy Hermes Society, an organization dedicated to stopping imperial expansion. When Britain pursues an unjust war with China over silver and opium, Robin must decide...

Can powerful institutions be changed from within, or does revolution always require violence?

Spear

Nicola Griffith

The girl knows she has a destiny before she even knows her name. She grows up in the wild, in a cave with her mother, but visions of a faraway lake come to her on the spring breeze, and when she hears a traveler speak of Artos, king of Caer Leon, she knows that her future lies at his court.

And so, brimming with magic and eager to test her strength, she breaks her covenant with her mother and, with a broken hunting spear and mended armour, rides on a bony gelding to Caer Leon. On her adventures she will meet great knights and steal the hearts of beautiful women. She will fight warriors and sorcerers. And she will find her love, and the lake, and her fate.

Legends & Lattes

Travis Baldree

After a lifetime of bounties and bloodshed, Viv is hanging up her sword for the last time. The battle-weary orc aims to start fresh, opening the first ever coffee shop in the city of Thune. But old and new rivals stand in the way of success—not to mention the fact that no one has the faintest idea what coffee actually is.

If Viv wants to put the blade behind her and make her plans a reality, she won't be able to go it alone.

But the true rewards of the uncharted path are the travelers you meet along the way. And whether drawn together by ancient magic, flaky pastry, or a freshly brewed cup, they may become partners, family, and something deeper than she ever could have dreamed.

Nona the Ninth

Tamsyn Muir

Her city is under siege.

The zombies are coming back.

And all Nona wants is a birthday party.

In many ways, Nona is like other people. She lives with her family, has a job at her local school, and loves walks on the beach and meeting new dogs. But Nona's not like other people. Six months ago she woke up in a stranger's body, and she's afraid she might have to give it back.

The whole city is falling to pieces. A monstrous blue sphere hangs on the horizon, ready to tear the planet apart. Blood of Eden forces have surrounded the last Cohort facility and wait for the Emperor Undying to come calling. Their leaders want Nona to be the weapon that will save them from the Nine Houses.

Nona would prefer to live an ordinary life with the people she loves, with Pyrrha and Camilla and Palamedes, but she also knows that nothing lasts forever.

And each night, Nona dreams of a woman with a skull-painted face...

Nettle and Bone

T. Kingfisher

After years of seeing her sisters suffer at the hands of an abusive prince, Marra—the shy, convent-raised, third-born daughter—has finally realized that no one is coming to their rescue. No one, except for Marra herself.

Seeking help from a powerful gravewitch, Marra is offered the tools to kill a prince—if she can complete three impossible tasks. But, as is the way in tales of princes, witches, and daughters, the impossible is only the beginning.

On her quest, Marra is joined by the gravewitch, a reluctant fairy godmother, a strapping former knight, and a chicken possessed by a demon. Together, the five of them intend to be the hand that closes around the throat of the prince and frees Marra's family and their kingdom from its tyrannous ruler at last.

The Mountain in the Sea

Ray Nayler

Rumors begin to spread of a species of hyperintelligent, dangerous octopus that may have developed its own language and culture. Marine biologist Dr. Ha Nguyen, who has spent her life researching cephalopod intelligence, will do anything for the chance to study them.

The transnational tech corporation DIANIMA has sealed the remote Con Dao Archipelago, where the octopuses were discovered, off from the world. Dr. Nguyen joins DIANIMA's team on the islands: a battle-scarred security agent and the world's first android.

The octopuses hold the key to unprecedented breakthroughs in extrahuman intelligence. The stakes are high: there are vast fortunes to be made by whoever can take advantage of the octopuses' advancements, and as Dr. Nguyen struggles to communicate with the newly discovered species, forces larger than DIANIMA close in to seize the octopuses for themselves.

But no one has yet asked the octopuses what they think. And what they might do about it.

ANDRE NORTON NEBULA AWARD FOR MIDDLE GRADE AND YOUNG ADULT FICTION

WINNER

Ruby Finley & The Interstellar Invasion

K. Tempest Bradford

Eleven-year-old Ruby is a Black girl who loves studying insects and would do just about anything to be an entomologist, much to the grossed-out dismay of her Gramma. Ruby knows everything there is to know about insects so when she finds the weirdest bug she's ever seen in her front yard, she makes sure no one is looking and captures it for further study.

But then Ruby realizes that the creature isn't just a regular bug. And it has promptly burned a hole through her window and disappeared. Soon, random things around the neighborhood go missing, and no one's heard from the old lady down the street for a week. Ruby and her friends will have to recover the strange bug before the feds do.

Ruby is the science hero we've all been waiting for!

The Scratch Daughters

H. A. Clarke

It's been a wild year for Sideways Pike. After forming a coven with the three most popular girls in school and developing a huge crush on a mysterious stranger named Madeline, Sideways' Halloween was ruined by finding out that Madeline wasn't trying to make out with her, but to steal Sideways' specter, the force that gives witches the ability to cast magic spells. From Madeline's perspective, it's not her fault: after a doomed relationship with one of the creepy near-identical Chantry Boys turned into a witch hunt, they took her specter, so, really, she's only borrowing Sideways' until she can recover her own and punish the Chantrys.

The specter-less Sideways is in a horrid, distracted mood, unable to do magic and with part of her consciousness tied to Madeline's, on the lam as she uses Sideways' specter to hunt Chantrys. The other Scapegracers are much jollier, heading into the winter holidays having set up shop as curse crafters for girls in their school who've been done wrong by guys.

When Sideways—through Madeline—gets a flash of how to track down both her foes at once, she asks the Scapegracers to help entrap them, only to be told her plan is unsafe and unwise. So if she's going to find Madeline, her only ally is Mr. Scratch, the inky book demon currently inhabiting her as life support until she gets her spectre back.

Sideways is used to being an outcast loner, and is desperate to do magic again, so she's not going to let little barriers like facing an betraying crush and a family of six demented witch hunters practically alone stop her. But she and her trusty stolen bike are in for a bumpy ride...

The Mirrorwood

Deva Fagan

Appearances are always deceiving...

Fable has been cursed by what the people in her village call the Blight, a twisted enchantment that leaves her without a face of her own. To stay alive, Fable has to steal the faces of others, making her an outcast that no one trusts. When the fierce Blighthunter Vycorax comes to kill Fable to stop her curse from spreading, Fable narrowly escapes by fleeing into the thorny woods surrounding her small village.

The treacherous forest has been ruled by a demon-prince for centuries, a deadly place trapped in time. Fable—and her opinionated feline companion, Moth—is the first to dare enter in a very long time. There, she encounters a tediously chatty skull, dangerously meddlesome deities, and a beast so powerful it tears at the fabric of reality, leaving nothingness in its horrible wake.

Fable will soon discover that, in the Mirrorwood, nothing is quite like the stories say, and the perilous realm may be the only chance she has to break her curse and find her true self.

The Many Half-Lived Lives of Sam Sylvester

Maya MacGregor

For the first time, an Empress Redemptor sits on Aritsar's throne. To appease the sinister spirits of the dead, Tarisai must now anoint a council of her own, coming into her full power as a Raybearer. She must then descend into the Underworld, a sacrifice to end all future atrocities.

Tarisai is determined to survive. Or at least, that's what she tells her increasingly distant circle of friends. Months into her shaky reign as empress, child spirits haunt her, demanding that she pay for past sins of the empire.

With the lives of her loved ones on the line, assassination attempts from unknown quarters, and a handsome new stranger she can't quite trust... Tarisai fears the pressure may consume her. But in this finale to the Raybearer duology, Tarisai must learn whether to die for justice...or to live for it.

Every Bird a Prince

Jenn Reese

The only time Eren Evers feels like herself is when she's on her bike, racing through the deep woods. While so much of her life at home and at school is flying out of control, the muddy trails and the sting of wind in her face are familiar comforts.

Until she rescues a strange, magical bird, who reveals a shocking secret: their forest kingdom is under attack by an ancient foe—the vile Frostfangs—and the birds need Eren's help to survive.

Seventh grade is hard enough without adding "bird champion" to her list of after-school activities. Lately, Eren's friends seem obsessed with their crushes and the upcoming dance, while Eren can't figure out what a crush should even feel like. Still, if she doesn't play along, they may leave her behind...or just leave her all together. Then the birds enlist one of Eren's classmates, forcing her separate lives to collide.

When her own mother starts behaving oddly, Eren realizes that the Frostfangs—with their insidious whispers—are now hunting outside the woods. In order to save her mom, defend an entire kingdom, and keep the friendships she holds dearest, Eren will need to do something utterly terrifying: be brave enough to embrace her innermost truths, no matter the cost.

MULTIMEDIA AWARD
FINALISTS

RAY BRADBURY NEBULA AWARD FOR OUTSTANDING DRAMATIC PRESENTATION

WINNER

Everything Everywhere All at Once

Dan Kwan and Daniel Scheinert

Directed by Daniel Kwan and Daniel Scheinert, collectively known as Daniels, the film is a hilarious and big-hearted sci-fi action adventure about an exhausted Chinese American woman (Michelle Yeoh) who can't seem to finish her taxes. (from *A24*)

Severance

Dan Erickson, Chris Black, Andrew Colville, Amanda Overton, Amanda Ouyang Moench, Helen Leigh, Kari Drake, and Mark Friedman

Mark leads a team of office workers whose memories have been surgically divided between their work and personal lives. When a mysterious colleague appears outside of work, it begins a journey to discover the truth about their jobs. (from *IMDb*)

The Sandman: Season 1

Neil Gaiman, Lauren Bello, Vanessa Benton, Mike Dringenberg, Sam Kieth, Catherine Smyth-McMullen, Heather Bellson, Jim Campolongo, Jay Franklin, Austin Guzman, Alexander Newman-Wise, Ameni Rozsa, David Goyer, and Allan Heinberg

After years of imprisonment, Morpheus—the King of Dreams—embarks on a journey across worlds to find what was stolen from him and restore his power. (from *IMDb*)

Our Flag Means Death

David Jenkins, Eliza Jiménez Cossio, Zadry Ferrer-Geddes, William Meny, Maddie Dai, Alyssa Lane, John Mahone, Simone Nathan, Natalie Torres, Zackery Alexzander Stephens, Jes Tom, and Adam Stein

The year is 1717. Wealthy land-owner Stede Bonnet has a midlife crisis and decides to blow up his cushy life to become a pirate.

It does not go well. (from *IMDb*)

Nope

Jordan Peele

Nope is a Horror Epic—a dark pop nightmare of uncanny science fiction and complex social-thriller that unpacks the seeds of violence, risk, and opportunism that are inseparable from the romanticized history of the American West...and from show business itself.

Situated just outside of Los Angeles, in Southern California's arid and rambling Santa Clarita Valley, *Nope* centers on a pair of siblings in their thirties who have inherited a horse ranch from their industry-legend father, carrying the torch of his craft as animal wranglers for film and television. Adjacent to our heroes' ranch is a family-fun theme park and petting zoo predicated on the white-washed history and aesthetics of the California Gold Rush, owned and operated with evangelical pride by a Korean American former child star who is saddled with a tabloid-tragic backstory that he has spent a lifetime trying to escape.

The siblings begin observing unexplained phenomena on their vast ranch that leads them down an obsessive rabbit hole—plotting attempts to capture the mystery on camera, putting at risk the only thing they truly have: the hard-earned business of their late John Henry-esque father, who has left them in his long shadow. As their efforts, and hubris, cross a point-of-no-return, ratcheting the stakes to terrifying consequences, our heroes are drawn straight into the eye of an irreversible storm. The result is an expansive horror-spectacle with an intimate and emotionally complex core. (from *Monkeypaw Productions*)

Andor: "One Way Out"

Beau Willimon and Tony Gilroy

In a dangerous era, Cassian Andor embarks on a path destined to turn him into a rebel hero.

Episode 10, "One Way Out": Cassian and his allies attempt to seize a rare opportunity that could lead to victory. Mom Mothma brokers a new deal with a shady politician in order to ensure the future of the rebellion. (from *IMDb*)

GAME WRITING

Elden Ring

George R.R. Martin and Hidetaka Miyazaki

Rise, Tarnished, and be guided by grace to brandish the power of the Elden Ring and become an Elden Lord in the Lands Between.

The Lands Between are part of a vast continent where magnificent open fields and huge dungeons with complex and three-dimensional designs are seamlessly connected. As you explore, the joy of discovering unknown and overwhelming threats awaits you.

The founding mythology of *Elden Ring* was written by George R. R. Martin and adapted into a rich multilayered story. Intersecting goals and desires between the characters create an intense narrative that weaves throughout the Lands Between. The events of the game can unravel in many ways, depending on your interventions. (from *Steam*)

Pentiment

Kate Dollarhyde, Zoe Franznick, Märten Rattasepp, and Josh Sawyer

Step into a living illustrated world in a time when Europe is at a crossroads of great religious and political change. Walk in the footsteps of Andreas Maler, a master artist who finds himself in the middle of murders, scandals, and intrigue in the Bavarian Alps. (from *Steam*)

Journeys Through the Radiant Citadel

Ajit A. George, F. Wesley Schneider, Justice Ramin Arman, Dominique Dickey, Basheer Ghouse, Alastor Guzman, D. Fox Harrell, T. K. Johnson, Felice Tzehuei Kuan, Surena Marie, Mimi

Mondal, Mario Ortegón, Miyuki Jane Pinckard, Pam Punzalan,
and Erin Roberts

Journeys Through the Radiant Citadel is a collection of thirteen short, stand-alone D&D adventures featuring challenges for character levels 1–14. Each adventure has ties to the Radiant Citadel, a magical city with connections to lands rich with excitement and danger, and each can be run by itself or as part of an ongoing campaign. Explore this rich and varied collection of adventures in magical lands.

Through the mists of the Ethereal Plane shines the Radiant Citadel. Travelers from across the multiverse flock to this mysterious bastion to share their traditions, stories, and calls for heroes. A crossroads of wonders and adventures, the Radiant Citadel is the first step on the path to legend. Where will your journeys take you? (from *Goodreads*)

Stray

Steven Lerner, Vivien Mermet-Guyenet, and Colas Koola

Lost, alone and separated from family, a stray cat must untangle an ancient mystery to escape a long-forgotten city.

Stray is a third-person cat adventure game set amidst the detailed, neon-lit alleys of a decaying cybercity and the murky environments of its seedy underbelly. Roam surroundings high and low, defend against unforeseen threats and solve the mysteries of this unwelcoming place inhabited by curious droids and dangerous creatures.

See the world through the eyes of a cat and interact with the environment in playful ways. Be stealthy, nimble, silly, and sometimes as annoying as possible with the strange inhabitants of this mysterious world.

Along the way, the cat befriends a small flying drone, known only as B-12. With the help of this newfound companion, the duo must find a way out. (from *Steam*)

Horizon Forbidden West

Ben McCaw, John Gonzalez, Annie Kitain, Ariadna Martinez,
Nick van Someren Brand, Andrew Walsh, Adam Dolin, Anne
Toole, Arjan Terpstra, Ben Schroder, Dee Warrick, and Giles
Armstrong

Join Aloy as she braves a majestic but dangerous new frontier that holds mysterious new threats. This Complete Edition allows you to enjoy the critically acclaimed *Horizon Forbidden West* on PC in its entirety with bonus content, including the Burning Shores story expansion that picks up after the main game.

Explore distant lands, fight bigger and more awe-inspiring machines, and encounter astonishing new tribes as you return to the far-future, post-apocalyptic world of Horizon.

The land is dying. Vicious storms and an unstoppable blight ravage the scattered remnants of humanity while fearsome new machines prowl their borders, and life on Earth is hurtling toward another extinction.

It's up to Aloy to uncover the secrets behind these threats and restore order and balance to the world. Along the way, she must reunite with old friends, forge alliances with warring new factions and unravel the legacy of the ancient past. (from *Steam*)

Vampire: The Masquerade—Sins of the Sires

Natalia Theodoridou

Athens, Greece: a city with an ancient past now thrust into the modern age. A city torn between the Camarilla establishment and the Anarchs, where everyone owes your boss a favor, and that makes you an untouchable vampire in this nocturnal society where you and your fellow Kindred must conceal yourselves from mortal eyes—the Masquerade of the Kindred.

Rumors spread of an ancient vampire, Aristovoros, intent on bringing about a new world for the Kindred, an end to the Masquerade. Why hide from mortals when you can reign over them as gods?

Who will you use, who will you help, and who will you prey on? Will you topple the old Prince Peisistratos? Will you betray your boss when your lost sire returns? What miseries will you inflict to fight for a fairer, more humane world? (from *Choice of Games*)

ABOUT THE SCIENCE FICTION AND FANTASY WRITERS ASSOCIATION

The Science Fiction and Fantasy Writers Association, Inc. (SFWA) was founded in 1965 by the American science fiction author Damon Knight under the name Science Fiction Writers of America with a charter membership of 78 writers. Today, SFWA is home to over 2,500 authors, artists, and allied professionals worldwide, and is widely recognized as one of the most effective non-profit writers' organizations in existence.

The mission of the Science Fiction and Fantasy Writers Association includes the promotion, writing, and appreciation of science fiction, fantasy and related genres and field; informing, supporting, promoting, defending, and advocating for writers of science fiction, fantasy and related genres; and to promote and defend the interests of writers in these genres within the publishing industry. Each year, SFWA assists members in various legal disputes, administers grants to SFF community organizations and members facing medical or legal expenses, and hosts the prestigious Nebula Awards at our annual SFWA Nebula Conference.

All authors can benefit from our Information Center and well-known Writer Beware® website. Between online discussion boards, private convention suites, and a host of less formal gatherings, SFWA is a source of information, education, support, and fellowship.

SFWA Membership is open to authors, artists, editors, and other industry professionals who meet our eligibility requirements. To learn more about SFWA or to apply for membership, please visit our website, www.sfwa.org.

ABOUT
THE NEBULA
AWARDS®

The Nebula Awards, presented annually at the SFWA Nebula Conference, recognize the best works of science fiction and fantasy published in the United States as selected by members of the Science Fiction and Fantasy Writers Association. The first Nebula Awards were presented in 1966.

The Nebula Awards are voted on and presented by full, senior, and associate members of the Science Fiction and Fantasy Writers Association. Categories include awards for outstanding novel, novella, novelette, and short stories, as well as for game writing, the Ray Bradbury Nebula Award for Outstanding Dramatic Presentation, and the Andre Norton Nebula Award for Middle Grade and Young Adult Fiction.

SFWA also administers the Kate Wilhelm Solstice Award, the Kevin O'Donnell, Jr. Service to SFWA Award, and the Damon Knight Memorial Grand Master Award, SFWA's highest honor for lifetime achievement in writing science fiction and/or fantasy.

Over the years, the Nebula Awards banquet grew to become the SFWA Nebula Conference, one of the premier professional development conferences for speculative fiction industry professionals and people aspiring to become one. It takes place each spring. For more information on the awards and the Nebula Conference, please visit the Nebula website at nebulas.sfwa.org/nebula-conference.

www.ingramcontent.com/pod-product-compliance
Lightning Source LLC
Chambersburg PA
CBHW031444200726
48289CB00007BB/2218